A MIDSUMMER NIGHT'S KILLING

A MIDSUMMER NIGHT'S KILLING

A Blanche Hampton Mystery

Trevor Barnes

William Morrow and Company, Inc.
New York

Copyright © 1989 by Trevor Barnes

First published in Great Britain in 1989 by New English Library, a hardcover imprint of Hodder and Stoughton, a division of Hodder and Stoughton, Ltd.

It is the policy of William Morrow and Company, Inc., and its imprints and affiliates, recognizing the importance of preserving what has been written, to print the books we publish on acid-free paper, and we exert our best efforts to that end.

Library of Congress Cataloging-in-Publication Data

Barnes, Trevor, 1955-
    A midsummer night's killing / Trevor Barnes.
      p.   cm.
    ISBN 0-688-11047-9
    I. Title.
  PR6052.A6688M5   1992
  823'.914—dc20

91-40964
CIP

Printed in the United States of America

First U.S. Edition

1 2 3 4 5 6 7 8 9 10

For my parents

'O Dieu, où es-tu? Es-tu là et ne te venges-tu pas? N'es-tu pas rassassié des meurtres de Moscou? – ou bien – ou bien – n'es-tu toi-même enfin qu'un moscovite?'

'Oh God, where are you? Are you there, yet do not avenge yourself? Have you not had your fill of murders by Moscow? – or – or – are you yourself nothing but a muscovite?'

Entry in Chopin's diary, 8 September 1831,
after the surrender of Warsaw to the Russian army

Acknowledgments

I would like to thank the following: Inspector Tom Millest of the Metropolitan Police for correcting points of fact (the inaccuracies that remain are my responsibility, whether through negligence or deliberate decision); the many Poles I spoke to in researching this book for their unfailing helpfulness and hospitality; Heather Jeeves, my agent, for believing in me; Carolyn Caughey, my editor, for making revision of this manuscript so painless that in drowsy moments I even thought it was fun; and most importantly, my wife, for her patience and constant support.

Chapter 1

Every day the fashion-conscious joggers puffed by. Courting couples ambled past and fretting mothers harangued their children. They all passed only yards away from the mutilated corpse, rotting in the dappled glade under branches of beech and lime snapped from the trees. In the end it was not we humans who found the remains. The English anyway are not a curious race. They prefer to leave bad smells alone, let them drift on the air for a few days and then fade. Bad smells, like arguments, are other people's business. It was a dog, a mongrel belonging to a Polish couple, that sniffed the body first on Hampstead Heath. For some strange reason its name lodged in the detective chief inspector's mind: Kisiel, a sweet Polish fruit dish which is at the same time distinctively sour.

The summer had been hot and unpleasant. For weeks the temperature had hovered in the nineties both night and day, and London was overcanopied by a limpid sky whose monotony was unbroken by even a single cloud. People threw aside pullovers and raincoats with joy; secretaries sunbathed in bikinis. She remembered seeing one businessman in St James's Park waddle past the pelicans to the centre of a lawn and strip off to his bathing trunks before laying his white, plump body down beside his briefcase. The heat became unbearable after a week or so. The pleasure turned rancid. Air-conditioning systems broke down. The litter, never so noticeable after rain, clogged the gutters and accumulated in the corners of alleyways. The fitful breeze flicked grit into tired eyes. From the endless banks of terraced houses south of the river, to the bleak tower blocks punching through the skyline to the east, where the Thames slouched past muddy banks down to the sea, to the leafy suburbs in the north and west – everywhere windows were left open to let the hot, sticky air blow through

1

during the day in preparation for the long, hot, sticky night. London had had enough of the heatwave.

Blanche Hampton had been hit by the heat as much as anyone else. The warmth outside had melded with anger inside to leave her in a state of incandescence. She had been married to her husband for almost five years and had suspected him of being a coward. When she had returned home a month before she had the final proof: an innocent letter on the kitchen table, her name scrawled in Roger's almost illegible handwriting as though a spider had committed hara-kiri on the sumptuous envelope (her mother had drilled into her that good stationery was as important as good breeding). Blanche had smiled. As she sat slumped on the sofa that Sunday afternoon recalling the letter, the memory of the smile rekindled her ire: it was the smile of the dupe, the smile of the trusting Caesar before Brutus plunged home the dagger. Roger's scribble announced that he had left her for another woman.

As she had read, her heart had pumped faster and faster and a hot flush prickled her flesh. She had wept for a full quarter of an hour, not just a temperamental bout of tears but great, heaving convulsions that she felt might burst her rib cage. The emptiness of self-pity filled up with anger as she reflected on Roger's cowardice, his inability to confess his unfaithfulness face to face. Disdain for his cowardice flickered into life again as the heat of the afternoon rolled over her T-shirt and nestled in the valley between her legs. A tattoo of irritation was drummed out by her long fingers on the arms of the elegant sofa. Her heavy-lidded eyes swung round the untidy room – cleaning had seemed pointless in the past few weeks – and came to rest on a corner of the Victorian sideboard that appeared unfamiliar. She remembered why. Their wedding photograph had stood there until four weeks ago, when she had slid it into the bottom of a drawer, believing she could bury painful memories under files and knick-knacks. She swung her robust thighs – wishing they were thinner in a rare pang of self-doubt – over the edge of the sofa, strode across to her desk and unearthed the photograph. Roger and she stood smiling, almost smirking, on the steps of the Registry Office. With placid determination, she peeled the tape from the back of the frame and removed the picture.

2

The blade of the scissors she held sank hungrily into their joined hands so that the photograph, and the couple in it, were split asunder. She was doubly glad she had always insisted on using her maiden name at work. Blanche was so deep in her daydream of revenge the telephone rang several times before she answered it.

'Detective Sergeant James of Hampstead here, ma'am.' The voice was a streetwise London drawl, the sort that said 'anyfink' instead of 'anything', the Hs dropped and the vowels flat. 'I got told to call you 'cause there's been a suspicious death on 'ampstead 'eath.'

He paused, expecting her to say something and take charge of the conversation. She did not immediately. Her mind was still set on marital vengeance.

'There's no 'ead on it.'

The scissors sliced through her husband's waist with a sharp snip.

The sergeant was nonplussed by the silence and staggered on. 'It's been there a while,' he murmured with a hint of disgust, as though the remains were stinking on the desk in front of him. 'Our detective inspector says it must be a sus' death. 'E wanted the Yard called in straightaway, ma'am, so that's why I'm on the dog.'

Blanche checked where she was to meet the Camden men. 'OK,' she said curtly, 'I'll be right over.' Her husband's legs disintegrated as the blades snapped through the knees of his suit. A grim smile hovered at the margin of Blanche's full lips as she dissected the photograph further until a jumble of tiny squares lay in a heap on the dining table. She swept them into a basket and an emotion she had not sensed for a month welled up inside, an unfamiliar warmth.

The chief inspector sprang up the stairs of the maisonette to change, the sweat dribbling down her back. The faint draught that had set the net curtains billowing a few minutes before had passed away. She realised with a jolt that she was happy: content with having completed a ceremony to help exorcise Roger's ghost and pleased with having work to do.

Everything was dusty and dry. The trees skirting the Heath stood in mute despair, their leaves ashen with thirst. At almost every entrance a seedy, unshaven man lounged beside a cart on two wheels hawking ice cream and Coca-Cola.

The constable who accompanied Blanche was called Flighty. He was young. Very young. He said he was twenty, but he could easily have passed for sixteen with his thatch of black hair, face of freckles and canary chirp. She parked her car by the public entrance and the constable hopped ahead of her down towards Kenwood House, standing solid and resplendent in the sunshine.

'It's the first murder I've been involved with, you see, Chief Inspector. And then discovering it's you that's leading the investigation. Me and the wife, we even saw your photo in the papers. That was some write-up.'

She knew what he was referring to: a feature article about her last two murder cases, with an unflattering photograph of her, feet splayed apart and hands on hips like a lumberjack. She had hated that photograph and when copies sprouted on noticeboards on her floor, Blanche crept round when no one was looking and ripped them down.

The memory reminded the chief inspector to keep her feet together while she walked. When she forgot they splayed out and emphasised her slight flat-footedness. For this reason she rarely ran anywhere, preferring a fast, rather ungainly, lope in her heel-less shoes. She was almost six feet tall and had learnt to stoop slightly to lessen the embarrassment of situations like the one she found herself in that afternoon, when she stood several inches above Flighty.

'Horrible smell. I was near to throwing up. To think the head had been sawn off. Not to speak of the . . . other things,' chirruped Flighty.

The chief inspector stopped and squinted her left eye in a certain way that was characteristic when she concentrated.

Flighty was puzzled and made nervous by the sudden halt. 'Didn't anyone tell you?' he mumbled after an embarrassed silence.

'Tell me what?'

The constable tugged at his sweat-sodden shirt to escape the chief inspector's stare. 'The body's been mutilated in other places as well.' Flighty's good humour faded completely. He curled his unlined face into a grimace of disgust, and

4

gulped before speaking. 'They castrated him. Just like a bloody animal.'

They emerged from an alleyway beside Kenwood House, thick with honeysuckle. Flighty pointed across the valley. 'It's over there. You can see the lads.'

Everyone who mattered was already at the top of the incline corralled behind ribbons of white plastic tape: the local investigating officer, a photographer scurrying among the bushes, the fingerprint man and the scenes-of-crime officer. The local investigating officer was a tall, thin, bespectacled man. He had a stray patch of auburn hair perched forward like an island on the margin of his receding hairline. Detective Inspector Petherton's face was florid and puffed from too much alcohol after hours. His lips set in a naturally cruel line that curled up at both ends when he smiled. For a tired man, however, he smiled a lot.

When they arrived he was standing next to a hut, which had been built beside a tarmacked path to provide shelter for visitors to the Heath. Blanche noted his uneasiness when she introduced herself. His bloodshot eyes gazed into the hazy distance rather than into hers and Petherton's right hand kept flicking at imaginary flies on the back of his head. The chief inspector knew he was expecting a male detective from Scotland Yard. The trace of West Country vowels lurking in his speech was heightened by his nervousness as he explained how the corpse had been discovered by the dog earlier that Sunday.

'The p.c. told me there was no head on it,' she said.

The inspector nodded. 'Looks as though it was sawn off. There's no sign of it round here either.'

Blanche had started to put Petherton at his ease with her usual skill by listening intently but felt obliged to scratch at a sensitive area of the murder.

'He also told me the man was mutilated . . .' Petherton lowered his bushy eyebrows as if it were a trick question and the chief inspector frowned with irritation at his over-sensitiveness. Once again, for a moment, Blanche resented the additional obstacles she felt she had to overcome as a woman police officer, obstacles created by her own colleagues rather than by the general public.

'Castrated,' Petherton spat through his teeth.

Blanche quickly changed the subject. 'Where's the pathologist?'

'You're lucky. It's Ruxton.' He led her with a conciliatory smile into the glade. It was much cooler. The sun was blotted out apart from dappled patches on the ground. They walked along a beaten track, infrequently used but recognisable, for about ten yards and then plunged into the undergrowth on the right, trees on both sides, the odd gorse and wild blackberry, even an eglantine battling for its share of the light. A few paces and scratches further on, she greeted a knot of CID officers and then saw the opaque plastic tent which protected the dead man from prying eyes. It reminded her of something. 'You haven't told the Press Bureau, have you?'

'You must be bloody joking.'

Blanche was pleased. She distrusted journalists as a breed and did not want the newspapers there until she was ready. They would learn about the murder quickly enough. All she could do was delay the inevitable.

She remembered she should have phoned her detective sergeant. She scribbled his name and number on a scrap of paper and told Constable Flighty, who was still hopping around behind them in a state of repressed excitement, to make the call.

Near the plastic tent her nostrils crinkled. Until that point, on the outskirts of the copse and as she walked with Petherton towards the body, the smell had only hung on the air with a neutral scent – unpleasant but anonymous, attractive and repulsive, apples rotting in an orchard. As she approached the tent, pulling out the thorns that snatched at her trousers, the sweetness of the smell became sickly. The first time she had breathed that familiar stench she too, like Flighty, had wanted to retch. In the stinking darkness of the copse, she felt she had left the summer day, the sunshine and the birdsong far, far behind. Blanche plunged through a gap at the side of the plastic tent.

Ruxton was alone and on his knees. He eased himself up with a grunt. She concentrated her attention on his face, leaving the corpse a confused blur at his feet. The stench was asphyxiating but Ruxton did not seem to notice. 'Oh, it's you again, Inspector Hampton,' he murmured. 'How nice to see you. Someone told me you'd been promoted?' It was as if he were greeting her at a macabre cocktail party, hosted by a corpse whom everyone was trying to ignore.

'Yes. To detective chief inspector. About six months ago.' Like many of the English, especially women, Blanche disliked trumpeting her achievements. She felt obliged to inject the compulsory English air of scepticism by shrugging her shoulders, smiling and passing as quickly as possible to the next subject. Pride was none the less there – a quiet, relentless pride that sometimes turned to obstinacy and was sometimes interpreted as arrogance.

'Congratulations.' The pathologist's speech was precise and accurate, like his reports. Blanche rated him. Ruxton's clothes had not changed for the past forty years of his adult life: the same baggy trousers, the same brown brogues, the same tweed tie, knotted tight. He wore these clothes, whether summer or winter, day or night. Blanche wondered how he could dress like that on such a stifling day and yet not display even a glint of sweat. He was short and bustling, with big ears that he made even more prominent by rubbing his forefinger behind them when deep in thought. 'Well, death has proved once again that it hasn't lost its sting. Shall we get down straightaway to our grave business?' His eyes twinkled mischievously at the appalling pun. The chief inspector made hers twinkle back. She wanted to thank him for turning out on a clammy Sunday afternoon by responding to his jokes.

The corpse lay on its back, the branches that had covered it placed to either side. The hands and the severed neck seethed with bloated maggots. The dead man was dressed in a navy-blue sports jacket of passable quality, a white shirt, a checked burgundy bow tie and grey trousers. The neck of the shirt and jacket were caked in blood where the head had been cut off. There were some splashes of blood over the shirt and trousers. All the clothes were dusty and stained from the rotting flesh and the branches that had been thrown over the body in its makeshift grave. The pathologist rubbed behind his right ear, which flapped forward as though on a hinge. His nose, flat and broad, did not twitch at all with the stench. Dr Ruxton's assistant, a buxom and grey woman in her forties and dressed in clothes from the same period, suddenly appeared in the tent and fixed the chief inspector with the disapproving eye of a chaperone. The assistant's lipstick was smudged and her perfume heavy enough to cosh the smell of the corpse. Whenever Blanche saw her, she veered unaccountably between sadness and merriment.

'I would say it's been here for around ten days,' began Ruxton. 'From the maggots. If a body is in the sunlight the first lot of larvae are all pupae after six days – they hatch only a day after laying, you see.' The pathologist had a tendency to treat most policemen as dull students who needed help with their examinations. 'But here we're not in the sunlight. The body was slightly hidden under those branches and leaves. I would say around ten days.'

'How was he killed?'

'No evidence of violence to the body. Except the decapitation and well . . . that.' He nodded towards the dead man's crutch. All Blanche could make out was a rip in the trousers next to the fly zip.

'Was that done when he was alive?' Blanche knew she could ask the pathologist, unlike Petherton, a question about the emasculation without embarrassment.

Ruxton stared at her for a moment and sucked at his breath. 'I think he was already dead, thank God, when the beheading and castration took place. Otherwise there'd have been much more blood round the neck and . . . round the genitals.' Ruxton rocked his head slowly from side to side. 'It's a very unpleasant aspect to the killing. The first time in my forty-odd years in the job I've ever come across anything like it.' He showed the amused detachment of an ornithologist who had just observed a rare bird of passage. 'There's no other evidence of violence to the body. No gunshot or knife wounds. That leaves the head. If and when it's found, that'll probably give the cause of death.'

Blanche asked whether the dead man had been killed on the Heath.

'Probably, Chief Inspector.' Ruxton refused to call anyone, except his assistant, by their christian name. Some of the chief inspector's colleagues resented Ruxton's formality almost as much as his puns. Blanche found these quaint. It was his occasional didacticism that rankled. She hated people who

8

patronised her. 'There's no hypostasis in the corpse – you know, blood in parts of the limbs inconsistent with the posture when it was found.' To Blanche's mild irritation, he had become the pompous lecturer again. 'So, he wasn't left somewhere else first and then moved. From the scuff marks on the back of his shoes, dirt on his trousers and marks on the ground, I'd say he was murdered over there by the hut, the body was dragged, head first, over the tarmac path, into the copse and then dumped here.' He talked about things that were the province of the scenes-of-crime officer with the blithe disregard of one who despised bureaucratic frontiers.

Blanche heard shouting in the direction from where she had come. One voice raised in protest twanged with Petherton's West Country vowels. The inspector appeared a few seconds later, his cheeks as taut and scarlet as tomatoes. 'The first of the camera boys,' he puffed, glancing over his shoulder. 'Says he's got some contract with Fleet Street. I caught him trying to creep up to the tent.'

She laughed and agreed to phone the Scotland Yard press bureau with some details to keep the newspapers off their backs. 'No sign of my sergeant yet, I suppose?'

'What does he look like?'

The chief inspector smiled more to herself than to Petherton. 'Don't worry, you couldn't miss him.'

Petherton shrugged and shuffled off to superintend the search and make sure none of the press photographers managed to come close. Blanche turned back to the pathologist, who was peeling off his rubber gloves. He asked his assistant for the dictated notes and sketchpad. Ruxton handed the gloves to his assistant unthinkingly in exchange. She took them with the cloying smile of a lovelorn spinster who still hopes to make a conquest. Blanche was relieved to be out of the tent and away from the sickly scent of death.

The pathologist flicked over the pages of the sketchbook, pointing with a stubby finger to the significant details. There was no nonsense with Ruxton. Blanche admired people who did not waste time. 'The deceased was about five feet eight or so in height,' Ruxton started. 'All the pockets are empty. Presumably the killer looked through them. The clothes are all marked C&A. My assistant' (the drab woman had followed them out of the tent and glanced at him adoringly) 'says that's some kind of department store.' Ruxton lived a cloistered life, Blanche knew, shuttling between the dissecting room and his colossal greenhouse, where he raised prize-winning fuchsias. 'No cleaning tickets or visiting cards hidden in the pockets, so you won't find any leads there, I'm afraid. Petherton will be telling you more about these scene of crime things no doubt.'

'What about his age?'

Dr Ruxton's ear flapped forward. 'Between sixty and seventy. That's why the body's not putrefied more. Youth, when it's dead, decays more quickly than Age. Old people have more fat than youngsters. Well,' he sighed abruptly, 'I think I've done as much as I can this afternoon. I'll carry out the post-mortem first thing tomorrow morning.'

Ruxton led the tortuous way out to the margin of the copse. The heat of the afternoon swung up from the parched turf and hit the chief inspector over the head like a club. Dr Ruxton hitched up his corduroy trousers and squinted into the sun. Without a word his assistant brought him a straw hat. His wide, deep-set eyes spotted her smile. 'Others may laugh at my little eccentricities. But ever since being a Boy Scout as a lad, I've believed in the motto, "Be Prepared". And that's what we are, aren't we, Margo?'

Ruxton's assistant blinked in gratefulness that her presence had been recognised. Her spinster's smile smudged on the powdered face made Blanche want to giggle.

The pathologist was finished for the afternoon. Despite the first dimness in the treetops, it felt hotter rather than cooler. The sky had slid into a dark, menacing blue and a fistful of clouds loured towards the south. The air oozed around them like treacle. A squadron of flies buzzed round Blanche's glistening forehead.

A figure – dressed immaculately in matching ivory-coloured trousers and short-sleeved shirt, a brown pochette slung under one arm, Italian leather shoes glistening in the sunlight – jumped playfully across the dry stream bed in the valley half a mile away and came swinging up the hill. He waved a muscly arm at the chief inspector who, without thinking, waved back. Detective Sergeant Dexter Bazalgette had that invigorating effect on some people, but not on everyone, for Dexter was a one-man walking minority unit: black, gay, and Catholic.

'My detective sergeant,' the chief inspector explained to Ruxton. The doctor flipped an ear forward with curiosity. His assistant's face furrowed with disapproval. Neither had met him before.

Ruxton and his assistant marched off along the edge of the copse towards a path on the crest of the hill. Two journalists sprinted over to try and cut off Ruxton's retreat but Blanche knew the pathologist had been employed long enough by the Home Office to be trusted to say nothing.

Detective Sergeant Bazalgette flashed his warrant card and sauntered across. Blanche greeted him with a frank smile. He was well over six feet tall. His skin was a warm chocolate brown and shimmered with his latest perfume. Dexter cut his curly hair short and neat. Energy surged from his body, a nervous energy that melted any fat and set his feet aquiver, or his fingers tapping, even at moments of rest. His face was usually open and friendly, especially when he shot a smile of dazzling white teeth. Dexter's nose had been broken when playing rugby as a youth and it lay, flat and spongy, in the middle of an otherwise handsome set of features. The nose imparted a nasal twang to his London drawl. Dexter fixed her with his sceptical, bloodshot eyes and sucked in the facts.

The fingerprint officer was called Jones, wizened and meticulous. He could sniff out a fingerprint – whether latent, visible or plastic – as some country people can unerringly brush aside leaves hiding a colony of mushrooms. Jones was also a car bore, the sort of man who debates the merits of a carburettor as though it were a Beethoven symphony. After descanting the praise of his undersealing, he revealed that the corpse would yield up a set of prints. 'The skin on his hands is tough and dry but a spot of the old formaldehyde and alum should do the trick. I'll get the results to you as soon as I can,' he grunted.

The chief inspector sensed rather than saw the whole copse grow still. The trees, the birds, even the crickets whirring in the long grass were silent and attentive. She felt stifled by the distant stench of the corpse and the rising humidity.

Suddenly the sun was eclipsed by black, leathery clouds

11

billowing up into the sky, and the woods in the distance sank into darkness. Policemen milled around while Blanche gave orders to the unlucky few to guard the body and start a search of the area. There was nothing more she and Dexter could do at Hampstead Heath. Petherton and some fellow officers ambled towards a snackbar at the side of Kenwood House. 'Don't think that's our scene,' commented Dexter, wiping a raindrop from his counterfeit Rolex watch, 'sipping tea among damp coppers and steaming tourists.'

Lightning crackled over the grey panorama of the West End. The Post Office Tower was smudged under black pencil lines of driving rain. Blanche relished the first cold speck landing on her cheek as she rushed towards her car. By the time she was on the road back to Scotland Yard, the drops of rain were bouncing off the tarmac like stones. The gutters swirled with the dust and grit and blood of a month-long drought.

Chapter 2

Blissfully the air-conditioning was working again and the corridors were cool and quiet when Blanche loped into work the next morning at eight o'clock. She liked to arrive early, sip black filter coffee which she made in the office and ruminate alone at her desk. From the odd room the chatter of a typewriter or the murmur of conversation curled round a half-open door. The noticeboards were the only decoration on the walls: details of wanted men staring down in Identikit stupidity; internal memoranda about canteen opening times; a Serious Crimes Squad summer ball. The number of people walking the corridors in uniform thinned out and then she was at the door.

All the desks in the office except hers were piled high with papers and files and, finding no more space there, they had slithered on to the floor and occupied the carpet with the rapacity of an invading army. Dexter and one of the two constables she shared the office with smoked and, despite the open window, stale nicotine clung to the furniture, the files, even the cream plastic blind. On the window sill Blanche had placed four plants whose health she watched over assiduously, chiding the smokers in the office for using the pots as ashtrays. Her tidy desk was on the far left next to the plants and was flanked by grey filing cabinets. On the side of one filing cabinet was a calendar made by her nephews of a bird escaping from a cage. The bars of the cage were threads of rust-coloured wool and the rest of the picture was made up of patches of felt stuck on to the card.

It reminded the chief inspector with a smile of the previous Saturday when she had celebrated her thirty-sixth birthday. She had passed the day with her younger brother in Somerset, crawled over by her two nephews, rubbed by an over-affectionate and sexually confused terrier, droned at by her brother's wife and depressed by the memory of her drowned marriage. The evening of her birthday was spent in a tandoori restaurant at Taunton. Waiters sauntered through the dimness with luminous smiles and chipped plates of curry which they slid noiselessly on to the tablecloth. Much to her surprise, Blanche enjoyed it. She was good at making the best of a bad job.

One detective constable was already in. He sat slumped at his desk with a coffee, smoke already curling from a cigarette and his nose chiselled into a newspaper. 'The chief super rang a couple of minutes ago, ma'am. He wants you to tell him about this Hampstead Heath job that's in the papers this morning. Says he hasn't had a written report.'

The chief superintendent's name was engraved in block letters on a plastic plate screwed to his door: Detective Chief Superintendent Brian Spittals. In fact it was not his door but his secretary's. No one was allowed direct access to Spittals. The secretary was a sweet girl who had once worked in Blanche's office. She was plain and bland and efficient at everything, except making tea, which for some reason always tasted of petrol when she brewed it. She nodded across to Spittals' door. He was expecting her.

When Blanche stalked in, he was standing by the window, rubbing his hands together, absorbed in watching a jumbo jet which swung lazily to the south and disappeared behind a curtain. He lingered by the window for a moment as if formulating what to say, and walked in his crablike way to the desk. The chief superintendent sat there, pretending to be relaxed, but just a little too hard. He gave the impression that he thought the chair was about to collapse beneath him at any moment. His black eyes darted less than usual and did not glisten with their familiar suspicion, perhaps because his angular face was softened by a newly acquired tan. Even Spittals' thick, mousy hair was better cut and more manageable than when he had left for Spain on holiday. He straightened his tie and leant back with what was designed to be a charming smile, rubbing his hands together frantically, fingertip to fingertip, as a tacit gesture of friendliness.

'How was your holiday, sir?' she enquired politely.

'Fine. Fine. Lots of sun. The wife and kids had a whale of

a time.' He paused, still rubbing his hands together, but more slowly now. 'But I didn't ask you to step in for me to bore you with my holiday. I was wondering how you were getting along with this new murder enquiry? There was no report on it in my tray this morning and I was just, well . . . wondering.'

His eyes flickered on her breasts for a moment and turned away. Some conversations with Spittals, Blanche knew with irritation, were an opportunity for mental striptease. He had never dared proposition her of course and he did not have the charm to flirt. But sometimes his eyes undressed with covert relish, confident of protection behind the authority of his job. He was a shy man of great cunning who had married a stupid woman too young. Blanche had met her at a police social function. Her clothes were as drab as her conversation. Spittals despised his wife but had remained with her for those most universal of human excuses: pity and the children.

'I was coming to see you first thing this morning, sir.' He liked being called 'sir'. He always insisted on it, because he believed it helped maintain a proper sense of hierarchy in the force. 'It didn't seem worthwhile submitting a written report to you until I'd got the results of the post-mortem and some of the forensic tests.'

'Fair enough, lass. But let me have something in writing as soon as you can, will you? I want to feel in control. Have things at my fingertips.' Spittals rubbed his hands again but this time so vigorously Blanche thought they might burst into flame. He relaxed and sat back. 'Oh, by the way, one of the reasons I called you in was to let you know about the press conference.'

'Press conference?' Blanche asked, squinting. 'What press conference?'

'About the murder.'

'But I haven't asked for one.'

'Precisely. That's why I've called you in,' said Spittals with a nervous smirk. To some extent he was in awe of Blanche, partly because she was a clever graduate and partly because he knew in his heart that she had little respect for him. Yet he yearned for her approval. There were times when he fêted her, and others when he ridiculed her upper-middle-class accent and intellectual pretensions. 'I fixed it for this morning. The commander rang me at home last night to say he wanted more publicity for the work of the Serious Crimes Squad. Enlist the aid of the public and all that.'

On the way out, the secretary whispered that Spittals was in a panic because he was to see the commander in ten minutes and all he knew about the case was what he had read in the newspapers, which was little enough. There was a sprinkling of paragraphs colourfully relating the discovery of a headless body on Hampstead Heath. There was no mention of the castration.

Ruxton had almost finished by the time she arrived at the mortuary. The air was cool and cloyed with antiseptic. Death for Blanche was less horrible when purged of its stench and the corpse – blackened, stained and broken – was exposed under arc lights. Drops of amber liquid dripped from a finger and foot on to the tiles surrounding the body. It had been soaked overnight in a Lysol bath to kill the maggots. Dr Ruxton, clearly recognisable despite the gauze mask and cap, nodded a welcome to her and murmured something to his assistant. The dissection table stood in the middle of the room, individual refrigerators for bodies covering one wall, each with a tin door and a label. The pathologist had filled glass jars standing on a trolley table next to him with specimens as he painstakingly removed each organ from the corpse. His eyes displayed no emotion as they surveyed the mottled and headless bulk before him, a few stray grey hairs on the corpse's chest catching the light, the forefinger of its withered right hand – which had a greenish tinge like the patina on bronze – pointing to the gash between the legs. For the first time the chief inspector could clearly see the dead man was old. The Lysol had seeped into the corpse overnight, swelling the tissue, so that the parts that remained were overblown and sleek compared to the day before, but still of great frailty. The skin reminded her of damp parchment about to tear of its own accord.

Ruxton checked his notes with a grunt. He folded back the flaps of skin he had cut in the chest of the dead man and walked across. His grey lady assistant edged along behind him. 'There isn't much to add, I'm afraid, Chief Inspector.

16

I'd drop his height to five feet seven.' The pathologist smiled wearily. 'He drank too much. He smoked too much. He had arthritis, so I should think he stooped a bit when he walked. What else?' He waved a pink hand for his notes which his assistant passed. 'I would also think he was a bit younger than I first thought – closer to sixty-five than seventy.' He glanced across sympathetically to the remains on the tiled table. 'Prematurely aged due to over-indulgence. Something,' and here he turned to the chief inspector with a twinkle in his eyes, 'that never happens to members of the police force.'

They stood at the edge of the room, the white floor tiles glistening and disinfected. The table in the centre displayed the corpse like an exhibit of modern art, the fragile skin taut over the cage of bones, the two mutilations imparting a mood of the emetic macabre.

Ruxton flipped his left ear forward and caressed it gently. 'The head was cut off, probably with a saw – you know, one with fine teeth. It wasn't chopped off. And the castration . . . Some sort of knife with a serrated blade. It wouldn't take too much force with a sharp one. There's no bone to cut through,' he added with a grim smile.

Back at Scotland Yard, the blonde on the calendar above the detective constable's desk taunted Blanche, her breasts golden and firm, nipples taut as thimbles. The glossy photograph eddied the memory that she had not made love for almost three months. She despised women who were no more than painted dolls, fetish objects for the stimulation of men, even though there was a part of her that wished to emulate them. With a certain pride she compared herself to the sexual icon of the calendar: rounded face, heavy eyelids, piercing mahogany eyes and shoulder-length brown hair. She rarely needed to bother with make-up and creams, a habit learnt from her mother from whom she had inherited a clear and glowing skin. Blanche preferred books to looks.

The press conference was the usual flummery. Spittals outlined the few known facts, with the exception of the castration, at great and self-important length, concluding with a photograph of the dead man's clothing. 'This, gentlemen' – because he was a shy man Spittals addressed the journalists like troops at a briefing – 'is what the dead man was wearing at the time he met his death. Since we haven't yet established his identity and there are precious few clues to it, I might take the liberty of exercising your profession and coin a headline, that he's "The Man With No Name".'

The assembled scribes stared impassively; a few made a wan smile; the trucklers laughed out loud. They knew the chief superintendent's little jokes. They were the 'responsible' journalists on the side of law and order, members of a privileged club. Spittals flicked a rotund finger at the press officer and asked him to hand round copies of the photograph he was flourishing.

The journalists scurried off, comparing notes to confirm they all had the same story. Their collective murmur hummed with preprandial expectation. Spittals, trailed by the press officer, strutted over to Blanche and asked her to record a couple of radio and television interviews. Blanche called him to one side and quietly refused.

'You know I hate all this, sir. I get very nervous and I really don't like doing it.'

'Well, if you think you get nervous,' he rasped, 'then what about me? You're meant to be the bloody university-educated superstar putting all us old-style coppers in the shade.'

'Please, sir,' she pleaded again, sensing her throat tighten and sweat ooze into her palms.

He did not bother to answer. Instead he swept her into the arms of a harried press officer with dandruff on his collar. A second or two later she was blinking into two spotlights erected by the television crew.

'OK, John,' she heard the cameraman grunt, 'we're rolling.'

The reporter leant forward, his face and teeth glistening under a spotlight, and asked the first question.

Her soaked blouse stretched over the skin of her back as she breathed in the cauldron of air in the office. Even with the blinds down, throwing the room into a slatted haze, and Blanche's eyes shut, the light glowed red through her eyelids for a quarter of a minute.

Blanche dialled the general number for SO7, the Fingerprint

Division, and was put through to Jones' extension. After ten rings, a voice that was not his answered with a flourish of bad temper. Jones had just gone out of the office for lunch. He had put the results into the internal despatch system along with his report. Jones had searched the computer and other files for a fingerprint match on the dead man but he had had no luck. Forensic were no more helpful.

The chief inspector closed her eyes with fatigue. The heat was unbearable again. She heard footsteps and opened her eyes to find Dexter standing in front of her, looking even more pleased with himself than usual. Blanche remembered how much she had disliked Dexter when she first met him. He was theatrical, impatient and acutely sensitive to criticism for a man of twenty-eight – features that now endeared him to her because they stemmed from insecurity and a desire to do a good job. They were drawn together partly because they were both minorities in the Serious Crimes Squad, he black and she female and a graduate. She was also intrigued by his Catholicism. Brought up a High Anglican at her girls' private school, she found her faith had ebbed away completely by the time she was sixteen. Dexter, on the other hand, went regularly to mass and confession. 'What's the fun of sinning,' he always said, 'if you can't go and confess afterwards?'

His parents were among the Jamaicans who had been swept to Britain in the fifties on a wave of hope, a respectable and hard-working couple who had slowly become disillusioned with the country which they had been brought up to consider a second homeland. Dexter's father had become a bus conductor, and the son watched his father's pride being eroded, month after month and year after year, by bad luck, racial prejudice and endless drizzle. Dexter and his three sisters had been brought up strictly by their gospel-loving parents on a council estate in Shepherd's Bush. At eighteen he rebelled, left home and became a Catholic. Two years later he joined the police.

Dexter had spent the morning with the Missing Persons Index on the police national computer.

'Let me guess,' Blanche yawned. 'You're about to tell me you've found the head that belongs to our corpse, and the murder weapon, and that the weapon's smothered in finger-prints. The prints were on the computer, and now the murderer

19

of a man we haven't even identified is safely under lock and key.'

Dexter shook his head from side to side and drew languorously on his cigarette; he blew the smoke out with a smirk; the insides of his lips were the pink of boiled shrimp. Dexter smiled coyly and leant forward so that no one else would hear. 'My love life has perked up.' He dropped one of his eyelids in a meaningful wink before sitting back, holding the elbow of his right arm in the palm of his left. 'And so has your luck, ma'am. Petherton's just phoned. They've fished a human head out of the Grand Union Canal.'

Chapter 3

London is a city that grew with the relentless anarchy of weeds. It seeped out along the tendrils of cart tracks and villages, a city that flowered and seeded, forever spreading, suffocating forests and fields and mills and streams. The past had nowhere to hide but underground, interred there under brick and concrete. London is condemned to mourn its buried history, like a spinster who broods on the withered opportunities of her life, the friends who died, the love she was too shy to welcome.

Blanche composed these somewhat flyblown thoughts as she stood beneath the two-hundred-year-old brick bridge which heaved Gloucester Avenue over the old Grand Union Canal and sent it slinking down towards the centre of London. Dr Ruxton, efficient as ever, was kneeling at her feet, examining the severed head. They were cut off from the rest of London above and around them, in a secret culvert that ran through the heart of the city. It was the most easterly of three bridges bunched together near Regent's Park. The cars that drove over the top were unaware of the knots of policemen beneath, as unaware as the passengers in the trains that thrummed and clanked their way across the two studded iron bridges a few yards away to the left.

Dexter's eyes rolled down from the brick vaulting under the furthest railway bridge to the green water below and then up again. Black patches of damp brooded among the bricks even though it was the height of a dry summer. Water dribbled down the side of the bridge in rivulets of glistening slime, as if a convoy of giant slugs had made it their motorway. Beneath the bridges the air was chill and concentrated, heavy with the stagnant smell of rotting vegetation. 'This place gives me the creeps,' he murmured.

Inspector Petherton smiled condescendingly. He considered

21

Dexter a black gay wimp who had only managed to enter the police because of positive discrimination. The inspector had been there an hour before they arrived and had cordoned off the site discreetly. Petherton told Blanche a lad aged ten from the local council estate had been playing with a friend beside the canal and spotted a black plastic rubbish bag bobbing in the water. It was amongst a scum of refuse – polystyrene, blackened twigs, leaves – in the lee of a derelict lighter moored under the middle bridge on the other side of the canal. Since the bag was tied into a bundle with string, the boy thought there might be something intriguing inside, so the two lads clambered down the farther bank and fished it out. An orange buoy now marked the spot where the head had been found. It showed clearly when the darkness under the bridges lifted as the police photographer's lights burnt away the gloom. The damp bricks seemed to shrink back in terror, like lice and centipedes startled under a rock by an inrush of daylight.

Dr Ruxton creaked to his feet. His assistant took the notebook from his outstretched hand. The bloated and anaemic head lay on its side on the concrete pathway of the canal, still on the black rubbish bag in which it had been wrapped. The eyelids were closed, the mouth partly open. The head looked as though it were made of wax. The dead man must have been imposing with his bony brow and beaked nose, Blanche thought, but otherwise she was disappointed: the water seemed to have washed away not only all the blood but with it any sense of character and animation. The decapitated head was like a mass-produced bust. Ruxton pointed to two neat holes at the nape of the neck. 'You don't need to look very far for the cause of death, do you?' he grunted. 'Shot through the base of the skull at point-blank range.'

'Not the sort of thing a mugger does,' Blanche commented.

'Yes. Feels like an execution, doesn't it? Neat. Clean. Efficient.'

Blanche squinted her left eye in puzzlement. The frigid efficiency of the murder seemed at odds with the mutilations.

'Perhaps it's a gangland killing,' suggested Dexter. 'One of the South London gangs settling an old score. Or drugs maybe. The old boy wanted too big a cut.'

Petherton raised his auburn eyebrows a disapproving quarter of an inch. 'You've been watching too many video nasties.'

Dexter bristled. He was over-sensitive to criticism. Anxious to dispel the tension, Blanche pressed Ruxton further. 'Is it the head of the guy we found on Hampstead Heath?'

The pathologist flapped forward his right ear and scratched behind it for a moment. 'Since there's a pretty limited stock of severed human heads in the London area at the best of times, I'd stick my neck out and say it *is* the same chap.' Ruxton giggled at his appalling pun, as did his lady assistant, whose neighing laugh resounded under the bridge. No one else thought it was funny.

'Do you think it's been floating on the surface all the time?'

The pathologist blew his nose thoughtfully. 'My guess is that whoever it was trying to get rid of the head tied some string or rope round the top of the bag and attached a weight to make it sink. But the bag slipped free and floated up to the surface.'

Blanche sauntered away and stood between the two railway bridges. The others followed. Through a gap of about five or six feet, the chief inspector breathed in the slab of pale blue sky. Behind her was a set of concrete steps leading up to Gloucester Avenue. The wall was smothered in a scrawl of multicoloured graffiti – pillar-box red, brown, lemon yellow, black. The indecipherable hieroglyphics of an alienated underclass. Eight feet above her, a buddleia sprang from the brickwork, and on its flowers fed three small tortoiseshell butterflies. Blanche was always moved by tokens of nature in the midst of the sterile city. 'Any idea of the type of gun, Doctor?' Blanche would follow the matter up with the experts at the police laboratory but always valued Ruxton's opinion.

She walked under the second railway bridge and into the sunshine. The pathologist waddled beside her, the fusty assistant bustling along behind with Dexter and Petherton. 'Can't tell yet. Haven't extracted the bullets. But I'd say it was probably a revolver with a silencer attached.'

'There was no violence to the head apart from the gunshot?'

'None at all. As I said, clean and efficient.'

They stood together silently in a knot and looked down at the impenetrable green of the canal. Blanche felt she stood in an impasse with no clear way forward. Ruxton sensed the same, for he waited a moment, sighed and murmured that there was nothing more he could do. He strode back towards his macabre package on the canal bank. His faithful assistant breezed along behind, having tossed the chief inspector a farewell glance of more than usual dislike.

A pleasure launch chugged round the bend on the left and was hailed by one of the constables on the towpath. The chief inspector nodded and Dexter waved the boat on. The captain revved up the engine with a whiff of black smoke and it glided under the bridges and between a row of handsome Victorian villas on one side, and a block of modern flats on the other. Also moored on the right, towpath side were several houseboats.

While Dexter went off with their detective constables to question residents of the block of flats and Petherton strode away to tell his men to rattle the brass door knockers of the Victorian villas on the other side, the chief inspector remained on the towpath and wandered towards the houseboats moored by the bank.

The first two had no signs of life. Gas bottles stood on the prows. Branches and odd pieces of timber lay on the roofs, ready to be taken below for fuel. The rear doors were padlocked shut. The third boat looked equally deserted. The scarlet paint on the sides was peeling and the prow was partially hidden under a patched tarpaulin. One of the side windows was not curtained and through it she registered five art gallery postcards stuck on to a cupboard that were curling in the sun, a jar of dried flowers and a filthy duvet cover that was once cream in colour. The last caused her to wince. Untidiness made Blanche vaguely irritable but uncleanliness was for her a form of bestiality. When her eyes became used to the obscurity, she made out beneath the duvet a man asleep. She rapped on the glass. He stirred. She knocked again but louder.

He sat up, rubbing his bleary eyes. 'Fuck off, will you?' he groaned without looking at her. 'This is a private home. I don't rent the boat out to anybody, I don't give directions to foreign tourists and I don't give guided tours – except to royalty.' He cantered through the litany as if he repeated it regularly.

'I'm the next best thing to royalty,' she countered.

'What's that?'

'Police.'

The man stopped rubbing his eyes and stared at Blanche through the dirty window. 'You've been reading too many newspapers. You believe you're as marvellous as they keep telling you you are.'

He threw off the duvet with a scowl and crawled out of sight down the hull to meet Blanche at the back doors, dressed in a dirty singlet and shorts. Between the makeshift bed and opening up the rear doors, the man underwent a transformation of mood, from morose to jocular. 'I'm Monty Turing, unpublished novelist and unemployed theatre director. Welcome on board the good ship *Cerberus*,' he said expansively, waving a pudgy hand in a mock bow. He was about forty-five, short and epicene, every muscle coated in white fat. Turing moved his body slowly. No energy was to be wasted. The only part of him with any spirit of quickness was his lips, which rattled at breathless speed.

She introduced herself and told him a severed head had been found in the canal. He whistled. 'They really should dredge out this canal more often, you know. People are just using it as a rubbish dump. I'll have to complain to the council.' He stepped down from the boat on to the towpath, setting his fat aquiver.

A smile slunk round his pudgy and unshaven cheeks like a cat that wanted to be stroked. The smile faded when the chief inspector did not return it. She found his bonhomie as empty as the bravura of his original rudeness.

'But I don't see what I've got to do with it,' he went on. 'I don't go around dismembering bodies and tossing bits in the canal. That causes pollution.'

'In that case, perhaps you can help me find the person who polluted it by throwing in this human head.'

Turing's horselike eyes swivelled to one side with suspicion. 'Unlikely. I haven't got much of the vigilante in me. I'm asleep most of the time.'

'That's one of the few things you've told me I believe.'

He nodded his head up and down. 'Really?'

Before he could stop her, Blanche jumped adroitly on to the platform at the back and plunged down the steps into the gloom of the hold. She heard Turing squeak with irritation

25

and follow her through the galley past a portable gas stove caked in grease and into the living accommodation. Towards the prow on a low table was a battered typewriter surrounded by overflowing ashtrays and sheets of paper. Turing stood in the doorway babbling with anger that she had no right to come into his house without permission. 'If you don't get out straightaway, I'm going to call my lawyer.'

Blanche glanced around the dimness. 'With what? Carrier pigeons?'

As the chief inspector moved closer to the table where the typewriter stood, Turing ran his tongue across his lips. Blanche picked up several sheets of paper, all marked 'page one' and with variations of the same dialogue. 'Writer's block?' she enquired, distilling a familiar scent from the fug of the room.

Turing shrugged lazily and said nothing. His tongue flickered over his lips again.

'I can't say I'm surprised,' she went on, fingering an ashtray.

The writer had gone strangely quiet. 'It's common enough. Writer's block.'

Blanche stared at him in mock sympathy before she lifted the ashtray to her nose and sniffed. 'Not for those who smoke this. When one's high on marijuana the words just flow out.'

Turing's cheeks tightened. His big, round, brown eyes drilled into hers to discover what the policewoman wanted. 'How long do you think the head's been there?' he murmured hesitantly.

She shrugged. 'Around twelve days.'

'So that would be . . . a week and a half ago?'

The chief inspector detected a veneer of meditation glued to his voice, a pretence of effort at remembering. Blanche turned the ashtray with the remnants of the joints round and round with her manicured fingernail. 'About then.' She looked up.

'Now you come to mention it . . .' Turing shuffled uneasily.

'Mention what?'

'The Thursday night before last.'

The chief inspector waited patiently.

'I was outside, sitting on the roof of the boat. I suppose it must have been about three in the morning.'

'Three in the morning?' she squinted in surprise.

'Yeah. Three in the morning.' He half swallowed an apologetic laugh. His tongue flickered once more over his dry lips, which moved faster when he spoke again. 'You see, when my muse is in form I work right through the night. I did it last night and slept through the whole day – until you woke me up.'

The chief inspector frowned with disapproval. She was suspicious of people with irregular habits.

'Straight up,' he continued. 'I wrote till six this morning. Anyway, the Thursday before last, I popped out for a quick fag at three in the morning to clear the mind. The night was peaceful, there was a sliver of a moon in the sky, just the odd star twinkling.' Turing was regaining his composure.

'No poetry, please, Mr Turing. Just tell me what happened.'

He blubbed out a pretence of wounded pride, then shrugged. 'Not much. I was on the roof of the boat and heard a splash. As if something had been dropped into the canal. I shouted out because we've had quite a few people dumping junk into the water at the dead of night. Bicycles, televisions, mattresses. You name it.' Turing took a deep breath and plunged on. 'Anyway, I disturbed whoever it was because they ran away.'

'How do you know?'

'I heard footsteps running away –'

'– One set or two?'

Turing pondered. 'Can't remember. It's one of those things I didn't take much notice of.'

'It made enough of an impact for you to remember it at all.'

He laughed nervously and edged forward, trying to be open and friendly. 'Look, I don't want to get involved in this. How do I know this guy isn't going to murder again and that I'll be the one to get it in the neck next time?'

Blanche waited, unimpressed. She wanted to exploit the glint of desperation in his eyes. 'How many sets of footsteps?'

He stopped about six feet from her and sighed. 'I don't know. Probably one. It was just a clatter, a car door slammed, the engine revved up and the car was gone.'

'How do you know?'

'I wandered up to the bridge. For Chrissake, I just thought it was a bit of junk,' he gabbled defensively. 'There were ripples in the middle of the canal and some bubbles gurgling up. But nothing else, so I just wandered back.'

Blanche nodded slowly. 'You didn't see who it was on the bridge? Whether it was a man or a woman?'

The nocturnal novelist shook his head like a wayward child refusing food.

Blanche told Turing she would need a statement from him. He whined but when Blanche started to twirl the ashtray with her finger again, he gurgled with laughter and said he would write the statement in the style of Raymond Chandler. It made her wonder how much of what he had told her was true. As she watched his animated, unshaven face and hairless arms restlessly cross and uncross, she decided he had embroidered the incident with unnecessary atmosphere but that the essentials were correct.

The police photographer and forensic officer were still scrambling over the bank opposite when Blanche climbed up past the graffiti on to Gloucester Avenue. Next to the canal was another brick factory, long and bleak. One part was occupied by a linen company, and from a window on the topmost storey a plaintive female wail quivered on the summer air. It was irresistibly foreign, a song of the casbah, a woman toiling for a few pennies and homesick for her native land. In all directions stretched lines of terraced Victorian houses, the street level stuccoed in rustic, the first floors with elegant cornices and buttresses. The odd car and pedestrian passed along, but the avenue would have been completely empty at three o'clock on any morning.

Four hours later, forty feet below where she stood, and twenty yards away from where the head was found, the divers brought up a second rubbish bag full of bricks and covered with mud and slime – the bag used to try to sink the severed head.

Chapter 4

There was no natural illumination at all, only two strip lights which bathed the gloss cream walls with a bluish hue. The room was in the centre of Kensington police station and blissfully cool. It was all so intensely familiar to the chief inspector, from the grey locker in the left-hand corner with papers and rags tumbling out around the half-closed door, to the smell of instant coffee limping through the air. The smell of the coffee explained itself quickly enough: a plump woman police constable bent down by the skirting board pouring water from an electric kettle into polystyrene cups. The girl sitting opposite with a sneer in her green eyes was to prove much more difficult to explain.

The call had come through that morning, two days after the severed head had been found in the canal. The collator telephoned from Kensington police station and said a young woman had just come in to report her father missing. Her description of him tallied with that of the unidentified murder victim. She had apparently just returned from holiday and found her father's flat in South Kensington empty.

'A warning though, Chief Inspector, before you arrive.'

'What?'

'She don't like the police one little bit.'

The woman was reading a feminist magazine and every line of her body, every article of clothing, every crease of the way she held the magazine oozed hostility. She was short and neat and angular, dressed in a purple silk shirt, baggy grey trousers and heel-less moccasins. Her corn-blonde hair was cropped rather than cut and was drawn together in a short ponytail at the back. Her face was freckled and suntanned, her nose aggressively pert. Her tiny eyes flew into Blanche's like darts.

She hardly stirred when the chief inspector walked in, just folded the magazine and looked up. 'So, is it him?' she asked.

The voice was educated and strident, the sort that would slice easily through a crowded room. As she spoke her bottom, almost prehensile, lip quivered. The enamelled rings on her fingers, the sort on sale at trendy craft stalls, trembled ethnically as she lit another cigarette.

The station officer, a harmless and friendly man in his early fifties, introduced Blanche to the girl, who was called Christine Mills. 'Tracy,' he murmured to the woman police constable, 'perhaps you would be kind enough to make two more coffees.'

'You should make them yourself,' snapped Miss Mills. 'Unless it's too difficult an operation for you male, senior policemen.'

The WPC reddened and looked down at the floor. The sergeant half opened his mouth but closed it quickly. The WPC moved to the door. She and the sergeant left.

Blanche pulled up a chair from the wall and sat at right angles to the girl. Sitting opposite someone, the chief inspector knew from experience, only encouraged confrontation.

Christine Mills snapped out her question again. 'So, is it him?'

'Who?'

'Don't be so bloody obtuse. The body that's been found. Is it my father?' Her chin narrowed to a point and, with the downward pout of the lips, added further to the sense of obdurate petulance. Black plastic earrings depended like prunes from her fleshy ears. They looked heavy enough to rip through the lobes, plummet down and make a dent in the tiled floor.

Blanche spread her hands in a gesture of innocence. 'I don't know. That's why I'm here.' She rocked backwards and forwards very slightly on the chair. She wanted to allow a few moments for Christine's aggression to dissipate. She glanced up at the harsh strip lights and down again. 'Do you happen to have a photograph of your father?'

The girl said nothing but rummaged about in a cheap red plastic attaché case. Christine Mills slid a colour portrait across the table with an ambiguous twist of the nostril, indicating either embarrassment at her emotion or dislike of her father. The corrupted features of the corpse Blanche had seen matched those of the man in the photograph. They were quite different from the artist's impression Dr Ruxton and she had commissioned, but the chief inspector was used to art and nature being at variance in police work.

An instinct stirred in Blanche as she scrutinised the creased photograph. It was bleached of all character, snapped in a studio as though for a passport or official archive. It reminded Blanche of the airbrushed portraits of Soviet leaders she had seen: emotionless icons rather than living men. The man was dressed formally, the knot of the tie constricted and tight. The shoulders were hunched, the head dominated by wisps of what must once have been blond hair, lazy blue eyes floating on red pouches of flesh and a prominent nose. The skin was clean-shaven and slightly mottled with age. A self-satisfied smile that just remained within the bounds of modesty twanged on the thin lips. Blanche had suspected the eyes were deeply set with pouches beneath but she had not expected the murder victim to have remained so handsome, even though his flesh had fattened with age. The only sure identification, however, would come when Christine Mills saw the body and the clothes.

'What was your dad's name?'

'Graham. Graham Mills.'

'And is the photo very recent?'

'Yeah. Dad had it taken a couple of years ago.' She laid a stress of displeasure on the word 'taken'.

'You don't seem to be very pleased with it.'

She sniffed. 'That's right. I *wasn't* very pleased with it.' Christine Mills spoke more to herself than Blanche.

'Why?'

Christine ignored the question. She had not heard. Her mind was elsewhere. 'Look, do you really think it was my dad who was found on Hampstead Heath?' Her voice was suffused with a momentary panic. With relief, Blanche noticed the façade of the girl's anger had cracked to reveal another, as yet unidentified, emotion beneath.

The chief inspector murmured that she did not know yet and thought it was the right time to ask if she could call her Christine, rather than Miss Mills. Christine waved a jewellery-encrusted hand, indicating she did not care a damn. Blanche repeated the question about why she was not happy with the photograph.

Christine shrugged and replied she was not sure. 'I suppose I was disappointed,' she said finally. 'I asked him for a photograph, you know, thinking I'd get something informal and relaxed. Something that was Dad. Instead I got that. There's no character, nothing of Dad in that at all. And he'd done it deliberately.'

Blanche knew just what she meant. It was a bureaucrat's photograph, a snapshot for officialdom, like those taken at her boarding school to send to proud parents and print in the school magazine. She pushed her chair back a couple of inches. The rubber tips of the feet caught on the floor. Christine tensed as the sound squeaked in her ears. Blanche paused for the tension to drain from her face and asked how she discovered her father was missing.

'I told the other guy at least twice,' the girl squawked, and stubbed out her half-finished cigarette as though she wanted to push it right through the ashtray. 'Why do I have to repeat myself?'

The chief inspector uttered some soothing banalities, despite her irritation at the woman's behaviour.

Christine exhaled to give the appearance of trying to keep her temper in check. 'I got home from holiday last night about nine. I wanted to ring him and just let him know that I'd got back all right. The phone just rang and rang. I assumed he'd gone out. So I tried later.'

'What time?'

'About eleven thirty. Still no reply. Same thing this morning. So, I drove round to find out what had happened. I was in a kind of panic. I thought something might have happened to him. He didn't answer the bell. It's a huge block and the caretaker said he hadn't seen Dad around for several days. I knew he had no plans to go away at all. He's very predictable like that. Anyway, if he was going away suddenly he would have left a message for me with the caretaker or on my answering machine.' She lit another cigarette and inhaled voraciously. Blanche waited. 'I panicked. I thought the old man might have had a heart attack or something. I started screaming and shouting, because at first the caretaker refused to smash the door in.' She glanced at her questioner but lingered for a fraction of a second too long. It had been calculated for an effect and the chief inspector wanted to discover which one.

'Haven't you got keys for your father's flat?' Blanche asked. She had always had a set to her mother's.

'You must be joking,' Christine replied with a derisive snort. 'Dad kept himself to himself. I asked him once if he would let me have a key but he said he'd rather not.'

'Why was that?'

'Deep down, he didn't trust other people. Besides,' Christine leant forward with the malice of a whispered confidence on her face, 'even though he was seventy, he was still a randy devil. Perhaps he was afraid I would barge in and catch him at it. You know what men are like.'

Blanche pulled in her bottom lip and rested her teeth on it. She had recently learnt how treacherous men could be. That did not stop her still liking most of them. Christine gave the impression of despising men generally and her father in particular. Blanche was intrigued but decided to disguise what interested her. 'How did you finally get into the flat?'

'The caretaker guy finally got a crowbar and knocked the door in. I don't know why but I expected to see Dad spread-eagled on the floor.' She smiled – a mean, dry, clever smile. 'But there was nothing. The flat was just empty.'

'What did you do then?'

'I called you lot. And then . . .' The cigarette shook uncontrollably in her hand. She gulped back the first sob but could control no more. Convulsion after convulsion quivered through her body. The chief inspector said nothing. She knew she sometimes had the dubious gift anyway for saying the wrong thing at the wrong time. Besides, Christine Mills' grief was edged with a sense of performance, of theatricality. Blanche felt like a spectator at the theatre. Drained by tears, Christine's eyes burned with less hostility. They were as flat and lustreless as two old coins. The electric clock, six minutes slow Blanche noticed with her usual exactness, buzzed on the wall.

The door opened and Dexter appeared. He sat down, alert and edgy, at the back of the room to the right of Christine Mills, forearms resting on the insides of his thighs. She deliberately caught his eye in a way that said, 'I'm no racist, I recognise you as a deeply significant human being.' Dexter smiled back vacantly.

33

'I'm afraid I'm going to have to ask you to come and look at the remains,' Blanche said softly.

'Can you stop being so apologetic?' Christine snapped. 'You mean come and see if it's my old man or not?' Her nicotine-stained fingers reached out for another cigarette, which she lit with a trembling flourish. The chief inspector was puzzled. Christine's tone oscillated between the transparently carefree and the apparently distraught, as easily as the feelings for her father swung from distaste to despair.

'Just before we go, I'd like to ask you a few questions about your father. I know he was retired but what did he do before that?'

Christine blew her nose petulantly. Her eyelids were swollen and raw. 'He worked for the government for a while. The Foreign Office or something.'

'Which department?'

'God, I don't know. I was born back in sixty-four. Dad had retired two years earlier and set up a business selling caravans, of all things. He sold out a few years ago.'

'When did he get married?'

'In 1961.'

'And what happened to your mother? Is she still alive?'

Christine flicked some ash from her cigarette by tapping it with her forefinger. 'Dad went back to playing around with other women – you know the way some men are, only interested in themselves – and after a while Mum had enough. They separated and got a divorce.' She stubbed out the half-finished cigarette and lit another abstractedly.

'Do you still see your mother now?' enquired Dexter.

Christine Mills injected a note of false sincerity into her voice. She wanted to make it appear she was speaking to a friend and the words suddenly began to flow more freely from her tongue. 'Not very often. We don't get on terribly well. We had a big row when I was eighteen – that's several years ago now – about me sleeping with a married man when I was at university. Things have never really been great since. She wants me to marry some boring chartered accountant, stay at home and look after his two point four children.'

'So what do you do instead?' Dexter asked sharply.

She scrutinised the sergeant to assess his motives. 'That's

34

none of your business,' she bridled. 'The police know too much about people like me already.'

Blanche decided to try irony on her. 'All policemen approve every single thing every single policeman ever does, you know.'

The chief inspector realised the woman was too earnest for irony. Christine only looked defensive, and felt the need to justify herself by boasting. 'Since you have it on file already, there's not much harm in me telling you. I'm a writer. I'm about to have several books published. I work for a radical collective in Islington called "Spark". That's also the name of our magazine. You should both read us, you know, trailblazing your way up this patriarchal and racist organisation.' She spoke the last sentence without even the ghost of a smile.

Dexter smirked knowingly at the word 'racist'. 'How do you know I don't read it already?' he asked.

'You wouldn't be here if you did.' Christine Mills turned to glare at Blanche, brimming with self-importance. Dexter hoisted his mahogany-brown eyes up to the ceiling. He thought Christine Mills was, in one of his phrases, 'talking shit'.

Blanche chuckled to try to release some of the tension before she ironed out her face into seriousness. 'Do you think your dad had any enemies? Was he in debt?'

Christine considered for a moment. 'He made a lot of money a few years back when he sold the caravan company and retired. He's always complaining about what he calls his "pittance". It makes me sick, with all the poor people in this country screwed into the ground by this mean bloody government. What he calls his "pittance" would feed an unemployed family in the North for weeks.'

'What about enemies?'

'I wouldn't know. He's a gentleman in his way. Sensitive, but also cold and hard right in the middle. Mum said once he has a fridge where his heart should be.'

'If your father dies, who would stand to benefit most financially?'

'I honestly don't know. Probably Mum and I.' She drew languidly on her cigarette.

'When was the last time you saw your dad alive?' asked Dexter.

She cocked her head to one side and pondered. Her skin was clear and smooth and covered in a layer of down like a fresh peach. She was not a beautiful woman. Her eyes were cramped together, her features too angular. But her complexion was beautiful, and Christine's concentration imparted to her face what in another woman could easily have been taken for charm had it not been crushed immediately by an outburst of irritation. 'I can't remember. I can't be bothered to remember.'

'Come on,' said Dexter, standing up and walking round beside the chief inspector, 'you must remember. Did you see him just before you left on holiday?'

Suspicion clutched Christine's eyes tighter together. She paused. 'A few days before, yes.'

Dexter pressed on. 'How many days?'

'I told you,' she muttered through clenched teeth. 'I can't remember exactly. Perhaps a week or five days. I went round to his flat. He seemed OK.'

'Did you phone him?'

She hesitated. She wanted to snap at him but Dexter was black and she felt obliged to be pleasant. 'Probably. A couple of days before I left.'

'You don't sound very sure?'

She crossed her arms, with a tinkle of jewellery. 'I told you all I can remember.'

'Did anything seem out of the ordinary when you saw him?'

'No. He seemed OK.'

Dexter twisted the extravagant gold ring on his right hand. 'Have you any idea why your dad might go to Hampstead Heath about a fortnight ago?'

'No idea. Dad doesn't like the outdoor life of walks and fresh air. He prefers a bottle of claret – or rather several bottles – and a good restaurant.'

Blanche interrupted. 'Where were you a fortnight ago, incidentally?'

Christine threw back her head and pronounced every syllable as though it were an enunciation exercise. 'I can't remember. Probably just about to go away on holiday.'

'Where did you go?'

'It's none of your business.'

'And who did you go with?' asked Dexter with a malicious smile.

'That's even less of your business.' Her lips were pressed tightly together again: a thin line of silence. She was going to say nothing more.

The assistant in the chapel of rest wheeled in the remains and casually flicked back the plastic sheet. The severed head had been placed back on the neck but lay at an unnatural angle to it. Christine whimpered under her breath that it was her father, turned as white as the walls and retched into a bucket in the corner.

The block of flats in the heart of South Kensington where Graham Mills lived reeked of respectable money. Blanche could tell at a distance from the well-pointed brickwork and the neat windows, the chauffeur in the car park buffing a Rolls-Royce, the tidiness. A different sort of block cast a shadow over her childhood: a postwar block that rose up three storeys on the corner of two suburban roads in Streatham. Putty sprang out from cast-iron window frames. There was no lift. The brickwork, although firm and solid, was ragged at the edges and in winter was sometimes emerald green with moss near the roof. They had lived on the top floor and Blanche remembered herself and her brother following the weary figure of their mother up the bare, concrete stairs to their flat.

Their uneventful and happy lives had been shaken when their father died suddenly twenty-five years ago. Blanche was eleven. In order to keep the two children at private schools, their mother sold their detached house and bought the flat. The service charge was exceptionally low. Blanche had been raised in shabby respectability, her mother continuously bewailing the sacrifices she was making on their behalf and instilling into her daughter a fear of failure that she had never lost. Her mother despised the neighbours with all the bitchiness of the upper-middle-class snob who has fallen on hard times. The neighbours responded by either pandering to her superior background or deriding her 'airs'. The chief inspector's mother had always been a dreamer. That was why she had called her daughter Blanche. She had once seen a stage version of *A*

Streetcar Named Desire, and insisted on naming her daughter after Blanche Dubois. She realised the character was mad but thought the name had an 'aristocratic timbre'.

The chauffeur in the car park narrowed his eyes as Dexter parked the car in a corner of the asphalted yard. 'This is private parking here,' he croaked haughtily. 'Residents only.'

Dexter bristled. They had no time to cruise around the streets to find a parking space.

The chauffeur hesitated and garnered what remained of his pride. 'If you don't move, I'm going to have to call the police.'

'Don't bother,' quipped Dexter with a toothy smile, 'we're already here.'

Inside the walls were panelled in oak and the green carpet – the green of a privet bush – stretched away into soft corridors without a speck of dust or twirl of white cotton. Red chrysanthemums lolled elegantly in a crystal vase. Above the desk a sheet of glass hung down from the ceiling engraved with the word 'Reception', and behind the desk lounged a girl with false eyelashes who was painting her nails. She told them the caretaker, Mr Reynolds, was upstairs watching Mr Mills' flat until the carpenter arrived to fix a new lock.

The door to Graham Mills' flat was ajar. Round the lock the wood was jagged and the paint bruised. They disturbed a man leafing through a book, which he had obviously taken from the glass-fronted case against the wall. He was taken aback: the look of the servant caught swigging from the sherry decanter.

Reynolds, like some of the older residents of Queensbury Court, Blanche guessed, had seen better days. His suit was clean and well turned out, but the cuffs had begun to fray and the elbows of the jacket had been patched. The time for repair was past. He hunched forward naturally but kept making strenuous efforts to jerk his shoulders back and stand up straight. His face was long and thin, as though it had been squashed between two flat irons.

An air of defiance hovered in the room. The wallpaper had begun to yellow, the paint around the picture rail to mottle. Near the door the carpet was frayed. The sitting room was relatively tidy for a man who lived alone. The books on the shelves were few but neatly arranged; the magazines – *Country*

Life and *Paris Match* for the most part although a *Playboy* peered out mischievously from amongst them – were in orderly piles on the two coffee tables. Everything was powdered with a layer of dust and motes were suspended in a shaft of sunlight that struggled through the net curtains.

'Have you found out where Mr Mills has gone then, miss?' Reynolds enquired as though of a neighbour. The caretaker eyed Dexter suspiciously. He wanted to ignore him, pretend Blanche alone was there. 'His daughter was quite beside herself this morning, you know. He's been away for spells before but she didn't seem too bothered then.'

Dexter showed his irritation at being excluded from the conversation by raising his voice and loping into the caretaker's eyeline. 'We think he's gone away permanently. He's been murdered.'

Reynolds turned to Dexter for the first time and his eyebrows jerked together. He threw the next remark at the chief inspector with a snort of disbelief. 'Your friend must be joking, miss. Mr Mills murdered!'

'We're not joking. His body's been found all right,' continued Dexter, a serious and intent stare on his face, nostrils flared with the insult to his ego. 'Head chopped off. Balls chopped off.'

'That's enough, Sergeant', the chief inspector interrupted. The crudeness Dexter had learnt on the streets offended her sense of propriety.

Reynolds' hard-boiled eyes swung to Dexter, to Blanche and back to Dexter again. His mouth flopped open as if about to say something but no sound emerged and his lips sank back into one grey line. He still thought Dexter was joking.

Dexter noisily began a search. Reynolds sank down into the sofa, which was of brown leather and of dubious taste, the tubular arms and legs made of glistening aluminium. The armchairs matched. The suite had slunk straight from the pages of an avant-garde design catalogue of the seventies and jarred with the rest of the furniture: reproduction Victorian, elegant and over-lacquered, and stained a hideous orange.

Blanche walked up and down the room. She decided to play the hostess, and smiled. 'You were saying that Mr Mills used to go away for odd periods?'

'On and off. For a few days at a time. Sometimes a few weeks. But he always told me when he was going away, mind. Until this time.' Reynolds examined his shoes with a look of surprise as if he had never seen them before. 'When his daughter came round this morning all of a kerfuffle like, I got quite alarmed. She started screaming the place down.'

'And he always told you when he was going away before?' interrupted Dexter.

The caretaker did not drag his eyes away from his shoes. 'Always.'

Dexter probed again, wishing to embarrass the man. 'Why didn't you call the police before? Surely you'd normally have seen him around the place – going in and out. Why didn't *you* get suspicious?'

Reynolds was aggrieved. His grey cheeks flushed with blotches of annoyance. But still he did not look up. 'It's not my job to keep checking up on the residents, finding out where they are at all hours of the day. It'd be more than my job's worth to carry on like that.' He calmed down and ran a calloused hand through his hair. 'The truth is, that I *was* getting a bit worried like, 'cos I hadn't seen Mr Mills round for a couple of days. But I didn't see it as my job . . .' Reynolds shuffled apologetically.

Blanche nodded. She understood Reynolds' reticence. Mills valued his privacy. He would not have appreciated the caretaker snuffling around after him. She had become irritated by Dexter's aggression, so she walked towards the caretaker and infused her voice with gentleness. 'So when did you see him last?'

'I couldn't say exactly. Somewhere between a fortnight and a week ago probably. He was always coming and going, a very pleasant sort of chap. Always pass the time of day with you, you know. Talk about this and that. He didn't have any side, did Mr Mills.'

'Did you talk about anything in particular?'

He thought for a moment, pursing his lips, relieved that Blanche had taken over the questioning. 'Not really. Except the war. He was in Germany about the same time as me, forty-four and forty-five. Talked about his daughter sometimes. On the one hand he seemed quite proud of her. On the other, he seemed a bit put out by her political views. Said she was a communist or something. Apart from that, it was the usual things. The weather and so on.'

'Was he a rich man?' put in Dexter, thumbing through some leather-bound volumes in the bookcase.

'Mr Mills certainly had a few bob until about a year ago. Someone told me he lost a lot of money in shares or something. He was on his uppers for a while and then, just recently, he seemed to perk up again.'

Steps thundered in the hall, steps muffled by the carpet but still distinct and determined, a group of men in a hurry. They materialised at the door, four of them. They stood framed in the doorway for a moment before entering. Two of them were thickset and suspicious, heavy heads protruding from heavy shoulders, dressed in heavy suits inappropriate for summer. Their leader – and it was clear he was their boss from the submissive look they gave him – was less clear-cut, short, effete and elegant. They were from Special Branch, Blanche knew intuitively. Policemen with sophistication, walking the no-man's-land between crime and subversion. If three were from Special Branch, the fourth man – youthful and bony – had an indefinable air of apartness.

'I'm Inspector Dickinson from Scotland Yard. Who are you?' asked the elegant Special Branch man, flourishing his warrant card. Blanche relished Dickinson's faint blink when he heard her rank. Special Branch look down on the rest of the police, cultivating their mystique of secrecy and supposed superior brainpower: Blanche knew all recruits were required to have shorthand or a foreign language. But rank is rank and she was one of the cleverest of the graduate recruits.

Dickinson asked one of his constables haughtily to escort Reynolds downstairs. He nodded to the other one to go outside with Dexter and stand guard outside the door. Dexter protested but the chief inspector ordered him to shut up and do as he was told. Only three remained: Blanche by the coffee table, Dickinson by the door and the fourth man in the shaft of sunlight – a diffuse, black profile. Blanche felt under attack by a group of men conspiring together, the only woman in the room. Something about the way these supposedly fellow police-men had barged in just at the moment she was interviewing a witness and presumed to squeeze her out – they had not yet said it but she sensed it in their manner – made the muscles tighten round her throat. A flush of anger rose in her cheeks. She breathed in slowly to prevent her voice quavering, and spoke with her most regal air. 'Would you mind telling me, Inspector' – she laid deliberate stress on his inferior rank – 'what interest you and the Branch have in Graham Mills? One moment I'm here, investigating a murder case, and then you appear.'

Dickinson understood her tactic. 'I'm afraid I can't tell you, Chief Inspector.' He seemed proud of his insubordination.

'The man who lived in this flat was a corpse found the other day on Hampstead Heath. It's his murder I'm investigating.' Blanche had no choice but to bluster on. 'I'm the investigating officer. I've got a right to know everything about the victim.'

'Of course you do, Chief Inspector.' The voice from the black profile was conciliatory. There was a Celtic lilt in it, the vowels clear and musical. Blanche found it reassuring. 'That's why we are here. To find out as much as possible about Graham Mills. Naturally, anything we find out that might be of interest will be passed on to you.' He had walked over to the inspector and stood beside him, slim and self-possessed, dressed in a cream summer jacket and red tie. His blond hair was trimmed short.

Instinctively Blanche knew she would have to retreat soon but was determined to learn as much as possible. She narrowed her eyes. 'Why are you so interested in Mills?'

Dickinson was about to reply but the fourth man answered on his behalf. 'You should know, Chief Inspector, that we're under orders to clear the flat of everybody at the present time. Unfortunately "everybody" includes the civil police. I'm sure you understand . . .'

An awkward pause swelled. The chief inspector masticated the words she had just heard. The way the fourth man spoke of 'the civil police' meant he was not one of them. The only people who accompanied Special Branch on jobs like this were from the Security Service, and the Security Service, MI5, would only be involved if the case touched on spying in the United Kingdom or counter-espionage in the intelligence services.

Blanche was helpless and they knew she was helpless. If she called Spittals or the commander, they would order her to get out and not cause any trouble. Spittals in particular hated 'trouble'. It did not lead to promotion. And she could not see the commander of her department coming off best in a wrangle with the deputy assistant commissioner in charge of Special Branch. The chief inspector was encircled and the MI5 officer pressed home the attack.

'Please do call your commanding officer back at the Yard, Chief Inspector,' added the blond man. The accent was softened Scots. He tried to make the tone one of genuine concern but the smile on his face – which Blanche could just distinguish against the light – was a touch too wide, the words tripped off his tongue too glibly to be convincing.

Blanche strode over to the telephone. She would not retreat unless ordered to do so. Spittals was in a meeting but agreed to take the call when the chief inspector insisted it was urgent.

'The Branch have an interest in this job then,' he meditated aloud. 'Hold on while I check it out with them.'

The line hummed when Blanche was placed on hold. She imagined one of Spittals' chubby fingers combing through the Yard's internal directory for the number of the Deputy Assistant Commissioner in charge of Special Branch. Dickinson and the MI5 man studied her, failing to suppress patronising smiles of confidence. Blanche smirked back at them as a defensive measure.

Spittals spoke again after a couple of minutes. 'I've vouched for the DI from the Branch. He's within his rights. Do as he says for the moment and the Branch say they'll contact you in due course.'

Blanche said nothing once Spittals had rung off. She did not need to. Dickinson and the Security Service officer knew they held the bureaucratic trumps. Blanche did not want to give them the added satisfaction of hearing her detail the success of their ambush. 'If you would care to leave now, Special Branch will be in touch very soon with all the relevant information.' The MI5 man stretched out a long, thin arm nervously towards the door. He showed a hint of hesitation. Blanche stood still.

'I know you're from MI5,' she said with deliberation,

squinting with concentration to filter out the details of his appearance. 'What's your name, please?'

The MI5 man pondered for a moment with a tuck in his lip which might have passed for a smile, as if her question were a riddle. He slid away from the window so that he was no longer a flat profile against the light. His skin was cratered with the marks of schoolboy acne, but so thinly that it added interest to what would otherwise have been an unremarkably handsome face. He smiled again. But this time genuinely. 'That's something you don't need to know. At least, for the moment.' He gestured towards the door again. 'I'm sorry.'

Blanche was cornered and she knew it. Taut with anger, she thumped out of the room.

Chapter 5

Graham Mills' former wife now called herself Mrs Madeleine Hawkins and had sounded distant at first on the phone, crisp and well-articulated, her voice falling away at the end of sentences. Her distress at the death of her former husband sounded genuine and she did not object when Blanche said she wanted to drive down to Hampshire that same afternoon to see her. The chief inspector sent Dexter and some detective constables to check Christine Mills' alibi and the dead man's bank account, and set off.

She followed the prewar road signs painted in white and black towards the village of Huntingsparish, weaving through the undulating country, past fields still swaying with corn. She finally blundered round a tight bend into the village and almost killed an old couple ambling out for a walk. They glared with annoyance as she swung the car to avoid them. Flies buzzed indolently through the summer air which seemed to have sent Huntingsparish into a deep sleep. The atmosphere in the village was too well manicured and schmaltzy for Blanche. She believed objects – whether people, buildings or landscapes – more beautiful when marred by the odd blemish.

Mrs Hawkins lived in a cottage, just beyond the church. The thatch was thick and neat, the walls a sparkling white except where the warm brickwork had been exposed. But as Blanche drew closer she saw indignantly that the front wall had been newly rendered with concrete, not smoothly but with finicky flicks of the trowel, like a badly iced cake. Worse still, a lych gate with a thatched roof had been erected on the far side of the cottage and a mock farm gate installed beneath. A beam curved up from the gate post to impart an air of even more studied quaintness. This construction marked the start of an entrance drive which snaked between two ponds, lined with multicoloured mosaics, where electric fountains splashed in the shimmering heat.

Madeleine Hawkins was still very handsome for a woman in her fifties. She was slim and held herself with pride. Her thick black hair was brushed back under a silk headscarf, her pixie features highlighted by discreet make-up. The bones in her face were finely formed and served to set off her almost flawless skin. She looked Blanche straight in the eyes, not with kindness but rather through a desire to patronise her. She was one of those women, the chief inspector decided, who prefer the company of men. After holding out a limp hand like a duster, the nails scarlet and well manicured, she led the visitor into the sitting room. 'So what can I do for you, Chief Inspector?' she asked as if Blanche had come to read the electricity meter. 'I will not be able to help you much. I have not seen Graham for about ten years, but I was of course shocked by the terrible news.'

As Blanche's eyes grew used to the dark interior after the blazing sun, she distinguished a copper warming pan shining on one wall and horse brasses glowing in the dimness opposite. The open hearth was crammed with logs waiting patiently for a distant Christmas. Sunlight oozed over the carpet in the hall, where a grandfather clock ticked loudly in a shaded corner.

Mrs Hawkins sat forward on the edge of her chair, one pale hand in the lap of her navy-blue slacks, the other jiggling with a gold chain round her neck. 'Do you think it was done deliberately? You know, planned?'

'I've no idea,' answered Blanche with complete honesty. She tapped her finger on the armchair in time with the tick of the grandfather clock. 'Do you know anyone who lives near Hampstead Heath who Mr Mills might have gone to visit?'

Mrs Hawkins contemplated her fingernails for a moment. 'When I was married to Graham, we did know a few people round there. There was a couple called Pollock, for instance. Bob and Eveline.'

'How did you know them?'

'Graham knew Bob through his caravan business.'

Mrs Hawkins gulped. She was pretending to be relaxed but resented being questioned about her private life. Blanche asked her to elaborate on the Pollocks.

'To tell you the truth, I found the wife bossy and loud. I liked Bob. I think Graham kept in contact with him after we broke up.' The tone was clipped and cold, with all the emotion mangled out.

'Anyone else?'

'There was a Polish man Graham used to go drinking with.' She passed on the name.

Blanche was cheered. She seemed to be getting somewhere. 'Anyone else?'

'Not that I can remember. We split up over ten years ago now. You form new friendships. Lose old ones. You know how it is – or perhaps you don't, being relatively young.' She laid emphasis on the word 'relatively', scanning the chief inspector's face eagerly for wrinkles, and tried to smother the barb with a glib smile. 'I married three years after the divorce and I've been very happy ever since.'

'What does your new husband do?'

She flashed an angry look as if Blanche had enquired not about her new husband, but the sort of contraceptive she preferred.

Mrs Hawkins hoped that by ignoring the question it would disappear. The chief inspector tapped her finger on the armchair five or six times and repeated the query.

The immaculately rouged lips hardly moved. 'Craig's a builder. A self-made man, as they say.' That, Blanche concluded, explained the ghastly excrescences in the garden – a man with money and drive, but no taste. Mrs Hawkins' eyes grew steely as they watched for a superior curl of the lip or an arch smile. The chief inspector resisted the temptation.

The grandfather clock rumbled, coughed and finally clonked out four thuds. A black cat was curled asleep on a chair in the kitchen. On the table there lounged a ripe fruit cake. Blanche was hungry and thirsty. Her hostess ignored the pleading look and gazed into empty space. 'Do you think Graham Mills had any enemies?' Blanche asked.

Mrs Hawkins laughed, a nervous chirp that fluttered in the rafters. 'Oh, no. He was far too charming for that. He should have had enemies, mind you, because he was a cruel man in some ways.'

Blanche furrowed her brow.

47

'Towards women, I mean. He had quite a number of them over the years. I suppose one of them, or one of their husbands, might have been upset enough to kill Graham.'

The chief inspector squinted with concentration. 'Did you ever feel like it?'

Mrs Hawkins laughed again. 'Once upon a time.' She meditated for a moment. 'He was rather unfeeling, not very sensitive to what other people wanted, in the way of love or behaviour.'

'What about his caravan business? Did he have any enemies there?'

'He had his rivals but caravans aren't drugs, you know. People don't kill each other for them.'

Blanche laughed, but from the blank expression on Madeleine Hawkins' face wished she had not. 'What about his employees?'

'He sacked a couple of managers, if that's what you mean. One of them was cheating the books and threatened to get his own back some day. But I don't believe it was serious.' The chief inspector made a note of the man's name.

'What about earlier on? I gather he worked for the government?'

'Yes. But that was a long time ago.'

'I have to check.'

Mrs Hawkins nodded. 'He worked for the Foreign Office doing some sort of secret work. He used to leave our flat in Richmond in the morning and come back in the evening. That's what he did from the time we married in 1961 until he retired and started his business a year later.'

Blanche wanted to confirm one possible reason for MI5's interest in Mills. 'Was he a spy, then?'

Mrs Hawkins shrugged. 'I suppose that's what one would call it. I don't take much interest in espionage and things like that.' Blanche waited, hoping she would say more. 'He never discussed his work and because it was secret I didn't ask him. I know you read in all these spy books about the burden of secrecy, how a chap wants to share it all with his wife, but Graham seemed to revel in it.'

Blanche looked beseechingly through the open kitchen door towards the fruit cake. The cat woke up, jumped to the floor and began to lap at the milk bowl against the wall. Madeleine Hawkins did not respond. Blanche was a visiting tradeswoman and she wanted to be rid of her.

'Most of the time we were together Graham was of course running his caravan business. He only sold it up a few years ago.' She paused for a moment. Her left hand went up to join the right, picking at the gold chain at her neck. She snatched a glance at her watch and breathed out a long, slow sigh.

The chief inspector was not to be budged so easily. 'Did Mr Mills have much of a drink problem, by the way?'

'How did that come out?'

'The post-mortem.'

She nodded philosophically. 'He was under increasing pressure before he retired from the Foreign Office. Graham was drinking a fair amount when we got married but as the years passed he drank more and more. By the end, when he sold his caravan business, he was finishing almost a bottle of whisky a day.'

Blanche tapped her finger patiently. Mrs Hawkins paused until she could bear the ticking of the grandfather clock no more. 'I kept asking Graham, as the drink problem got worse, if anything was the matter. But he just ignored me, as if I wasn't there. I was very hurt. That was part of the problem, you see. He always wanted to appear tough and strong, without any weakness. He hated people whom he called "soft". "So and so is really soft," he would say with a sneer. He meant that they were willing to admit they had faults.'

She was in full flow for the first time, talking more to herself than to the chief inspector, a rapt glint in her wide eyes, the pupils little black pools of memory. She stopped and looked out of the window. Her complexion was still smooth for her age, Blanche noted enviously. Only a few wrinkles tugged at the edges of her mascara, and the skin was only now starting to pucker round her throat. 'I must remember to pick some more of the tomatoes,' she exclaimed abruptly, changing the subject. 'I'll need some for supper.'

'Was drink the only reason your marriage broke up?'

'You've been talking to Christine, have you?' Her tone was calm but edged with bitterness. 'I shouldn't expect to get the whole truth from her!'

'I gather you don't get on terribly well?'

'I wouldn't say that at all, Chief Inspector. We get on fine. When she lets me.' She was defensive. Blanche had touched the raw nerve of family honour. The former Mrs Mills was willing to admit that her marriage had gone awry, but not the relationship with her daughter. 'We don't see eye to eye on a whole range of issues but we get on very well. Her father was rather more indulgent towards her than I, and I didn't approve. She's a headstrong girl and has some very strange ideas. That's all.'

'And what about the other women?'

Mrs Hawkins pulled in her nostrils and used them to look at the policewoman like a soldier squinting down the sight of his gun. 'Other women?' she queried.

'Yes. Other women.' Blanche tried to repress any sign of enjoying the embarrassment she was causing. 'Christine said Mr Mills was rather a Casanova.'

'Graham was a charming man. Good manners. Well dressed. One of those men who grow handsomer with age. I was attracted to him as soon as we first met.' Her embarrassment had made her lose her self-control, Blanche noticed. She was almost beginning to gabble. 'It was at a party in Chelsea held by an old school chum of mine. My friend warned me that he had a reputation as a philanderer but I was so in love that I didn't worry. He proposed to me and I was overjoyed. I thought, well, I have some power over him that other women don't. I was proud of myself. Too proud of myself as it turned out.'

She glanced through the window again, wishing to slake her bruised pride in the summer haze, the oaks at the far side of the field soft-touched by the shadows of afternoon. 'It was all right for a while and then I found a letter sent to him by one of his women, a shop assistant on the cosmetic counter at Harrods as a matter of fact. He said he'd break off the affair and,' she smiled wistfully, 'as far as I know, he did. But it started again. That, as well as the drinking, became too much. I got a divorce in 1975.'

'Did you see much of him afterwards?'

Mrs Hawkins looked out of the window again, this time nervously, as though she were looking for something or somebody. Blanche had to repeat the question.

'We sent each other Christmas cards. We met once or twice for a meal but even that stopped when I remarried. My new husband insisted. I didn't feel bitter towards him so much as sorry, and of course I feel even sorrier now, with this horrible murder.' She did not sound sorry, however, rather grimly self-satisfied. A personal incubus had been exorcised.

'You see, I've started a new life here in the country. And I don't want it spoilt by the past.'

She stood up abruptly and looked into the mirror on the wall, bringing her hands up to her ears to check the alignment of the headscarf. It was mutually understood that the chief inspector was dismissed.

Blanche hesitated. Graham Mills had been a British spy and British spies have a certain reputation. 'There's one last question I'd like to ask. Was Graham Mills a homosexual?'

Mrs Hawkins flushed angrily. 'No, Chief Inspector. Quite definitely not.'

They walked towards the door, Mrs Hawkins tapping the barometer in the hall on the way with a well-manicured fingernail, and they shook limp hands on the gravelled drive.

As they did so, a new Jaguar saloon car swung round the corner and scrunched to a halt a few yards in front of them. Mrs Hawkins jumped back in surprise. The driver squeezed his tanned bulk past the steering wheel and swaggered across.

'Craig, I keep telling you to come into the drive much more slowly,' she cried angrily.

He waved a stubby hand to dismiss her comment. A heavy gold chain jangled round his wrist as he did so. He was about fifty, wearing a navy blue T-shirt that was stretched to breaking point around his waist, and slacks. The buckle of his white belt would have covered a tea plate. ''Ello,' he said, extending a hairy paw. 'Since the wife's not introducing me, I'd better do the honours meself. I'm Craig 'awkins, builder of this parish.' His accent was working-class London, friendly yet suspicious.

Blanche knew what Mrs Hawkins had wanted her to avoid: her new husband.

The chief inspector introduced herself.

Craig's bonhomie dissipated. 'What are you doin' round 'ere, then? Maddy,' he growled, without taking his eyes from

51

Blanche, 'you didn't tell me nothing about the old Bill comin' round 'ere this afternoon.'

'I didn't know, Craig,' she whined. 'The chief inspector only phoned around lunchtime . . . besides, it's nothing to do with you . . .' Her explanation trailed off.

'What do you mean, nothing to do with me? The old Bill comin' to see my wife. Course it's something to do with me.' The voice was harsh and aggressive, used to issuing orders. Hawkins instinctively moved across to stand in front of his wife.

Blanche took a step backwards. He was a big, strong man, even if overweight. 'You don't need to worry, Mr Hawkins, I'm just going.'

He looked from one woman to the other, gesturing with his open paws. 'For Chrissake, is one of you goin' to tell me what this is all about?'

The chief inspector waited. Madeleine Hawkins was pale with fear of her husband's temper. She was not going to say anything.

'Graham Mills, your wife's former husband,' explained Blanche gently, 'has been found murdered.'

The muscles in Hawkins' forearms relaxed. His mouth opened slightly and he grunted through his teeth, 'Cor blimey.'

From her car, Blanche watched Madeleine Hawkins pick her dainty way over to the greenhouse to harvest the tomatoes. She reminded Blanche of a flamingo – head high and steady, the stiff legs choosing safe ground. She intrigued the chief inspector. It was a combination of the timbre of her voice, the self-knowledge of her middle-aged beauty, that English aloofness. Blanche's fascination had made her forget to ask for more details of the women Mills had had affairs with: she should have enquired, but did not, sensing that Madeleine Hawkins would have waved away the question by appearing to answer it. Mrs Hawkins had adored her former husband and been bitterly and regularly betrayed. Her adoration had turned to dislike, the dislike to hatred.

Madeleine Hawkins scurried back into the cottage to prepare afternoon tea. It was almost five o'clock. Blanche was hungry and thirsty and irritable. In the kitchen she imagined Craig's cavernous mouth chomping into a wedge of fruit cake. She hoped it made him sick.

Chapter 6

Back at the Yard, Dexter was in a fury. When the chief inspector came in to the office she found him stalking a wasp with a rolled-up newspaper. Rather than wait until the wasp settled and then strike, Dexter's arm was lashing out at the window in a frenzy. Such little things as flies could easily distract him, Blanche knew, and he could do no more work until the source of annoyance was stilled.

The newspaper rose menacingly, fell with a whoosh of air and landed on the glass with a thud. 'Fuck, fuck, fuck,' shouted the sergeant, thrashing the desk with the newspaper to underline each expletive as the wasp buzzed to safety. 'The little bastard just won't sit still. I've been trying to kill it for the past ten minutes,' he screamed through clenched teeth. 'I winged it once but rather than lie there and let me smash it to pulp, the bloody thing took off again.' As if to emphasise its triumph, the wasp buzzed round the room in a victory flypast. Blanche felt like ignoring Dexter. But her reputation among some of her male colleagues of being arrogant and misanthropic – based on her private-school and university background, polished accent and inability to suffer fools gladly if at all – dictated a more diplomatic approach. 'I read somewhere that a fly can't deal with two threats at once,' she suggested. 'You get two pieces of tissue paper and kill it in a pincer movement.'

Dexter loped from the room and came back with some folded sheets of toilet paper. By then, he was sweating with frustration and anger. He waited until the wasp settled on the window again and advanced. 'Right, you little bastard, I've got you now.' First the right hand edged forward and then the left. Dexter crouched, tense and alert. The wasp, a black spot on the window, sat obligingly still. The toilet paper in Dexter's left hand rustled as it moved to within a foot of the victim.

The right hand was also in position. The whir of the electric fan on Dexter's desk was the only sound in the office apart from the background hum of the traffic. The sergeant's long, elegant fingers trembled and plunged towards the wasp. He gasped as if to say 'Got you at last'.

For the briefest of moments there was silence. Dexter bellowed out a piercing howl of pain and started to jump around the room clutching and shaking the forefinger of his right hand, his face puffed out with rage. He fled from the room to douse his throbbing digit under cold water, and ululating yells of 'fuck, fuck, fuuuuuuck' echoed down the corridor.

On her desk was a note scribbled in Dexter's italic handwriting. Dickinson of Special Branch wanted her to ring him back urgently. Spittals wanted to speak to her about how the case was going. She called the chief superintendent first to get him off her back.

Dickinson refused to talk over the phone. They haggled about where to meet. Neither wanted to be at a disadvantage by seeing the other on foreign territory: his on the top floor of the Yard, where ordinary policemen felt abashed; or hers in the Serious Crimes Squad offices, where Dickinson might feel the chief inspector would pull rank. They decided to meet fifteen minutes later in a hamburger bar in Victoria Street.

Dickinson was not there when she arrived. The aroma of sizzling meat and french fries overcame her initial lack of appetite, created by the blanched photographs over the counter of hamburgers oozing cheese and exotic dressings. They looked as if they had just been in a car crash. She remembered she had not been given any cake by Mrs Hawkins and asked the indeterminate Asian boy behind the till for the largest hamburger they had, with fries.

When Dickinson sidled across five minutes later he threw an accusing look at the hamburger and fries she was shovelling down her throat. He held a polystyrene cup of black coffee between finger and thumb as delicately as if he were drinking Earl Grey from Meissen china. Dickinson carried his jacket over his arm, looking, as before, very pleased with himself. His white shirt had a marble-smooth front and creases down the arms like knife blades.

'I promised we'd be in touch.' She noted the royal 'we'. He refolded his jacket and laid it like a baby on the seat. 'I had a word with the relevant people and they okayed me telling you a few things.' Dickinson spoke fast and fluently in a lazy London drawl. His lips were thin and well chiselled, his features as clean-cut and neat as his hair. He smelt of a heady body perfume.

She decided to bluff and pretend she had already built up an accurate portrait of the murdered man's past. 'Perhaps you could just fill in a few details about Mills' time as a spy. Let me know why MI5 are so interested in this murder.' Blanche knew that Special Branch, as only the police arm of the counter-espionage experts in MI5, would not have initiated the investigation.

The inspector impaled her on a reproachful stare. 'Do, please, try and keep your voice down a little.'

'Hamburgers have ears, do they?'

The inspector did not smile. Instead he leant forward with a frown. 'Who told you that by the way – that Mills *was* a spy?'

'I have to protect my informants.' Blanche paused, with as enigmatic a smile as she could muster. 'It's obvious anyway, with all of you sniffing round Mills' corpse. He left the secret service back in 1962. That's a long time ago. He wasn't working for them afterwards, was he?' she enquired with a desperate casualness.

He shook his head, gazed round the restaurant and spoke in a whisper. 'As far as I can make out, it's routine. The kind of thing that happens when any former spook dies and no one knows why.' Dickinson sipped his coffee. The chief inspector waited. 'MI5 like to do a check to see there's nothing, how shall we say, that threatens national security. They wouldn't like any classified documents, diaries and so on to get into the wrong hands. They like to check just in case there's some espionage connection.'

'What, you mean suicide or assassination?'

Dickinson nodded sagely.

'Mills couldn't chop off his own head and testicles, so it's not suicide,' Blanche whispered back, with a flash of annoyance at the inspector's indirectness. 'And this hardly looks like a KGB assassination.'

Dickinson raised a finger in admonition. 'Don't you believe it. The Russians are a rough bunch. But the enquiry isn't a serious one. Just routine,' he clucked reassuringly. 'Looks to me that Mills got mugged by some sadistic loony. Whoever it was took all his money, credit cards and stuff like that. Or perhaps he was a poof,' he added with the conspiratorial smirk of a flirt.

She did her best to imitate an alluring pout. She reasoned that if Dickinson fancied her, she might as well exploit his lust. 'I didn't appreciate being hustled out of the flat like that.'

'Rules are rules. If the all-clear's given you'll be able to carry on with the case.'

'Hold on a minute,' she bridled. 'No one's taken the case away from me yet.'

The inspector's eyes twinkled so patronisingly that Blanche wanted to kick his shins under the table. 'You've just got to hold your horses for a bit. Wait until the Security Service gives the all-clear.'

'What do you mean the all-clear?'

'When MI5 decides the murder case doesn't have any espionage implications.'

'What sort of cooperation will they give me then?'

Dickinson took out a tin of snuff from his jacket pocket. He lifted a pinch to his chiselled nose and sniffed, leaving a residue of chestnut-brown powder round his nostrils. 'Not much.'

'Will they let me look at Mills' file?'

The inspector's face creased with a suppressed chuckle. 'No way.'

'So how will I know the murder isn't linked with what Mills was doing while he was with MI6?'

Dickinson raised his eyebrows. 'MI5, the counter-espionage experts, take that decision for you.'

'And I can't question it?'

'You're catching on fast.'

Blanche tried to wipe the grease from her hands with a paper napkin but they still felt slippery. She downed the dregs of the now tepid coffee. 'A policeman's lot, Inspector, is not –'

'– a happy one?' he smirked.

'Not so much happy, as simple,' she murmured, narrowing her eyes. 'It's complicated most of all by fellow policemen.'

Dickinson stood up and lifted his jacket from the moulded plastic seat. His brow tightened with irritation as he spotted a squashed french fry that had lain unnoticed beneath and stained one arm. Dickinson slipped into the jacket and took a pinch of snuff to overcome his annoyance. A few seats away, two French girls with serious faces exchanged glances.

Dickinson patted his pockets and made ready to leave. 'I'm so glad I could help you,' he concluded. From his neutral features she could not tell whether he was aware of the irony or had been so well drilled in the value of secret titbits that the comment was offered at face value.

He swaggered out, trying to catch the eye of the two French girls. One giggled back coyly.

Outside, in the dimness of evening, Victoria Street was bloated with people and cars. Horns screamed, children shouted, lorries and coaches lumbered into gear with a spurt of blue exhaust; a drunk gabbled to himself in a doorway surrounded by his belongings in plastic bags; the pure white vanilla of an ice cream dropped on the pavement had turned to a grey gamboge liquid creeping towards the gutter. There was already a sense of the day coming to an end. As Blanche walked down Caxton Street, Nino's Café sported a closed sign and inside she saw the proprietor wiping the silver cylinders on the counter that provided boiling water. She saw the nineteen storeys of New Scotland Yard tower up ahead of her, the venetian blinds drawn down against the setting sun. The chief inspector studied the web of aerials – shaped like forks, television antennae and threads of cotton – that sprouted from the roof. She had seen them before but for the first time, that evening, etched against the sky, they made her feel uneasy.

'I checked out Mills,' Dexter said with an impatient flick of the head. He was still smarting from his encounter with the wasp. They were alone in the office. She ran a finger along the window blind, and decided her ragged nails deserved a manicure. The finger ploughed a furrow through the dust. She felt sweaty and dirty and found it difficult to concentrate. Dexter was saying, 'I found out most of what you wanted. Mills' solicitor was a nice old guy, half-moon specs, about sixty. He was gay. I could tell he fancied me from his eyes. I like my game well hung,' Dexter grinned with a camp flick of the wrist, 'but not hung that long.'

Blanche liked his coarse humour when corralled within the limits of propriety. 'So what did you find out?'

'The will was drawn up about ten years ago. Mills had a basic one before that and just altered a few bits.'

'How much did Mills leave?'

'Ten grand or so plus the value of his flat. Mind you, that's worth another three hundred grand. Apparently Mills had almost all his money – half a million – invested out in the Far East. But the company he was involved in went bust and his money was wiped out overnight.'

'So what did he live on?'

'Mills had a government pension and the money in the building society. At one stage, after his money in the Far East got wiped out, Mills had to think about selling off his flat to make ends meet. But somehow or other he struggled through –'

'Who gets the money that's left?' Blanche interrupted. She was bored by irrelevant detail and sometimes found it difficult to curb her impatience.

Dexter twisted round on his chair and took a notebook from the inside pocket of his jacket. 'The former wife, the woman you went to see, gets £2,500. Pretty mean, I thought, and certainly not enough to kill for.'

'Unless you thought you were getting more.'

'You're only guessing.'

'Many things are done on the basis of supposition,' Blanche murmured without conviction.

Dexter, understandably, looked doubtful. 'The rest of it's split in thirds. One third goes to the daughter, Christine – the charming girl we've already met. Now that *could* be worth killing for. The next third goes to a woman called Tatyana Nowak, who lives in Chiswick apparently. Have you come across her, Chief Inspector?' Dexter only used her title when he feared he might be appearing too familiar. This happened rarely.

Blanche shook her head. 'Did the solicitor know why this Nowak woman gets so much money?'

Dexter shook his head mournfully. 'Didn't have the faintest idea. He just came across her name in the will. I've got the address. Anyway, the rest is split in four between some Polish cultural set-up in Hammersmith; the Polish government in exile; the Sikorski Institute – the solicitor guy said it's a Polish museum. And the fourth share goes to the London office of the Polish free trades unions. Mills seemed to have a big thing for Poland, didn't he?'

'Did the solicitor have any idea why?'

Dexter raised his forefinger like a teacher with the answer to a tough question from a clever pupil. 'Said Mills knew lots of Poles during and after the war. He felt like helping them out.'

Dexter eased his torpid bulk from the chair and dragged on his jacket. The aimlessness had disappeared from his face. He was off to do something.

'What's up?' Blanche asked.

'I thought I'd do a Registry check on this Nowak woman and the names you got from Mills' divorced wife. You never know, there might be something on one of them.'

The chief inspector was always willing for Dexter to do battle with the Police National Computer rather than her and so she nodded assent. 'Mind you,' she murmured in a flat tone of melancholy, 'it will be a waste of your time if MI5 and Special Branch decide to keep the case.'

Dexter hesitated and rolled his eyelids down and up like window blinds. He thrust out his arms, palms open in a gesture of entreaty. 'We must find out why they're so interested. If only so that we know the gossip.' He bowed low, a mischievous smile painted on his face, and disappeared with a roll of his buttocks.

Blanche meditated on the tremendous sunset pulled like a mantle across the London skyline. Dickinson, she thought, was a flirtatious messenger boy. Although she disdained him, the chief inspector realised with a surge of pleasure that she still enjoyed the power to draw men. It swept away an intermittent gloom that had hung about her since the morning, when she emptied the rubbish basket where she had tossed the dismembered photograph of her wedding. The act of destruction had cheered her at the time, yet, coming across the diced photograph days later, it seemed more like a petty act of revenge. Dickinson's flirtatiousness warmed her. She found the messenger boy as ridiculous as the message he carried with all the self-importance of an initiate in a secret craft. Ridiculous messages, Blanche decided, deserved only to be ignored.

Chapter 7

'I look at it this way,' Spittals grunted the next morning, and rubbed his hands so hard Blanche feared they might ignite. 'The probability is that those Special Branch devils up on the nineteenth floor will hit the ball back into our court in a week or so. You just carry on as normal. Take my advice and treat it all as a straightforward piece of police work.'

'Nothing is ever a straightforward piece of police work, sir.' She fought to suppress a smile that always twanged on her lips when the chief superintendent burbled homespun police philosophy.

He stopped rubbing his hands and glanced up as if to say, 'Don't play clever with me, young lady,' and then continued. 'Play it by the book. That way no one suffers in the long run.' Spittals had shaved around his moustache that morning and scraped off some spots that peppered his chin. He fingered one of them gingerly in fear of its bleeding again. Something was niggling at his innards, worrying him out of his usual placidity. His overriding motive was to protect himself from trouble. He believed the way to achieve this was to respect established hierarchies and never buck against them. He could sense 'grief' and had sniffed out already that the Mills murder case, with the involvement of Special Branch and MI5, was a potential source. He leant forward and looked square into Blanche's eyes. 'I don't mean to interfere. But sometimes you young fliers who were lucky enough to have an education I never had the chance of, don't always appreciate the demarcation lines there are in the Force.' Spittals thought a private education, even at a dreadful minor girls' public school like hers, and university, automatically meant privilege.

'Has anyone . . . ?' Blanche hazarded.

'No, of course not, Chief Inspector. No one above has said anything so far.' Spittals' hands whirred across each other like

61

bobbins, while his eyes bored into hers for signs of insubordination. 'Remember, just treat it as a normal piece of police
work. Which reminds me – you better let me have a sit. rep.
by tomorrow afternoon. The paperwork's always important
and I'll have to decide whether or not we need another press
conference. Let me have that report on time, won't you?'

Spittals wanted Blanche to mark time. She was determined
not to, although when she dictated the report for the chief
superintendent, it was a depressing reminder of her squad's
lack of progress. No murder weapon had been found. There
were several possible suspects but none had a clear motive.
She and Dexter and the other officers had followed most of the
leads given by people who said they had seen anything out of
the ordinary around Hampstead Heath at the time of the
murder. All had come to nothing.

As the former Mrs Mills had suggested, a Dr Stefan Wyzinski had lived in Hampstead until four years ago but then
moved up to Nottingham to live with relations. Dexter spoke
to Wyzinski over the phone. He was terribly shocked – he was
sure the famous round-the-world Scotland Yard would soon
bring the offender to justice – no, he had no idea whatsoever
what Mills might have been doing on Hampstead Heath.
Did he know why Mills had left so much money to Polish
organisations and people? Graham Mills liked Polish people,
came the reply, had good relations with the community, especially when in the Foreign Office. Graham Mills had told
Wyzinski once that he had a guilty conscience about Poles,
believed they'd been let down badly by the West – surely the
sergeant must know about the tragedy of Yalta and how
Churchill and Roosevelt . . .

'What did you think of him?' Blanche asked, sitting down
at her desk.

'Sounded harmless enough to me. Even rather gaga. I
checked out his story as best I could. It seemed to stand up.'
Dexter shrugged.

The chief inspector took out her notebook and scratched a
pencil line through Wyzinski's name on the list of people with
possible connections with the murder. The next name on the

62

list was Michael Smith, the manager who, Mrs Hawkins said, had been sacked for fiddling the books.

Smith's used-car business was one of several set along Cricklewood Broadway, as Shoot Up Hill tired of climbing past council flats and flopped down towards the North Circular Road. The showrooms were constructed from former shops whose fronts had been knocked out and replaced by sliding glass windows and loud plastic signs. Outside Smith's shop, cars tried valiantly to glisten despite the lack of sun. A spotty youth was polishing the window of a Mercedes. He confirmed with a flick of his dyed head of hair that the 'guv'nor' was inside.

Blanche had decided to dislike Smith even before she met him but the man in all his ample flesh only confirmed her predisposition – curly black hair dusted with dandruff; ferret-like brown eyes set in a face of rippling scarlet blood vessels; languid cigar; grey slacks splitting at the crotch and specked with stains.

Smith's greasy façade of salesmanship cracked when he discovered who the visitors were. He immediately wheezed out an invitation to coffee and waddled back into his 'office' at the back, which was no more than a glass cubicle. After the opening pleasantries Smith acknowledged, with what he hoped was disarming frankness, that he had in the past been involved in one or two 'dubious little business deals. But all strictly within the letter of the law, you understand, Chief Inspector. You see, I was very much on my uppers after I resigned from managing Mr Mills' caravan business.'

'You didn't resign, you were sacked for fraud, weren't you?' said Dexter with relish.

'Pure calumny,' Smith mumbled past his cigar. 'No criminal charges were brought.' The broken blood vessels on his face flushed even redder in mock anger. 'Who on earth is going around telling such unwarrantable lies about me – me, a respectable businessman, who trades on the basis of an unblemished reputation.'

Smith opened a drawer in his desk and pulled out a half-empty bottle of whisky and three tumblers. The digital clock on the wall clicked up six minutes past eleven. 'Can I offer you officers of the law some refreshment?' Dexter and Blanche refused. Smith slopped himself out a measure which he gulped down to assuage his outraged innocence.

Smith blanched when Dexter put to him that he harboured a grudge that led to murder. The whisky tumbler tinkled as Smith's trembling hand poured out a second glass. 'That's just bloody stupid. Why should I wait so many years to do it? Huh?'

He puffed greedily at his cigar. The ash was curving under its own weight and Blanche cast round for an ashtray: she disliked sloppiness. Outside, an old London bus ground its way to the peak of Shoot Up Hill at a speed which outraged the vehicle's better judgment. A red blur flashed across the mirror, on the back wall facing the street. 'Mills was a hard man – all very smooth and kind on the surface. But he was tough as old boots underneath. I know other people who knew him who would disagree with me, it's up to them – live and let live is my motto – but I don't think he had a heart.' Smith thumped his chest sentimentally to indicate that unlike Mills he had one. It might be choked with cholesterol, but he had a heart. 'I could honestly say that if Mills thought his interests and those of anyone else were, how shall I say, in conflict, he'd sacrifice that other person just like that.' Smith lifted his right hand and made a courageous attempt to snap his middle finger and thumb. Rather than a sharp crack, the sound he produced was a greasy whisper.

Did any Poles come round to the office of the caravan company? People were always coming in and out, and a few were Poles, Smith supposed. 'Mr Mills himself was a wizard salesman, one of the best. Had a marvellous way with words. He could sell a caravan to an Arab' (he pronounced the first 'a' of Arab to rhyme with month of May) 'to cross the desert with, pulled by camels if he wanted. Wasn't that he was loud and clever. Mr Mills was quiet, unassuming. Lovely voice. Rich and creamy. Like sweet sherry. I told him once. I said, you should go into the adverts.' Smith's blubbery lips were no longer shaping the words clearly. The syllables slid together like strands of weed in a river. His drinking had started very early in the morning.

Dexter asked whether Mills had any enemies.

Smith's bloodshot eyes rolled round to his and struggled to focus. 'I certainly wasn't one of them. I have my enemies . . . my bank manager for one.' He snorted at his own joke and lit another cigar. 'But old Mills didn't seem to have any.'

Dexter leant forward. 'Did you ever see Mills scared?'

Smith paused and fuelled his memory with another whisky. His breath reeked of the heavy scent of scotch. 'Can't remember anything.'

Blanche was irritated that she had frittered away so much time listening to a drunkard and had learnt nothing. She consoled herself, as usual, with a stoic shrug: it was good sometimes to sit back and observe the human comedy. The used-car supremo slopped out another generous measure and slouched deeper in his chair. The digital clock whirred on to twelve thirty. As Dexter and Blanche rose to leave, Smith staggered to his feet and invited them to go for some 'runchtime lefreshment'. The pungent reek of scotch and cigar smoke, laced with motor oil, was becoming emetic.

'Sshh funny how the ol' memory works, you know. Talking of Mills bein' scared . . . I remember one day when he really blew his top. This geezer turns up at the office. He burst in on Mills.'

'How do you know?'

'I was there, weren't I? After a few minutes, it heated up and this bloke started screaming blue murder in some foreign language or other. Mills just exploded.'

'What was the row about?'

'I dunno.'

'What was the guy's name?' asked Blanche.

'No idea.' Smith's mind had staggered deeper into stupor. His eyelids were dragged down by the weight of alcohol. 'Hold on, wait a mo'.' He scratched his head. 'Perhaps it was Polanski or something like that. That's what he said when he arrived anyway. Polanski.'

'Do you remember anything else?'

Smith's unfocused eyes blinked straight through her and he shook his head so that the flesh under his chin wobbled. 'No. Mills kicked me out of the office when the geezer arrived. And I just 'eard the screaming through the door. Never 'eard a barney like it.'

'What was it about?'

'No idea. I think the foreign geezer must have been the husband of one of Mr Mills' fancy women. He had quite a few of them,' he said with a leer.

The chief inspector nodded. 'What did this foreign man look like?'

Dexter scribbled some notes while Smith burbled. 'Oh – it'sh ages now. Short, tubbyish. Tiddly little 'tache. I got an amazing memory for faces. I mean there was this chap I was trying to sell a Merc to –'

'– anything else you can remember about him?'

Smith still carried the whisky tumbler with him and swilled more of the amber liquid down his throat. He swayed back and forth. 'Only a big gap between his front teeth. And when I say big, I mean big. Room to stick a pencil in it.'

Smith swayed sideways now, from side to side, yawing slowly like a boat. His eyes were opaque like worn-out marbles. A film of sweat glittered on his skin. 'I'm shorry, I've . . .' He staggered back into the gloom of his glass cubicle and slumped senseless in his chair. Dexter followed him but returned a few seconds later to report he was sound asleep.

As they squeezed their way out past the loud and brassy cars, the spotty youth whistled appreciatively at Blanche's legs. 'Cor, the standard of the old Bill's recruitment ain't half going up these days.'

She laughed and tapped her forehead. 'They let me in for what's up here. Not what's down there.'

'That's what they all say.'

'You better lock your boss up in his office,' warned Dexter, 'otherwise I'll have to nick him for being drunk and disorderly. Then you'll be joining the dole queue.'

The youth squinted against the sun. 'Shouldn't worry, mate. With this boss I'm always out of a job after lunch as it is.' He slouched back over to his barstool by the glass doors, donned a baseball cap hanging from a convenient peg and began to doze.

Chapter 8

Bob and Eveline Pollock still lived in Hampstead in the same house in Frognal Gardens as when Graham Mills and his wife used to go round to dinner. It was solid and patrician, surrounded by silver birches behind, and shaded at the front by a stunted monkey puzzle tree. Robert Pollock was a tall and courteous man, by turns friendly and serious. He was not quite sure when, or whether, to laugh: a diffidence that only strengthened his trustworthiness for the chief inspector. His wife was short and shrewish with a bundle of ill-kempt black hair which she tried in vain to keep in place with several tortoiseshell combs. The nervous tic on the right side of her lip did not check her talkativeness, and the combination made her comic.

Eveline Pollock, punctuating her inconsequential chat with pauses for her tic, led Blanche, who was beaming to prevent herself laughing out loud, through to the reception. 'I suppose the last time Graham Mills came round must have been only about a week before he was murdered. He was his usual, cheerful self. Graham talked a lot, I remember, about Christine and how he thought she was now at last coming round to behaving more sensibly and getting a proper job on Fleet Street, rather than living in Hackney in some run-down house with a bunch of left wingers.' Mrs Pollock gabbled all this in one breath and in a staccato voice. Blanche felt she was being fired on by a verbal gatling gun. But she liked Eveline Pollock, who was open and friendly and did not hide her opinions. She scampered out to make more coffee.

Mr Pollock lounged back in the sofa by the window and lit his pipe, puffing contentedly. 'Graham and I used to meet frequently – either here or at Graham's club, the Garrick. I used to have a quiet drink with him and some of his friends. He kept contact with a lot of his old Foreign Office and intelligence buddies.'

'Tell me, did Graham Mills seem at all different in the weeks before his death? You know, worried about anything?'

The aroma of shag tobacco drifted across the room. Unlike cigarette smoke, Blanche found it vaguely arousing, irresistibly masculine. A shaft of afternoon sunlight fingered the blue curlicues of smoke rising to the ceiling. 'He seemed a little on edge, distracted. I would be saying something to him and look round and he would be staring into space. He was very good, you see, like most loners – and he was a loner at heart – he was good at hiding what he really felt.'

'Did you try and find out what caused this nervousness?'

'It was nothing I could put my finger on really. Someone who didn't know him so well' – and his eyes half glanced towards the kitchen in a shared confidence – 'wouldn't have noticed it. He'd been like that before on occasions when he had something on his mind and I knew from experience that he would never tell me what it was. Usually he'd just mumble something about overwork or Christine or "a little local difficulty".'

Pollock smiled to himself in fond remembrance. Blanche raised her newly plucked eyebrows with suspicion. 'What did that mean?'

He reached out his long, gaunt arms and knocked the contents of his pipe into an ashtray. 'His love affairs. Graham loved the opposite sex. I must say I was rather surprised when Graham introduced me to his wife. I didn't think he'd marry such a woman. Madeleine was rather innocent.'

The words echoed those of Blanche's mother seven years before when the young policewoman had announced her engagement. The chief inspector remembered the humourless but loving face, admonishing her daughter for throwing herself away on an 'arrogant coxcomb'. Mrs Hampton disliked her future son-in-law because he mocked her snobberies and illusions and because he was handsome. Unbearably handsome, thought Blanche with a surge of pride and defiance, imagining her mother shaking a theatrical finger: 'I told you so. I told you so. Running after a floozy from the office. I told you so.'

Blanche realised with a start that she was daydreaming – a trait she despised in others. She hurried on to another question. 'Did he talk about any "little local difficulties" to you before he was killed?'

'Oh no. As I said, it was just a feeling I had that he was worried about something. I've no idea what that something was.'

'Do you think an angry husband decided to get his own back?'

Robert Pollock curled his lip with uncertainty. 'It's possible, I suppose. But most of Graham's women were divorcees in the older age bracket.'

Eveline Pollock bustled back bearing a tray of coffee cups – small, elegant ones rather than mugs, Blanche noticed, her eyes well tuned to class distinctions in drinking vessels. 'Really, darling, you're giving the chief inspector quite the wrong impression of Graham! I only know for certain of one affair after he'd divorced Madeleine. That was with that Anne Lorenzo woman.' Bob said nothing. With an inscrutable smile he relit his pipe and flopped back further into the sofa. Eveline poured the coffee, her mottled forearms as powerful as a boxer's. 'Tell me,' she gushed with her staccato tic, 'do you think the murderer really was a jilted woman or a cuckolded husband? Have you found any good clues? Your job must be terribly exciting.'

Blanche for the most part liked her job but disliked talking about it. She parried Mrs Pollock for a few minutes, sipping the excellent coffee and hinting that she had some leads which might come to something. Neither had any idea why Graham Mills should have been on Hampstead Heath just over a fortnight before. He had certainly not come to visit them, and was not in the habit of coming out to north-west London to take a walk.

Robert Pollock said Mills had once worked for Britain's foreign intelligence service, MI6, but that the dead man never talked about it in any detail. 'I was in military intelligence myself during the war. A lot of chaps still think they're operating "sub rosa" years after. They love the sense of belonging to a club. I only knew Graham once he was out of the spying game of course, because he retired – or from little hints he gave me *was* retired – from MI6 in 1962.'

The chief inspector stirred uneasily in her seat. 'What do you mean? *Was* retired?'

Her host's good humour was unscratched. 'Just early retire-

69

ment, that's all. I joked with him once and said it was because he was working for the Russians.' Pollock chuckled. 'He didn't take that too well.'

'And *was* he working for the Russians?'

Mills' friend froze in mid-puff, and exhaled slowly, his eyes burning with scorn. 'Of course not.'

'Did he ever tell you what he did exactly in MI6?'

Pollock knocked out his pipe. His good humour seeped back. He was enjoying himself, giving a lecture. 'Just after the war, from what I could gather, he was a main liaison with the exile groups, because lots of Poles and Czechs and Hungarians and others came to Britain. They all thought they could get rid of the Russians from their homelands, with our help and that of the Americans.'

'Was that why he knew so many Poles?'

'Probably. Part of Graham's job was to mix with these groups and find out what they were up to. He made lots of friends, especially among the Poles. After that Cold War time Graham got increasingly vague, although piecing things together, he seems to have been involved on the Soviet desk, doing pretty routine clerical work by the sound of things.'

Blanche had waited patiently for a pause in the conversation to pick over one point that intrigued her again. 'Did Mills ever tell you why he left MI6?' She noticed Eveline was sipping her coffee and staring out of the window. She was bored.

'Graham said he was fed up with the Service and disillusioned. Felt distrusted and had various people manoeuvring against him behind the scenes. It's the same in all organisations – especially secret ones.'

The chief inspector tried to hide her disappointment at the reply by pressing on. 'Do you think there could be a connection between Mills' time as a spy and his murder?'

Eveline had lost interest completely and bustled out to clear the lunch table. Pollock pondered. He shook his head with solemn finality. 'Of course, the war and all that Iron Curtain business with the emigrés must seem distant to you, Chief Inspector. Probably all happened before you were born.'

Blanche nodded. The absurd and obscure events Pollock referred to were probably taking place around the time of her birth, nine months after an unsuccessful solicitor from Shrewsbury had made love to his wife of three years in the front bedroom of a detached house in Streatham. It was then, sitting in the Pollocks' drawing room, the sun having taken on the golden glow of late afternoon, that Blanche realised that she had become Mills' chronicler, his biographer, trying to snatch his life from the yawning oblivion of other people's memories. Every other case she had worked on had had some motive anchoring it to the present – love, jealousy, anger, greed – some indication about the route to follow. But with Mills there was nothing substantial. Only moods and hypotheses. She could do no other than clutch at the past, which she sensed retreating from her at a pace she could never hope to match; clutch at it and hope that there, somewhere, might be a sign pointing to the murderer.

The chief inspector murmured that she had to be on her way. Pollock said nothing until they reached the front door. He was assembling his words. 'Graham always gave me the impression that there were secret facets to his life, little compartments, that were completely separate. It was true for his women. Once or twice I came across somebody I knew and we would talk, and Graham's name would come up. I discovered Graham knew them as well. But he never told me . . . It was as if he wanted to keep us apart, to stop us exchanging notes.'

In the garden the light had thickened to an afternoon gold. The lawn was smooth, although at odd intervals an unruly blade of grass, unwilling to be regimented by the roller, blinked in the sunlight. 'I think you're exaggerating things as usual,' grumbled Mrs Pollock. 'Just because Graham knew a couple of people you were acquainted with in the caravan business and didn't tell you.'

'Well, they were people who had dealings with the Eastern bloc. Graham went there many times, you know, after he retired from secret work. I only discovered it a couple of years ago.'

'Why did he go?' Blanche enquired.

'Business, he told me.' His eyes, smoky-blue and rheumy, meditated on the garden before swivelling back to his guest. He held out his hand to give a strong handshake. The telephone clanged out behind them.

Eveline scuttled off to answer it. 'It's for you, Bob,' she

shouted down the hall. 'A chap called Urquhart. Says it's a private matter.'

Blanche thought nothing of that telephone call at the time. Certainly not enough to stay and eavesdrop. She walked down the path to the garden gate and on to the road. Later, she was to wish she had stayed.

That evening Blanche recognised the car too late. She had taken in its colour and shape without understanding the implications, like a feature in a long-familiar landscape that suddenly changes. It was only when she was walking along the pavement towards the front door of her flat in Ealing, past the pollarded willows, that she noticed the door of the car open. The energetic and slightly stooped figure of her husband, Roger, in his crumpled journalist's suit, slipped out. A smile was glued on his face as if he had just been away for a few days at a party conference rather than walked out on his wife many weeks back. He bustled across the road and cut her off just as she reached the front door. A voice inside Blanche – the voice of her upbringing and schooling, of a certain English femininity – whispered in favour of retreat. But another, stronger voice – of anger and betrayal and pride – ordered her feet to keep walking.

'Have you forgotten something?' she asked, with a squint of concentration.

He stood in front of her, hands in pockets with the easy confidence of a handsome man. 'Like what?'

'Contraceptives?'

The smile, always slightly lopsided, remained in place for a moment and then melted. 'That's unworthy –'

'– but of course, I forgot. Now you'll be wanting to start a family. So you don't need any.'

Roger shifted his weight from one foot to the other. 'Blanche?' He sucked his lips to wet them. She waited, her eyes searing his. 'I wonder if we could talk.'

She drew her head up and articulated every syllable. 'I don't talk to cowardly, promiscuous little ticks.'

'Look here, Blanche . . .' She knew from the huskiness of his voice that he was angry. 'I didn't just come here to be insulted.'

'Well you may not from your point of view, but you have from mine.'

'Always so clever, aren't you?' he sneered. 'Always so bloody clever.'

She recalled his over-sensitivity about lacking a university degree but now, rather than pandering to it, she enjoyed scraping it raw. 'Now, will you please get out of my way.'

He stood unmoved. 'Only if you talk to me.'

His obstinacy angered her. 'I do not want to talk.'

'Blanche, I want to come back.' He staggered forward, hands outstretched to embrace her.

'Don't touch me, Roger. Don't touch me,' she hissed through clenched jaws.

'Forgive me.' He staggered on. 'I'm sorry. I'm sorry.' Blanche felt the anger at his cowardice and betrayal flare inside and, as his arms looped around her, her clenched fist chopped into his stomach. His face froze for a second in its attitude of humility before the mask was twisted beyond recognition with gasping pain. He sank to his knees clasping his innards.

Blanche picked her way past him and went up to the maisonette. She sat on the sofa and burst into tears.

Chapter 9

'I heard a couple of hours ago,' Dickinson began. 'How did they put it? I've got the memo here somewhere – "The Security Service have no further direct interest in the case and are satisfied, on the evidence to date, that there are no national security implications." So there you are, Chief Inspector. Over to you.'

The message that Blanche was to ring Dickinson had been taken by a constable the next day while she drank with Dexter in a pub just behind the Yard. 'What sort of cooperation can I expect from you and MI5, if I decide Mills' time as a spook did, after all, have something to do with his death?'

Blanche knew she had asked the question before but hoped he had forgotten. He had not. 'When something like this happens, it's MI5 and MI6 who decide whether or not there could have been any spying connection, not you. For the moment, you must simply take it as read that that period of Mills' life – when he was spying abroad for MI6 – has nothing to do with his murder. That's official. And final.'

'So, no cooperation?'

'None. But obviously if you turn something up, let us know.'

The chief inspector realised the conversation was slipping away from her, drifting like a boat from its moorings. That boat had on board an invaluable cargo of information and she knew she had to board it. She recalled, with a cynical twist of her lips, those tight little eyes roving over her breasts and neck in the hamburger restaurant. 'I really must say, Inspector, I'm sure we could settle this amicably one lunchtime over a drink. You could perhaps give me a few more details. Just to flesh out the bare bones of what I've learnt so far.' Blanche cringed at her oleaginous charm: surely Dickinson would recognise it as fake.

'Just because Mills was a spy for a time during his life

doesn't mean that he was killed *because* of it. There's probably a much simpler motive, so they told me, like money. Or perhaps it was a jilted woman. Mills spread it around a bit. Did you know that?'

'I *did* actually.'

'While we're on the subject of espionage . . .' Dickinson went on in a jocular way. Blanche's fist was strangling the telephone so tightly, her forearm ached. She consciously relaxed as she realised Dickinson was not going to hang up immediately. 'Let me give you one scrap of information on good authority about Mills, which puts him in a class of his own among the British spies of his generation.'

'What's that?'

'He wasn't a poof.'

'I already know that.'

'From a good source?'

'As good as they come. His former wife.'

'What does a *wife* know?'

'Enough. At least I can rule out the possibility of a midnight tryst of two geriatric gays.' She sensed him smile. Not chuckle, just smile. Special Branch officers have a certain reputation to maintain. Now was the moment to ask the favour. 'Why don't you tell me something I *don't* know? Like who that guy from MI5 was who was with you in Mills' flat?'

'Who, the case officer?'

'Mmm.'

She held the conversation by a delicate thread. If she pulled too hard it would snap. The phone crackled and, for an irritating moment, she heard nothing at all. She thought she had been cut off. Dickinson had rebuffed the invitation to lunch, and an instinct whispered through her bones that he was under orders not to discuss Mills with her again. 'That's just the sort of information that I'm supposed to protect very carefully, Chief Inspector.'

'But as one copper to another . . . ?' she murmured with mock matiness. The minim in their conversation stretched to a semibreve.

Dickinson breathed conspiratorially. Blanche knew he enjoyed playing conversational poker, and so did she. 'His name's Urquhart.'

'Telephone number?'

The inspector chuckled. 'Mine or his?'

'Both.'

Dickinson dictated seven digits almost in a stage whisper. 'That's his of course.'

Before she could say more he replaced his receiver.

Urquhart. That was the name of the slim, shadowy man. It was also, she remembered, the name that Eveline Pollock had called out to her husband the afternoon before. Was it the same Urquhart telephoning Robert Pollock? If so, why? For the same reason she had visited him?

The muscles in her neck, stomach, arms and legs were taut with tension and impatience. She had been dragged suddenly from out among the spectators, dumped on stage and told to play the lead. The old fear of failure that goaded her on and on had re-awakened. Dexter was rocking back and forth on his chair, apparently asleep after his lunchtime libation of vodka and orange. She thought she detected a snore alternate with the squeak of his chair, but as she sat back, one heavy chocolate eyelid creaked up. Dexter knew intuitively that her mood had changed, from languid curiosity to fierceness – a burning fierceness that annoyed him. There was so much to do, Blanche told herself. She scribbled out the list of people to contact on a memo pad, and those Polish organisations – what are they? The Sikorski Institute and POSK? Dexter stood up and stretched with the arrogant grace of a cat. She handed him the bottom half of the list. Blanche took the top half. At the head of the column was the name Tatyana Nowak.

Her eyes burned with an alien intensity, an other-worldliness which disturbed Blanche: an amber enamel laid over a base of turquoise, the turquoise allowed to run in streaks like cirrus clouds, and all these parts transmuted into an even more exotic whole by pupils that resembled strokes from the pen of a Chinese calligrapher, so clear, so sharp, so feline that the chief inspector could do nothing but stare. The effect was all the more surprising because those disconcerting eyes were secreted behind an ugly pair of spectacles, twig-thick brown frames and thumb-thick lenses. She took them off with a distraught sweep of the arm and fixed those eyes on Blanche like pincers. They

76

were the eyes of a tragic innocent: one whose fate it was to fight against destiny and suffer without cause.

The door of Tatyana Nowak's house had juddered open but was restrained by two chains. Mrs Nowak's suspicious look turned to a crease of fear when Blanche said she was from the police. She motioned for the chief inspector to come in with a nod of the head. She was tall and made sterling efforts to carry herself well, although wrinkles of pain crossed her forehead every time she took a step – due to the arthritis that had distorted and knobbled the joints of her fingers and legs.

A sweet, stagnant smell wafted across – roasted coffee beans, pungent sausage and cigarette smoke. The air fermented into a richer brew as each new layer of aroma was added. It hung, palpable in the rooms, day after day, turbid with her memories. Motes swung in the sunlight, which was filtered on to the oriental carpet through muslin blinds at the windows. But as if to contrast with the air of neglect, every object in the living room was spotless: the elegant mahogany furniture, Chinese vases, black-framed etchings of fierce eagles bestriding their quaking prey, well-nourished bookshelves. An eccentric and cultured woman who had fallen on bad times, Blanche concluded, as she was nodded towards a sturdy armchair.

The detective took out her notebook. 'It's about the murder of a man called Graham Mills.' It was then that Mrs Nowak took off the spectacles and unleashed those eyes on her. Blanche was so fascinated she simply stared for a moment. Those deep, wide eyes could not hide the genuine surprise and grief. Blanche had already registered her dyed brown hair, lifted up and pinned with a tortoiseshell comb, the prominent nose – neat and firm, but with flaring nostrils, and the cheap but svelte grey dress set off by a leather belt of faded red. Her accent was dusky, the vowels sometimes misplaced and the Rs rolled, but her English was completely fluent. She oozed gentility: the gentility of the 'salon', gentility in decay.

'You mean Graham is dead?' The voice was tinged with falsetto.

The chief inspector had the time to hear her take two deep, rasping breaths. Then Mrs Nowak sobbed. The muffled cries rose and fell, rose and fell in an arpeggio of grief before finally subsiding into silence. She dabbed at her ravaged face with a handkerchief. 'I'm terribly sorry. The news you brought . . . took me completely by surprise.' Her chest heaved erratically. She picked up her spectacles and began to wipe the lenses mechanically. Blanche offered to make some coffee. Mrs Nowak did not move all the time Blanche was preparing it and sat in a trance when she returned with the tray. The woman's voice was strong but cracked.

'I don't keep up with the news much now. I can't really see the point. It all changes so fast. So much of what we read in the newspapers one morning seems unimportant two weeks later.' She smiled apologetically and put her spectacles back on again. Blanche explained when and how the corpse had been found. Tatyana Nowak rocked back and forth, hugging herself, and whispering 'Poor Graham, poor Graham'. Finally, she took a deep breath but did not sob again.

Blanche waited patiently. 'How did you get to know Graham Mills?' She had to repeat the question to shake the older woman from her reverie.

Mrs Nowak blew her nose with a silk handkerchief and settled herself. 'That was a long, long time ago. I managed to escape to London during the war. And here I met my husband, Zbigniew Nowak. He worked with the Polish government in exile and we were married in 1942. It was around then we got to know Graham because he was interested in our work.'

'And you've kept in contact ever since?'

'Yes.'

'How close to him were you?'

Mrs Nowak looked at her so suspiciously Blanche was surprised. 'Zbigniew died when I was pregnant with my son, Marek. It was awful. That was in 1950.' She paused and breathed in deeply again to stem any tears. 'I was left all alone with my young son. I knew some Polish people in London but not too many. Because he was such a close friend of Zbigniew's, Graham seemed to feel some responsibility for me, as a widow and mother. He was very helpful and openhanded after my husband's death and we remained good friends until he got married.'

She stopped as though she had finished. Blanche paused and then prodded. 'What about afterwards?'

'We just kept in contact. His wife was a bit jealous of him

being friends with other women. We saw each other more after the divorce. We'd occasionally go to the cinema, theatre or just bridge parties together.'

'You never remarried?'

She shook her head wistfully. 'No. I had to stay faithful to my dead husband. His death was such a tragedy. I could never love another as I loved him.'

The chief inspector nodded in sympathy – knowing it was mock and wishing it were real. Words like 'love' and 'loyalty' had become childish for her in recent months, blurs of meaning in an adult world. Perhaps, she considered, that was another message to be decrypted from Mrs Nowak's eyes: help me, a child in a world of grown-ups, for I am lost. 'What about your son? What does he do now?'

'Marek still lives here with me. He's a teacher,' she added proudly. 'It would have been nice if he'd married but he just hasn't found the right girl so far. Perhaps if he'd had a proper father . . . Do you mind if I smoke?' she asked abruptly. 'This has all been an awful shock.'

She sat upright in her chair, her bare and mottled arms laid on the rests. The skin was like that of an apple that was beginning to wrinkle. She turned to an occasional table by her side, loaded her ivory cigarette holder with a cigarette and set it smouldering with a silver lighter encrusted with garnets. The hand she raised to her lips glittered with rings and shook so violently that it could hardly hold the cigarette. She drew in thankfully the first lungful of smoke and rested her arms back on the chair again. Blanche decided Tatyana Nowak must have been a very beautiful woman twenty or thirty years ago.

'As you can see,' the Polish lady said finally with an apologetic smile that revealed a clean line of false white teeth, 'the news you brought has upset me.' Blanche opened her hands in a silent gesture of sympathy. 'Oh, it's not your fault. It's just that as you get older, friends and memories get more and more precious and when you lose them, they can't be replaced. After the war, you know, they rebuilt Warsaw brick by brick. The city rose up again like a phoenix from among the rubble. Dead friends are not like that.'

'Did you go back to Poland after the war at all?'

'I was in a state of shock for several years after my husband was killed. He died in a car accident back in Poland you see – on a visit in 1950.' She hesitated for a moment, staring at her distorted hands and avoiding Blanche's eyes. Whether because she was nervous or wished to hide something, the chief inspector could not decide. 'I went back on holiday eventually. In the sixties and seventies. It was very strange being followed everywhere by two secret policemen. I became so depressed, seeing what the damned communists had done to the country.'

Blanche gulped down a mouthful of coffee and savoured the heavy flavour on her tongue. 'Did Graham Mills leave you anything in his will?'

Mrs Nowak met her gaze and looked troubled. 'What? You mean he *did* leave me something in his will?' There was no hint of the surprise Blanche was expecting. 'I suppose he just left me some money, did he? Or did he leave it to Marek? Graham always valued money more than I did.' The tone was one of disappointment and regret, as if she was half expecting the money all the time but was hoping for something else.

'You'd been told then that you'd benefit from Graham Mills' will?'

Those troubling eyes took on a withering glint of contempt and drilled into the chief inspector's, excavating for a motive. Tatyana shook that fine, handsome head of hers from side to side and flicked the ash ostentatiously from her cigarette. 'No, no, no. You have got it completely wrong. It's true I'd always considered it a possibility that Graham might leave me a little bit of money when he died – should I survive him. A little legacy, how shall we say, for memory's sake. But to suggest I would murder an old and loved friend for what I'm possibly getting. That's ridiculous.' She laughed: a deep, throaty laugh that was faintly hysterical in that quiet, well-ordered room, the echo of a carefree schoolgirl from years gone by.

'Has anyone told you how much Mr Mills left you in his will, Mrs Nowak?'

Still giggling, she gurgled out, 'No. A few hundred pounds, I expect?'

'We're talking about over a hundred thousand pounds. Before tax.'

80

It was as though someone had dropped ice cubes down the back of her dress. The laugh dropped from her face and she froze with astonishment. 'You are joking?'

'I'm not joking.'

'And you suspect me . . .'

'I don't suspect anyone in particular. But if you could tell me – just for the record – where you were on the third to the fifth of August I'd be grateful.'

She ignored the question. She seemed transported to a dreamworld of rapture. 'A hundred thousand pounds. That's a lot of money. I can move out of this house to somewhere more respectable with that. Some of the neighbours are awfully noisy.' Tatyana Nowak reminded Blanche of her mother when she said that. The hysterical current in Tatyana's laughter now flowed through her voice: distant but none the less detectable.

After Blanche had reminded her of the question, Mrs Nowak tottered over to the mahogany desk. She seemed frail, much frailer than when Blanche first walked in through the front door. Mrs Nowak thumbed through the pages in her diary, an expensive one bound in red Moroccan leather. She said she played bridge on the third of August, stayed at home on the fourth and went to the cinema with a friend on the fifth.

Blanche said she would need to talk to both her son and the friend some time later. 'Do you have any debts, Mrs Nowak?'

Tatyana sat down at the desk on a high chair and crossed her legs elegantly at the ankle. She tossed her hair back from her eyes and glowered. 'The only debts I have ever had since I've been in this country are debts of honour. I have managed to pay even most of them back too. No, I am not in debt, Chief Inspector.'

'Did you have a debt of honour to Graham Mills?'

'If anything he had one to me,' she exclaimed.

'What do you mean?'

She laboriously and ostentatiously pushed another cigarette into her ivory holder and lit it. 'I was joking. It was I who owed a lot to Graham,' Mrs Nowak murmured tonelessly, as if she needed to convince herself. 'He was so kind to my son and me just after my husband got killed. We were so alone then.'

The policewoman hesitated. Mrs Nowak was after all a

woman of a different generation who would draw the boundaries of privacy more widely. 'Excuse me asking but was there ever . . . any . . . relationship between you?'

Tatyana laughed with what Blanche found a forced naturalness. 'Of course there was a relationship. We were friends. But there wasn't any love affair, if that's what you mean.' She said this decisively before looking down and turning one of the rings on her left hand round and round between her forefinger and thumb. 'It was better that way,' she added pensively.

'Meaning you regret there wasn't one?'

'Perhaps,' she sighed.

'What about enemies? Do you think Graham Mills had any?'

She swung her spectacles off again, unleashing her eyes. 'Only people with German or Russian blood could have murdered Graham in such a way. For they have deep down less humanity than other peoples. Just look at what they have done between them to Poland!' The shine in her eyes told Blanche that she meant her views to be taken seriously. 'As for other enemies, Graham certainly left a trail of jealous women, and where there are jealous and disappointed women, there are always men not far behind.'

Blanche asked for names but, like the Pollocks, Mrs Nowak was vague on detail. She gazed towards the veiled window and pondered. A fly buzzed across the ceiling and settled on a framed photograph on top of the chest of drawers. The photograph was one of several.

'Do you think Graham had any enemies from his time in British intelligence?'

Mrs Nowak thought for a moment, turning the ring on her finger round and round. 'No, that could hardly be of any importance,' she said, shaking her head from side to side.

'What's that?'

'I was talking to Jozef once and he told me there were several Poles who had turned against Graham for various things he was responsible for just after the war.'

'Who's Jozef?'

'The friend I went to the cinema with.'

'What did he say?'

Tatyana spoke with an offhand wave of her cigarette holder,

to tell the chief inspector she was purveying stale and inaccurate rumour. 'Graham was supposed to have let some people down in one way or another. But people were so sensitive then. Poland had been terribly, bitterly betrayed. Half our homeland was just handed over to the Russians at Yalta. Despite all the promises, all the words. Never trust any politicians, ever. And the Russians above all.' Blanche shook her shoulders in a noncommittal way. Unfortunately Mrs Nowak saw her. 'It's all very well, you just shrugging your shoulders like that,' she snapped. 'It's just history to you. The past. But to us Poles, you understand, we have to live that betrayal out. Day after day. Year after year.'

As she became angry, her accent reverted to the clean vowels and slushy consonants of her native country. She ended by punctuating the words with blows from her fist on the arm of the chair. The last one clumsily caught the end of the smouldering cigarette resting on the side table and catapulted it on to the carpet several yards away. Blanche was so surprised by the outburst, she sat stunned in her chair for a moment, before retrieving the burning tobacco from the carpet.

The policewoman waited for Mrs Nowak to calm down. Her eyes wandered to the four photographs in thin, lacquered black frames. The first was of a baby, a tiny blurred face surrounded by a halo of white linen.

Mrs Nowak answered the chief inspector's unspoken question. 'My son, Marek. The next photo is of me with my family back in Poland. It was taken before the war.' The picture showed a group of people picnicking on the margin of a pine forest. They had, so it appeared, just finished eating. The mother and father sat in the centre, formally arrayed, the mother wielding a parasol against the fierce summer sun. Around them, like petals, some standing, some lounging, stood three young men and two young women. There was a strong family resemblance between the brothers and sisters: tall foreheads, small, straight noses and smouldering eyes. The two girls – in their middle teens – were in summer dresses. One sported a floppy straw hat.

'I'm the one with the hat on,' murmured Mrs Nowak helpfully. Already, at that tender age, Tatyana Nowak knew how to pose for effect, one elegant hand lifted to the brim to emphasise her profile. 'My father had bought some bottles of champagne. Not to celebrate anything in particular, but simply because he was like that. That day in June, with the scent of the pine trees in my nostrils, I drank my first glass of champagne. The bubbles tickled my nose and floated straight through my head. It made me feel so grown up. I felt so happy then.' She mused and fell silent.

'Did any of your brothers or sisters come across to England with you?'

'No. They were all killed in the war. My sister by a German bomb. Two brothers by the Gestapo and one by the Russians.'

'I'm sorry.' Blanche understood now why Poland's betrayal had gnawed into Mrs Nowak's soul.

'"Never be sorry", Chief Inspector. That's what my father kept telling me. "Never be sorry for anything," he said, "that's not your fault. Otherwise your tears will run dry."' She lit another cigarette. The decadent perfume of the tobacco oozed and insinuated round the room, flowing in and out of the beams of sunlight. 'I could never believe him. I always *did* care. I *do* cry when terrible things happen. It's my Polish sense of tragedy, I suppose, a feeling that things are always against us.'

The third photo was of a rugged-looking man, handsome and rakish. She told Blanche with a smile of sentimentality that it was of her late husband. The chief inspector stood up and walked over to the chest of drawers. She picked up the fourth photograph of a young Tatyana on Westminster Bridge – beaming, slim and beautiful – arm in arm with Zbigniew, with three men behind them in double-breasted suits. Big Ben towered behind. The buildings round about were pockmarked and battered as a result of German bombing. 'When was this taken, Mrs Nowak?'

She hesitated. 'It was taken the morning before Zbigniew went back to Poland. That's him with me in the photo. The spring of . . . 1950. Do you recognise one of the men behind us?'

Blanche scrutinised the three faces behind. One seemed familiar, like the opening chord of a song she had heard somewhere before but could not remember when. After a moment or two she understood. She cut away the well-groomed mop of hair, added the marks of old age and recognised Graham Mills. She nodded. 'Who are the two others?'

'The one on the left is Jozef Taczek, the friend I was telling you about.' He was stocky and running – at least to judge from his jovial expression – carelessly to fat. There was a twinkle in each narrow eye and a wide gap perched charmingly between his two front teeth. Blanche pulled the photograph closer and, with a surge of excitement, remembered Smith's description of the man who had had an argument with Mills at his office one day. She asked the next question with deliberate calm. 'Your friend, Jozef. Did he get on well with Graham?'

Tatyana twisted her head to one side in surprise. 'Of course they did. They were the very best of friends.'

'Always?' Blanche scrutinised her face.

The Polish woman paused, as if she understood Blanche was preparing a conversational ambush. 'Yes. Always.' Her eyes were troubled.

'You don't sound very sure?'

'Well,' she replied gently, 'if you know something why don't you tell me rather than stand there smirking?'

Blanche sucked in her breath. 'I heard they had a bad quarrel at Mills' caravan business.'

'Chief Inspector, what are you telling me? All good friends have arguments.' Tatyana laughed in her raucous way, with relief, Blanche thought.

'What about the last man in the photo?'

Tatyana scrutinised it and, with the directness of honesty, said she had forgotten. He worked under Graham at the Foreign Office. He just happened to turn up that day and was no particular friend of anybody.

Blanche asked if she could copy the photograph and Mrs Nowak did not object.

She looked down at her wedding ring again, twisting it round and round with a venom that marked the skin. Her personality had suddenly slumped somehow, aged in just those few minutes the chief inspector had been with her. She was a strange woman: a mixture of pride and self-pity, hope and despair and also – Blanche sensed – of dishonesty. The chief inspector only winnowed the truth from the half-truths much later. And, even then, not from Tatyana Nowak's lips.

85

Chapter 10

Blanche woke early the next morning. She was troubled by the vision of her husband clawing for breath at her knees two nights before: one part of her relished the memory, while another, the side of her that abhorred all violence, churned throughout the night. Usually she passed the hours of darkness in dreamless sleep but that night she was restless and her gloom curdled when she finally dragged back the curtains at six o'clock in the morning. The sun peeped above the Ealing horizon, flecking the roof tiles opposite with a cheerless glow. The washing lines drooped, the garden sheds and stunted trees dripped with morning wetness. Everything was draped in a drizzling mist that blunted all edges to blandness.

The chief inspector was rarely depressed, but when she was she ate, ate in gargantuan quantities until her skin lost its early wrinkles and she felt like one of the rotund birds that bounced over her lawn. She munched through two bowls of muesli, four slices of toast and three eggs. The clouds had thickened and specks of rain dotted the windows as she slumped into her car an hour later and threaded her way through the dreary backstreets of Acton and up on to the Westway. A few street lamps still guttered lemon-curd yellow in the mist.

She hoped Dexter, in his intermittently sensitive way, would recognise her low spirits, and give her some sympathy when she arrived. 'About time,' he murmured simply, putting the phone down and disentangling his lanky legs, as she came through the door. He leant forward with an expression which was often mistaken for a leer. In fact it was a look of glee. The sergeant treated the passing on of important police information as a form of high gossip. 'Have I got news for you.'

'What?' she asked in a dry monotone.

'That woman you went round to see yesterday, Tatyana Nowak. Dead. Topped herself last night.' Blanche scrutinised the glittering eyes, set in hollows of his smooth skin, and the half-open mouth for the shadow of a smirk, indicating it was a practical joke. 'Must have been your dress sense.'

Blanche ignored the ill-timed humour. 'Are you serious?'

There was no hint of a smile on his face. 'How did she do it?' the chief inspector asked with a steadiness that surprised herself.

'Overdose. The son was taking a morning cuppa to her in her bedroom, got no reply when he knocked on the door, went in and found the body. He probably didn't fancy his breakfast after that.'

'Very funny,' she commented without enthusiasm.

'I try to be.' Blanche knew the sergeant was deliberately playing the jester to lift her spirits but his jollity only grated. He went on, 'The son was hysterical and put under sedation.'

'I sometimes wish *you* could be put under sedation.' Blanche was serious.

'I am already. Remember I work for the Metropolitan Police.'

The chief inspector's lips tightened into a smile despite themselves. Tatyana Nowak's suicide, assuming it was suicide, came as a complete surprise. Mrs Nowak was distracted the day before and the news of Mills' death had certainly taken her unawares. But the journey from distracted shock to suicide, as the chief inspector knew, is a long and tortuous one. It seemed almost too much of a coincidence that Mrs Nowak should die the very night after Blanche's visit.

Marek Nowak, Tatyana's son, lay sleepily in the hospital bed as the sister took the chief inspector into the ward. The sister, an earnest woman whose spindly limbs were too short for her body, placed Nowak's clothes in a neat pile on the single chair beside the bed and reminded him to vacate the bed as soon as possible. The figure in the bed grunted.

His moustache imprinted him with an unmistakable Polish air that was almost caricature. It was thick and black, and drooped. Dark bristle was glued around his cheeks. The thin yet muscular arms that lay on the top of the blankets quivered with nervous energy. His eyes were not so alarming as his mother's: the brown of old pine, slightly exophthalmic and guarded by heavy lids. He avoided her gaze, swivelling his glance around the room to avoid eye contact. He said nothing. The distant hum and clatter of the hospital seemed to rise in volume. He did not invite her to sit down and there was only one chair; Blanche could hardly dump his clothes on the floor.

'I'm sorry to have to come and chat with you at a time like this, Mr Nowak. But as you probably know I came to visit your mother yesterday and . . .' She hoped he would pick up the conversation and carry her through the embarrassment. He said nothing, staring so fixedly at a point just behind her left ear that she turned to discover what fascinated him so much. There was only the plastic curtain. When she turned back, his narrowed eyes were scrutinising her face, but as soon as her glance crossed his, they skidded back to where they had rested before. She introduced herself and asked if she could move his clothes on to the bed so that she could sit down. He nodded.

The policewoman found the conversation tortured, largely monosyllabic on his part, yet he was curiously talkative when he saw an opportunity to extract some information about why the chief inspector had come to visit his mother. He murmured that the suicide had come as a terrible shock. He had come home late and had a brief conversation with his mother. She always stayed up late, he added, because she loved to listen to the radio or records. Nowak's voice was deep but the tone was curiously lifeless and monochromatic.

Had she talked about Blanche's visit? Yes, in passing. She had said the police had come round and broken the news of the murder of an old friend of hers, Graham Mills. Marek said he knew his mother was fond of Mills and saw him every few weeks. More frequently, Blanche reflected, than the dead woman seemed to imply. No, he didn't know exactly how many times because he didn't spy on her. No, he didn't know Mills particularly well at all. In fact, Nowak hadn't met him, face to face, on a personal basis for several years. He used to be closer to him when Nowak was a youngster but now he was older – well, he didn't care either way about Mills and he hadn't bothered to keep up the relationship. Despite the swivelling eyes, what he said made sense and seemed reasonable to the chief inspector. He'd read about the murder of Mills in

88

the newspapers but hadn't told his mother because he knew it would upset her – no, not upset her enough to make her commit suicide, but upset her all the same. He must have known she would learn of the murder eventually? Oh yes, but he would have prepared the ground in his own way, and besides, he argued, the later his mother learnt about Mills' death, the less she would be hurt by it. Blanche gently said she disagreed, at which he grunted and shrugged his shoulders.

Marek described how he could not sleep well the night before and had risen early at about half past six. He began to get worried by half past seven because his mother was always up before him, and had finally got so concerned that he went into Tatyana's bedroom a quarter of an hour later with a cup of tea. He found his dead mother, three empty aspirin bottles beside the bed and a glass that smelt strongly of whisky. There was no suicide note.

He probed with fascinated precision about Blanche's visit to his mother. His yearning for knowledge was natural to Blanche and, from a glint of resentment beneath the hooded eyelids, she guessed he blamed her in some way for the death of his mother. He made it clear that although Tatyana suffered bouts of depression through being in exile, she had no record of mental illness and had never tried to commit suicide before. 'She told me once that she was desperate when she heard Dad had been killed in Poland. She said she thought about suicide then. But she didn't do it – for my sake. I was her memory of him, if you like.'

'What do you remember about Graham Mills? When you were a kid, for example.'

'Not much.'

Blanche sat back in her wobbly hospital chair. 'What do you mean?'

'Precisely what I said. Not much.'

The policewoman recalled her meeting with his mother the day before. 'Your mum told me he did a lot for both of you. He was a sort of uncle, almost a replacement father if you like.'

The eyelids lifted and he looked straight at her for a moment so curt she could easily have missed it. 'No. He was never anything like that.' The eyes were hooded again as quickly as they were unloosed. His wiry fingers picked at the blankets covering his waist. Blanche sensed he was affronted by the question in some way but Marek Nowak knew how to control his anger. 'No. He was never a replacement father,' he uttered with finality. 'Simply a friend who helped us out of some tight spots. We didn't have much money then.'

Disdain for Graham Mills was the ground bass in his voice. She paused and decided to attack directly. 'Why didn't you like Mills? Had he ever done anything to annoy you?'

There was no flash of those poisonous eyes, simply a shrug. 'No. I just didn't like him very much.'

'And what about your mum? Do you think she had any reason to want to see Mills dead?'

Marek's brows met in a tortured knob. He scratched his clump of crow-black hair and a few flecks of dried skin floated on to the neck of his pyjamas. He shook his head from side to side with a whiff of theatricality for such an introverted man. 'No. She had no reason she knew about.'

Blanche knew he was an intelligent man who used words as precisely as he used them sparingly. She decided to play out his legalistic game of definitions. 'What about reasons *others* knew about?'

He glanced up and his lips curled into a superior smile. 'I wouldn't know about those.'

'Did she tell you about the legacy Mills had left her in his will?'

'What legacy?' Marek murmured, failing to conceal his surprise.

'Mills left her a considerable amount of money. She seemed pleased about it, as if it would take a load off her mind – you know, money worries.'

The eyes were unhooded again as he fathomed the implication of the question. 'If you think my mum killed Mills for some godforsaken pile of money, you must be bloody mad. OK, she was worried about money because she was always trying to keep up appearances. But . . . to commit murder for it. You must be mad.' He shook his head vigorously and tightened his cheeks to stop any tears flowing. 'It just wasn't her. Anyway, she was . . .'

'What?'

'Nothing. I was just thinking, you never really know what

anybody can do. I think I know my mother but – how much money was it, by the way?' He was improvising, pirouetting from one view to another, first denying his mother could possibly have killed Mills and then changing his mind. He was in a calm phase now, contemplating the material benefits that would flow to him from his dead mother. Blanche respected his intelligence but not his integrity.

'No one knows yet. The lawyers still have to sort out Mills' affairs. Your mother's share of the estate will be a hundred thousand pounds or so.'

There was no whistle of appreciation, no pleasure, the sort of reaction that Blanche half expected. 'I see. My mother could have used that money.' It was a bald statement of fact, as though he were preparing an inventory of her expenses.

The plastic curtain round the bed rustled and the spindly sister appeared, reminding the chief inspector that Mr Nowak was very tired and that anyway she wished the patient to get a move on. Blanche replied with an apologetic shrug that she just had a few more questions. 'Can you remember where your mother was on the nights of the third to the fifth of August? She said you would probably be able to confirm her alibi.'

'Look. I can't remember what the hell I was doing then, let alone her. I don't have a diary or anything. I'm not Samuel Pepys.' He was not confirming the alibis Tatyana had given her. The policewoman divined several possible reasons for this but could not decide which was the true one. His eyelids lifted again. Blanche had scratched another raw spot. 'All I know is, I've just lost my mother and you come barging in here and imply she was involved in some way with murder –'

Blanche raised her hands in a conciliatory gesture. 'No, no, Mr Nowak. I was simply asking you in case there was some sort of link between the suicide and the murder, the sort of link that perhaps you couldn't see but I could.'

'Well, there isn't and that's it,' he snapped. 'Do you mind clearing off while I get dressed?'

Blanche nodded. He resentfully gave her the telephone number of the comprehensive school in Clapham where he worked as a history teacher. She left him slumped in the bed, eyes closed, exuding the timelessness of a translucent marble memorial in a country church.

As she drew the plastic curtains closed behind her, the spindly sister clicked up in her sensible shoes, brandishing a piece of paper. 'This is for you, I believe.'

It was a message to ring Dexter urgently at the Yard.

'The NHS shouldn't be used as a telephone answering service, you know.' She marched off over the linoleum tiles before Blanche could answer.

Blanche was annoyed with herself. She had forgotten her bleep and had no idea how long the sergeant had been trying to find her. She balanced a polystyrene cup of national health tea by the public telephone, ducked her head under the plastic globe, and dialled the direct line.

'What's the problem now?' she snapped when Dexter answered.

'Nothing.' Dexter sounded defensive.

She knew her tone had bruised him but could not stop herself. 'Well, what is it, for Christ's sake?'

'They've found the weapon.'

'What sort of gun is it?'

'Hey, cool down, guv! If you carry on like this, I'll wish I hadn't phoned you at all.' She sighed. Outside the sky was a uniform, concrete grey. She detected a slow indrawing of breath at the other end of the phone.

'It's a Beretta with a silencer. With it was a small saw with a blade about two feet long. Made in Sweden, where the porn comes from.'

Blanche smiled faintly: she appreciated Dexter's efforts to dispel her bad humour. 'When were they found?'

'Two days ago. The Underwater Search Unit found it in one of the ponds on Hampstead Heath, about half a mile from the body.'

'Why on earth did we only get to hear today?' Blanche spluttered. She hated incompetent individuals who smothered efficiency. 'God, I'll stick one on the idiot responsible.'

Dexter snorted gently at the other end of the telephone. 'The USU say the delay was caused by all the junk they found in the mud. They had to work through golf balls, wire netting, prams, milk bottles.'

'The artefacts of modern civilisation, eh?'

'Arty what?' The sergeant knew his boss was cheering up.

'The truth is, someone's dropped a bollock and they're all rowing for shore like crazy.' Dexter, lazy and inefficient in his own way, liked to puff himself up and berate other departments at Scotland Yard. 'Anyway, the result came through late this morning. There's an exact match on the old man.'

'What, the calibre of the bullet?'

'Yeah. And the remnants of blood and hair on the saw blade.'

'Any prints?'

'You want everything, don't you.'

'It's the human condition.'

'Your trouble is you read too much.'

'Vaccinated with printer's ink.'

The chief inspector's attention was attracted by a bulbous bluebottle, glutted with the heat of summer, strutting over the outside of the plastic globe. She thought aloud. 'Whoever it was who topped Mills, slung the gun and the saw in the pond, perhaps in a panic, and then threw the head in the canal. No trace of the knife of course?'

'What, the one used for the . . . ?' Dexter was still very coy about the emasculation.

'Yes.'

'Yes.'

'Yes, what?'

'Yes. The knife was there was well.'

'Just get on with it, Dexter,' she crackled angrily, running her eyes around the rim of the plastic globe of the telephone booth.

Without any warning he paused, a nervous buzz twitching the telephone line. He was stung, Blanche knew, hurt by her tone as he was by a handful of his lovers. He spoke to her of his conquests, most of whom he treated with disdain. A few, however, clutched beneath his skin and it was these who invariably tossed him away like a piece of wrapping paper. Dexter found a certain self-flagellatory joy in talking about his unhappy affairs. By reliving the agony, he wanted to dull it. Blanche sensed he suddenly wished to tell her some more secrets of the heart. She did not share his desire: he was her sergeant, not a client for psychological counselling. 'Get on with it,' Blanche repeated, but this time more softly.

'There's an exact match on the knife as well. Also I got an interesting phone call from that slimy janitor, Reynolds, at Mills' block of flats.'

'What did he have to say?'

'You know the way people forget things and then remember them – well, he said Mills thought he was being followed in the days leading up to the murder.'

'What did he mean "being followed"?'

'He wasn't too open about it. He told me a guy from security –'

'What, the one who arrived at Mills' flat when we were there?'

'The description fits. Anyway, this character warned Reynolds not to say anything to anybody – even us – once he'd given his statement to him and the Branch. Talked of official secrets and all that.'

A memory twitched in Blanche's mind. 'Seems rather heavy-handed.'

'Reynolds said he felt guilty he hadn't told us earlier. Felt we ought to know. Very generous, I thought, especially since he treated me like black scum.'

'Just cut the anti-racist agitprop, Dexter, and tell me what happened? Will you?'

She imagined Dexter smiling at the other end of the phone, lips drawn back, white teeth glittering with amusement.

'One evening, a couple of days before the old boy disappeared, Mills came down and on the way out asked Reynolds to follow him to the doors at the entrance of the flats. Mills told the caretaker to look across the road, and he pointed to a man sitting at the window table of a restaurant opposite, and said something like, "He's been sent to watch me". Reynolds couldn't work out whether Mills was being serious or not.'

'Any description of the man in the restaurant?'

'No. Too far away.'

Blanche replaced the telephone in its cradle.

A chord hummed inside her head, a mysterious chord like harmonics, confirming that somewhere there was reason and order behind Mills' murder. If anyone knew he was under surveillance it would have been Graham Mills. As a former spy, he could recognise a 'follow' and, whatever people had

94

said, no one had described him as a fantasist. Out of the blur of the past few days, she heard the echo of some words of Robert Pollock: 'He was a little more on edge than usual the last couple of times I met him.' Blanche was sure Mills was in danger in the days leading up to his death. And he knew it.

An old lady, stooped over her sticks, shuffled along the corridor in her dressing gown. A young mother skated by, frantically chasing her two offspring.

The memory that had twitched distantly during her conversation with Dexter surfaced. She would try an experiment.

She picked up the telephone again and dialled Robert Pollock's number. He answered. She asked if she could call round and see him later that day and ask some further questions.

The pause was so long, the chief inspector thought she had been cut off. 'Look, I'm not meaning to be rude or anything like that, Chief Inspector. And I would really like to help you further. But I'm not allowed to.'

Blanche nodded. 'What do you mean?'

'Well, I've been told that I can only talk about Graham Mills to people authorised by the Security Service.'

'Who told you?' Blanche decided to risk a bluff. 'Urquhart?'

'You know him, do you?'

'Of course I do,' she lied, her heart thumping with anger and excitement as her prophecy was confirmed. 'But he's got no right to tell you that.'

He sighed. 'That's as may be. But I'm afraid I'll have to check back with him first.'

Blanche clenched and unclenched her fists to keep calm. 'What did Urquhart tell you?'

'I'm not sure . . .' Pollock sighed again while he pondered, but decided to speak. 'Well, he asked to come round to see me. I told him you had already interviewed me and he sounded rather miffed, saying he was in charge of the investigation. Anyway, it was too late by then. He told me not to talk to anyone else in the future, including you, without MI5's permission. Look,' he said suddenly, 'are you sure this is all right?'

'I'm working with Urquhart. He didn't mind me calling you.'

'Well, I'll just give him a call and check . . .'

'No, don't bother.'

'It's no trouble. I'll call you back.'

'No. Don't!' she just had time to say, before Pollock replaced his receiver.

She would just have to wait on the consequences of her bluff. At that moment Robert Pollock was probably ringing the same number for Urquhart that Dickinson had given her. Blanche took a swig from her polystyrene cup of tea and grimaced. The tea was as chill as Dr Ruxton's mortuary slab. She chuckled, pleased that her intuition had not deserted her.

Chapter 11

When Blanche arrived back at the office from the hospital, Dexter was on the phone, complaining about a wistaria he had bought which he had carefully planted and fertilised, and which had shown singular ingratitude by dying. Dexter's only obsession, apart from handsome men and work, was his roof terrace. The detective constable was not there because Dexter had despatched him to discover more about Mills' tangled love life. He had already found the woman called Anne, a divorced and wrinkled Sloaneish secretary in blue tights, with whom the dead man had had an affair. There was no jealous and angry man on the warpath behind her and she herself lacked bitterness over Mills' infidelity.

Blanche was relieved to find there were no messages from Robert Pollock or Urquhart. A memo placed strategically on the chief inspector's desk by Dexter announced that Spittals wanted another interim report on the Mills case. It scraped the chief inspector into irritation. Blanche felt that as a woman and a member of the police, Spittals believed she had to prove herself three times better than any man.

While dictating the report that afternoon, Smith's description of the foreign man who had had an argument with Mills came back to mind, especially the gap between the front teeth. Jozef, the friend in Mrs Nowak's photograph, had such a gap. Blanche recalled she had foolishly not asked Mrs Nowak for Jozef's address or telephone number. She did not even have his surname. She phoned Marek Nowak's number in Chiswick and the droning, monotonous voice she had encountered first at the Paddington hospital finally answered. Nowak said he had just arrived home. She asked if he knew the man.

'Jozef Taczek?' He sounded doubtful.

'Your mum had a photo of him in a group with your dad.'

'Yes, I know. I'm puzzled because it's disappeared.'

'Your mum said I could take it and make a copy.'

He sounded both apprehensive and relieved. 'I'm not sure I want you to.' He breathed nervously for a moment. Blanche imagined him rasping his tongue along the line of his moustache. 'It's my photograph now, you know, and it's got a lot of sentimental value.'

'I won't damage it. I'll make sure you get it back as soon as possible.'

'Just make sure you do look after it. If not, there'll be hell to pay, I promise.'

Blanche was puzzled by his concern over the photograph. She wondered whether his bad temper was just due to his nervousness but decided there was no point in arguing. She had already arranged for copies to be made anyway by the Photographic Section, and said she would return the framed photograph the next day.

'What do you want Jozef for anyway?'

Blanche weaved past the question. 'How do you know him?'

'I know *of* him. It's rather like Graham Mills. He knew my dad well, and has always been friendly with my mother. She used to see him pretty often. What's he supposed to have done?'

'Nothing, as far as I'm aware. Your mother mentioned him. Have you got his address and telephone number, by chance?'

'I haven't.'

'Whereabouts does he live? London?'

'I don't know,' he answered sullenly.

Blanche paused, wondering whether Marek's unhelpfulness had a motive other than shock at his mother's death. 'Why are you trying to protect him, Mr Nowak? You must know at least which part of London he lives in.'

The chief inspector knew the man's surname. There could not be many Poles called Taczek living in the Home Counties. She could have threatened Nowak but, after a few seconds' hesitation, he gave her no need. He spoke fluently, as though a psychological dam had burst, freeing his tongue. 'He lives in Earls Court. I don't know his number. I've no reason to ring him. And when . . .' He trailed off.

Blanche asked what he was going to say.

'Let me give you a warning when you go to see him.'

98

'Warning?'

'Don't trust a word he says.'

'Why do you say that?'

'Advice.'

'From whom?'

'My mother,' he concluded, slamming down the telephone.

Dexter and Blanche lunched the next day at the pub near the Yard patronised by the Serious Crimes Squad – the sergeant on Chablis and she on single malt whisky. They had sat in the garden at the back because the heat was stifling again, but when assailed by a choir of drunken Australians in T-shirts yodelling 'Waltzing Matilda', they retreated to the interior. The fug and smell of stale beer inside the pub were almost unbearable but at least familiar. They were joined by some heavy-jowled colleagues in Crimplene suits who breathed out some feeble cracks about how honoured the pub was that day to be graced by the 'Brains and the Brawn', as Blanche and Dexter were known. They laughed the laugh of the good-humoured surrounded by the tiresome.

They left their colleagues behind and walked back under a muslin sky. Ever since the discovery of the body, the weather had been unsettled and oppressive. One day the heat pressed down from under a ceiling of grey cloud, the next, wind scattered the cloud and raised goose pimples in the shade. Dexter slunk off to check up on the alibis for Christine Mills and her mother.

Blanche suddenly found herself alone in the office, an alien in a place she knew like a sister. A gentle murmur stole into the room from the offices close by, conversations punctuated by the chirrup of a telephone or a commanding shout. Feet padded past the door. The phone rang on the constable's desk. She took a message. The time had come. She checked in her diary and dialled the seven digits Dickinson had given her for Urquhart.

'Hello.' The voice was distant and neutral.

'Is that Mr Urquhart?'

'Yes. Who's that?'

'Detective Chief Inspector Hampton of the Serious Crimes Squad. We met a few days ago in Graham Mills' flat.'

'Don't worry, Chief Inspector. I remember you. In fact I was going to give you a ring some time. By the way, how did you get my number?'

It was now the calm, relaxed voice she remembered from Mills' flat.

'I have my sources.'

'So do I.' He paused. Blanche thought she heard a click over the telephone and remembered that their conversation might be recorded. Their opening banter would have the transcribers groaning, she thought. 'So why have you rung me?'

'Information.'

'About Mills?'

'And about you.'

His tone changed from the sardonic to the official. 'The amount of help I can offer is extremely limited.'

Blanche gabbled on, hoping he would be deceived by the flow of words. 'It's simply this: I've discovered Mills was being kept under surveillance just before his death.'

She heard nothing for several seconds: enough time for her to doodle on the cover of a maroon file a shape that the pure in mind would interpret as an airship, and the lewd-minded as a phallus.

'Who gave you this information?'

She could not be sure, but sensed she had caught him off balance, had thrown grit into the cogs of machinery that before had been interlocking smoothly. 'So you're confirming the tail was from MI5?' She played the knowing coquette.

His Scottish accent grew thicker. 'Not at all. In fact I was going to say that I can't help you. You see, the Security Service has – as I'm sure you'll understand – access to certain information which it can't allow individuals outside to see without special security clearance. We and Special Branch are called in, as a matter of routine, to investigate the violent death of a former employee. Secret information is gone through very thoroughly from every angle to discover if there could be any possible link between us and the death.' It was he who was gabbling now, tossing out words to form a verbal smokescreen. 'Once we come to a conclusion about this, the decision is final from the point of view of the uniformed police. As I'm sure you'll appreciate, we just can't allow any old Tom, Dick or Harry to start ploughing through our files.'

'What happens if you've got it wrong?'

'Our investigation can be reopened at any time if anyone presents new evidence. But really, Chief Inspector, I think you're off beam if you think there's more to this than an attack by some mugger.'

Urquhart's mellifluous yet crude vowels annoyed her. In Mills' flat he was diplomatic and shadowy. Now he was pompous and schoolmasterly, lecturing her – like Spittals – but with more elegance. Another change intervened. His voice relaxed and he spoke to her like a confidant in a hasty whisper.

'Look, Chief Inspector . . . I understand the quandary you're in. I'd help you further if I could but things are – how shall I say – rather more complicated than you might think.'

'What do you mean?'

'I can't talk here. Let's meet for a meal some time and we can chat about it then.'

They fixed on a restaurant in Notting Hill Gate for the following evening.

Blanche studied the doodle she had made on the file during the telephone conversation with a weary smile. She was as puzzled by his swinging changes of tone as by his friendliness. She suspected he wished to ask her as many questions as she wanted to pose him, but her doubts were stilled by the dinner invitation. She was more flattered by it, she felt, than she should be.

She circled the squares between Kensington High Street and Cromwell Road until she found a parking space. The houses were mid-Victorian, each with a flight of steps leading up to a porch supported on two marble pillars. The façades were stuccoed and painted a cream which had been darkened by the ubiquitous London dust. There was a garden in the middle of Allen Square. It was guarded jealously by a chainlink fence and hemmed in by dusty trees. The gates at either end were locked. Signs proclaimed the garden only for the use of residents. While she skirted the fence, a downtrodden nanny unlocked one of the gates and escorted two raucous infants inside to play.

The answerphone at the house where Taczek lived sported a blotched, brass nameplate. Blanche prodded the white plastic button and the voice of the young man she had spoken to earlier on the telephone to fix the meeting crackled an invitation to come up. Taczek lived on the second floor and she was embarrassingly out of breath as the door opened. Blanche resolved to take more exercise.

The Voice on the telephone took on human form. He was a pretty youth, shorter than her, and beautifully proportioned. The hair was a mass of black locks, the nose firm and strong, the features chiselled, the lips red and pouting. He swayed willow-like in the doorway, one hand stroking the cravat at the neck of his white shirt. The eyes were black as coals. They roamed with a glitter of horror over Blanche's crumpled outfit and came to rest, with one last shudder, on the scuff marks on her navy-blue shoes. She realised she had been intending to polish them for the past fortnight but had been too busy.

'Chief Inspector Hampton?' the Voice enquired witheringly.

Blanche noted approvingly, and with a twinge of jealousy, that the interior was decorated with taste and refinement. Three original Hogarth etchings hung in the hallway, while the lounge – high and spacious – breathed an air of intellectual luxury that was not produced by mere expenditure. A few choice antiques had been scattered strategically to add the elegance of age to the room. As she walked in, a man strode across the room to greet her, chunky hands outstretched in welcome.

Even on the sofa, Jozef Taczek exuded energy – a restless charm that sprang, along with sweat, from every pore. It flowed through his hands as they shaped curlicues one moment and chopped the air the next. At regular intervals his right hand would spring upwards to adjust his thick-rimmed spectacles. There was no need for the gesture: it was simply an endearing nervous tic. His accent was as thick and solid as his body, which – contrary to the impression given by Tatyana Nowak's photograph – had not grown flabby. Although in his late sixties or early seventies, Taczek was well preserved. There was only a tuck or two under his chin indicating the dewlap to come, and his neck rose like a tree trunk to display the fine head, eyes lively and mobile, hair swept back, the moustache

102

brushed outwards with a dapper air. 'Charles, would you be kind enough to go and make some tea?'

The Voice nodded and went out obediently. Taczek smiled broadly. The gap between the front teeth, Blanche saw, had not closed with the intervening years.

Blanche explained that Tatyana Nowak had mentioned his name to her.

'It is sad, Tatyana. Very sad that she should take her life. I loved her very much. And then, suddenly, to go and do this . . .'

'When was the last time you saw her?'

'It must have occurred about three weeks ago. We went to see a film. It's quite old now. A Hungarian film – a very good one – about an actor and his rise to fame in the Third Reich. How he turned a blind eye to the collective faults of the regime in exchange for individual glory. I found the hero not unsympathetic,' he added with a cryptic smile.

'What do you think could have made her commit suicide?'

He lifted his eyebrows. 'Tatyana always was to me a romantic woman, a lady who would have wished the world to be other than it is – and thus a little credulous, even innocent. In addition, she was an impulsive woman. Of great warmth. But there was a dark side. Of depressions, when she knew not which way to turn.' His English had an antiquated air, learnt from some dusty grammar published when atlases of the world were still predominantly red and people in real life tried to speak like the characters in Oscar Wilde's plays. Blanche was confused by his comments about Tatyana: each in itself seemed full of insight but they did not add up to a coherent picture. She furrowed her brow and was pleased to find Taczek responding without a verbal prompt. 'It's all right for you British. So secure in your history and your character. Great Empire. The Mother of Parliaments. Mrs Thatcher. The Falklands. Economic Recovery. With Poles it's different. Your Shakespeare summed it up rather well in that line. "As flies to wanton boys, are we to the Gods –"'

'"– They kill us for their sport."'

Taczek chuckled. A twinkle of humour appeared in his eye. 'It is reassuring to know the famous Scotland Yard is not staffed alone by unlettered fools and drunkards. Ah! Charles!

You have brought the tea. I hope, Chief Inspector, that you will join us in this civilised English custom?' Taczek did not so much speak as declaim, like a retired actor whose visitors are now his sole audience.

He poured the tea without stemming the flow of words. Blanche was accustomed to such overwhelming personalities but Taczek's language made her feel rather drunk and light-headed. The Voice meanwhile had sunk into an armchair and listened raptly. 'I think personally, assuming Tatyana was not murdered – and who knows, there might have been some secret motive somewhere? – that she took her life in despair, the despair of the exile, perhaps disillusioned with the West and its lack of stomach in recognising the evil of socialism. In such a despair, she may have taken her own life.'

Blanche shuffled in her chair, doubting the man's good sense. 'But you know of no specific reason?'

'No. Not at all.' He sipped his tea and smiled mischievously. 'Of course, nowadays we all get suicide out of perspective. In ancient Rome it was a noble gesture of despair. It still is in Japan.'

'I've never understood that,' Blanche replied warmly. 'I always thought suicide was just bloody stupid. The last refuge of those without hope.' The swear word rang embarrassingly in the room, like a single singer in a choir who is out of tune. She hated death, its finality, its mystery. She loved life even during its blackest moments. This was why she tracked those who took it with such dedication: it was a personal quest to create only a little justice in an unjust world. Suicide simply bloodied the face of all her instincts and values, her personal crusade to uphold life at all costs, the residue of her religious faith that had ebbed two decades before.

He inclined his head to one side patronisingly. 'You are neither old nor an exile. In time, you might understand.'

'I doubt it,' she replied, before asking Taczek how badly Tatyana Nowak would have been hit by the murder of Graham Mills.

Taczek prodded his spectacles and pondered. 'Very, I am sure. You see, I knew them both. Tatyana and her husband, Zbigniew. A marvellous man. Did you know about him going back to Poland?' Blanche nodded. 'It was dreadfully sad.

Zbigniew didn't like smoggy London at all. He missed Poland terribly and thought he'd go back there to see some relatives.'

'Mrs Nowak told me something about a car accident?'

He hesitated. 'Yes, yes, that's right. Zbigniew took a corner too fast and he came off the road. He died instantly. It was a tragedy.' He said this with conviction, as though the memory was still raw.

Blanche asked when that was exactly, probing for details now that she believed she had gained his confidence. She was a gifted confessor, as Dexter had once remarked, complaining that as a woman she was lost for ever to the priesthood of the Catholic Church.

Taczek fixed her with his pale eyes. 'I can't remember exact dates any more. I think it must have been the spring of 1950. A long, long time ago. Yet I remember as well as if it were yesterday how badly the news hit Tatyana. She was shattered, distraught. Her whole life had been based around Zbigniew. She adored him. There he was, just going back to his native land for a holiday, and fate intervened.' He sipped some more tea, his little finger twitching in the air, a ring sparkling. He glanced up to check whether he was believed.

Blanche stored up that look. The Pole's eyes slithered together, as much in suspicion as in an effort to recall. 'I think the only thing that made it bearable was that she had within her Zbigniew's child. It gave her a reason to live. Marek was born and of course I did my utmost, along with other friends, to help her.'

'One of those other friends was presumably Graham Mills?'

He nodded slowly. 'Poor Graham. Dying in such a sordid and sadistic way.' He lifted a finger in the air. 'Such things never happened when I first lived in London just after the war. You English are so much more violent now.'

'Do you have any theories as to who killed him?'

His eyes twinkled. Taczek obviously relished gossip. 'It's just my, how do you say, pet theory that one of Graham's ex-lovers, or else one of their husbands, organised the whole thing.'

'Have you got any evidence?'

Taczek hoisted his eyebrows even higher than usual, so that they almost met his receding hairline, and opened his eyes wide. 'No, of course not. I don't deal in evidence, Chief Inspector. But in tittle-tattle and speculation.'

Blanche picked up her cup of tea and leant back in the armchair. It had taken time for her to crack the carapace of her upbringing and appreciate good living with a clear conscience. The china was antique Crown Derby. The Voice proffered sugar with a frown of dislike. Blanche proffered him in return her special smile: the facial equivalent of a kick in the kidneys. 'How close were you to Mrs Nowak? Her son said you saw her quite often.'

'Tatyana was a dear, dear friend. We knew each other – well, from the time I arrived here in 1945. When Zbigniew was alive and in London, we formed a very close group –'

'– along with Graham Mills, I gather?'

Taczek adjusted his spectacles again with a flicking motion. He leant towards her, eyes keen and sharp. 'You're well informed.'

'I have a photograph of you all together,' she continued, watching him intently. 'Tatyana Nowak showed it to me. Of you all on Westminster Bridge with Big Ben in the background.'

Taczek said nothing for a moment, his face blank and puzzled. He simply stared at her. 'How charming. Presumably it's the one she has on her chest of drawers?' His eyes dropped as he sipped more tea.

'Cake?' The Voice had crept behind her chair and thrust a plate of chocolate sponge almost into her face. 'Cake, Chief Inspector?' he repeated with a smirk of malice. She was so startled the cup rattled on her saucer, spilling Earl Grey over her dress. Blanche breathed deeply to cool her temper.

Her host nodded and poured out some more tea, instructing his catamite to refill the pot with boiling water. 'You were asking me how close I was to her . . . I suppose I saw Tatyana once every two or three weeks. We either met in town or else I would pick her up from her house.'

'Did you go in?'

Taczek chuckled. 'Of course. For a quick drink sometimes. I never stayed long. To be quite frank, I found her house rather drab and depressing.' He gulped down the last mouthful of lukewarm tea before Charles returned with the boiling water. 'Sometimes Marek was there, sometimes not. He's a rather strange young man. I have the impression he does not like me very much now. I have tried my best to be kind to him, help him through hard times, help with some research he was doing into his father. But then, the young are never grateful – are you, Charles?' The question was tossed playfully across the room like a tennis ball.

The Voice uncurled itself from the electric kettle. 'What have we to be grateful for, Jozef? Pollution? Nuclear weapons? Modern architecture?' A laborious game was being played. Blanche knew policemen who squirmed in the presence of 'benders', 'bum-bandits' and 'turd-burglars'. She found most homosexuals, like Dexter, congenial and intelligent, but the Voice's sybaritic pose and rudeness were unpleasant.

She asked Taczek where he was at the times Mills was murdered and Mrs Nowak committed suicide. He said he was away in his country cottage in Wiltshire and turned to the Voice, who corroborated his master's testimony with a nod.

'Were you and Tatyana Nowak ever lovers, Mr Taczek?'

The Voice snorted into his tea. Jozef merely smiled, flicking a look of irritation at his companion. 'No. Never. We were nothing more than just good friends. Very good friends.'

She had one last dart to sling at him – a blunt one and from a long distance. 'How often did you visit Graham Mills when he was at work at his caravan business?'

He shrugged his shoulders. 'Once or twice, maybe.'

'The former manager remembers you on one occasion bursting into Mr Mills' office. And you had a big argument.'

Taczek lounged back very slowly indeed and the chief inspector noticed his miniature paunch for the first time – little changed since Tatyana Nowak's photograph was taken decades before. He watched his stubby fingers drumming on his stomach for a moment. 'Oh yes! I remember. Graham and I had an embarrassing argument about money. He refused to pay me back or something. He was bad like that.'

'And did he pay you back?'

He prodded his spectacles. 'Graham always paid one back – finally. He loved vendettas. In fact that argument was the major reason why our friendship ended. We met occasionally afterwards at social gatherings but we didn't seek each other

107

out. What I heard about Graham came largely through Tatyana.'

Mrs Nowak had not told her of this quarrel, Blanche remarked. Taczek replied that Tatyana preferred to gloss over it because she lived in a past of fantasy when all three of them were young and happy and friends.

'What were you called then, by the way?' Smith, the used-car salesman, had said the foreign gentleman who argued with Mills was called Polanski.

'What do you mean?' His forehead knotted with concentration.

'Were you called Taczek or were you known by some other name?'

He shuffled from one plump buttock to the other and prodded at his spectacles. He was winning time to frame a cautious reply in case he was caught out. 'I think – I must – I have always been Jozef Taczek.'

'You sound surprisingly unsure.'

'When one reaches my age, one is never sure of one's identity.' He glued on a feeble smile.

'You didn't use a different name when you had that row with Mills?'

'Why should I?'

'I was told you called yourself Polanski then.'

Taczek sat upright and drew himself in protectively, like a snail snatched by a child from a garden path after rain. He stared at her for a moment, the eyes little roundels of cold blue glass. 'Whoever it was, was obviously mistaken. I have never used that name. Are you sure we talk about same event – a dispute at Graham's office?'

'Your description fits exactly.'

He had regained his composure now, she sensed. His horns emerged tentatively from their shell and he erased any further minor errors from his English. 'It's obviously a mistake, whatever this anonymous person says. I did go and see Graham once or twice at work and things did get a little heated on the occasion I referred to. But I never called myself Polanski. You British people have great difficulty in pronouncing Polish names, let alone remembering them.'

The Voice had fallen asleep in its armchair and did not stir when Taczek bustled around to show Blanche out, once again courteous and self-composed.

'I am so jealous of the untroubled sleep of the young,' he said, passing the sleeping Voice.

Blanche recalled the cake thrust into her face and the stain on her dress. Charles had balanced a cup holding lukewarm dregs of tea on the arm of his chair. Blanche deliberately brushed it with her thigh, tipping the brown liquid over the white shirt of the dozing Adonis. He awoke with a pampered scream. The chief inspector apologised far too profusely and tried to dab him with a handkerchief. He patted her away and fled to the bathroom.

The children and their nanny had left the garden in the square. The gate was securely locked again. Blanche noticed as she passed that someone had lubricated the padlock recently, and a brown stain was spreading inexorably over the pavement where the surplus oil had dripped. The sight echoed Blanche's reaction to Taczek: suspicion and distrust. He had lied about several things, the chief inspector concluded. She was certain Polish exiles did not go back to their mother country at the height of the Cold War 'on holiday', for a start.

Chapter 12

Blanche had spent a lot of time, relatively, on her make-up. It was not every night, she reflected, that she dined with a secret agent. In the cracked mirror of the restaurant's toilet, she admired the extra blusher on her cheeks, the blue pencil over her fleshy eyelids, the coral lipstick. Her face was not so much beautiful as interesting, she told herself, her hair thick and full, her eyes alive and sparkling.

Her good humour rapidly dissipated once out in the restaurant. Urquhart was late, very late. Blanche read a copy of the *Decameron* until she could bear it no more and finally took a table, hidden behind a flourishing aspidistra, in a corner of the restaurant. She told the waiter someone was due to join her and waited. For half an hour. The waiter, a cocky Italian who flicked his buttocks at her at the least opportunity, eyed her patronisingly and made attempts to chat her up in feeble English. She finally called him across and ordered for one. A pink carnation smirked at her from a transparent vase on the table. She brooded on this flower with a desiccating look.

A thin, tall shape slipped into the chair opposite. 'Sorry about the delay. Important business, I'm afraid.'

She smouldered. Bad time-keeping in general was high in her canon of sins but not as heinous as bad time-keeping in the particular: spoiling her dinner. 'You're only an hour late,' she said with staccato coolness. 'So I've already ordered.'

'For two, I hope,' he replied with desperate good humour.

She massacred the attempt to gloss over his lateness with a stare. It was the first time she had a chance to look at him closely. The light, a single bulb in an ethnic basket, was suspended from the ceiling and lit just the table. The area round it was hidden in the penumbra. Urquhart's face was thrown into eerie relief from the light which shone downwards and so deepened his eye sockets, yet also bounced upwards and painted a smudge of white on his chin. He was neither young nor middle-aged. Any age between thirty and forty would have stuck to him equally well. He was clean-shaven with a face that had been ravaged by acne when younger. As Blanche had decided before, the effect – now he was mature – was not unsightly. It added interest to a face that otherwise would have appeared too white, smooth and bland. A crest of wavy, blond hair was loosely rooted on a magisterial forehead. His eyelashes were extravagantly long, tar black and as thick as the teeth on a comb, and his lids were gently slanted, harbouring eyes of an electrifying blue. They had something Celtic in them, dark and brooding. Blanche's irritation crackled on the air.

He jabbered about football for the first five minutes to smother her angry silence. Not about the great figures of the game but of the subtle strategies behind it: the financial deals, how players could be disposed in different formations on the pitch. He even transformed the table into a football pitch and by pushing a salt cellar here, and a napkin there, explained how a good manager and team could win the advantage. Soccer had the same effect on Blanche as bad wine: drowsiness and a headache. She realised that Urquhart had neither the grace nor sensitivity to apologise and she wondered whether it was due to shyness or boorishness.

'I have the same involvement in soccer as I do in your case,' he concluded. 'I'm a spectator, watching with an informed interest. I don't actually play football any more, you see. That all stopped when I got a back injury at school. All I can do now is go to games and watch Glasgow Rangers from the Copeland Road stand.'

'The trouble is, Mr Urquhart –'

'– please call me Robert.'

She preferred the surname alone. It seemed more appropriate for a faceless spectator. 'The trouble is, I don't think people on the sidelines are going to help me very much. I want more people – to carry on with your footballing metaphor – to join my team, to kick the ball for me. I need more people like my detective sergeant who rolls his sleeves up and gets on with the job.'

He sat back calmly and rubbed the end of his neat nose. He

summoned over the waiter, who was chastened now that a man had arrived, and ordered wine to supplement Blanche's mineral water. The waiter swaggered away.

'You see,' the chief inspector went on, 'I've come to a dead end.' Urquhart did not blink. He listened intently. Blanche thought she detected a flicker of self-satisfaction, as though she had confirmed what had been for him until then just a suspicion. 'I've got various suspects. It could have been the wife or daughter, wanting his money. The man he sacked for fiddling the books of his business. A jilted lover. Or her husband.'

'Or there's the chance Mills got murdered by a sadistic lunatic,' Urquhart added.

'And always the possibility he was killed because of something to do with his time in the secret service.'

His lips tightened. 'In theory, yes.' His eyes flickered to left and right, with hardly a turn of the head. It was the automatic and well-oiled gesture of someone used to trading in secrets. 'I'll do my best to help you. What do you want to know?'

'Not very much.' She paused and squinted at him. 'Who killed Graham Mills and why.'

Urquhart laughed and drummed his fingers on the table. The knuckles were white, the fingers well scrubbed and bony. Healthy hands, dentist's hands. 'I don't know.'

'Come on! What *was* the result of your enquiry into Mills' murder? It's the least you can tell me after keeping me waiting for an hour!'

'Didn't Dickinson tell you anything?' He smiled mischievously. 'Apart from giving you my private phone number?'

'I guessed you wanted him to give it to me anyway,' she punched back.

The fingers stopped drumming. He flattened his hand on the table. 'Of course. Should you need help.'

Blanche was pleased. He had come to realise she was no puppet to be manipulated. 'Which I do. Dickinson said he couldn't give any and I should just go and get on with it.'

'He was being honest.' He pursed his lips. Blanche waited and watched him intently, mouth open, one eye half closed. 'I was in charge,' he continued in an offhand way. 'It seemed to me a fairly routine enquiry.' He scratched the side of his nose.

112

'Mills left the Secret Intelligence Service – that's MI6 if you didn't know –'

'– I did know.'

'Good.' He nodded, as though impressed, before leaning forward. 'He left SIS back in sixty-two but kept some contact with the service for at least a decade afterwards.'

'Doing what?'

'Can't say.'

'Come on! It can't have been that important.'

Urquhart looked at her impassively. 'I just can't tell you. Six sent me a summary of his career but even refused *me* access to all his personal files.'

Blanche had her face in what she hoped was an alluring pout of disappointment when the wine arrived. Urquhart gulped down three glasses almost without a pause.

'They're obviously not going to let just anyone go burrowing through their Registry willy-nilly. The whole tone of my contacts with them was that Mills was,' he paused to scratch his eyelid, '"burnt out". He wasn't privy to any really sensitive stuff that could have put him in danger – that's according to my liaison fella in SIS.'

'Who's that?'

'My business.'

The chief inspector smiled winningly. 'Please call me Blanche.'

He chuckled gently. 'Whatever I call you, it's still my business.' Urquhart gulped down a fourth glass. 'Blanche.'

'So, what did you say in your report?'

'The truth.'

'Which is?'

'There's no evidence of any espionage connection.'

'Are you always so sure of the truth?'

'I'm sure there's no evidence if that's what you mean.' He shrugged. His hand gestures were slightly more generous, but there were no other signs of the wine he had drunk. He ordered a second bottle. 'It's almost impossible to prove anything in the spying world. The not-proven verdict is standard. Besides, the KGB doesn't go in for assassinations these days.'

Blanche looked sceptical to draw him out.

Urquhart lifted his chair with both hands and moved it

113

round so that he could cross his legs. 'OK, so there was poor Georgi Markov a few years ago in London. Poisoned by the Bulgarians. But the KGB and the CIA don't think assassination's worth the candle any more. Too afraid of the propaganda implications.'

'So it doesn't happen at all?'

'Selected targets occasionally. More often than not, one of their own, who some people might say deserved it – a defector usually.' He said it without emotion, like someone discussing the death of turkeys in an abattoir.

Urquhart had come straight from the office and was still wearing a grey suit with a red tie. He loosened the tight knot round his throat. His eyes had come to rest less on the table and more on her. His bony shoulders were less hunched.

'Did you find *anything* suspicious?'

'No. Mills wasn't gay, so that ruled out a killing of that sort. You've gone through the other possibilities. They're far more likely.' Conversation with Urquhart was like grappling with warm jelly. Every solid fact slipped out of Blanche's grasp as soon as she believed she grasped it. Like her, she thought, he had developed the skill of talking endlessly but saying little.

'Any doubts at all?'

Her companion stared at her, as if to fathom her motives. He propped his right elbow on the table and rested his chin on the cupped hand – the pose of a football manager pondering how to redeploy his players when neither side has shown any likelihood of scoring a goal. 'I couldn't make my mind up about exactly why Mills resigned from SIS in 1962. He was in a fairly senior position. He seemed to lose more than he gained.'

'Perhaps,' the chief inspector remarked flippantly, 'he was a Soviet agent and decided to get out while the going was good.'

Urquhart looked at her impassively. His eyelids were raw and red. He leant forward and spoke in a grim whisper. 'This is highly confidential, you understand?' She nodded. 'There is a lot of circumstantial evidence that Mills *did* work for the Russians.'

Blanche chewed the last mouthful of spaghetti bolognese to

help her absorb the implications of this discovery. 'And you don't think that can be related to his murder?'

He shook his head. 'Lots of Brits who spied for the Soviets died peacefully in their beds.' Urquhart was enjoying himself. He was in control, the keeper of the secrets. He poured himself another glass of wine from the second, half-empty bottle.

Blanche refused. She wanted to keep a clear head. 'Have you come across a man called Taczek?'

The MI5 officer's lips tautened. 'Yeah. His name cropped up as an acquaintance of Mills.' He looked steadily at Blanche, watching for a reaction. 'He did some freelance work for MI6 in the late forties and fifties. Keeping contact with emigré groups and so on. Taczek told me he could think of nothing from those times that would have made Mills any sort of target for a KGB assassin – or any other sort of assassin come to that.'

The waiter arrived with Urquhart's main course, insipid rolls of an unidentifiable substance masquerading as 'involtini siciliani'. He picked at it while she pondered the results of his visit to Taczek.

'That's what Taczek told me as well,' she remarked. 'But Tatyana Nowak said to me a number of Poles had a grudge against Mills for something or other – she didn't say what, and I had no chance to find out.'

Urquhart lifted a bony hand in a gesture of resignation, his mouth chomping heartily. He ate the peas from the cradled fork, not from the back of it as Blanche's mother had taught her. The chief inspector remembered the photo she had borrowed from Mrs Nowak. 'What about another man who worked with Mills back in the early fifties?'

'Who's that?'

'I don't know his name. He's in a photo of Mrs Nowak's taken on the day her husband went back to Poland. She told me he worked under Mills in the same department of MI6.'

Urquhart widened his eyes slightly, whether as a gesture of surprise or warning – since the waiter came up behind her just then and was about to remove their dirty plates – she could not be sure. The waiter asked whether they wanted dessert. Urquhart declined. She ordered an ice cream. 'Can't help you if you don't know the name.' He pushed himself back in his chair. 'Did Mrs Nowak make a special mention of him or something?'

'No. He was just in this photograph she had on her dresser.'

'What did it show?'

'You sound very interested.'

Urquhart shrugged to pretend indifference. Blanche stared into his face but could read nothing from it. It was as blank as a stone worn by aeons of tides on the seashore. 'What else did she talk about?'

'She tried to spin me a yarn about her husband going back to Poland on holiday in 1950 and being killed in a car crash. What do you know about it?' Blanche expected him to mutter with disbelief as she had when she had digested the story.

Instead he rubbed a bony finger along the flank of his nose. 'The story about the car crash is true, as far as I know. As for the holiday, I agree with you, it sounds a wee bit unlikely. But not as unlikely as you think. The Poles were almost as keen to get foreign currency then as they are now and they allowed certain visits to relatives.'

'You haven't answered the question,' she prodded, turning an empty wineglass in her hand. 'What *was* Tatyana's husband doing back in Poland?'

'Snap.' He bared his clean, white teeth in a smile. 'I don't know. My investigation didn't cover irrelevant things like that.'

Robert Urquhart did know more than he pretended, Blanche was convinced, but she was not convinced about the thoroughness of his investigation into Mills' murder. His attitude towards it was dismissive and arrogant, almost as though MI5 had decided the result before the enquiry had begun. His loftiness irritated and intrigued her. 'Mrs Nowak was surprised by the amount of money Mills left her. Were you?'

'Not particularly.'

'Didn't you go and see her?' The chief inspector knew the answer before he spoke it.

'She wasn't relevant. It would have been a waste of time.' He gulped down greedily the last few drops of red wine. They had finished two bottles. His pale cheeks had taken on a ruddy glow. Neither of them were drunk but she became aware of how warm her bare forearms were, their curves emphasised

116

by the down caught in the back lighting from the restaurant. They were ripe and plump, she reflected, worthy of caresses, and she grasped her right bicep in her left hand. She held the grip for a second or two, released it and then stroked her fingertips along the edge of the muscle. She caught Urquhart's glance when she looked up, a musing and erotic stare that swerved away. He blushed, like a gangly adolescent Blanche once caught ogling her breasts when she wore a bikini on the beach. She found Urquhart's look, strained through those black eyelashes, oddly arousing.

The waiter conducted two unsteady businessmen to the empty table beside them. Both had leaky eyes and cheeks etched with scarlet lines of burst blood vessels. They were smartly dressed in silk ties and well-cut suits. One, with a tousled bundle of greasy hair, waved his arms about in mock anger. At the table beyond, two blowsy women and four men were on a works outing from the Midlands. They flicked ash from their cigarettes into the empty wine-glasses and shouted each other down in vain attempts to be witty. Urquhart looked to the ceiling in a gesture of comic despair.

Blanche saw her moment. 'You were rather mean by the way to tell everyone I spoke to – or was about to speak to – not to talk any more to Scotland Yard. You told Reynolds, the caretaker, to keep quiet. And Robert Pollock.'

Urquhart blushed – a hue that was even more scarlet than that created by the wine suffusing his skin. He looked down with a smile. 'Yeah, I got a call from Pollock.'

'And since he didn't call me back, you obviously told him to keep quiet.'

'I've heard a couple of so-called radical journalists are sniffing around, pushed on by Christine Mills. I was playing safe. That's all. Besides, that time of Mills' life has got nothing to do with his murder. I've checked it. You're wasting your time.'

Urquhart ordered a third bottle of wine from the waiter with flicking buttocks. He had drunk over a bottle and a half already but showed little outward sign of over-consumption, except for his accent curdling into a thicker Scots. For lack of anything better, she asked Urquhart where he was from. 'Glasgow, that's my home city. Born in Govan to Calvinist parents. They thought the life of their only son could be fulfilled through belief in Jesus Christ, hard work, a good education and keeping the Sabbath.' His blue eyes twinkled. 'Their only son thought a bit differently.'

He said he had two sisters but that he was the only and beloved son. His father was a shipyard worker, made redundant when the yard was closed. 'He and my mum live alone in a council flat in one of those awful blocks in Easterhouse. Because of the cuts in the repair budget, the roof leaks, the windows leak, the walls run with condensation. I don't suppose you know much about life on council estates?' he asked sardonically.

She prickled at the implication that she had led a soft and protected life. But he was right. She did not know much about it. Her childhood hardships had been limited to undergoing doting but humourless tirades from her mother.

His voice softened when he saw her reaction and became more confident, as though he could now say what he wanted rather than what he ought to say. 'Dad was made redundant when the yard was closed in seventy-three. He and Mum were moved out to the new estate. The work was meant to follow the workers. But it never did. It broke his heart, never working again. He just shuffles round the house. Sits in his armchair for hours and says nothing. Just wheezes.'

The waiter arrived with the third bottle of Valpolicella and Urquhart poured himself a glass with the same relish as if it were his first. 'Glasgow's had a facelift in the past few years but it's no more than that. It hasn't given people proper jobs. The schools are changed in ways people don't want. They're made to pay taxes they didn't vote for. Some of the Scots feel they're living in a colony. Down in Westminster Thatcher's got no idea.' He spoke passionately, even wildly – a tone that was the complete opposite of his usual, cool manner. He leant forward on the table, emphasising the points with a thin finger. 'Think of yourself first and damn the rest. Ye shall be judged as ye can spend. And if you're old or poor or handicapped or just think there should be more to life than this – then go to hell. I tell you, the times are out of joint.'

He offered her another glass of wine. She shook her head. He poured himself another, swilled it down with a grim smile and cradled the empty wineglass in his hands. 'I'm sorry,' he murmured. 'I tend to get carried away when I've drunk a wee bit too much. Imitate the way my dad goes on.' He chuckled. 'And, my God, does he go on.'

Blanche scanned Robert's face for his true beliefs but in vain: his features had collapsed back into inscrutability.

The waiter smacked a plastic plate containing the bill on to the corner of the table and glared at them. There was a queue of customers chattering by the door and waiting for places.

'Your expenses or mine?' asked the MI5 officer.

'Yours. You can launder them better.'

He chuckled and wiped the back of his hand across his lips. 'Malicious rumour.'

'Incidentally, *was* it your lot or Special Branch who were tailing Mills just before the murder?'

Urquhart's hand stopped dead in its trajectory towards the bill. He dropped his chin and examined her over imaginary spectacles. 'Where did you get that from?'

'An informant.'

'Don't be silly. Who told you?' In his voice there was a squeak of alarm. The policewoman was surprised because she assumed he would have been privy to everything about Mills. She realised that even the keepers of the secrets did not know them all. She refused, gently and firmly, to tell him. She did not want Reynolds troubled again. Urquhart polished his nose in silence for a few seconds. He was irritated, the chief inspector decided, by her obstinacy, and hovered on the edge of asking her again. But his pride did not allow it. He rose pensively, and a little unsteadily, from the table and disappeared out of sight behind the woven rush lampshade, the same tall shadow she recalled from Mills' flat.

Outside the evening air swept over her like a refreshing bath. Somewhere behind a block of flats at the top of the street, a rectangle of deep inky blue in the twilight, a dog barked. A couple strolled past on clicking heels which echoed from one side of the road to the other. She sensed Urquhart's presence beside her. 'We should meet in a couple of days' time. I might be able to answer a few more of your questions. I'll give you a call.'

She was not sure whether she wanted to meet Robert

119

Urquhart again. He had given her little useful information and spoilt her digestion. Before Blanche could turn to reply, he was already striding away up the road in his suit. She noticed for the first time that he was wearing a pair of white socks, glowing incongruously in the twilight.

Chapter 13

'Haven't you found out who did it yet?'

'We're doing our best, Miss Mills.' The formality, Blanche hoped, would help to calm her. She had been half expecting the call from Christine ever since Urquhart's warning.

'It's bloody pathetic. It's the same with these terrible rape cases. The police just piss around, taking fingerprints, interviewing people. They never tell the women in the area when they're in danger.'

'They can't go around alarming people on the basis of flimsy evidence.'

'Alarming people! Alarming people for Chrissake, you *should* be alarming people. Just like my dad. There's a bloody killer out there, Chief Inspector. A sadistic madman, wandering around free to murder again. For Chrissake, why haven't you arrested anybody yet?' The torrent of words tumbled out of the phone pell-mell, a flood that the chief inspector was unable to stem.

Blanche decided to become familiar again to try to tame her hysteria. 'Look, Christine, we really are doing our best. We're talking to anybody and everybody.'

'Doing your best!' Christine Mills spluttered. 'The only thing the Met does best is beat up blacks and sit in front of bloody computers planning how to crush the coming riots of Thatcher's underclass.'

'That's ridiculous.'

'Hardly any of you are out on the beat trying to catch murderers and rapists.'

Blanche said nothing. She wanted to say, 'I've had enough of your hysterical phone call, you spoilt, confused little bitch.' But she knew from experience that it was as dangerous for policemen to speak honestly to the public as for members of the royal family. The woman detective wondered what had driven Christine to phone her at Scotland Yard. Genuine frustration? A guilty conscience? Delayed shock? She allowed the silence to hum on the line, hoping it might make Christine Mills understand how ridiculous she sounded.

'Are you still there, Chief Inspector?'

'Yes.'

'Well, have you got nothing to say?'

'Nothing to add, no.' Blanche wanted the conversation to finish, otherwise she might become irate and blurt out something she regretted. She disliked losing her temper against her will because it rarely achieved useful results and symbolised impotence rather than strength: always better to channel anger than display it, she thought. 'I'll obviously be in touch if I have any news.' The policewoman waited with a certain mischievous expectation.

'Look, I have some influential friends, you know, Chief Inspector. People who might be interested in your lack of progress.'

'Is that a threat, Miss Mills, or a promise of promotion?'

'You think you're clever, don't you?'

'Not particularly,' Blanche lied. 'But above average.'

The phone clicked into a hum as Christine Mills slammed down the receiver. Blanche wished her patience had lasted longer but she shrugged stoically.

She harried the detective constable who was checking Christine Mills' alibis. Christine's live-in lover had confirmed the holiday dates she had given: they had travelled abroad around the date of the murder, and he had vouched for her staying at home in the days leading up to the death. Blanche was disquieted but not sure why.

Christine Mills' call reminded Blanche that she had no description whatsoever of the killer. After tedious checks a clutch of people who had been seen on Hampstead Heath around the time of the death had been traced but none could be linked to the murder. Spittals read the reports his female graduate detective had been sending him and, by one of those acts of intellectual percipience for which he was renowned, concluded that she was far from knowing the identity of the murderer.

He rubbed his hands together frantically as usual. 'I'll have

122

to re-allocate you to another job soon, Chief Inspector, unless you can show some progress.'

Blanche noticed he said 'some progress' rather than 'more progress'. 'I'm doing my best, sir.' She realised with a suppressed groan that she was forced to justify herself to the chief superintendent in the same terms as she had defended herself against Christine Mills.

'Of course you are.' Spittals even managed to impart a patronising rustle to his whirring hands.

Blanche was about to describe her meeting with Urquhart and hopes of covert sources of information. But she swallowed the words. 'Please don't do it yet, sir. I'm just starting to make progress.'

The chief superintendent stared at her colourlessly and tightened his lips.

The day after, Blanche was telephoned by a callow and panic-stricken press officer. A well-known columnist on a liberal newspaper – short and fat and pompous, the inspector knew from seeing him interviewed on television, and presumably an 'influential friend' of Christine Mills – was demanding details of the latest developments in the Mills case. He had hinted darkly of rumours of police incompetence and attempts to smother establishment scandal. Blanche told the press officer to invite him round for an 'off the record' briefing. If he accepted, Blanche would be able to cross-examine him but if, as she suspected, he proffered an excuse and refused, the chief inspector could ignore any threat. Meanwhile she decided to hold Spittals at bay by investigating the dead man's links with the Polish community in London.

Tadeusz Swod did not smile. Life, Blanche soon discovered, had given him few reasons to do so. He gestured with a long, withered arm for her to follow him up the stairs. His house in a respectable street in Balham smelt damp and cold, an effect enhanced rather than discouraged by the adopted English cosiness of the decoration: patterned carpets, patterned wallpaper, smoked-glass lampshades and brass knick-knacks on the walls. Swod's name and address had been given to Blanche by a librarian in the Polish Centre in Hammersmith – the one to which Mills had bequeathed a legacy. The librarian smelt of almonds for some reason, and assured the chief inspector that Swod was a respected historian who knew much about the Poles and their links with the British secret service.

The historian had turned his front bedroom into a study. Books and papers in neat rows and piles crammed all the available space between floor and ceiling. His hunched figure padded across to the desk in the bay and Swod gestured for the police officer to sit down. His face was remarkable: gaunt, wizened and pale, the skin pulled taut across the prominent bones. His stare was made the more intense by his ability to hardly blink at all. His eyes were like black pools of water, his hair a hoary white, prickly and short, with a parting down the middle which looked as though it had been cut by a Stanley knife.

Blanche was disappointed. She had expected for some reason a warm and well-fleshed figure, dressed in tweeds saturated in the comforting perfume of unsmoked tobacco. She chuckled at her romanticism: even most of the historians who had taught her at Cambridge sported tattered leather jackets and greasy jeans.

'Could you show me your identification please, Chief Inspector?' She expected his suspicion and passed across her wallet of blue plastic. Rather than glance at it as most people did, he reached out and took it gently from her grasp. He studied her warrant card intently, as though there might be some real doubt about her identity, and then returned it to her without even the glimmer of a smile.

She explained why she had come. He spoke deliberately, weighing each word. 'Graham Mills and the Polish emigrés in London . . .' He grunted. 'Do you have pen and paper?'

She nodded unenthusiastically. It was going to be a lecture but she hoped a more interesting one than most of those delivered by neat men with grey hair at the Police College.

Swod raised his smouldering eyes to the ceiling to remember a quotation, and recited it with the relish of an evangelist preacher. '"I keep my Death's Head battalions ready without mercy or pity to kill men, women and children of Polish origin. That is the only way to get the 'Lebensraum', the living space, we need."' The Pole scratched his head with an emaciated finger. 'Hitler said that in 1939 and he had his way. The Poles

124

were slaughtered in millions.' He leant forward in his chair accusingly. 'Did you know only sixty per cent of Poles with university degrees survived the war?'

The chief inspector shuffled in her armchair. Not a single fact she had heard so far was relevant to the case. His unblinking eyes registered her impatience. 'All of this may not seem important to you, but in history who is to say where understanding of a particular series of events starts? The point I am making is that Poland was like some living body that had all the life blood sucked out of it at the end of the war.'

Swod paused and looked down at his typewriter. It was an old-fashioned one, as heavy and solid as a lorry. He was wearing a thick grey cardigan over a white shirt and it reminded her of how chilly the air was in the house. Swod was of the generation that reached for an extra layer of clothing rather than turn the heating on. He looked up again, the head dignified and earnest. 'But people hope against hope. It is one of their most endearing characteristics,' he said, as if they were fools. 'Some Poles hoped that although things were desperate, the West would do something after all. In that spirit WIN was set up in 1945.'

'What's that?' she asked with her usual directness.

'It stood for "Wolność i Niepodlegtność", meaning Freedom and Independence in Polish, and it was formed from the remnants of the Polish Home Army. The Home Army had fought against the Germans in the Second World War. So WIN was revived with the support of the Western Allies to help the Poles fight against their new rulers, the Soviets. The Central Intelligence Agency and Britain's MI6 provided funds.'

Blanche nodded. She knew at last what the historian had been approaching. Swod allowed himself a quarter smile at her recognition but his body was so unused to this display of emotion that he began to cough. He finally wiped a dribble of saliva from the side of his mouth before continuing. 'It was doomed to failure. Poland was divided against itself to begin with: the communists and the WIN anti-communists hated each other. And after the horrors and destruction of the war, people were tired out. They had had enough of fighting, no matter against whom. And of course, the Soviet security police were so efficient.' He paused and moved in his chair, as if his bones ached. Blanche scribbled the odd note: she needed few because her memory was retentive.

'The German Gestapo weren't a patch on the Russians in terms of efficiency. I was captured by the Gestapo during the war and was terrified because I had on me a number of incriminating documents, lists of names, maps and so on. They didn't search me straightaway because it was time to change the guard at six o'clock precisely. The Germans are very orderly. So they wasted time by changing the guard, and I had all the time in the world to destroy the documents. The Russians on the other hand would have stripped me naked, even if the temperature was far below zero, and then would have sliced every article of my clothes, even down to my shoes, into tiny pieces. With the Russians I would have been executed on the spot. With the Germans, I just spent two years in Auschwitz.' No wonder, Blanche realised, Swod could only pinion his face into the imitation of a smile. He waited until his visitor finished a note.

She shivered in her armchair through cold and impatience, thinking that Swod relished a captive audience but that she hated forming it. Suddenly he leaned forward and a note of pain quavered in his voice. 'In 1947 people were rounded up, some were executed. Everyone in the West thought WIN was finished.'

Blanche saw the opportunity to prod the historian towards her goal. 'And this is where Mills fits in?'

Swod stared at her, unblinking, lifting a hand in a gesture of patience. 'Just before WIN was smashed by the KGB, it sent out delegates to Paris and London and Washington and soon afterwards these delegates received news through various sources that WIN was being built up again. Would the British secret service, MI6, and the CIA help? And *this* is where Mills starts to fit in.' His eyes widened to accentuate the point and reprimand Blanche for thinking that he was straying from the matter in hand. Swod paused, as though expecting everything to be clear now to the chief inspector.

But to her annoyance it was not. He reminded her of a mathematics mistress who had taught her at school. She never finished her explanations of formulae because she used to stop halfway through for the cleverest girls to give the answer. The cleverest girls always knew the answer of course. Blanche never did, and had hated maths ever since. 'How *does* he fit in?'

'MI6, as you probably know, is the British intelligence service charged with spying and secret operations abroad. Mills worked for it and was the officer responsible for any new Polish operations, amongst others. He also had some involvement in attempts to land agents and arms on the Baltic coast. It's all a long time ago now of course. People have rather forgotten about it, although that doesn't stop the government taking legal action against former agents who want to write about it.' Blanche adopted a quizzical expression. She knew little about espionage and, until this murder case, cared less. One instinct whispered that spying, like some police work, was a necessary but grubby business and so should be secret. Another told her spying, again like police work, was a sacred cow, the subject of pompous statements of loyalty from over-protective politicians, and so should be regularly threatened with the abattoir.

'I don't suppose you would know much about MI6's history would you?' he went on. 'Pretty chequered at the best of times. The Russians know all about it. It's only the British people who are kept in the dark.'

The chief inspector twiddled her ballpoint pen. She wanted the digression to end.

'MI6 and CIA pumped in money, arms, radios. They even parachuted in some agents. But WIN was leaking like a sieve, the Polish militia were told in advance and the men were picked up as soon as they touched the ground. Then the KGB decided it was time to roll up the whole operation.'

'How did they do that?'

'They arrested about a hundred people. On Radio Warsaw in December 1952 WIN was revealed to have been a puppet of the KGB since it was revived in 1948. The West had just been sending gold straight to Stalin's coffers.' Swod pulled the skin back even tauter over his cheekbones. 'Some were put in jail for two to three years. A few . . .' His eyes were still directed at her but seemed to turn inwards, glistening with memory. 'A few were tortured and executed in secret. Those were the days of Stalin.' A gust of wind whisked a patter of rain against the window.

Blanche shuffled in her chair, agitating her toes to restore the circulation. She wondered whether Swod suffered the cold as a form of endurance. It fitted his ascetic character. 'How was Graham Mills involved with all this?'

'You think it has something to do with his murder?' he asked pointedly, narrowing his eyes. 'I have been wondering about it ever since I first heard. I thought I might receive a visit from someone – but from security, not the police, checking up.'

With a flutter of surprise, the chief inspector recalled Urquhart's desultory enquiry. 'You weren't seen by MI5 then?'

'No. But then, all this business happened a long time ago. Decades ago. People forget. People forget there were rumours going round that WIN and some of the other spies were not just penetrated in Poland, but betrayed by an agent inside SIS in London – apart from Philby.' He glanced up, an actor keen to verify whether he had achieved an intended effect. The chief inspector was fascinated by him: a farrago of high seriousness and mischief.

'Are you saying Mills was a traitor, that he helped to mislead us into thinking WIN was genuine?'

Swod stared at her impassively and said nothing for a moment. He ran a skeletal hand over the bristles of his hair. His will was cold and sharp, like a steel blade. 'No. What I am saying is that Mills was one of the MI6 officers with responsibility for WIN. He knew about the whole organisation. He also kept in touch with Washington, CIA liaison and all that. Your people in security have very strong suspicions.'

Blanche frantically wiggled her toes inside her shoes again to try to warm them. 'Is there any proof?'

He shrugged. 'Espionage, Chief Inspector, is not like arithmetic. The answer is . . . to so many decimal points, plus or minus so much. Unless someone confesses, the answers are grey, not black and white.'

The conversation was destined to be elliptical, the chief inspector concluded, however hard she tried to make it more direct, and decided to make her questions more oblique. 'How grey was Mills?'

128

Another flurry of rain whipped across the pane. Swod twisted in his chair to look, hollow-eyed, out of the window. 'Mills was investigated at least three times. Once in the mid fifties and again about 1964. Then he was investigated again in the seventies. There was evidence that could be seen to point either way and so the verdict was left open. As an historian I would agree with that judgment.' He picked a stray, white hair from his cardigan.

'How did you know him?'

Swod raised his hairless eyebrows in surprise. 'I assumed someone told you. I helped set up WIN after the war and was one of its representatives in London. I met him then. After Auschwitz, WIN gave me some hope.'

A hope that was soon crushed, the chief inspector reflected, scrutinising Swod's stern face. 'Is there anyone you know who thought Mills was a traitor and cared enough to see him dead?'

'No,' Swod answered simply. 'Besides, why wait so long to do it?'

'Perhaps the murderer only had enough evidence now to decide on revenge?'

'Fanciful, Chief Inspector. Fanciful.'

Blanche pressed on. 'Perhaps Mills confessed?'

'To confess one needs a sense of sin. Mills did not have that.'

'A sense of sin isn't always necessary. Just unbearable pressure.'

Swod pursed his lips with faint irascibility: his 'bon mot' about Mills had not been as conclusive as he hoped. 'That's always possible. But the evidence against Mills was circumstantial. Hardly the sort that makes a chap confess.'

'How often did you see Mills recently?'

'Hardly at all. Occasionally, perhaps once a year, I caught sight of him at Ognisko, the Polish Hearth, in Prince's Gate. He'd come across for a coffee, wish me all the best. He used to tell me about the odd trip to Eastern Europe on business. Then sometimes I had some news of him too through my acquaintance, Jozef Taczek.'

'He was close to Mills too?'

'Oh yes, much closer than me. They were real friends, at least until they quarrelled.'

129

The detective's pen hovered in the air. She had guessed Taczek had not told her the whole truth of his relationship with Mills but now had confirmation. 'What was the cause of their quarrel?'

'Jozef wanted him to do some sort of favour and Mills refused.'

'It must have been something important to break a friendship over.'

'Quite right. But I do not know what it was.'

Blanche believed him. 'Jozef Taczek didn't talk about WIN when I saw him.'

'None of us like talking about that period very much,' he replied. Blanche smiled to herself as she realised that he was unaware of the irony. 'And we have to be careful who we speak to.'

Taczek, Blanche realised, could also have been asked to keep silent by Urquhart. 'There was a young man round at Mr Taczek's flat when I went round to see him.'

The skin puckered at the side of his lips again, this time into a sneer rather than a smile, although with Swod Blanche found it difficult to tell the difference. 'His secretary. Jozef is a friend and one forgives a friend many things. He is obviously less discreet than he used to be.'

Blanche asked how well he knew Tatyana Nowak.

'Tatyana? Yes, her suicide is very sad. I knew her and her husband. That was sad as well.'

'What was sad?'

'Her husband.'

Blanche saw her opportunity. She decided on false naïveté as a cover for her suspicions about Zbigniew Nowak. 'I heard he returned to visit relatives.'

Swod blinked slowly and impassively, like an owl. 'I don't know who told you that. He went back to act as a liaison with WIN and as a spy. Hasn't anyone told you about this?' he added, with a spark of genuine surprise.

'No. I thought he died in a car accident.'

The Pole turned to stare out of the window, his expression once again as bleak as the sky outside. 'That was a cover story. The truth was he went back to spy. I don't think Zbigniew's marriage to Tatyana was going too well at the time. Like Mills

130

he was always chasing women. He even tried to seduce my wife once.' Swod twisted his face into a look of disgust at the memory.

'But he was patriotic. And courageous.' He coughed and his breath rattled like a pebble in an empty can. The chief inspector suddenly understood that the historian's self-important but indomitable spirit was housed in a broken body. She felt protective towards him and he sensed her warmth. He dabbed at his mouth with a handkerchief. 'It's still an official secret. But I'm old and secrets don't seem so important any more.' He gulped. 'After the war the Russians encouraged the Poles in Britain to return home and so a number of army people – including Nowak – went back. Zbigniew returned in early 1950. Some of them, good patriots, agreed to spy for the West. Zbigniew was one of them. Most were corporal or second-lieutenant level. Some found jobs in the post office. Some in factories. A few even got back into the army. A few rose to very high levels indeed and sent back invaluable information. I cannot tell you their names because some are still alive.'

She clutched and unclutched her toes – but now more with excitement than to combat frostbite. 'And what happened to him?'

'Betrayed and executed. The story about the holiday and the car accident were put about, even told to his wife in the beginning, so that none of the others still in Poland should be put in danger.' He coughed again – the same painful choke – and wiped the saliva from his lip. 'He knew he was betrayed by someone in MI6. He knew, and he tried to get out of Poland.'

Blanche sat motionless, afraid to move in case Swod understood the value of the information he was giving her.

'From the time Zbigniew Nowak arrived in Warsaw, he had the feeling something was wrong. His belongings were searched. He was followed. Information that he knew was hard to find, proved easy to locate. But any information from behind the Iron Curtain was treated like gold dust in those days. The people at the very top of MI6 insisted Nowak stayed in place.' Swod rubbed his knees with a groan. They were arthritic and starting to throb. 'But Zbigniew finally had

131

enough. He smuggled out a message saying he'd discovered who in London had betrayed him and that he was going underground to escape. He apparently made his way north to Gdańsk and organised a merchant vessel to carry him to Finland. Details of the ship were forwarded to MI6 in Helsinki and two agents went to Turku to meet him.'

'What happened?'

Swod rubbed his knees again. 'They waited and waited. Zbigniew did not come off the boat. They found out from the crew that the ship had been boarded the night before a few miles out from Gdańsk by a Russian naval vessel and that a Polish passenger had been arrested and taken off. That man was Zbigniew Nowak.' The historian sat back, his eyes glowing with tearful anger.

'So you believe Zbigniew Nowak, as well as WIN, was betrayed by Mills?'

He shook his head. 'No. I just say it is a strong possibility. No one has any firm evidence.'

'Mills and Zbigniew Nowak were friends, though, weren't they?'

'What are friends?' Swod paused for a moment, as though in doubt. 'Nowak trusted and admired him, I think, but whether Mills deserved . . . but I'm digressing.'

'You didn't like Mills at all, did you?'

The frail hands opened in a gesture of mock candidness. 'It's like when one sees a snake. There's an involuntary shudder and, however hard one tries to control it, the shudder is still there. It was his attitude to women that shocked me.'

Blanche sensed his dislike must have had some personal grounds. 'Is that all?'

'No. I might as well tell you. I've told you everything else.' His eyes bored into hers, unblinking. 'He had a short affair with my wife a long, long time ago. We forgave each other. She died four years ago. But the scar never heals.'

Blanche nodded with genuine compassion. She found herself agreeing with the historian's distaste for Mills' personal morality. She used not to be so censorious of others' behaviour but her own betrayal had, she thought, seared her more than she understood. She made a note in her pad. 'Chase solicitor about divorce.' The chief inspector did not believe the man sitting

132

in front of her had murdered Mills, but he had a motive, and she would have him checked.

'At the Polish centre they told me that Marek Nowak had been looking into his father's life. Did he come and see you?'

'A couple of times. I referred him to various people who knew his father, including one or two working in the Eastern European section of MI6 at the time.'

'Who?'

Swod closed his eyes in thought. 'Various fellows. One's called Capron. In MI6 he worked under Mills. He transferred across to MI5 later, though, and he now works for the Security Service. But I doubt if he agreed to talk.' Swod brought his hands together as though ready to pray and raised them to his lips. The pauses had lengthened and Swod's eyelids drooped more and more frequently, due to fatigue, boredom or perhaps just the sunshine breaking through the clouds and sending the odd flash through the window. Blanche closed her notebook with a sense of achievement. Thank God, she thought, Urquhart had not spoken to Swod first. The historian contemplated the ceiling wistfully. 'I'm afraid I have no useful contacts in MI5 or MI6 nowadays. It's the officers working now who are the only ones who can really tell you what went on in the past. They're the ones who can look at the files. And with the present government they're more scared to talk now than ever before.'

He rose languidly from behind the desk and padded to the door. Blanche followed thankfully. She needed to move and restore circulation to her frozen limbs. He tendered a dry, crisp hand to her on the doorstep and inclined his head in farewell.

Chapter 14

The chief superintendent stopped rubbing his hands and burst into his cackling laugh which descended into a cough. Blanche had just asked him for permission to approach the secret services formally and inspect their files on Graham Mills. 'Blanche, I'm telling you, it's a waste of bloody time going to the spooks. They wouldn't even tell their own mothers what size socks they wear, in case it got out to the papers.'

'I think it's worth a try all the same.'

'MI5 and MI6 will just tell me to piss off. They'll say, "We've done our own investigation, Chief Superintendent, and concluded there's no link between the murder and espionage. You don't need access to the files. So, please, sod off."'

He smiled and spread his ruddy hands in a gesture of helplessness, wanting her to smile too. Blanche did not. She stared into space instead. The same tired Spittals litany, she thought, to justify causing no trouble. It was too much to ask her boss, a creature of the system, to challenge it in any way. Spittals' hands began polishing themselves again – in irritation at her obvious disdain. 'There's no point in being annoyed about it. That's my decision and it's final.' She let out a sigh of disappointment.

Spittals' red eyes followed the curve of Blanche's bottom on its gyrating course to the door. The chief superintendent had something else to tell her. The commander had reminded him only the day before of the need to use manpower more efficiently: the government was no longer inclined to keep tossing money at the police force without seeing results. Spittals was still one inspector down on his personnel establishment and had not seen any evidence of progress on the Mills murder. 'By the way, Chief Inspector, can you give Ken a ring and think about giving him a hand with that robbery case? You'll find it more productive than the one you're on at the moment.'

She turned and held the door open. 'Is that an order or a request, sir?'

The chief superintendent dabbed at the stubble of his moustache with a finger. Although he was irritated by Blanche's upper-class accent, cleverness and rapid promotions, Brian Spittals secretly admired her obstinacy and willingness to buck the system. He also liked to be popular with his officers. 'I haven't made my mind up yet. I'll see what I can do.' He winked at her like a cheery market tradesman selling substandard goods, already thinking of the lunch he had planned with an old colleague from the Manchester force. 'I'll let you know. Carry on for the moment.'

When Blanche had left, Spittals rang a friend who worked in the office of the deputy assistant commissioner in charge of Special Branch. He explained what his chief inspector wanted to do and asked advice. The friend said he would make some enquiries and ring back later that day.

Just before he was due to pack his case, tidy the papers on his desk for the last time, and go home, Spittals was surprised to receive a call from the commander of the Squad, who asked the chief superintendent to call in before he went home.

The commander sat in a pinstripe suit behind his desk, an island of teak in a sea of purple carpet. He rose and guided Spittals towards the low, black sofa in the corner. Although they met several times a day and were on good terms, the chief superintendent always felt uncomfortable in the commander's presence: he was an earnest, church-going man who never laughed, never drank, never swore and rarely showed emotion. They exchanged banalities for a couple of minutes.

'Brian, I think we might – potentially – have a little problem with one of our cases.' Spittals rubbed his hands with concentration. 'I got a call this afternoon from the Branch. Apparently you'd referred some request to them – for access to MI5 and MI6 files.'

Spittals could not understand his boss's motives. Was he to be reprimanded or not? He licked his suddenly dry lips. 'It wasn't *my* request, sir. It was DCI Hampton. And the request wasn't a formal one. I was just after some informal advice from a friend who works in the main office, really.'

The commander held up gentle, well-scrubbed hands. 'Oh,

don't worry. I'm not upset about anything you've done. You behaved perfectly correctly.' Spittals relaxed. 'I'm just a bit puzzled, that's all.'

'Why's that?'

'Well . . .' The leather of the sofa squeaked as the commander uncrossed his legs and leant forward. 'Did your friend ring you back?'

Spittals shook his head. The chief superintendent was seething that his friend had obviously spoken to some other people in Special Branch and that the commander was now involved. His irritation showed.

The commander nodded his head in understanding. 'That's what I'm thinking, Brian. Why involve *me*? Why not just call you back and tell you what they told me? – what you obviously knew all along, that there's no hope at all of looking at secret files.'

'Perhaps there was some other reason why they called you.'

'There was. Special Branch say MI5 think it would be for the best if Hampton was taken off this Mills murder case.'

'Did they give a reason?'

'Said it was nothing to do with her professional integrity, just that she was pursuing the spying line a bit too vigorously. Probably likely to turn up something a bit embarrassing for national security.'

'I did warn her, sir. But like a lot of these graduate entry people, she feels she's got something to prove.'

'Woman in a man's world, Brian. It's hard for her.'

Spittals nodded, unconvinced. 'So, what do you think we should do, sir?'

The commander stood up and smoothed his trousers. 'Take her off the case, of course. We don't want any trouble, do we?'

'I have a confession to make,' declared Urquhart that night in the restaurant. The MI5 man had arrived a few minutes before and handed his grubby Burberry raincoat and umbrella to an unctuous waiter by the door. Blanche found the dishevelled air he always seemed to carry about with him endearing. 'I didn't agree to see you last week because I wanted to give you any information. The idea was to find out what you'd discovered.'

136

He had rung her in the afternoon and suggested they met. Blanche had accepted breathlessly.

The chief inspector smiled smugly at Urquhart's remark. It confirmed what she had already thought. 'I thought you might be a poacher rather than the gamekeeper you were pretending to be. But I said nothing.' She swigged a mouthful of wine with relish, irrigating her tongue to savour the bitter fruitiness. Her mouth remained parched and she swilled out another glass. Her thirst sharpened even more. 'Talking of poachers, what did you find out about the ones who were stalking Mills just before he was murdered?' She looked flirtatiously at Urquhart and held his gaze before he dropped his eyes to the table. She squirmed in her seat and tugged her dress down over her knees. Suddenly the restaurant seemed sultry.

His eyelashes flickered into life as he looked up again – a shy, delicate glance, like a cornered deer. He seemed a little taken aback by her directness. 'I'm not sure yet. It seems there was some sort of watch on him, yes. Special Branch probably.'

Her forehead crinkled. 'Why? Were they expecting him to meet someone?'

'Haven't the faintest idea. I only found out yesterday that there was some sort of operation. You've got to allow me some time.'

'There may not be much more time,' she countered. 'My boss hinted this afternoon at asking me to work on another case.'

'Really?' said Urquhart in a tone that was meant to indicate disappointment but whose neutrality hid an element of satisfaction. 'That's a pity. I'm beginning to like these candlelit dinners at the expense of Her Majesty's government.' He sounded genuine at least about the candlelit dinners, which pleased Blanche. He smiled to himself rather than to her, the mark of a shy man who was intermittently confident with women, she hoped, rather than the smile also of someone who enjoyed cheating on his expenses. Urquhart cupped the glass of wine in his hands.

The wine mellowed the atmosphere between them, and Blanche felt less hurried than the week before to extract information from him. She was becoming less interested in any tittle-tattle he might purvey that might help her with the case than in himself. She had never talked to a spy properly before. She scrutinised the spare figure before her in crumpled navy-blue suit and silk tie, and tried to penetrate his sunken eyes. 'You're not exactly James Bond.'

He chuckled. 'Beneath this bland exterior . . . No, you're right. James Bond in real life might pull the women but he wouldn't pull many spies.'

'Which do you reckon's the most important?'

He pondered the question, as if she had posed it seriously, then he leant forward and whispered conspiratorially. 'I may have to arrest you, Chief Inspector, for flirting with a member of Her Majesty's Security Service.'

His gravelly Scots voice pleased her more than the last time she met him. Urquhart held himself with the same appealing forcefulness as when he walked. They did not talk for a minute or so, studiously examining every inch of the tablecloth or the other diners.

'So what have you been up to?' he asked finally to crack the silence.

'Not much.'

'Have you been to see anyone?'

'A guy called Swod.'

'Apparently he knows a lot about Mills' time in Six.'

'Then why didn't you bother to go and see him?' she asked suspiciously.

He smoothed the tablecloth emolliently with the flat of his palm. 'I didn't know it at the time. But I've learnt a few things since.' She waited. She was determined not to ask questions. 'Mills was thoroughly investigated once in the fifties, once in the sixties –'

'– and once in the seventies. I know. Swod told me.'

Urquhart breathed in deeply. 'Did he tell you the results of those enquiries?'

'Open verdicts. Not enough evidence either way. But Swod himself didn't trust Mills an inch.'

'Probably with good reason.'

'What do you mean?'

'Well, the first investigation left the verdict open, according to the files in the Registry, and put a question mark against him. The second investigation was just one of hundreds that were done in the sixties. MI5 decided to do a trace on pretty well everybody who'd been to Cambridge and Oxford during the thirties and showed communist sympathies. The last was set up in the seventies when apparently some defector had cast some doubt on Mills. Everything added together puts Mills very much on the side of guilt rather than innocence.'

They said nothing but listened to the chatter in the restaurant, the clatter of cutlery and tinging of glass. The first bottle of wine was already empty. Urquhart ordered a second. Beneath, deep beneath their feet, an underground train rumbled past into oblivion.

'Why, by the way, didn't you bother to go and see Swod? He thinks there are some people around, some Poles, who might still have a grudge against Mills, and might be happy to see him murdered.'

'It wasn't part of my brief. I was asked to do a straightforward paper chase, as we call it, and a few interviews. Look for any glaring inconsistencies, any obvious clues in the files, any leads, any untied ends. There weren't any.'

She had been misled again. She had assumed, when she was told that Mills' murder had been checked thoroughly for any spying connections, that the enquiry had at least had the semblance of efficiency, if not diligence. Instead an intelligence officer had ploughed through Mills' personal effects and leafed through a random selection of files. She was too dumbfounded to be angry.

'There's no way I can look at those files, I suppose?'

He swung his head from side to side. 'No way.' A dim shadow passed across his face. 'Even I couldn't see some of them last week. They'd been withdrawn by somebody.'

'Who?'

'Don't know. I learnt by various devious means,' and here he winked at her, 'that they'd been taken out by someone in the section that deals with the interrogation of defectors from the Soviet Union. There might be a new big fish, a defector, who's been landed by us. Mills, you never know, might have been somehow involved and that might be the reason why he was under surveillance.' His face turned thoughtful as the waiter approached with the main courses. 'We'd better carry on with our conversation a little later. This restaurant's too public.'

They sidled down Holland Park Avenue, the huge white villas on the left towering up behind solid brick walls. Leaves danced curlicues on the pavement as the wind ripped them from the plane trees and sent them scurrying along the ground. The branches above murmured to each other and refracted the light from the street lamps into kaleidoscopic shapes on the pavement, shades of concrete grey, forming and reforming, overlapping and separating. Urquhart almost had to shout above the roar of the traffic sometimes, lunging forward with his umbrella, in a patch of sulphurous light one moment and in shadow the next. She had never seen him with an umbrella before. He wielded it self-consciously, as though he had never owned one before and had just bought it in a Harrods sale.

She was drowsy with the wine. She shook herself vigorously to throw off the fugginess in her head. 'So, is there some new big fish, as you put it, who's about to defect?'

Urquhart sauntered along thoughtfully for a moment, stopped and turned to face her. 'No idea. Information like that is guarded very carefully. Besides, defectors are handled first by MI6. We in MI5 come in a bit later. But the odd rumour has gone round that Six has been operating someone big, someone quite high up in the KGB. Someone with an elephant's memory who might be about to finger Mills once and for all.'

'And who is this person?' she enquired innocently.

He lifted his eyebrows and sighed with irritation. 'How do I know? Finding out things in my line of business isn't like going to the bloody public library. I'm helping you as much as I can.'

'Sometimes I wonder just how helpful you are being,' – she paused to stress his name with ironical friendliness – 'Robert. And I also wonder why you're doing it. MI5 have got no real reason at all to help the Met.'

He poked the leaves with the point of his umbrella, a wrinkle of pain on his forehead. 'I thought I made all that clear. I originally decided to meet you because I'd heard the civil police weren't letting "sleeping spies lie". I wanted to find out why you were so keen on the espionage angle – just in case I'd missed something.'

'So it was a form of self-protection?'

He nodded. The spy turned his face to the road and watched a red bus clatter past them down the hill, one solitary passenger sitting in the brightly lit interior. 'I still reckon you're wasting your time.'

A hint of desperation tremored in his voice. He looked lost and alone. The street, the shadows, the branches rustling above, the cars accelerating up the hill, became menacing and alien. Her eyes were drawn by the impenetrable blackness of the alleys between the parade of houses opposite, a clutch of raucous youths tumbling out of a Victorian plastic pub on the corner and a drunk dressed in a greasy jacket sitting on a bench set back from the road. A black cat edged soundlessly along the top of a brick wall behind them, his two eyes luminescent in the reflected light from the street. London had lost its infant summer and begun the long descent into winter.

'How long ago since the murder now? Eight weeks? Nine weeks?' Urquhart murmured between clenched teeth, stabbing the pile of dead leaves at his feet with venom.

She started walking again, crossed the road and headed up one of the streets of Regency terraced houses. Urquhart followed. 'Why didn't you tell me about WIN by the way? And Mills' involvement with it? Was there anything in those files you talked about?'

'Mills had his fingers in lots of pies. Nothing, how shall we say, suggestive came my way.' He paused for a moment. 'It was some of the WIN files that had been withdrawn from the Registry – the dossiers cross-referenced from Mills' personnel file.' Urquhart meditated.

Away in the distance the ululating cry of an ambulance rose and sank in the night.

'Did you come across Taczek, Swod or Tatyana Nowak in the files?'

'There were references to all three, yes. Taczek was on our books during the fifties and sixties as an informant on the Polish community – what the Polish government in exile was doing, contacts with emigrés who might have useful information and so on.'

141

Blanche bristled with anger now she knew the truth about Taczek.

'It was all very informal,' he went on. 'He wasn't a proper agent. Just dined an officer or diplomat now and again. He still feeds us the odd titbit, apparently.'

'Thank you very much,' she said, ladling on the irony. 'Taczek must have laughed up his sleeve at me all the time I was interviewing him. I thought he was just a friend of Mrs Nowak and nothing more.'

Urquhart brushed her annoyance aside.

'Did you know Swod didn't trust Mills an inch?' she asked.

'I'm not surprised. Those suspicions of Mills were very heavy. My guess is that Swod blames Mills for a lot of the operations that went wrong.' Urquhart slowed his pace and glanced around, his head picked out by an orange-yellow from the street lamps. A knot of youths swaggered along the pavement opposite along a wall sprayed with graffiti. Urquhart inclined his head and seemed to listen to the wind. It gusted through the council estate they were now in, picking up sweet papers and whisking them a few yards down the street. The council houses were low and comfortable.

'I wish I'd been brought up in one of these,' he said, 'rather than a tower block. Fat chance of you even getting a council house nowadays.' He was irritated again. He began to walk faster, as if he had remembered something and had work to do. His tone became brisk and businesslike. 'We're in a bizarre situation, aren't we, with me having access to some of the files and a few contacts in the Service and you doing the interrogations?'

Without any coherent sense of direction she turned right again and they found themselves in an almost deserted Portobello Road. It was Saturday. The stalls of vegetables and fruit had been dismantled hours before, leaving the gutter choked with cardboard cartons, waste paper and bruised brussels sprouts. The heady smell of fish and chips wafted from a take-away shop. 'The powers that be in MI5, by the way, believed enough in Mills being a KGB agent to offer him immunity from prosecution in exchange for confession and cooperation. That was back in the early sixties. It helped push him towards resignation.'

142

'What was his reaction?'

'Mills laughed in their faces and told them not to be so silly.'

Blanche was still thinking about Tatyana Nowak. 'Was there anything in the files about Zbigniew Nowak, Tatyana's husband?'

Urquhart stabbed his umbrella through the heart of a cardboard box lying helplessly on the pavement. He looked at her with a hint of suspicion. 'Only that he was an agent for SIS and had some involvement with WIN, and went back to Poland in 1950. He was arrested and was executed – when was it? – about September that year.'

He withdrew his umbrella from the innards of the cardboard. 'What did Swod tell you about Zbigniew Nowak?'

'Pretty much the same as you. Taczek and Tatyana Nowak, on the other hand, fed me a cock and bull story about Zbigniew Nowak being killed in a car crash. The same story you told me the last time we met,' she said with a sneer.

The clean-shaven figure in front of her smiled patronisingly. 'Ah, but that was when I was only pumping you for information, not giving it to you. That story, you see, was invented originally by the Russians to cover up the fact that Zbigniew was badly tortured by the guards before they shot him. British intelligence – and that includes me – tagged along to cover up their embarrassment. Mrs Nowak and Taczek must have got to know most of the truth and stuck by the cover story. People like to be in on a secret.'

They were now on Ladbroke Grove, completing the fourth side of the rectangle. Her thoughts about Mills were as confused as her emotions towards Urquhart. Mills was suspected of having worked for the KGB. The suspicions were behind his enforced retirement in 1962. But why should murder him decades later because he betrayed his country and worked for the Soviet Union? Unless the KGB feared Mills was about to expose one of its agents. Did Mills possess such prized information? How did he gain it? She was irritated with herself for thinking like a spy, for slipping into Urquhart's world of suspicion and conspiracy, and as she became more irritated with herself, she became sharp with her companion. 'The trouble with you intelligence people is that you love the back alleys and cul-de-sacs, don't you? Much prefer them

143

to the open streets. You drool when someone tosses you a conspiracy theory.'

'Perhaps you're right. But everything I've said to you is based on the Registry files.'

'It's all right for you. You can look at those marvellous files. I can't.' A flurry of tissue paper used by the market traders to wrap oranges rustled at her feet. 'I don't trust things or ideas. I trust people. And I've only ever trusted one person completely in my life. My mother. And she's dead.'

Urquhart was grave again. He spoke to the trees like a man speaks to a priest in the confessional. 'I trust my parents too. They're so honest, so straight. I know whatever I do they'll love me.' His voice was infused with a huskiness she had not heard before. It disappeared quickly, to be replaced again with a bitter, haunting, angry tone she had heard once before, and it puzzled her. 'Sometimes I just despise you people down in England. Not you personally, of course. The English in general. Their superiority. Their snobbery. Their materialism. It's the English that vote Thatcher into power again and again and the Scots seem to take the brunt of it. The Labour Party is a busted flush and can do nothing about it. There's no opposition in parliament any more to keep her in check. It's one-party rule for the foreseeable future and I find it depressing.' Urquhart pulled himself up short with a laugh: a dry laugh, empty with insincerity. 'But we in the spy world love Thatcher because she adores us. Just say "national security" to her and she has an orgasm.' He chuckled, this time Blanche thought genuinely. 'Don't take me seriously. We all talk like this when we're off duty. Keeps us sane.'

She said what followed without thinking. Perhaps it was the air he possessed of inviting confidences. She told him her husband had left her a few months before for another woman. Since then, she told him, sometimes she was lonely, sometimes she was happy, but she was cynical about men.

'Cynicism breeds loneliness,' murmured Urquhart. Blanche thought he sounded sincere. 'Without trust you can't have friends.'

Blanche couldn't remember later how they kissed first. The weight of his arm slipped across her back, round her waist. Until then she had always imagined him to be somehow insubstantial, a shadow of a man. But suddenly he seemed to blossom out and take weight, like a ghost deciding to cross back over the frontier from the land of death. His lips were firm and damp enough, the hand that caressed her face dry and sinewy. His breath smelt of mint. She thought they must have looked ridiculous, two people over thirty surreptitiously clawing at each other through layer upon layer of raincoat, wool and cotton. But none the less she was excited. Urquhart guided her into an alleyway along Ladbroke Grove and their tongues intertwined, playing and toying with the other. His nimble hands unbuttoned her coat, quested down the back of her skirt and stroked the cleavage where her buttocks divided. She suggested Urquhart should come home with her.

She did not sleep well that night. Lovers never do on the first night. Their new partner snores, or talks in his sleep, or tosses and turns. There is a tension in the air, each person lying awake yet pretending to sleep, aware of every sigh or murmur from the other's lips. The air is too hot or too cold, too fresh or too fuggy. The night creeps by in restless anticipation of the morning. She slid into sleep as dawn approached but rose early to make tea.

She had forgotten the telephone answering machine the night before. There were two calls. One was from her husband asking for a meeting. With Urquhart upstairs, Blanche felt the satisfaction of post-coital revenge, as she listened to Roger's crackly voice, pleading for a meeting. She really would have to see him some time. The other message was from Dexter. Christine Mills had called several times to say she wanted to see the chief inspector urgently because she had 'something very important' to tell her about the death of her father. Dexter had also been phoned by Mills' accountant. Blanche and Dexter knew Mills had recovered from his deep financial difficulties the year before and the accountant had at last discovered how: substantial payments had been paid into Mills' Swiss bank account in the months leading up to his death. No one knew where the money had come from.

Urquhart sat upright in the bed and unstuck a bleary eye. She told him about Dexter's messages. He sipped his tea thoughtfully.

145

Chapter 15

The shops – those endless lines of shabby, plastic-fronted London shops, the paint peeling, the windows steamed up – finally reassembled themselves into council flats; they disintegrated again and reappeared as boarded-up warehouses at Dalston Junction, weeds sprouting vigorously from cracks in the brickwork. More blacks walked the streets now, loose-limbed and casual, before Blanche and Dexter appeared at the side of Hackney Downs. The leaves had fallen earlier here and some of the trees were already skeletons against the autumn sky, mingling their inky branches with the black cables of the electric pylons. At the eastern end of the downs shivered a solitary pub, the walls on two sides scarred with mortar, the whole building dwarfed by the tower blocks striding round about. Christine Mills lived a few hundred yards away.

Dexter parked and switched off the engine. Blanche listened to the silence. An old man staggered across the empty space of the Downs. His dog scoured ahead, sniffing at crumbling turds and chasing its own mangy shadow. The chief inspector caught the suspicious glance of two girls who stood against the wall of the railway embankment. Their skirts were drawn up to the crotch, the heels high, the legs bare, the skin chafed by the cold. Dexter locked up the car carefully.

The Victorian block of flats where Christine Mills lived had been painted a dark green a decade ago and the wood of the frames now showed through in parts, black and rotten. In the lobby, there was no carpet on the tiles, only lino. The scent of boiling greens saturated the air.

Christine held a cigarette between the fore and middle fingers of her left hand. She dusted some ash from the sleeve of her black, Chinese-style padded jacket. It floated down to the threadbare navy-blue carpet, some settling on the bedroom slippers she wore. Her hair was dishevelled and her green eyes full of sleep. She showed no surprise. 'I thought you'd have phoned first,' she yawned.

A flat male voice from the Midlands crawled round the corner of an open door behind her. 'Who the fuck's that, Chris?'

'That policewoman I was telling you about,' she exclaimed over her shoulder. Her voice sounded alien, clipped and upper-class, in the dingy flat. 'With a colleague.' She smiled at Dexter.

'What, the one who's meant to be finding out about your dad?'

'That's right.'

'I'll go back to fuckin' sleep then. Will you bring us a cup of coffee in an hour or so?'

'OK.' The same hostility Blanche had first encountered in the police station still crackled, but tempered by sleepiness and familiarity. Blanche had summoned up a tearful of sympathy for Christine Mills when she learnt of her father's death. Tears tend to melt most dislike. But the more she had discovered about her – pampered upbringing, an unearned regular allowance from her father, a handsome legacy in Mills' will – the more Christine's hypocrisy rankled. It was to be revolution not on the rates but on a private income.

The girl swung round as a silent invitation to follow, and led them past a tangled bunch of bicycles and a wall of political posters to hopeless causes. In the main room a patterned, violet carpet had been laid in the centre of brown lino. Piles of books lounged on the floor, a portable typewriter with newspaper cuttings and papers on a table and withered pot plants on both window sills. Visible through the windows, behind the plants, were the blank walls of another block of flats opposite, veined by dismal branches of trees in the street below. An electric fan heater thrummed away on the floor next to the table while the two bars of the electric fire in the hearth burned like red-hot pokers. She lit another cigarette and pushed the remains of a croissant away from her across the table. 'Well, are you going to ask me questions or do I just start off?' The old aggression flashed.

'Since I've got no idea why you wanted to see me, you'd better tell me what's on your mind.'

147

The ring-bedecked finger holding her cigarette quivered. 'There's no point in beating about the bush, I suppose. I lied to you. I saw my father the night he was murdered.' The smoke curled from her mouth and mingled with the harsh, dry heat from the electric fire.

Blanche pushed her chair back a couple of paces. Her cheeks were already burning from the heat. She knew there was a reason behind Christine's nagging phone calls and now she had discovered it: a guilty conscience. 'Why did you and your boyfriend lie?'

'I don't know. I was just stupid. I was afraid of being suspected of the murder, I suppose.'

'You didn't even know what had happened to your dad when you came to the police saying he was missing –' added Dexter with venom.

'Look! I didn't bloody murder him if that's what you're saying!'

'I'm not saying that at all. But I want an explanation that makes sense.' Blanche peeled off her raincoat and hung it on the back of the chair. She found the beating heat oppressive and wanted to ponder the implications of what Christine had just said. She walked over to the window. The chief inspector was inwardly elated: at last she had a witness who claimed to have met Mills on the night he was murdered.

Christine sucked on her cigarette. 'I used to see Dad every now and again, say once a month, and we usually spoke over the phone at least once a week. If I met him we'd go out for a meal. He'd always treat me. A few years ago we had rows all the time about politics but more recently we kept off the subject most of the time. But that particular night, the fourth of August, it . . . But I'm jumping ahead of myself. Dad phoned me up the day before and, knowing I was about to go away on holiday, suggested we meet the next night, on the fourth of August. So round I went to Daddy's flat.'

Blanche was not content to rely on her story alone. She had already been deceived once. 'Did anyone else see you?'

Christine pondered a moment. 'I don't think so. That looks bad, doesn't it?' She looked at them nervously, stubbing out her unfinished cigarette and lighting another. 'I can't remember. I always arrived and went straight up. Daddy was there and we had a drink. He was in a strange mood. As if he had something on his mind. You could always tell because he would tap his feet on the floor. Finally it came out. He said he'd been followed for the last week or so. I told him he must be going mad, imagining things like that, but he insisted. Then – this was the really weird part – he asked if I would stay the night round there. He'd never asked me to do that before. As though he was scared of something.' Christine flicked the ash from her cigarette into an empty lager can on the table. Blanche leant against the window sill and crossed her arms, scrutinising her intently. 'He was drinking even more than usual that night. He said he wanted some company because he was lonely and worried. He wouldn't say why, just said it was one of his morbid moods. I said I couldn't stop the night because I was going away on holiday early the next morning. Do you want a cup of coffee by the way?'

They shook their heads.

'Well, I'll just go and make one for me and Jake. All this talking gives me a dry throat.' She padded out with the plate of unfinished croissant.

In the street Dexter watched three kids start to kick a football against a brick wall. He wandered over to the table. 'I told you she talked shit,' he hissed. 'And of course that drippy boyfriend of hers backed her up.'

The top file next to the typewriter was labelled 'African Feminists', the one underneath 'The Female Phallus'. A groan issued from the bedroom next door as Christine brought Jake his coffee. She reappeared with her own mug.

She sat down at the table again. 'As I was saying, I went round and Daddy took me to a French restaurant he knew.'

'What did you talk about there?'

'It's difficult to remember. Nothing important.'

'Could you try?' Blanche said, with deliberate emphasis on the last word.

Christine glared at her, the eyes smouldering like emeralds. 'Don't patronise me.' The chief inspector thought the girl was going to spit at her. Blanche did not care: she was angry with Christine Mills and would spit back.

Christine stubbed out her latest cigarette with a shaking

hand and lit another to regain her composure. 'He said he was going out to meet a friend.'

'Who?'

'He said it was someone out of his past. I'm sure it was that meeting that was scaring him.'

'He didn't say anything more than that?'

'No,' Christine said with a jangle of her jewellery. 'He just said he was meeting this "friend". I assumed it was a woman. I asked him why the hell he wanted me to stay the night when he was going out later, and he just shrugged his shoulders and said he was in a funny mood and didn't know what he was saying.' She suddenly began to gnaw her knuckles and paused for a moment, plunged in memory. 'I asked him whether the person he was meeting was anything to do with him being followed, but he just laughed.'

'Did he say anything about where he was going for this meeting?'

'After he told me what I told you, that was it. He started on a kind of – well – what Mum and I used to call one of his damage limitation exercises. He always sort of backpedalled whenever he'd exposed his feelings.' Christine shuffled uneasily in her chair. 'He was really weird that night. By the end, he acted as if he'd said nothing to me at all earlier about being worried, being followed and everything and he turned the conversation round to me and my future. He kept wondering how I'd look after myself when he'd gone.' Christine was gazing into space, talking more to herself than the police. 'Looking back, what he said is really strange, bearing in mind he must have been murdered a little while later.'

'How do you know he *was* murdered that night?' asked Blanche.

She looked up suspiciously. 'I don't. I'm just guessing. I'd never seen him so strange before.' She looked down at her hands again. 'He started going on again about me going into mainstream journalism, how a friend of his had contacts in Fleet Street, why the hell didn't I grow up and settle down like normal girls, why did I go around with Jake. And that was it.' Christine stopped talking, wringing one hand through the other.

'Did he threaten you if you didn't?'

150

She looked up again, with a flash of helplessness in her eyes. 'What do you mean?'

Blanche repeated the question.

Christine pulled on a sallow smile. 'I thought you'd ask that. He said he'd cut me out of his will and scrap my allowance.'

'And that wasn't all, was it?' added Blanche.

The dead man's daughter looked across from Dexter to the policewoman. 'No. We started shouting at each other. We both said things we didn't mean and made stupid threats. Finally I stormed out.'

'What time was that?'

'I don't know. Some time between nine and ten.'

The hum of the electric fire was the only sound in the room. Dexter bent over a withered fern on the window sill and plucked off some desiccated fronds.

The anger inside Blanche against Christine had dissipated. Instead, she felt tired and drained suddenly as she walked across to join the sergeant at the window. They gazed down at the innocent football being kicked back and forth against the wall outside, the thwack of the ball booming in the street amongst the traffic noise. The three boys should have been at school with their ragged clothes, crew cuts and sullen eyes. She swung round to face Christine again, her voice calm. 'It would have been useful if you'd told me all this at the beginning.'

'Hindsight's always perfect.'

'What sort of threats did you make during the row?'

Christine squirmed in her chair and stared at the carpet. 'I can't remember. I probably told him to go and jump in the river.'

'You didn't say you'd like to murder him?' interrupted Blanche, knowing the answer that was to come in advance.

Christine's eyes glittered angrily as she looked up. She half opened her tight, thin mouth and held it on the verge of speaking. Her mouth closed after a moment and she said nothing. She sat devoid of energy and aggression. Her right cheek twitched and she ran a hand over her head to brush down some stray, dyed hairs. 'Yes, I did. I did threaten to kill him.' Her eyes were blank and colourless with remembered grief. She shed no tears. She sat still and silent. When she did

151

finally speak it was in a whisper. 'I didn't want to tell you I saw him that last night, for . . . well . . . I knew you'd get to know about my legacy in the will, the fact I was short of money, the row – and the whole thing just blew up in my mind. I panicked even before I knew he was murdered.' She spurted out a tinkling laugh and flicked more cigarette ash into the lager can. 'Daddy was always trying to use the money as a stick to beat me into changing my way of life. But I wouldn't.' The irregular thud of the football floated up from the road.

'So, your alibi for the night of the murder was a false one?'

Christine looked across and for the first time a defensive flabbiness crawled across her face. 'Yeah. I got Jake to lie, and say I went away on holiday earlier than I did.'

From the moment Blanche first met Christine Mills, the taut, angry little figure had irritated her. She developed in the chief inspector the emotional equivalent of a skin rash, and made her wish for nothing better than to discover Christine was the 'friend' her father had met on Hampstead Heath. She was close enough to the dead man to arrange to meet him at an isolated spot without arousing suspicions. She had a motive.

'You probably don't believe it,' Christine offered with a sneer, 'but I do have a conscience.'

'It only seems to work intermittently.'

'It's like my clapped-out car.'

'Sounds like they both need a good service,' muttered Dexter.

'Most policemen need theirs serviced before mine.' She sipped some lukewarm coffee from her cracked mug. 'But my conscience is the only reason I'm telling you this, all the same. I'm sorry.'

From her tortured look, Blanche understood the curt apology cost Christine's pride dear. It did not, however, wipe out the waste of time and effort caused by her foolish decision to lie. The detective was philosophical: time, in this world at least, only flows in one direction and can never be summoned back. 'Can you think of anyone who might have paid large sums of money into your dad's Swiss bank account in the last few months?'

Mills' daughter laughed. 'I didn't even know he had one.

I'm not my dad's accountant, you know. Only his daughter.'

'You know your father almost went bankrupt about a year ago?'

She drew the cigarette from her lips and blew out the smoke thoughtfully. 'You're joking?'

'No. I'm not. All his investments in the Far East went bust.'

A shadow of green disappointment passed across Christine's angular face. She gulped audibly. The pink drained slowly from her already pale cheeks until they turned the colour of timeworn ivory. 'The old bastard! I really need all the money I can get. Trust him to screw up even when he dies.' She teetered between tears and the hectic flush of anger. Christine obviously thought she was going to get much less than she expected from Graham Mills' will. She had forgotten about the payments made into the Swiss bank account and the Kensington flat. 'I loved him in my own way. So did Mummy. We both know he made far more from the caravan business than he ever admitted to. There he was, gallivanting around with his ageing tarts – you know, the randy widows on the cocktail circuit who eat nothing but spinach leaves.' She made a hollow laugh and flicked some more ash into the lager can. 'We both thought he'd be called to account in the end. That there'd be some justice. We were relying on it.'

She stomped over to the window beside Blanche, her voice suddenly strident with anger and sadness. 'I was going to be free from his constant nagging. I'd have been free to travel, to write, able to do exactly what I wanted with my life.' She snatched up the fern from the window sill and for a second Blanche expected it to soar through the air and sow its parched soil across the carpet. But Christine put the fern back on the sill and deflated herself into an armchair by the window. 'Is there anything else you want to know?'

Blanche decided to strike while her defences were down. 'Did you murder your father?'

The reply was murmured into the string of turquoise shark's teeth she wore round her neck. 'I didn't. But sometimes I wish I had.'

The policewoman decided to believe her for the moment. The door squeaked open. Jake had ventured to investigate Christine's raised voice. 'Are you all right, Chris? Have they been going at you again?' He sported designer jeans, three days' growth of beard and an elegant leather jacket that he had thrown over his shoulders against the cold. Clothes, Blanche guessed, that Christine probably paid for. He was good-looking but of the rough, hirsute kind. The detective was constantly surprised at the men that some women deigned to have relationships with. He addressed all his remarks to the chief inspector through Christine in the way that Blanche disliked. 'Look, you,' he said, finally turning to the chief inspector, 'what do you think you're doing?'

'You, shut up,' Blanche cut in firmly, 'or I'll arrest you for wasting police time by giving us a false alibi.'

Jake stood, arms akimbo, on the threshold of the room, nonplussed. Christine blinked wearily. Her lower lip twitched as though plucked by an invisible finger. Jake's eyes looped round her protectively. He shrugged and slunk away. Blanche knew he was a coward. Just like her husband, she thought.

Blanche nodded to Dexter and pulled on her Aquascutum coat, noticing how threadbare it looked. She made a mental note to rifle her deposit account to buy a new one. Her night with Robert had reawakened her interest in her appearance.

Christine remained motionless. Her eyes drilled into the innocent carpet. The two police officers moved towards the door. The only alteration in her face was the pucker of her lips melting into a pout of unrelieved gloom as they shut the door behind them.

Back at the car, the two tarts still slouched against the wall next to the railway embankment. Dexter jumped inside and inserted the ignition key. He did not turn it straightaway. The windscreen was splattered with spittle which had dribbled down the glass and dried. The girls, elbows propping up against the wall behind, hips thrust forward, blew them two almost toothless smirks as the windscreen wipers cut a valiant swathe through the dried spittle. It was only when Dexter parked the car back at the Yard that they noticed in the paintwork of the boot two long, deep scratches.

Chapter 16

The chief superintendent stood by the window watching the descent of the autumn sun through a cobweb of grey cloud, his hands in the pockets of his trousers, which, Blanche noticed, were always slightly too tight. The office gossip was that his wife insisted that he wore his suits until they fell apart. 'Why didn't you come this morning, Chief Inspector? I left an urgent message in your office.'

'Sorry, sir. I had to go direct from home to interview an important witness. I didn't think you would mind.' Blanche noticed he was not rubbing his hands together: a sure sign that he had something of significance to impart. On second thoughts, she wished she had not uttered the last sentence.

His eyebrows beetled with irritation. He swaggered to the desk. 'Well, I *do* mind.'

He gestured for her to take a seat. Blanche decided to be placatory and repeated her apology.

'I suppose this witness was in connection with the Mills case?'

The chief inspector nodded. 'The dead man's daughter.'

Spittals drummed his fingers on the desk for a moment. He was, Blanche knew, honing the next phrase in his mind before he uttered it. 'I'm ordering you off the Mills case with immediate effect.'

The clumsy phrasing lodged in Blanche's mind as much as the content. Why not say 'immediately' rather than 'with immediate effect'? But the content appalled her. Since Spittals sat behind his desk with a smile of ineffable self-satisfaction and gave no indication of offering an explanation, the policewoman asked for one.

'I'm not at liberty to offer one, Chief Inspector. Orders from a higher authority.'

Blanche had heard rumours about the pressures on police

manpower but knew from the chief superintendent's manner that that could not be the reason. She guessed someone in Special Branch or the intelligence services had objected to her enquiries and that Spittals or the commander had simply capitulated. 'If I might say so, sir, I think this is absolutely dreadful. I'm put on a murder case. I'm told MI5 will investigate any espionage background to the killing. They find no clues – so they say. But the more I discover, the more I think Mills' time in MI6 *was* probably the reason why he was killed. Just at the moment I seem to be getting somewhere, I'm dragged off the case.'

She spoke with such vehemence that Spittals was taken aback. He had sympathy for her, although he was irritated by how many of the new high-fliers questioned orders rather than carried them out. He tried to cover his embarrassment by starting to rub his hands together with more than the usual combustive force, and was secretly rather proud of how she had managed to annoy Special Branch and the intelligence services. He did not like their arrogance and exclusivity.

Once Blanche saw his hands whirring over each other, she knew there was some hope. She had to appeal to his pride. 'Isn't there anything you can do to help, sir? Delay things for a few days?'

The chief superintendent quite liked the idea of embarrassing Special Branch and MI5 but only if there were no risk to himself. After all, he had been ordered directly by the commander to take Blanche off the case. 'I'll offer you a compromise. Officially, you're withdrawn from the case with immediate effect.' Spittals liked the phrase 'with immediate effect'. It had the right bureaucratic timbre and, besides, was a favourite of the new commissioner, littering his memos. 'But if you carry on for a few more days on an unofficial basis, that's your business. If you create any problems with the funnies, you're on your own.'

'The "funnies", sir?' She had never heard the word before.

'Spooks. Spies. Policemen of *my* generation call them the funnies.'

When she came back into the office Dexter sat comatose, his eyelids drawn down like the venetian blinds, the only sign of wakefulness his fingers flicking absentmindedly through the pages of a gay magazine he had hidden inside one on gardening. The wraith of a smile was still strung across the chief inspector's lips – a configuration they fell into naturally when the brain behind them was puzzled – as Dexter unglued one eyelid and focused his eyes on her. He wiped the boredom from his forehead with an immaculate white handkerchief.

'So,' he groaned, 'when are you going to arrest Christine Mills?' Dexter, for all his patience and intelligence in most matters, faltered when it came to the moment to arrest the people he investigated. From a chance remark, an eccentric squint, a shifty gait and nothing more, Detective Sergeant Dexter Bazalgette liked to pronounce on the guilt or innocence of an individual. Like a Shakespearian monarch he would have liked to be able to send the guilty ones straight to the scaffold, to be despatched on a block still steaming with the blood of the last condemned prisoner. Deep down, Blanche sometimes thought, he adored the violence he was supposed to quell.

Dexter coaxed his gold-plated gas lighter into flame and lit a cigarette. 'I shouldn't leave it too long. Any evidence there is in her flat might evaporate. Anyway,' added Dexter, 'if you're not going to arrest the Mills girl, then perhaps you should go for someone else. Mills' first wife. Taczek. Smith the car dealer. I don't know. But Spittals is going to want to see results in a day or so otherwise we're off to do some time on that robbery job.' Such a wilful mood of Dexter's bordered on a sulk. He closed the gay magazine with an elegiac glance at a pair of swollen male buttocks.

Blanche wondered whether Spittals' order to her had leaked out to Dexter already, but decided not. Dexter's strictures, about the need to make progress soon, because otherwise they would be withdrawn from the case, fizzed in her mind. Spittals, like some demented bailiff, would soon be foreclosing on her debt. She ploughed the phone through the scattered papers on her desk top and pressed the digits corresponding to the school where Marek Nowak worked.

'Yes?' croaked a high-pitched male voice.

'Mr Nowak, please.'

''Old on a minute, will yer? I'll just put you through to the staff room.' A succession of clicks followed and finally the subdued sound of the phone ringing again as if through water. It was answered by a woman with a military snappiness. 'What do you want?'

'Mr Nowak, please.'

'He's in hospital.' Blanche sucked in her bottom lip with a presentiment of bad news. 'As he was cycling into school this morning a car ran him down.'

The hospital stood, square and blank, in the autumn sunshine. The architect who designed it twenty years before, Blanche reflected, had drawn inspiration from childhood memories of dog-eared graph paper – neatly ruled green squares within a darker grid of ruled squares. Since the new hospital had not been large enough from the moment it had been built, prefabricated huts bred fissiparously, and straggled now under the shadow of the main building. There was no wind to bend the plume of black smoke rising from the hospital's incineration chimney. A few leaves still clung optimistically to the lime saplings planted either side of the path leading to the reception.

The local police had told the sergeant that Marek cycled to school every morning to keep fit and to save money. That morning, when he was about a quarter of a mile from the school gate, a Volvo estate car drew out from a side-road and drove straight at him. A freckle-faced child heard the burst of acceleration and screamed at Marek. He swerved and avoided the worst of the impact, but was catapulted on to the bonnet of the car and then on to the pavement. The car drove off at speed, the tyres screeching, and disappeared into the endless bricks of suburbia. Marek was knocked unconscious for a minute or two. A parent who was taking her children to school noted down the number plate. It was false. Witnesses gave only a vague description of the driver, concentrating on his clothes, for the only thing visible inside the car was a blue, fur-edged anorak, the hood pulled up tight. The local police sounded surprised by Nowak's apparent lack of cooperation. He grunted, they said, and weaved and ducked like a prize fighter when asked questions.

When Blanche and Dexter arrived he was mumbling to himself on the side of the bed, hands clasped in the lap of his dressing gown. The chief inspector waited at the end of the

158

room and tried to siphon off his individual murmur from the swell of coughing and clattering round about. The words slipped pell-mell into one another, as if Marek were talking in his sleep. Their harsh footsteps on the tiles attracted curious stares from the other patients and, as they neared him, they caught Marek's attention. He trembled as intensely as a fly whirs its wings, and stopped talking.

He looked down at the floor again. 'Poetry,' he sighed. 'Old poetry.'

Dexter turned round one of the gold rings that adorned his fingers and made a stab at humour. 'I was told poetry was dead when I was at school.'

Marek was impassive. 'God may be dead. But poetry will never die! For centuries civilised man thought poetry was the pinnacle he must reach for –' He caught himself suddenly and smiled for the first time Blanche had known him to, the embarrassed smile of a passionate devotee who suddenly discovers that everyone around him, whom he thought entranced by his obsession, was in fact sniggering behind his back. Marek blushed and scratched his hair.

'Whose poetry was it?' asked Dexter with a strange tenderness that surprised Blanche. She remembered the sergeant had never met Marek before, and introduced them.

Marek looked up and slid his hands on to his knees. 'You wouldn't be interested.'

'Try me,' asked the sergeant.

Marek eyed them up his nose for a moment, breathed in and recited two verses, his head flung back, his eyes damp. His toneless voice caught fire and was blessed with new colour and depth. The mottled old man two beds away stared at them with poached eyes.

Nowak's face glittered with febrile urgency. He was no longer mean with his words, speaking only in monosyllables, as he had when Blanche first met him. The chief inspector recognised the classic symptoms of shock in his talkativeness, but intermingled with fear. Fear of the driver who had tried to run him down? Or fear of her? She examined him protectively, for he was, she reflected, the only surviving member of the Nowak family. Dexter shook his long limbs loose and a frown of puzzlement bunched his forehead.

'What does the poem mean?' Dexter asked impassively, scrutinising every hair, every pore, on Marek's face. It was as though Dexter had met Marek somewhere before: an invisible thread of emotion bound them and excluded her.

'I'll try a translation but it's never quite the same,' Nowak murmured apologetically. He eased his body back on to the bed, tucking the dressing gown fussily round his legs. 'It's from a poem called "My Will and Testament" by Słowacki. My mother used to recite it to me often when I was a kid.' He caught his breath. '"Here behind me I leave no heir to either lute or name. This name of mine vanishes like lightning and its echo shall ring – but hollowly – in the mouths of future generations. But you who knew me, pass on these words: that I squandered my youth for my country, that while the ship was fighting I kept to my post up in the cross trees and, when she sank – I went down with her."'

He gazed at the cream wall opposite, unblinking. When he spoke again, Marek reverted to that low, colourless tone of his, and spoke more to himself than to her. 'I look ahead sometimes and wonder what people will think of me when I'm dead. How little I've done. That poem reminds me that I did my best, did my duty if you like.' His fingers tugged at his moustache.

Dexter chuckled, that big, broad, white smile of his. 'No one talks about Britain like that any more. The Empire's dead and buried.'

Marek gently lowered his eyelids and laughed. He had gained a sense of humour, or perhaps of irony, since Blanche questioned him the first time. 'It's not Britain I'm talking about. It's Poland.' He jutted his chin out proudly and his voice regained its animation. 'I was born in England, true enough. But I've stuck with Poland and done my duty by her.'

'How?' Blanche enquired.

'Various things,' he murmured.

'Such as?'

His gaze swung back to the wall as though Blanche's features held no more interest. She had that feeling of insult often felt at a party when the person one is talking to focuses his gaze on people round about all the time, searching for someone more interesting, powerful or sexy to talk to.

She waited for a second, hoping Marek would turn and

catch her eye. He did not. His eyes resolutely scanned the wall and bed opposite. There a bundle of balding, middle-aged man lay asleep, a blissful smile on his face, exhausted by the tedium of hospital life. She was taking a long time to come to the attempt on Marek's life that morning. It was better that way. Marek asked how much progress she had made in her murder investigation. The question was posed with almost too obvious an innocence. She replied, 'Some.'

'Have you arrested anyone?'

A mischievous twinkle lurked in Dexter's eyes.

'No one yet,' she said. Marek was fencing with her, keeping her at bed's length. His impassive, fierce stare reminded her of an owl squatting on a fence post, watchful and ready to plunge at the first rustle in the undergrowth. 'I think though that I'll soon have to open another murder investigation to add to the one on Mills – yours.'

The eyes widened and the pupils, floating on a reef of chestnut, dilated a fraction. She saw fear slither across his face. It had been there all the time hidden beneath the forced gaiety, the conversational duelling. 'You're not suggesting that what happened to me this morning was attempted murder, are you? It was an accident. That's all there is to it.' The words flowed out of his bristly lips with unaccustomed swiftness. He clasped and unclasped his hands nervously. 'From what I can remember this lunatic just accelerated out from the side of the road. Probably didn't look where he was going – you know, the usual story – and he knocked me down. That's all there is to it.'

Marek snatched up a bunch of grapes from the bedside table. He plucked and ate them with surprising sensuality, sucking out the juice and spitting the pips into his left hand. Sensing her disbelief grow and surround him, he flashed with petulant anger. 'Look, I should know. I just wish you'd leave me alone. It was like this at the time of Mum's suicide, you police just wouldn't leave me alone.'

Even when Dexter took over the questioning, Marek said he remembered nothing about the car or its driver. Nor could he think of anyone who would want to kill him. He showed no surprise when Blanche told him the number plate of the car was false, and Nowak emphasised he did not want the police to press charges if the driver was found. He thought the whole incident had been blown up out of proportion.

An old man by the entrance began coughing. A nurse scurried past with a covered bedpan.

Blanche found the man in front of her an enigma, impenetrable and secretive. She knew hardly anything about his life: just a few disjointed notes. 'Why didn't you marry? Was it your mother?'

Marek lowered his eyebrows a millimetre. 'I never really wanted to. I never met the right woman. I loved my mum too much perhaps.'

'She must have missed your father a lot?' Blanche fished, tickling him into keeping up the conversation.

'She never stopped thinking of him. Father's memory was always there. It was there for both of us.'

Blanche was confident enough to probe deeper. 'How did your dad get killed, by the way? I've heard lots of different stories. I gather you've looked into the whole thing.'

'Who told you that?' he flashed.

'Dr Swod among others.'

Marek's tremble quickened, as though he were on the verge of taking a decision. He closed his eyes and opened them again. She could not tell whether their new dampness was the result of emotion or blinking. 'It's a horrible story. Not everyone has their father betrayed and then executed.' Blanche waited for his shaking to give him the momentum to carry on. 'You know he went back to Poland to spy for the West?' Blanche nodded. 'Well, he went back on the twenty-third of April 1950. St George's Day. The English national day. My mother engraved it on my memory.'

'And did you manage to find out who did betray your dad?'

Marek scratched his receding clump of hair. The gesture was clumsy and theatrical, the policewoman considered, the pause a beat too long. 'No. Various people have talked about possible traitors in MI6. You know, Philby and that bunch. But whether it was him or someone else . . . or just bad luck.'

'But Dr Swod told me there was a rumour of someone particular in MI6, possibly Mills, being the traitor. He must have told you that, you went to see him.'

Marek blanched behind the protective layer of half-grown

beard. 'He did suggest it. But I never confirmed it.' Abruptly Marek's hands stopped shaking. He lifted the skeleton bunch of grapes – now with only a few fruit clinging on precariously – back to the metal bedside cabinet. He clasped and unclasped his wiry hands two or three times as though wringing out a rag, pulled his legs on to the bed, sat back and replied in a raucous whisper. Blanche knew he was concealing something but she was unsure what. 'I found nothing out that pinned the blame on him. There were three or four people who could have betrayed my dad.' His voice wavered with a hint of uncertainty.

'Just how well *did* you know Mills?' asked Blanche.

He began trembling again. 'As I told you, I hardly knew this guy Mills. He was just a friend of my mother.'

'Come on, Mills was really close to you when you were a kid –'

'– a kid, sure. When I was young he did us lots of good turns. I knew him pretty well then.'

'You're not seriously going to tell me that a relationship like that just ends, when the guy still meets your mother every few weeks or so?' A woman with candyfloss hair glared at them in open-mouthed amazement, for their voices had risen little by little. She had moved quickly since learning of Marek's accident, Blanche thought with pride.

The sun stood uncertainly on the horizon, a disc of perfect orange, hovering above the smudge of suburban parks and tiled roofs, the same sun Spittals had been admiring a couple of hours before. A jet signed an elegant loop across the eggshell sky. The sun flooded the ward, painting a red halo round Marek's head and throwing Dexter's face, which looked down at the floor disconsolately, into purple shadow.

'Autumn always makes me sad,' Marek grunted. 'You can see the year balancing. Just waiting to tip over into the chill of winter.' He uttered this with the finality of a poem's last line. The conversation was over. He stopped trembling as quickly as he had begun a moment before, and seemed to withdraw down the dark passage to the daydream he was locked in when they first arrived. The man was neurotic, if not mad, Blanche decided. She nodded to Dexter and they walked away.

They had reached the main corridor when a hand touched

her shoulder. It was Marek. With a gesture he drew them to the side of the corridor. The fever in his eyes flared. 'You saw I was het up in there? I just couldn't talk with the old bag next to us flapping her ears to catch every word. Look – I've got something very important to tell you.' It had been an exhausting day, Blanche reflected in the matter of a second: Christine Mills had unburdened her thoughts, Spittals had ordered her off the case, and now Marek Nowak had chosen that moment to reveal another fragment of the truth. He looked at her directly. He had done it so rarely, she almost flinched. 'Look – before my mum died she told me Jozef Taczek had confessed to her, confessed that he'd murdered Mills because of the betrayal. That was why I think mum must have killed herself.' He glanced skittishly up and down the corridor. 'One old friend had killed another. It was more than she could bear. I'm only telling you this because . . . well, it's obvious who killed Mills. Taczek. You've got to arrest him. And quick.' He trailed off breathlessly.

'Are you sure Taczek doesn't want you dead as well?'

Marek's mouth hung open. 'He might,' he said unsteadily.

'When did your mother tell you all this?'

'The night before she committed suicide.'

'And why are telling us this only now?'

'I didn't believe it before. And then this car ran at me. It started to make sense.'

'And Taczek confessed to her that he'd murdered Mills?' asked Dexter earnestly to confirm what they had heard.

'That's what Mum told me.'

The confession fitted neatly. The sergeant preened himself. Marek glared, challenging them to arrest Taczek. Then a hunted look dribbled into his eyes. 'If anything else happens to me,' he murmured, wetting his lips, 'look round my house. You might find it worthwhile.' He turned on his slippers and into the protection of an irascible nurse.

Blanche was happy as she walked out, confident at the end of the afternoon that she had at last found an explanation for Tatyana Nowak's suicide, and the first direct link between a particular human being and the murder. Dexter was abnormally silent as he swaggered down the drive. He spoke only when they arrived at the car. 'You realise,' he said, turning the gold ring on his finger again, 'that Nowak was doing his best to cover it up.'

'What?'

Dexter spread his hands in mock supplication to the heavens. 'That he's gay, for God's sake!' The chief inspector realised his explanation accounted for the batsqueak of sexuality that had passed between them. 'And what's more,' said Dexter with a mocking smirk, 'I think he fancies me.'

Chapter 17

No dithering, Blanche thought. Marek had told them Taczek had confessed to the murder. That would be sufficient to arrest the old Lothario. Under the gloomy strip lighting of a police interrogation cell he might be stripped of his self-possession, and confess. Like Dexter, she had had enough of grappling with the bundles of facts she had accumulated, facts that did not slot together to form a coherent pattern, but dissolved and reformed into new patterns every time she touched them. They reminded her of the cardboard kaleidoscope she had as a child, packed with coloured fragments, which she looked into for hours, turning and watching, turning and watching.

They drove up the ramp from the underground car park at Scotland Yard and out on to Victoria Street at 8.40 p.m.

The trees around the garden in the centre of Allen Square were spread with golden syrup under the street lamps. The square was deserted. A couple of streets away the traffic rumbled but here, in the heart of London, all was tranquil. Blanche looked up and searched the sky, seeking some prophecy of success or failure, but found only a sprinkling of stars brave enough to outshine the lemon gleam of the city's lights.

Taczek stood in the hallway of the second floor outside his flat, solid arms akimbo, the smile dissolving from his face as he saw them climb the stairs. 'I see you chose to visit me in force on this occasion. If you had told me in advance, I would have prepared a few canapés for your arrival.'

He seemed only mildly surprised when she asked him, in the appalling police jargon that made her cringe, to accompany her to the local police station. He said he would come only if arrested. So she arrested him. He chirruped with animated amusement as she explained it was on suspicion of murder. 'This is all rather jolly,' he gasped finally. 'I've seen this done so often in the films but to be arrested myself . . . It's pure heaven.' Jozef paid a theatrical farewell to his young lover, telling him not to forget to make the phone call he had promised.

He gabbled all the way to the police station about his favourite *films noirs*. He said he adored hard-bitten policemen. Blanche was irritated and entertained by his nervous chatter in equal measure. All the time she prayed in desperation that the constables would discover something incriminating back in the flat: perhaps letters from Zbigniew or Tatyana Nowak, bloodstained gloves, she did not care. But something.

The Voice slipped the magnetic card into the slot of the public telephone, consulted the number he had been given by Taczek, and dialled. His breath curdled on the night air. Cars skimmed past on the Earls Court Road, their headlights drawing his shadow again and again across the back of the booth.

'Yes? Can I help you?' The enquiry was distant and neutral.

'A friend of George with a message.'

'Just a second, please.' The young woman on night shift high up in a tower block near Lambeth Bridge yawned. 'Just wait a second, please.' She confirmed the tape recorder was working and examined her computer terminal for instructions. 'What is the status of the message?'

'Red.'

'And what is the message?'

'George needs help. The police have arrested him.'

Taczek remained sprightly even in the interview room and treated the first half hour of questions as a party game. He sat opposite to the chief inspector and Dexter, behind a narrow wooden table, hands gesticulating, with the face of a bridge player. 'You have no reason to arrest me,' he kept repeating. 'You'll just make yourself look very foolish.. It will do you no good in the end.'

Blanche slumped back in her chair and decided to attack circuitously. She relished the intellectual challenge of an interrogation. 'I advise you to answer all my questions truthfully. Last time we spoke you told me some lies.'

'Really?' Taczek took off his spectacles and a gleam twinkled in his face. 'What is truth anyway?'

'You told me Zbigniew Nowak was killed in a car accident. That's untrue.'

Taczek unclasped his hands and relaxed. 'If that's all you're worried about I can explain simply enough.' He stood up and began to pace restlessly round the room, stopping occasionally by the door to squint out through the perspex porthole, by the table to lean across it and impale her on his eyes, or by the wall where he sent his hands into spirals of explanation. 'You see, the last time I spoke to you, I didn't realise that all this investigation was serious.' She spluttered and pointed out that it was a murder enquiry. 'I didn't see the relevance of something that happened a long time ago. An incident that was dead and buried.'

'It was up to me to decide that. Not you,' she replied waspishly.

'I beg to differ with you a bit there. Because I knew all the surrounding circumstances. I might as well tell you now that I have done some freelance work for Her Majesty's intelligence services.' Blanche nodded in mock amazement. Taczek leant forward and lowered his voice to a confidential whisper. 'As a result I know some background to what Zbigniew Nowak was involved in. It's still highly secret. A careless word from someone and people could still be compromised.'

'Nothing you've told me is new,' she snapped. 'And none of it gave you the right to lie to me. If you lied over how Nowak died, you probably lied over more important things. Mills was probably murdered because he was working for the KGB. At one time I thought Tatyana may have done it, but now I have evidence it was someone else.'

Taczek froze by the door. He digested what she said by twisting his head to one side and pushing his spectacles higher up his nose. His voice moved up a register, from baritone to tenor, and it was tinged with irritation for the first time that evening. One of his thick fingers began stabbing the air at her. 'Young lady, you don't have the faintest idea what you're talking about. That's all complete and unmitigated rubbish.' He waved his arms at her patronisingly. 'I've had enough of this charade. I've played along with you for the past hour. But now I want to go home. Get back to the book I was reading.'

His arrogance made her even more determined than before. She tightened her lips into a straight line. 'You'll be released when I decide.'

Taczek hoisted his fist and smacked it down on the table with a hollow bang. 'This is outrageous. I demand my solicitor. You just don't know what you're letting yourself in for, meddling with me.' His cheeks were the colour of dough and his eyes sparkled with anger. He puffed up his chest like an exotic bird engaged in a courtship dance.

The chief inspector had seen businessmen before, stopped for drunken driving or speeding offences, who adopted the same tactic. 'How dare you,' they puffed. 'Do you realise who you are talking to, young woman? The chief constable is my personal friend.' All the time they stroked their nicotine-stained moustaches and exhaled noxious fumes from their foam-flecked lips.

The door of the interview room swung open and a detective constable swaggered in. He said nothing. He slipped a folded piece of paper across the table. She unfolded the first section. 'Nothing found so far.' It was then that her stomach began to yaw, for it occurred to her that she had no solid evidence at all with which to tackle Taczek. She had not even thought about persuading Marek Nowak to write down what he had told her. All she had were some notes she made in the car, witnessed by Dexter. She thought she would take the statement tomorrow or the next day, when he was out of hospital. She felt the blouse stick to her back as the sweat began to dribble. Her cheeks were assailed by minute pinpricks of fire.

She unfolded the second section. 'Man called Urquhart phoned. Wants you to call him. Urgent.' The pleasure of this was almost enough to wipe away immediate fears about what to do with Taczek. After reading the note, Blanche thought she would dispose of Taczek somehow with the same ease with which she refolded the slip of paper and slid it into her handbag. Dexter detected her change of mood and examined her quizzically.

'Aren't you going to ask me any more questions?' demanded Taczek with a peremptory prod at his spectacles. He was thoroughly disgruntled. His features had dried into a venomous grimace, the spade-like hands resting in his lap.

She had to appear calm and justified in arresting him. Interrogations were like poker, an old detective inspector had once told her, they depended on bluff. 'I know you think Mills betrayed Zbigniew Nowak.'

The Pole glanced up and gave his spectacles another prod. 'Oh really? And who told you that fascinating little fairy tale?'

'A little bird.'

'A little bird with no respect for the truth.'

'So, it's not true?'

'No, it's not true. Necessarily. I've no idea who told the KGB my friend, Zbigniew, was spying for the British.'

'But someone did?'

'Possibly,' he said, checking himself. 'I have no real idea what people have been telling you about my involvement with MI6 at the time. It has always been pretty marginal.'

She was glad at last to have a use for information from Robert: it justified her relationship with him and her decision to press ahead with the case. 'I know for a fact that you were as close as anyone to what was going on between us, the Americans and Poland during the Cold War. So stop playing innocent and answer my questions, please. Who betrayed Nowak?'

The room was silent except for the rustle of Dexter's pen and the jingle of his wrist chain on the table as he wrote. The irregular echo of footsteps passed backwards and forwards along the corridor outside. Taczek put his hands on his knees and studied the grain of the plastic floor tiles. 'Look, Chief Inspector, I am finding this extremely tedious. You are doing yourself a lot of harm by keeping me here like this interrogating me about matters which are protected by the official secrets legislation.'

Blanche paused. She did not care a damn whether the information was protected or not. She was investigating a murder and Taczek's prissy regard for guarding secrets irritated her. 'I'll ask you again. Who betrayed Zbigniew Nowak?'

He let out a tired sigh. 'I might as well tell you – if only so that you'll let me go home.' Taczek muttered to himself, 'There are four or five candidates '

'I already know that.'

Taczek prodded his spectacles with irritation. 'Do you want me to tell you or not?'

'Go ahead.' She waved her right hand in imitation of one of his patrician gestures. 'And one of them was Mills?'

Taczek nodded.

It was time to deploy Dexter's tactic of unsubstantiated allegation. She put no special inflection into the question but eased it out naturally. 'Is that why you killed him?'

Taczek threw back his sculpted head and chortled: a healthy, hearty laugh that Blanche judged genuine enough. She noticed his teeth for the first time: small and irregular, like pieces of gravel on a driveway, but sparkling white. He slapped his chunky thighs with hilarity. 'Oh, you are a joker, Chief Inspector. I adore your little jumps of logic. Your non sequiturs.' He leant forward and wagged his finger at her again. Blanche found the gesture patronising, symbolising the way she was treated by many of her superiors at the Metropolitan Police or creatures from the male world of spies. 'Just because I knew Mills was suspected of betraying someone does not *necessarily* mean that I had anything to do with his unfortunate death. Knowledge does not imply volition.'

The chief inspector disliked his arrogant manner, his jocularity at her expense, particularly when the only weapon she had was bluff and she was vulnerable for having pressed on with the case against Spittals' opposition. If things went wrong, she would be blamed, and her career as a detective – the career she had fought for so tenaciously, against the depredations of her husband, against male prejudice, against policemen who drove up back alleys on patrol when she was a constable and groped for a kiss – that career might crumble to dust. 'But a confession to me – admittedly a plain, simple person – implies guilt. I know you've confessed to murdering Mills.'

Taczek looked with narrowed eyes from her to Dexter and then back to her. He seemed too stunned to speak before snorting with mirth again. 'I was mistaken in thinking that false confessions are confined to the Soviet bloc. Now they've obviously been exported to this country.'

'You've confessed to one person. Now you can confess to me.' Bluff, Blanche hoped, might just work.

Taczek took off his spectacles and polished them with a handkerchief. 'How on earth can I confess anything to you? No pope has yet admitted women to the priesthood,' he said with a sarcastic smile. 'You – and no other human being, for that matter – are competent to hear my confession.'

Dexter laid down his pen. He took an informed interest in the sacred value of confession. 'They say a soul feels lighter for getting rid of its burden of sin.'

Taczek turned his head to face him. 'I do not have the sin of murdering Graham Mills on my conscience, young man.' He whipped back to Blanche again. 'To whom, incidentally, am I supposed to have bared my soul?'

Dexter looked at her. Blanche nodded. 'To Tatyana Nowak,' explained the sergeant.

Taczek pushed at his spectacles. It was a gesture, Blanche thought, to allow him time to absorb the information. He propped his chin in the palm of his right hand. 'If I said this to her before her death why are you taxing me with these preposterous allegations only now?'

She said nothing. Dexter's notebook rustled as he turned over another page.

'Unless . . . it was Marek who told you and not Tatyana.' Taczek hoisted his spectacles again and revealed his row of cone-like teeth. 'I had nothing to do with the murder of Graham Mills. I never even discussed it with Tatyana.'

Dexter glanced up again, the artery on his forehead throbbing. He was losing patience with the slow progress. 'That's a bit weird, isn't it? Someone both you and Mrs Nowak know gets murdered and you don't even talk about it?'

Taczek studiously ignored the question. 'I met Tatyana only once between Graham's murder and her suicide. She led her own, isolated sort of life. Only listened to classical music on the radio or her beloved Chopin on the gramophone. I waited for her to bring up the subject of Graham's murder because I knew she would have been very upset. She'd heard nothing and so I said nothing.'

Blanche noticed that both Jozef Taczek and Marek seemed very sensitive about giving Mrs Nowak the news of Mills' death. 'I know,' she said. 'I broke the news to her.'

'Did you? I expect she was shocked.'

172

'I find it strange you didn't bring the subject up. But if you murdered Mills it would have a certain logic, wouldn't it?' Blanche added with a measured snideness.

His smile shattered like a glass hitting the floor. 'I don't find that funny. Marek's suggestion, and I assume it is Marek's, that I discussed Graham's murder – let alone confessed to it – when I was with Tatyana that night is total lunacy. Marek's mad. He's got hidden motives. You shouldn't trust him.'

Before Taczek could say anything more someone tapped rapidly on the door. Dexter eased himself across the room and spoke in a whisper. She sensed his glistening cheek brush her hair and his breath warm the side of her face as he bent forward to murmur in her ear. 'Spittals on the dog. Says it's urgent.'

'Can't he wait?'

'No. Says he's got to speak to you now.' Dexter's voice was imbued with a seriousness that was unusual to Blanche.

Taczek leant back, slung his arms behind his head and stretched his chunky arms as if waking from a deep sleep. The detective spotted a playful glint gleaming in his eye. Although he was in repose the same energy she had noticed when she first met him oozed through his body.

A constable led her along the corridor past fluttering notices and an electric clock that had stopped. He showed her into another bare cubicle where two hatchet-faced men were scribbling, and pointed to a phone that lay scratched and bruised on the desk.

'Hello.'

The harsh, flat voice of Spittals was unmistakeable. He sounded calm, even distant. A sure sign of anger, Blanche thought. 'What the hell are you playing at, for Christ's sake?' Spittals barked before pausing for a reply. When she said nothing, his language degenerated into grossness. 'I've just had a call from the commissioner's office saying you've arrested someone with security links. They got called up by the Cabinet Office. You've got to release him straightaway or else they'll have my balls to play snooker with.' She remained silent. 'Are you still there?' She grunted. 'For fuck's sake, and I don't care who the hell he is – release him, throw him back on the streets and don't touch him again. I thought I told you to keep clear of the funnies, for Christ's sake!'

All she could manage was a burbled apology.

'See me first thing tomorrow morning.'

She gulped. How had the commissioner become embroiled so quickly? Let alone the Cabinet Office? Christine Mills did not have any really influential friends but Taczek certainly did. Her skin fried with embarrassment. The two officers who were scribbling eyed her curiously. She smiled at them weakly. She hated making mistakes. She hated even more being made to look a fool. She was powerless. She had to obey or be sacked. She believed Spittals would somehow have treated a male officer differently – spoken less patronisingly, with more respect. The chief superintendent seemed to revel in the reprimand he issued to her. The final insult, Blanche knew, would be the smile Taczek would sport when released.

She slunk back to the interrogation room. Dexter looked up expectantly, a loop of ash dangling from the end of the cigarette he had lit in her absence.

Taczek drummed on the table with the tips of his fingers. 'I did try and warn you, Chief Inspector. I did say you had made a mistake.'

She wanted to take that thick neck of his and press her fingernails, long and freshly varnished for Urquhart's benefit, deep into the flesh until the cocky smirk on his face was replaced by a grimace of pain. He did not even wait to be told the subject of the phone call. Taczek thrust himself up from his chair and patted his jacket and trousers to remove any creases. 'I'm sorry I couldn't stay longer but it was getting rather boring.' Without being asked, he strode over to the door and waited, moving his weight from one foot to the other and tugging his shirt cuffs out of his jacket sleeves. Blanche nodded wordlessly to Dexter who, with a show of reluctance, opened the door and disappeared with Taczek to arrange the formalities of release.

She stood alone in the glimmering, grey room, hair in a squall, face drawn up in a squint of concentration. She was thinking of a bleak room in a small block of flats in Streatham, the curtains drawn to keep in the heat, the walls weighed down with the knick-knacks of a happy life: the flat she had been

174

brought up in. She was angry with herself then as well. She had come to pick up her mother's possessions: the cracked Harrods dinner service, souvenirs of trips to Brighton and Bournemouth, the frayed and tired linen, the cooking pots, the scarlet tea cosy her mother had knitted, the family photograph albums she valued so much. Mother's objects were the detritus of a life scraping for pennies, making things last beyond their natural span, so that her fatherless children should be happy. Although Blanche had been sad standing there in Mother's empty flat, she had been overtaken then by the same feeling she sensed come over her in the interrogation room that night after Taczek had left. Starting in her stomach, a warm glow suffused her body until it set her fingertips tingling and her scalp crackling. It was an ancient emotion for Blanche, calling her home from the wasteland of tension and anger she had tramped across for the past few months. Happiness. A sentiment that ambushed her at the coldest moments. Urquhart had called. And he might have an explanation.

Chapter 18

Blanche tumbled through the front door of her flat just after eleven o'clock. The red light of the answerphone was flickering. She expected Urquhart but found first a message from her brother inviting her down for the weekend. She groaned with guilt at not having phoned him before. The only other one was from her unfaithful husband.

'Look, Blanche, I know it's all a mess. I really, truly am sorry.' The words sounded hollow when played back in the emptiness of the flat, like an extract from a vacuous, romantic novel. 'It was a terrible mistake. Let's get together again. Please.' The tape crackled for a few seconds and then hummed as he replaced the receiver.

The chief inspector kicked off her shoes and poured a slug of single malt whisky. She stretched herself out on the sofa, bought in a fit of extravagance from Harrods five years before, admiring the sumptuous material. She adored her flat, decorating it with a classical sparseness that niggled Roger, preferring a few excellent things – whether wallpaper or china – to many mediocre ones.

Urquhart's work number at MI5 rang and rang. Blanche realised that Robert had never given her any other. It was finally answered by a man who spoke with an artificial, lazy drawl and was suspicious when she asked for Urquhart by name. When he demanded who Blanche was, and why she was phoning so late, she rang off. What was Urquhart playing at? He called her and raised her hopes. Then he disappeared.

She prowled nervously about the flat and poured another whisky. It had been a long, long day. Clips of her conversations with Christine Mills, Marek Nowak and the encounter with Taczek floated before her, flickered like a silent film as she ran her manicured fingernails along the spines of her many books.

Upstairs and ajar was the door to the main bedroom.

176

Through it, in the ghostly light from the street lamp, she distinguished the tangled duvet, her dressing gown slung over an ebonised chair and a French Empire mirror with a sphinx carved at the apex, of which she was particularly proud. She considered what the previous night meant to her: two acts of 'love' in the space of seven hours. Urquhart was not in love with her, she was sure, and she was not in love with him. Yet. It was a night of physical fulfilment, a pleasing confirmation of her desirability. Love was a different matter. She had experienced it with Roger, for a while, that confidence and happiness in the presence of another. Then it had faded, had been mislaid without her exactly knowing when or how – like a childhood toy that is suddenly no longer there, tossed into the rubbish bin in a moment of carelessness. Blanche controlled her emotions well. She committed them, like a good general, only when sure of victory. She liked Robert Urquhart and was attracted to him, even trusted him, unlike Spittals who was no doubt gleefully stabbing her in the back at that moment. Christine Mills, Marek Nowak and Taczek were all liars. Robert Urquhart was her only hope, her only ally.

It was too late to phone her brother. She dialled the number her husband had given her, which belonged to one of his old school friends, a television producer. The friend answered and a note of panic entered his voice when he discovered who it was. She heard Roger's name being called.

'Blanche?'

'Yeah. It's me.'

'Thanks for calling. Sorry to keep chasing you but, well, I wanted to make sure you knew I was serious.'

Even though he was a journalist, Roger's strength was never clear communication. 'About what?'

'About wanting to meet you. Look, I was sorry about what happened round at the flat. It was . . . well.' The detective waited to hear whether Roger would apologise. He never apologised. It was always she who made the peace overtures. 'Just one of those things.'

'Yes. Your fault. You attacked me. I said I didn't want to talk and you attacked me.'

'Hold on a minute, Blanche. It was hardly all one . . .' She sensed him draw in his breath with great effort. He was a weak, cowardly man, she reflected, who wanted to be popular with everyone, yet whose deep insecurity drove him to self-righteous pomposity and chill cruelty. 'There's not much point in carrying on talking really, is there? You hardly seem in a mood of Christian charity.'

Typical Roger, she murmured to herself, trying to throw the blame on to her and make her feel guilty. 'Why should I be? You haven't shown any repentance.'

'But I am repentant. I am – look, why don't we meet for a drink soon and talk face to face? I'm standing in Nick's hall, so everyone can hear. Can't we meet somewhere?'

Blanche considered. She was not a coward and she would have to meet Roger eventually. 'OK. How about next week?'

He sounded relieved. 'Can't you make it earlier?'

'No. We've both got to prepare our scripts.'

'True.'

'I just hope they are better than tonight's.'

Her limbs ached and mouth tasted as though some incubus had emptied the contents of an ashtray into it while she had been asleep. The telephone was still shrieking. She reached out from her bed, waited for another chirrup in case the caller was going to ring off, and snatched the receiver irritably. She heard the rapid bleep of a public call box. It was Urquhart, telling her to meet him in half an hour outside the Dorchester Hotel in Park Lane. She gagged with irritation and he told her, with a forced gravity weighing down his voice, that it was connected with the Mills case. The conversation was over before it had started. She felt she had dreamed it.

Mechanically she looked in the mirror. She pencilled on a new crust of eyeshadow and lipstick. Her hands shook so much that she smudged the rouge and had to start again. She smacked her lips together, dragged a comb through her hair and marvelled once again at how even simple artifice improves the human face. It was 1.15 a.m.

Urquhart slipped from a shadow and placed his hand under her arm without a word. He dragged her across Park Lane, dodging a last, straggling taxi, almost threw her over the guard rails on the far side of the road into Hyde Park and strode

178

ahead into the looming darkness of the trees. Urquhart's eyes were battened tight down into slits and he said nothing. As they walked towards the centre of the park the city lights merged into a distant, phosphorescent haze and the velvety darkness closed in about them. The undulations in the grass were heightened by the long shadows, and she tripped over. She had forgotten to bring her gloves and so the hand that she thrust out to break her fall sank into the cold, muddy turf. A dusting of moisture was already starting to form on the blades of grass as the temperature plummeted. Her shoes oozed into the ground and, as the breeze sliced through her light coat, she shivered.

Urquhart stopped and turned a few yards ahead of her. Washed in shadow he looked as mysterious as when she first met him. He stood motionless and listened. The traffic was no more now than a hum, an occasional pinprick of light edging along Bayswater Road and Park Lane. Nothing else moved. The city was dropping into its restless slumber.

'Look, Robert, I've had enough. Tell me what this is all about. I thought it just might be some sort of lovers' tryst – not some bloody SAS training exercise.'

He tried to relax for the first time. His muscles creaked as the tension began to loosen. He was well wrapped against the cold in a navy-blue gaberdine coat, a tartan scarf thrown round the neck, and his hands were covered by heavy black gloves. White socks winked from underneath his trousers. His eyes had been rubbed a raw red by fatigue and cold and had a harried glitter. His breath smelt strongly of alcohol.

'MI5 have been watching me. That's what's wrong. I've been ordered not to see you again.' His breath spumed on the night air.

She looked down and shuffled her feet inanely. Why all this mystery? Was he telling the truth? Was he tired of her already? She could read nothing from the parchment of his face. It was turned from her and draped in shadow. His tone had been matter-of-fact, as if he were reporting to a committee.

'Who ordered you to stop seeing me?'

'My boss. A man called Capron.' Tension crackled on the cold air. His eyes flickered over her shoulders.

The name, Capron, tugged at her memory. She asked

whether it was the same Capron who was in the photograph she had borrowed from Tatyana Nowak, and who Marek had been to see. Urquhart looked at her suspiciously. 'No idea.'

'Don't you know?'

'My boss is the head of K8, the MI5 sub section that looks into suspicious resignations and so on. But the Capron you're talking about worked for MI6, not MI5.'

'But Swod told me he transferred – from MI6 to the Security Service. Perhaps that's why your boss wants you to stop seeing me. He knows something about the murder he doesn't want you or me to find out about.'

Urquhart stared at her for a moment and then shattered into a hearty laugh, much too hearty to be genuine to Blanche's ears. 'Talk about conspiracy theories!'

'What's he like, this Capron?' she asked angrily.

'Very smooth. A safe pair of hands.'

'Is he about the right age to have worked with Mills?'

'I don't know. Why don't you show me this bloody photo?' he asked with a snap of irritation. His face was draped in shadow and unreadable. What light there was brushed the back of his head, highlighting a few strands of blond hair. Blanche decided Urquhart could not be trusted with the whole truth.

'I haven't got it any more. I gave it back to Marek Nowak.' The detective had retained a copy of the original.

Urquhart paused. He turned away, musing, and walked away into the gloom.

Why was she conspiring with him to talk around the subject rather than come to the point? Relationships with other people work like a ratchet. Time is passed together, monuments visited, meals consumed and a common stock of memory accumulated. The wheels turn, the ratchet clicks, the two people approach. Something ineradicable happens and assumptions are made about kindness or fidelity – based on how often the ratchet has snapped. But in Urquhart, standing there facing him that night, she encountered a ratchet that had broken free of its retaining spring and was spinning in reverse. She felt further away from him than ever.

The two figures stood, isolated and alone, in the depths of Hyde Park at two o'clock in the morning. He had withdrawn behind his shield of mysterious self-possession. What the hell did she care about whether his boss Capron was a good operator? Her career, her desire for physical love, had led her to devalue, and so betray, herself. Blanche sensed the anger of outraged pride. She was not willing to let herself be betrayed and used by Urquhart. She would not allow him to sidle away into the night leaving her to kow-tow to an irate Spittals in the morning.

Her chest shrivelled with anger. She could no longer support men closeting their secrets. She would prise Urquhart's out at screaming point. 'All I want is the truth – for once. Not office gossip or patronising shit about trusting the Registry files. No tales about defectors and what the Brits got up to in the Cold War. I've had enough of that. Just tell me the truth. Crawl out of that little shell of yours and tell me the truth. About what you feel for me. And then about Mills.'

Days, hours before, that distant body had shed its casing. She had seen it naked. The tight, round buttocks; the blond hairs on his shoulders backlit by the bedside lamp; the curve of his back rising and falling; the bony rib cage, hard and muscled; the warmth of his breath scalding her neck. She thought she had begun to know him in those intimate moments.

Urquhart slowed after a few steps and then stopped. She had not moved. His shoulders rose as he took a deep breath like a diver about to plunge. He slowly turned to face her. 'I'm sorry. I should have told you at the beginning. For a spy, I'm not very good at deception.' Urquhart kicked at the turf with the toe of his shoe. 'I'm married. I have a wife and a young son.'

She was numb, frozen by surprise. She wanted to feel some emotion straightaway but found none. 'You bastard,' she hissed. She wanted, but could not bring herself, to hit him.

'Things are never that simple. You must know that.'

'Things like that *are* rather simple. A man is either a faithful bastard or a faithless bastard. You're in the second category.'

Urquhart winced. At least she thought he did. It may have been a trick of the light. He said nothing. The chilliness in Blanche's feet and hands was replaced by a pulsating warmth as her mind raced with the implications of what Urquhart had told her. She had come to suspect that her affair with him would not be straightforward, that he was not sent by heaven

181

to redeem her from chastity. But she had not consciously considered he might be married. She had always promised herself she would never have an affair with a married man. Yet she was in precisely that situation. Deceived. Betrayed. Her betrayal probably meant little to Urquhart, she considered, when he was charged with preventing the betrayal of a nation. The betrayal of a nation was too distant to make her care. It was the betrayal of her trust that made her flutter with anger. The state – like communism – was too abstract, too vague for her.

Looking into her churning heart as she stood there that night, she knew she felt an affection for the man opposite and believed he had some affection for her. She could not say it was 'love' because she had always found it difficult to define the border between 'love' and 'friendship'. There are no infallible guides, no accurate maps, to the territory of the heart. You are a pioneer every time you enter that unknown land.

She was not thinking clearly and she prided herself on thinking clearly: priorities, motives, objectives. These were her watchwords. She wanted the truth from Urquhart if it did not bruise her, untruth if it did. She told herself she did not care about the fact that he was already married but was equally scarred by the knowledge that he did have a wife. His shadowy presence created an irresistible desire for her to stretch out – just an arm's length away – and caress him, but that desire was counterbalanced by nausea at the prospect of his body coming into contact with hers again. Perhaps her husband was not such a shit after all, Blanche thought, just a human being who experienced the same tangled skein of feelings as held her then. She stood in limbo until he spoke again.

'You know what I mean.' She shook her head. She could pretend no longer. She did not know what he meant. 'My wife and I live separately. Most of the time. I've been back now and again to stay for à while, hoping it would all work out. We've stayed sort of together because of our son, for his sake if you like. I don't know what we'll do – stay together or split up.'

'Presumably you're going back to her now? For another little experiment?' A cold and neurotic performance, she told herself, as the words tumbled out.

182

Urquhart studied the ground intently, scouring the turf for his words. 'As a matter of fact, I wasn't. It's early days for us, you and me, if you like. I think we got too involved too quickly.' She laughed out loud, since it was he who had set the pace. 'But I wanted to make sure that, well, I wasn't just being cynical about it all, making use of you. I am very fond of you.' The words were wrenched out like rotten teeth. She could almost hear the tearing of the flesh. 'But I'm not willing to break up with my wife and son yet. Although I may be forced to.' He was pensive, as if his words contained hidden meanings.

'And how do I fit into these plans – if at all?' Her words stung with sarcasm.

Urquhart flung his arms back and forth across his body to warm them up. 'I'm cold. Let's walk for a bit.'

He insinuated his right hand under her arm and tried to ease her towards the Bayswater Road. She resisted. 'Answer my question, for Christ's sake! How do I fit into these plans of yours?'

'That's precisely why I asked you to come here at such a bloody ridiculous time. To tell you.' They began to walk. Blanche listened to the squelch of their feet, the soughing trees, the swish of a distant car on the damp road and behind it all an amorphous hum. 'I had an appointment to see Capron, this afternoon. It was meant to be routine. An update on various reports. Everything went through on the nod. His mind seemed to be somewhere else. I was just about to put my papers away, when he said he had something "delicate" to talk about. Capron said it had come to his attention that I'd been meeting you and that it had to stop.'

'How did he know?'

'No idea. I thought you might have said something to somebody.'

She glanced at him scorchingly. 'Thanks for your trust.'

The sarcasm went unregarded. 'Capron said he knew you were working on the Mills case and that we must have discussed it together.'

'He couldn't prove it.'

'That's what I told him. But he went on to say he knew I'd spent the night at your place. Someone must have been watching us.'

A balloon of disgust inflated within her. A man must have lurked in a car parked between two lamp standards, noting the time of arrival, the minute the curtains had been drawn at her bedroom, the second their shadows met and intertwined behind the window. During the long night, the car would have been joined silently by another. The first would have slid off into the darkness. Those men, balding men with families, would have written their reports with a knowing smile, omitting anything too indelicate, and the contents would have been passed on to Urquhart's boss, and then probably on to Spittals. He was going to carpet her not only for arresting a part-time MI6 agent for murder without sufficient evidence, but also for fraternising with the 'funnies' between the sheets.

With a swell of panic, she looked round at all the wintry trees. Each could hide a Special Branch man. Had a car not followed her a long way along the Bayswater Road when she was coming to meet Urquhart? Why had she not realised earlier? 'Is there anyone here tonight?'

He shook his head. 'Capron said he'd call them off now he had the information he wanted.'

'Didn't you protest? Say it was appalling that they spied on us like that?'

'Course I did,' rejoined Urquhart wearily but with little conviction.'He just looked at me and said our affair had to stop. He mumbled about official secrets and civil service discipline. He said you'd been sticking your nose in where it wasn't wanted, and hadn't heeded warnings from your superiors about giving up finding an espionage connection with Mills' murder.'

Blanche understood the people who must have put pressure on the commander to take her off the case: MI5 and Urquhart's boss, Capron.

'There is a link,' she groaned. 'I'm convinced.' Urquhart looked at her suspiciously.

'Did Capron ask you straight whether you'd given me any help?' Urquhart nodded. 'And what did you say?'

'I admitted it. It would have looked a lot worse if I hadn't a proper motive for meeting you in the first place.'

'And what did he say?'

'He looked at me with one of those amiable stares of his,

184

said I was overworked and I should take some time off. Said I was talking poppycock, had signed the official report anyway and that – from his point of view – that closed the investigation.'

It occurred to her suddenly that she had forgotten to tell Urquhart what had gone on during the day, especially what Marek Nowak had told her and the disastrous arrest of Taczek.

Urquhart's face lengthened as she related the two episodes. He was particularly fascinated by what Marek Nowak said. He thrust his gloved hands in his pockets and trudged on, his face closed and looking inward. Occasionally a faint glow from the city brushed the edge of his cheek and she was reminded how handsome he was, the smooth chin, his lines as clean as a lengthening shadow. 'I reasoned with Capron. But well – I didn't have that information you got from Nowak for a start, saying Taczek had confessed. Capron ended up by saying I was barred from all files that have anything to do with Mills. The Registry's been told. I haven't got access to what we need most – written evidence.' The MI5 man kicked the grass and dead leaves with his brogues. 'Capron said if I met you again I'd be sacked.'

'But he can't do that!'

He pulled his coat about him, his face dark against the city. 'That's what you think. There are no industrial tribunals in Her Majesty's Security Service. A rumour circulates and someone is shuffled off to some distant department. Why should they have to explain? They're secret. And this government wants it to carry on that way.' They plodded on. She was tongue-tied with fatigue and cold.

Urquhart glanced into the looming trees and smelt the wintry air.

In one of those swings of mood she experienced, swooping backwards and forwards like a pendulum, Blanche was frothy again. Word loose and fancy free. She stopped and planted her stiletto heels in a puddle of mud. 'From what you've said I assume you didn't resign for my sake. After all, we do live in the real world.' The sarcasm stung the night air. But it was hypocritical sarcasm because she knew she would have done the same as him. No one in their right mind sleeps with a person once and sacrifices their career on the altar of one

185

night's pleasure. She would not have done it, but was disappointed that Urquhart did not make the gesture.

'As you say, we live in the real world.' His cold tone made her want to vomit over his white socks. She restrained herself. 'I've got responsibilities. I need the salary. Besides,' he said, with the archest piece of self-justification, 'what help I can offer you now, I can best give from the inside. If I'm pushed out, I'll be just like you. Helpless.'

'Scurrying round to pick up the few crumbs that fall from the table?' She looked at him, bleary-eyed and depressed. Her feet were freezing again, sprouting chill mushrooms. He stared back at, and through, her. She had to hit him, dent him, somehow. 'You like the freemasonry bit of it, don't you? The secrecy. The clubbiness. Admit it. The real reason you tugged your forelock to Capron was that you were afraid of being kicked out?'

He shrugged his shoulders. She hated his indifference, the lack of passion, the buttoned-up calmness, that was somehow emphasised by the Scottish burr as he spoke. 'I suppose you're right. We're all afraid of being thrown out of the club. Especially if you've paid or done a lot to get in – whether it's the snooker hall or the Garrick.' He chuckled softly. 'Whatever you belong to it always hurts when you're kicked out. Outside the club, you go back to what you were before – being alone. Just a human being without power or importance.' Urquhart thrust his hands in his pockets and brooded. He pulled his gaberdine coat closer around him. 'I'll do whatever else I can to help you, Blanche, but you've got to realise I'm being watched all the time now.'

She wanted to go home and sleep. Sleep for days. Above all she wanted to slide far away from Robert Urquhart. He sensed her disgust and hatred stinking in the air. He wanted to dissipate it and leave her with a last impression of him that was not totally unpleasant. He glanced across the flickering, urban horizon. The Serpentine lay away to the west, the black slate of its surface ploughed by the chill breeze. A tall hotel broke up the skyline of the night. 'I'm sorry it's had to end like this. I'll give you what help I can.'

Blanche walked away from him back towards Park Lane. She did not care whether he followed or not. The soles of her shoes had turned to tongues of ice. Her hands throbbed with the hastening October cold. What few cars there were when she arrived had disappeared. Park Lane was deserted. From an open apartment window six storeys up, rock music thumped the damp night air.

She turned round as she reached the pavement to discover Urquhart a few steps behind. He called her name. He repeated it, but louder and more insistent. She ignored him and did not turn again until she reached her car. Urquhart was still with her. He fumbled for a kiss as she unlocked the car but she twisted her cheek away. She smelt the staleness of alcohol on his breath. He did not try again and she drove off. She kept sight of him in her mirror – hands in pockets, bedraggled – until she turned the corner, hoping that image would be the last she would ever have of him.

Chapter 19

Spittals' hands glowed from the diligent rubbing he was applying to them as she came in through the door at ten o'clock. He halted only for a second, enough to narrow his eyes and purse his lips into a look of utter disgust, as though a dog's turd had grown legs and scurried on to his carpet. The rubbing resumed as vigorously as before and slowly drew the tension from his lips and cheek muscles. The rustling of Spittals' hands, one across the other, backwards and forwards, was the only sound in the room apart from a demented fly. It had been woken from its sleep by the central heating and in a state of despair and paranoia dive-bombed the double glazing in a vain effort to escape. Blanche felt like doing the same.

'So, you've really got me in the shit now, haven't you? Arresting a former MI6 man with high-up connections. Very high up indeed. The Commissioner's Office got a call from some pinstriped twerp in the Cabinet Office.' She blinked and looked demurely down at the grey and red carpet which squelched across the floor like a rabbit that had been run over by a lorry. Spittals had insisted it should be laid when he took over the office. 'So. Come on then. Give us your side of it.'

Spittals rubbed his forefinger across the stubble of his moustache as she flopped into an explanation. While she gabbled on Spittals stopped rubbing his hands and, with his eyes on the demented fly, expressed disbelief by taking off his jacket and cradling his head in his hands. He was more irritated than angry – irritated that the Commissioner's Office had called him direct to demand an explanation. But melded with the annoyance was a certain satisfaction that the model-graduate chief inspector, whom he thought much too clever and ambitious for her own good, had made a grave error. 'Lack of maturity,' he had mumbled the night before, 'no experience of real life. Women don't understand these things.

Promoted just a little too quickly in my opinion.' But the chief superintendent knew he had to counterfeit genuine anger when he confronted Blanche, tear her off a strip, and put overweening ambition in its place. So the colour in his cheeks darkened to a ruby red. His feet began to tap more and more loudly beneath the desk and his jaw quivered more and more violently as Blanche put her side of the story and pleaded for more time to finish the investigation.

Finally he jumped up, when he thought the appropriate moment had arrived, and whipped a blast of abuse across the table. It was accompanied by a squall of spittle. She could do nothing but batten down the conversational hatches and wait until the storm blew itself out. She stared at him defiantly, and after he had ranted for a minute or so, the chief superintendent felt vaguely ridiculous so he lowered his frame into a cowering chair, and resumed the final polish of his palms.

'I warned you before, I'd have to take action if you carried on as you were. So, from this moment, I order you off the Mills case. There are no exceptions this time. You stop now. The file is closed.' He emphasised each word with a stab of a well-fleshed finger that bore his brassy signet ring. He remembered the call he had also had that morning from a senior man in Special Branch. 'Words like "national security" and "Official Secrets Act" are being bandied around in my hearing and I don't like them very much. They make me come out in spots. Words like that mean trouble, big trouble, and I've got enough of that in my department as it is without you importing any more. Is that clear?'

Blanche nodded with such studied attention it verged on caricature. The chief superintendent was pleased with himself. He smacked his lips and stroked his moustache with surprise. He was annoyed by Blanche's defiance yet he also admired it. His deepest sympathies sided with her against the plum-mouthed bureaucrats of the Cabinet Office. 'You realise of course that this Taczek character might take it further. Sue the commissioner for unlawful arrest or something like that.' He leant forward confidentially over the desk. 'But we should be able to fend him off.'

He wanted her to show gratitude and deference, but she simply murmured 'Thank you, sir' with no conviction. Blanche did not like the chief superintendent glowing smugly over her mistake. Spittals resumed his rubbing again because at times like these she made him nervous. Blanche did not respond like the other ambitious young officers he knew.

She walked towards the closed door. 'Take my advice this time, Blanche. A call from the Cabinet Office means some very big people indeed risk having their noses put out of joint. If you don't bail out now, it could well be the sack or demotion. Just leave the funnies alone, will you?' Spittals picked up from his desk a silver cup he had won in his youth in the Manchester Bowls League. It was the only sport he had ever practised and he was inordinately proud of it. He breathed lovingly on the silver and polished it with his sleeve. 'The Force has got enough obstinate and bloodyminded men as it is, without adding any females.'

Dexter came off the phone and scribbled a line or two of notes when Blanche loped into the office. 'I've been looking for you everywhere. Then I discovered you were with the chief, being ticked off,' he said mischievously. The sergeant took a languid drag at his cigarette. He always smoked cigarettes sensuously, as though each one was of a special vintage and he wanted to fix its particular flavour on his palate. 'Our friend who got knocked down by a car, Mr Nowak, has fallen into a bad coma and he's on the critical list.'

Blanche had no energy left for bad news. She wanted to sleep. Not for hours but for days and days. Her arms and legs throbbed with tiredness. The coffee she drank tasted like creosote. 'So what? Let the bastard die,' she wanted to say. It was he after all who had led her to arrest Taczek, he who had indirectly led her into the chief superintendent's office that morning to have her face sprayed with warm saliva.

'It looks to me as if someone tried to murder him,' whispered Dexter as an afterword.

A detective constable was working away in a corner. Blanche winked at Dexter and nodded for him to follow her outside with his coat. He said nothing until they were outside New Scotland Yard and had left the security men far behind, stamping their feet against the cold outside the main door.

She explained to Dexter why she could not talk about the

Mills case at work. If news wended to Spittals that she had any more interest in the Mills murder she would be suspended immediately. Great, round clouds rolled slowly across the sky like whales and a chill wind slapped their faces as they clattered along the pavement to Angelo's Café. They collected steaming mugs of frothy coffee and sat down opposite the gleaming silver water boiler. Beneath lay a line of glum sandwiches, a Perspex dish of an unidentifiable fish meat and a mutilated leg of ham.

Dexter explained in his nasal twang that an unknown woman had passed Nowak's bed the previous evening during visiting hours, tripped over a chair and fallen on him. Marek was asleep at the time but as soon as the woman hit the bed Nowak woke up with a scream. The woman apologised and hurried out of the ward before anyone could stop her. The detective constable who was supposed to be guarding him was out of the ward at the time chatting up some nurses. Nowak was still dazed by sleep. He said nothing for a minute or two and told the person next to him that he was having a bad dream when the stranger woke him up. He asked whether anyone knew who the woman was. No one did.

An hour or so later, Marek started to rub his leg and called across a nurse because his head ached. She found a spot on Nowak's calf that was red and swollen like a severe mosquito bite. It seemed a minor problem. Within another hour Nowak's temperature was high with fever, he was rolling and twisting in the sheets, his body soaked in sweat. He uttered odd bits of English and Polish – a word here, what people took to be an odd line of poetry, names. The nurse summoned a doctor in alarm, and just as a sedative was about to be given, Marek began to scream. His eyelids peeled back, the eyeballs rolling wildly in their sockets. He shouted, so the doctor told Dexter, as if he were crying to someone a great distance away. With the sedative, Marek drifted into sleep but he did not wake up. He was in a deep coma. The mosquito bite on his leg had swollen into a scarlet hillock. The patient was moved on to a life-support machine and another set of X-rays was ordered in case the first ones had not revealed internal injuries caused by the car accident. They showed nothing. Close examination of Marek's skin round the swelling, however,

191

showed a minute mark, as if a needle had been inserted.

Blanche could not go to the hospital herself. It was too foolish. She told Dexter what had happened in the meeting with Spittals and how he had ordered her off the case, and she asked Dexter to go on helping her. He tugged at the knees of his well-pressed trousers and watched Angelo pour out a cup of tea for a florid man with a limp. 'Provided it doesn't get me the sack. I'm black, remember, and jobs aren't too easy to come by, even for someone as good-looking and intelligent as me.'

Dexter agreed to go to the hospital and find out what he could. He hoovered up the dregs of his coffee and scurried out of the café. Blanche remained to think, clutching a second cup of coffee. The owner of the sandwich bar swabbed down the counter again and whistled an aria she recognised from *La Traviata*.

A fragment of conversation with Urquhart bubbled up in her mind. In a sudden panic of sadness, she pictured him – the tall, thin frame, the stubby nose, the waves of golden hair tumbling over his forehead. She closed her eyes to the image, waiting to hear only the words and shut out the pain. She had asked whether intelligence services still commissioned murders of their enemies. Urquhart chuckled and said 'some'. MI6 and the CIA were forbidden by internal guidelines to assassinate, but that did not mean, he continued, that they did not employ 'freelancers' to eliminate the odd opponent. And what about the KGB? They used, Urquhart whispered, to have a whole sub-department dedicated to murder during the Cold War. Nowadays, and especially under the younger leaders of the Soviet Union who had not known the horrors of the Second World War, they used assassination very sparingly indeed. He talked about the bad publicity for the Russians flowing from an incident in London a few years before, when the Bulgarian secret service murdered a political exile in London. The publicity surrounding the death was carefully orchestrated by Western intelligence services, said Urquhart with a smirk, to cause the maximum amount of embarrassment to Russia and its allies.

Her erstwhile MI5 lover had imparted a cruel twist to his lower lip. 'We know there were some red faces in KGB headquarters. But their problem was being found out. The

KGB's next victim won't be left dead with a poisoned pellet in him, like a wood pigeon that a kid takes a pot shot at with his air gun. There'll hardly be a mark.'

She smacked her hand down on to the saucer without realising she still held the cup. The crack of china resounded round the café as the saucer split in half. A lady with a drained face wrapped in a nylon scarf and sitting at a table near by glanced up with a scowl.

Blanche blamed herself for Nowak's coma. She should have been more suspicious. One attempt had been made to murder Nowak the day before. Why would the killer, especially if it was the KGB, stop after one go? Marek Nowak was the only witness to Taczek's confession to the murder of Mills. With the suicide of Tatyana Nowak and a successful assassination of her son, the confession would vanish from memory. The spoken word, after all, only becomes history when it is recorded.

Nowak's attempted assassin was a woman. If Taczek *had* murdered Mills, he could not have administered the poison that had thrust Marek into a coma. Christine Mills perhaps? Blanche was still suspicious of her decision not to tell earlier of the quarrel with her father on the night of his death.

Perhaps Nowak might recover. Perhaps he might not. She had to discover evidence of Taczek's confession to the murder of Mills that might survive Nowak's death. There was one place she might come across it that she had not yet properly explored. She had to visit it herself and risk dismissal. Was it worthwhile? She had never considered the possibility as likely until then. Blanche was proud of her tenacious progress in the Metropolitan Police and had sacrificed much for it – children, so far; social life; feminine sensitivity. But the motive behind her achievement was not self-interest alone, nor the desire to carry aloft the banner of feminism. She wanted both of these to some extent but only in a police force whose integrity she could believe in. When her principles and her career clashed, she had to sacrifice her career.

She could not be issued with a warrant for her visit. The search would have to be illegal and secret – the sort of operation she knew Urquhart's organisation carried out regularly under the generous blanket of 'national security'.

193

She regretted she would not be seeing Urquhart again for only one reason, or so she told herself. She was convinced the defector he referred to vaguely was important and Urquhart was her only source of information about him. Perhaps Marek Nowak was a KGB agent and was about to be named by the defector. The person who recruited Nowak, or who had been recruited by him, would be trembling with anticipation. Nowak would have been a likely target in such circumstances. Or perhaps Graham Mills was about to be named by the defector just before his murder. Perhaps Tatyana Nowak took her life for fear of the ignominy of exposure as a spy. Perhaps, perhaps, perhaps. She could invent hypotheses as often as she sipped her tepid coffee. None of them, however, suggested a random death for Graham Mills. His murder had to be linked to Tatyana's suicide, the poisoning of her son and the betrayal of the father. That family, like their beloved homeland, was a trinket of the gods.

She dropped a one-pound coin on the table to pay for the smashed saucer. She intended it to lie flat and silent. Instead the coin began to roll and described a series of ever smaller circles, until all movement died with a final rattle. The Italian behind the counter beamed with a set of saffron-coloured teeth.

Outside the café Inspector Dickinson of Special Branch was inhaling snuff from the back of his hand. Behind him, parked at the kerb, a red Ford Granada revved its engine. 'Someone would like to have a chat with you, Chief Inspector,' he stated with a sniff.

'Someone in the car?'

He nodded. Blanche could just make out a flabby shape in the back seat. Dickinson opened the door to allow Blanche to get in and ordered the driver to move off. The car pulled out into the traffic, leaving Dickinson behind. The man sitting next to her was like a porcelain buddha, rotund and self-contained, the skin without a wrinkle despite being fifty or so years old. His mousy hair, on the other hand, had been eroded by the years. It was thin and ragged, and folded forward to hide a growing bald patch. The man's skin was the matchless white of a person who preferred study to sport and shadow to sunlight.

'Sorry to just snatch you off the pavement like that, Chief Inspector, but I felt we ought to meet.'

'Who are you?'

His thick lips chuckled but the goatee beard crushed the effect of the smile, imparting an air of superiority to the epicene face. He reached inside his tweed jacket and passed across a Security Service pass – the sort used by MI5 officers to identify themselves when in trouble. His name was Andrew Tait. 'If I may, I'd like to come straight to the point. What did Marek Nowak tell you before he went into his coma?'

Blanche told him. Tait tried out his smile again. He gave the impression of being perpetually amused by, and yet far above, the foibles of fellow human beings. It showed not only in his smile but in his voice, which was gentle with a mischievousness lurking beneath, the mischievousness of a mind that loved to irk convention. His dress was far from conventional too: a shirt of cream silk, a spotted bow tie and black brogues.

'So who was it who got Taczek released so quickly then? You?' asked Blanche with a squint of concentration.

The MI5 man pondered for a moment and stroked his beard. He looked down at the other hand neatly folded in his lap. 'No, it wasn't me. It was an old friend of Taczek's. You may have come across him in your investigation into Graham Mills' murder. Capron. Hugh Capron.' He flicked up his eyes, small and blank, holes that sucked in everything around him, but gave nothing back.

Blanche stared at the back of the driver's head to win time to think. The man who released Taczek was also the one in Tatyana Nowak's photograph. 'Capron knew Zbigniew Nowak, didn't he?'

'Apparently. Have *you* come across Capron?'

'Only the name. In passing. I know nothing about him at all.' She decided not to tell Tait about the photograph.

The car purred on, the driver looking neither to left nor right, the picture of inscrutability. Tait stroked his beard again with long, elegant fingers, appraising her with colourless eyes. He looked vaguely sad. 'I gather you've had some contact with a young MI5 officer called Robert Urquhart?'

There was no snideness in his tone so Blanche decided to remain aloof. 'How do you know that?'

'Phone calls in and out of our buildings are often recorded. Standard security.' The MI5 man eased his bulk round in the car seat to face her better.

'Urquhart was in charge of the Security Service investigation into Mills. So I met him a couple of times.'

The car had stopped at some traffic lights. The driver twisted his head round for instructions and Tait told him gently to carry on. 'What did you make of his investigation?'

Blanche held no loyalty to Robert now. She told the truth. 'Not very thorough. That's one of the reasons I've carried on with mine.'

'Carried on regardless, some might say.' Tait's smile was so faint it needed a microscope to detect. 'Not very thorough, eh? Why do you say that?'

She shrugged. 'Just an impression.' She did not want to be specific so that Tait could press her further.

The MI5 man turned away from her with a thoughtful sigh, as if he knew what thoughts were passing through her mind. He rested his hands on his protruding stomach. 'Did Urquhart mention Capron at all?'

'Like I said, the name came up in passing. Capron is his boss.' Blanche did not want to mention that it was Capron who had forbidden Urquhart to meet her again. She wanted to forget that night as soon as possible. She scrutinised a dilapidated man on the pavement outside who was passing from rubbish bin to rubbish bin, rustling around inside and placing everything of interest in a plastic bag.

'Nothing else?'

'No.'

The MI5 man seemed to suddenly shake his bulk to wake himself up and remind himself that the chief inspector was still in the car with him. 'So, tell me, Chief Inspector, why have you persisted in this investigation – into the espionage side of things, I mean? It should have been made quite clear to you from the beginning that MI5's word on this would be final.'

She swivelled to face him. 'No one should have the right to be investigator, judge and jury in a murder case – let alone one like this.'

'One could argue precisely the opposite,' continued Tait

smoothly. 'Just because this case *is* like it is, it's essential that the government's secret service *is* both judge and jury. And let's face it,' he added with a malicious smile while he examined his fingernails, 'with a government like we have at the moment we're encouraged to do so. Without even a trace of guilty conscience.' He glanced up at her over a pair of imaginary spectacles. 'So have you stopped your investigation?'

'No choice. I've been ordered off it,' she sighed. Tait nodded with barely concealed satisfaction. 'Although I'm almost certain Mills was murdered because he'd worked for the KGB.'

Tait puckered his lips and nodded slowly in a gesture of admiration. 'You've done your homework, I'll give you that. And it's a plausible theory. Except there's a fundamental mistake behind it.'

'What's that?'

'Mills never worked for the KGB.' The car wove through the traffic on Hyde Park Corner and purred up Park Lane, the grime-grey hotels flashing by on the right. Blanche twisted uneasily in her seat. 'Zbigniew Nowak was betrayed all right. But not by Mills.'

'Who by then?'

'We're waiting for more evidence. Mills was amoral and untrustworthy, but we've known for a while now that he definitely worked for us.'

'When will you know who *did* do it?' she probed, in as casual a voice as she could manage. 'When you find the KGB agent who tried to poison Marek Nowak?'

Tait twitched, as though at the end of an invisible wire, and his dead eyes flickered into life for a moment. He tried to cover up the flutter of surprise by leaning forward and telling the driver it was time to return to New Scotland Yard. 'We will know in the end who betrayed Zbigniew Nowak.'

There was no point in pressing him. Blanche leant back into her seat and glued on her most charming smile. 'Now I'm officially off the case, I wish you'd tell me more about this mysterious Zbigniew Nowak.'

Tait seemed relieved. He seemed to have made up his mind in advance that he could reveal a certain amount of information about the past rather than the present. When he spoke it was as if he were dictating a letter to her, concentrating on the correctness of his grammar and syntax. He was obviously proud of his memory and intellect. 'Zbigniew Nowak was just one agent who was captured and executed. He met a particularly unpleasant death.'

Blanche recounted what Swod had told her.

'He did not paint in the ghastly but important details then. So I had better tell you.' Tait ordered the driver to continue down Victoria Street and strike south towards the Thames. 'He was an unlucky man. But then the Poles are an unlucky people,' he began. Tait folded his hands, one across another, in a gesture of resignation. He sat silent for a moment, glancing with a look of displeasure at the cars jamming them in on either side. 'After his capture on the boat off Gdańsk, the torture began.' He looked across to confirm Blanche was paying attention. Like her, she reflected, Tait did not suffer fools gladly. 'The two interrogators were drunk on vodka. They heated up pokers until they were red hot, and branded him. They wanted Nowak to confess. They needed him to confess. Probably,' the MI5 man interjected with a thoughtful stroke of his beard, 'to stop themselves being sent to the camps as Western agents. They wanted names. Of other spies. Of the people in London. They pulled out his fingernails. Still he did not submit. Finally the interrogators must have lost their patience, or perhaps it was just the heat of the vodka. But the final horror was the same.'

The MI5 man paused for a moment to stroke his beard again and a hint of emotion, of disgust, entered his voice for the first time. 'They castrated him. And then shot him dead.'

Blanche felt vaguely sick. 'How do you know this?'

'The KGB had an enquiry. They didn't object to the torture and the shooting. That was standard under Stalin. They were angry because it was carried out unofficially – without the prior approval of the Party. The Party, you see, wanted a show trial. They couldn't hold one with a defendant who was just a mangled lump of flesh.' Tait yawned into a white hand, the well-disguised yawn of a man whose only knowledge of torture was confined to that inflicted by sitting through committees.

'Presumably MI6 had their own enquiry?' asked the chief inspector in a self-righteous tone.

Tait nodded. 'It concluded that someone must have betrayed Nowak and that he probably knew who it was. Philby was discounted and everything pointed to Mills – a senior man in the Soviet bloc department. Odd pieces of evidence about his movements and early life were all dragged up. Eventually Mills was suspended. Nothing was proved beyond doubt, but no one felt they could take chances. Mills was demoted and sent to another department.'

'But you're telling me all the suspicions about Mills are unfounded?'

The man from MI5 nodded, his aquiline nose in black profile against the car window behind him. 'Mills was deliberately besmirched by the KGB. And I must say,' sniffed Tait appreciatively, tugging out a silk handkerchief from a pocket to blow his nose, 'they were very clever about it. They never fed information into the system that appeared conclusive against Mills, just highly suspicious.'

Tait told her that some of the information about Mills involved a KGB agent, whom he called 'Nikolai' for lack of anything better. After his demotion inside SIS, Mills became a little unconventional in what Tait called his 'fieldcraft'. He liked to take risks. One of the biggest was to take on the identity of a businessman and travel behind the Iron Curtain. The Russians obviously knew who he was and kept him under surveillance all the time. On a couple of these trips in the late fifties, Mills fell in with 'Nikolai' in Moscow. 'Whether Mills knew then that he was KGB, we'll never know, but they certainly got on very well together. The Soviets fed some disinformation back to us about the meetings with "Nikolai", hinting that Mills was working for them and using the meetings to pass information across.'

The car plunged into the chaos of Trafalgar Square, taxis honking, buses spewing out black clouds of exhaust, pigeons swirling in indolent flocks around the monuments. In silence they passed down the grandness of Whitehall, hemmed in by the blank façades of bureaucracy, ministries where men and women toiled in cold obscurity. The gothic spires of parliament shimmered in the autumnal sunlight as they drove to the far side of Parliament Square and turned right towards Victoria.

Blanche absorbed the implication of what she had just been told: Mills had not betrayed Zbigniew Nowak and so could not have been murdered because of it. And Robert Urquhart had been shown to be lying to her about more than his affections. 'So why did Urquhart keep telling me Mills probably *was* working for the Russians?'

Tait stroked his beard with a look of puzzlement which faded after a moment. 'He probably doesn't know the truth. He wasn't told. We keep our staff in a certain amount of darkness. And the public, of course, in complete darkness.' He made a hollow smile, the smile of the high priest and mandarin through the ages, the smile of the keeper of secrets.

As though by an immaculately timed piece of theatre, the driver pulled up opposite the front entrance to New Scotland Yard. 'I'm sorry you can't pursue your investigation any further, Chief Inspector,' concluded Tait. 'But . . .' His soft voice trailed off. 'I'm sure you understand. The interests of national security and all that.' He made a final, half-hearted attempt at a smile that could have been a yawn. Blanche's door was already being held open by the driver. The chief inspector got out.

'Oh, by the way,' called Tait. He leant across the back seat so that he could look up and see her face. 'This conversation is confidential. Not to be mentioned to anyone.'

'Anyone?'

'Anyone. Goodbye.'

He pulled the door shut himself, discreetly so that there was the minimum noise. The car accelerated off and disappeared into the late afternoon traffic.

Chapter 20

The chief inspector extinguished the lights of her car, turned off the ignition and sat motionless for five minutes. She counted them off, one by one, on the dial of her watch up to two o'clock. The street lay silent and deserted. Most of the street lamps had switched off automatically but, by an irritating quirk of fate, the one that had not was almost directly in front of the Nowaks' house. A withered tree protruding from the pavement cast a shadow across the bay window. The wind had risen powerfully during the evening and now thumped against the side of the car, whistling through its hidden but inevitable apertures.

She sat and thought about the events of the day. Dexter had been to the hospital, where Nowak still lay in a coma. No one had taken much notice of the woman Blanche assumed to be the attempted assassin, and Dexter garnered a description that could have fitted Christine Mills – and a hundred other women equally well. The hospital had started a set of poison tests when Dexter arrived but as yet nothing suspicious had been found.

As she closed the car door gently, she whispered thanks to the wind for smothering any noise. It snatched at the windows in the nearby houses and set them rattling in their frames; it whooshed over the slates and plucked at the loose ones, prising them away and sending them spinning to the ground; it scurried down through the garden gates, hoisted up handfuls of dead leaves and paper and kicked them scurrying down the pavement. The night was full of the rasp and scrape of branches as the wind made the limbs of the trees beat against one another. No lights were on in any of the houses and the only living thing in sight was a brindled cat who froze on the pavement, surveyed the bleak October night, and padded arrogantly across the road. Above, a gibbous moon fought a brave but doomed battle to be seen through the scudding cloud, occasionally emerging to spill its light like a bucket of whitewash over the slates.

She knew Marek's bedroom was at the back of the house. The door to his room had been closed and locked when she visited the mother, and she had not bothered to come to the house when Tatyana committed suicide. If she had searched his bedroom earlier, she thought ruefully, she would not have been shivering on the pavement in a black pullover and jeans at two o'clock in the morning, carrying a large screwdriver. About fifty metres from the car she discovered a passageway which sliced between the terraces.

With one last glance along the empty street she plunged into the blackness, treading warily on the soles of her training shoes. When she emerged from the tunnel, she was hemmed in on either side by wooden fences. At the junction she turned left and skirted the walls that ran behind the houses. One pale light shone at an upstairs window. She watched and nothing moved: a landing light left on through forgetfulness or fear of the dark. Lines of tiles shimmered in the slivers of moonlight. Chimney pots stood out in black profile like squat, ebony gargoyles. Slack linen lines whistled and whipped in the wind, tugging at their concrete posts. A loud crash ten yards to the right made her start.

The bang came again but softer, and she made out the squeak of rusty hinges against the din of the stormy night. The door of a garden shed had swung open. The door banged once again. She waited but heard no more. It had jammed. She tiptoed by a well-mown lawn, then a garden jumbled high with broken washing machines, bicycles, empty flowerpots and scraps of wood.

The next house was the one owned by the Nowaks. She clambered over the mossy wall at the bottom of the garden and edged round a shed. The shed windows were broken and stood out black and jagged by the reflected light of the moon. The grass in the garden was uncut and came up to her calves. The fishpond was almost overgrown. She edged tentatively into the lee of the house to hide in a deep shadow and bumped into a broken rainwater pipe which smacked on to the concrete patio. She swore softly but no one seemed to wake up. Blanche forced the screwdriver up into the crevice between the two halves of the sash window and heaved. The lock snapped and the detective levered up the bottom section. She pushed the curtains tentatively apart and listened. Nothing except the wind howling in the empty night.

The chief inspector climbed in over the sill, eased down the window and found herself in the hall. The same smell of stale tobacco hung on the air that she recalled from her only meeting with Tatyana Nowak the day before her suicide. She switched on her torch and turned to the right. The door to Marek's bedroom was a blank rectangle before her. She turned the heavy, white porcelain door knob and pushed gently, then switched off the torch in case she was seen by someone at the back of the house, and entered the bedroom. She could make out nothing in the darkness at the beginning except a jumble of bric-à-brac and the outline of a colossal eagle crucified on one wall. She tiptoed past the hazy outline of an unmade bed to pull the curtains closed, switched on her torch again and played it round the room like a searchlight. Marek's bedroom was unkempt, not the anarchic mess that follows the visit of burglars but the slovenly disorder of a certain type of bachelor. The bed was a tangled pile of grey sheets and stained blankets. Around the room, encumbering every available perch, were mugs and glasses. She picked up one mug and by the light of the torch saw a pea-green mould on the dregs of coffee. The floor, desk and chairs were strewn with books and papers. Many were in Polish. Even the ones in English had a Polish theme: the rise and fall of Solidarity, Eastern Europe, the Soviet Union. Her nose twitched to the smell: mouldy and fetid like sweaty clothes left to stew in a plastic bag.

The eagle on the poster dominated the room, tall and black and proud on a scarlet background. Fierce and unforgiving. As her torch toured the room it alighted on an extraordinary sight. On a low table in the far right-hand corner was a black and white photograph of a man: handsome, clean cut, direct in his glance. Blanche tiptoed over and remembered the face from the photograph of Tatyana's that she had borrowed. It was a portrait of Marek's father as a young man. The son and the father looked very different. Arranged around the photograph were bouquets of plastic flowers: virulent scarlet poppies with green leaves, straggly ivy, lemon tulips, alabaster roses – all out of season and radiating out in a baroque flurry from the central shrine. Blanche shivered with unease, as though she had stumbled into a crypt.

If anything was to be found it would not lie in the open. She ransacked the wardrobe which was bursting with piles of unwashed clothes and unironed shirts. One was splattered with red stains. She could not tell in the torchlight whether it was ink or blood. A battered desk stood beside the wardrobe. It ached under the piles of books, papers, clothes and junk. The torch picked picked out a doll in Greek costume. As she disturbed them, a film of dust rose up like an atom cloud. Three of the drawers in the desk were locked. She used the screwdriver to force open the first one. Inside were a couple of building-society account books and a few bank notes. She pocketed them to make the break-in look authentic.

The second drawer was harder to force. Blanche blinked with surprise. Under a newspaper was a pile of gay magazines. Handsome, sculpted men pinioned her with their glances: not an ounce of fat, tight buttocks ripe and ready for piercing, hands and tongues rippling up and down their bodies. Dexter was right about one thing, Blanche thought with an indulgent smile.

She broke open the third drawer with a snap. Inside was a brown exercise book. The cover was unmarked except by three inkstains and the name Marek Nowak. The writing was unkempt and messy, blotted and scrawled as Marek's fountain pen crept across the pages. She began to read by the mooned light of the torch.

'My guilt is so deep I can't rub it out. For the first time in my life I could not confess all my sins to the priest. Father Jankowski looked at me so kindly I could not tell him. I thought he might have guessed I was not normal. I was shaking and sweating so much in the confessional I thought I was going to faint. I wanted him to tear it from me so that I had no excuses. All he had to do was ask, and my guilt would have flooded out. But he didn't. I have to write this to get some of the weight – the choking weight – off my chest. If I don't, I'll go mad.'

Was it a literary exercise or a true confession? Blanche wondered.

'I better start at the beginning for lack of anywhere else,' Marek continued.

Blanche thought she heard a bang outside. Perhaps a dustbin had tumbled over or another tile been flung from the roof.

For many years, Marek wrote, he had believed his mother when she said his father had been killed in a car accident. Jozef Taczek had always substantiated the story. When Marek went to Poland for the first time, when he was eighteen, a place of pilgrimage had been his father's grave. He had gone there to lay a wreath on every visit since. The headstone of the grave, in a grey cemetery on the outskirts of Warsaw, was of plain granite and gave simply the dates of birth and death. When Marek saw the headstone for the first time no one in the neighbourhood whom he asked knew anything about the man who had been buried there. Old women nodded their heads and chomped their false teeth, young men smiled sympathetically but no one could shed any light on the mysterious car accident that had killed his father.

'It was then that the uncertainties began. It was not an obsession then, only a gnawing doubt. When I plucked up the courage to ask my mother about it she just burst into tears and I could not bring myself to question her again. I was on my own.

'I was alone in this new search as I was alone when I discovered I loved my own sex. I only discovered that late as well when I became friends with John at college. I had to keep it secret. I found that part of me disgusting. Disgusting but necessary. I need it like nothing else – more than food, drink, art, everything. I need to be loved. Loved by another man. I could never tell mother because she despises homosexuals. She spits out the word like she splutters the word "Jew". She thinks we're perverts, condemned by the Church, men who've allowed their normal natures to be twisted by depraved men. Look at Oscar Wilde, she'd say! Read the transcripts of his trial! Pederasts were not born pederasts, they were made into them. She thinks a man like me learns his sexuality like someone learns to ride a bicycle or learns how to swim. She couldn't get it into her thick skull that being gay just happens. I wanted to confess to her once but balanced that against the need to be loved by her. The two just could not coexist.

205

For her to love me, I had to carry on with my secret life. God, I hated her vindictiveness sometimes, hated her little petty bourgeois intellectual fart-arsed snobberies! But all that hate can't wash away the guilt. She's dead and I caused her death.'

Blanche looked up for a moment to chew the implications of what she had just read when another alien sound impinged. A key was rattling in the lock of the front door. Her heart vaulted into her throat.

She thrust the exercise book into a coat pocket and scrambled to the window by which she had entered. She yanked upwards on the two rings at the bottom of the window. It did not move. She heaved again. She was aware of footsteps running through the house. She pulled desperately, thinking the muscles in her arms would crack. The window flew up about a foot and stuck. It was wedged in one of its tracks. She pushed out her right arm for protection but it was too late. Hands fastened round her neck and threw her sprawling across the floor. She just had time to make out a black profile against the window before a shoe slammed into her chest with the sound a beanbag makes when it hits the floor. Blanche rolled away and started to run towards the front door. The man, and she was convinced it was a man now, tried a rugby tackle in the dark. She heard his body crump on to the floor behind her. But he managed to catch one of Blanche's flying feet and as she fell her skull caught a glancing blow from a table.

Stunned, she staggered to her feet. She heard hoarse breathing near by. Blanche flailed her fists out towards the noise and tensed as one blow crunched into flesh and bone. A fist sizzled into her stomach like a flaming sword, skewering her innards. Her lungs burst into fragments of agony so infinite that her lower lip could do no more than flop open and dribble out a feeble croak. She sank to her knees. Then he fired the single shot. Even though there was a silencer on the gun, the detonation and the whack of the bullet burying itself in the floorboards were unmistakable. The chief inspector froze.

The house was suddenly silent. A distant floorboard creaked. The wind still howled through the chimney pots and rattled through the cracks of the window frames. The man was still in shadow, his hoarse respiration mingling with the chief inspector's rasping breath. 'OK. That's enough, Blanche.'

She didn't recognise the voice for a moment. It was so familiarly distant. But then, in a gasp of stifled anger, she knew.

Urquhart stepped forward out of the blackness, his profile framed by the window. A thin splinter of moonlight caught the blond stubble of his beard and sliced like a glistening needle across the snout of a .45 revolver. The tiny hole of the barrel was pointed at her chest and was as unnaturally black as a beauty spot on an expanse of white bosom.

Chapter 21

Urquhart flicked the main switch and she blinked as the room was washed by the harsh overhead light. He looked pale and serious as his eyes scampered round the room until they found the telephone. Then he smiled. 'You're obviously a bit tired. Why don't you sit down?' He raised his golden eyebrows and nodded towards a chair. As she moved to obey, the black spot of the gun followed her unerringly across the sitting room. It was the same room where Blanche had sat and talked to Tatyana Nowak so many weeks ago. He ordered her to empty her pockets on the carpet in front of her. Blanche obeyed. Nothing explicit had been said but she knew her relationship with Urquhart had crossed a new frontier: he had become an enemy.

Holding the revolver in his right hand, Urquhart searched the chief inspector for a weapon and, finding none, picked up the pile of possessions from the floor. 'So what are you doing here?' he said finally.

'Probably the same as you.'

'And what's that?'

'Looking for clues.'

'I better look at the ones you found, then.' He sorted through Blanche's things deliberately, one by one, and only stopped when he came to the building-society books she had purloined and Marek's exercise book. A frown of puzzlement creased his brow when he looked at the cover. 'Interesting?'

'So why *are* you here?' she asked, ignoring his question. 'Insomnia?'

He snorted out a chuckle. 'Unfinished business rather.'

'Yes. It *is* a bit strange you only searching this place now, isn't it? I was only telling a colleague of yours today that the investigation into Mills' murder left a lot to be desired.'

Even though hooded by shadow, Blanche sensed Urquhart's

eyes narrow and bore into her like hungry grubs. 'Who was that?'

'My business.'

'What did he want?' he murmured with theatrical calmness.

'A chat.'

'What about?'

'Early Buddhist scriptures.'

Urquhart stepped forward menacingly. His voice rang with the irritation of the anxious. 'What about?' he repeated, enunciating each word carefully.

'It's a secret.'

He smiled slowly and relaxed. 'Everything's a secret. That's the bloody trouble.' Urquhart opened the exercise book and skimmed through a few pages with furious concentration before stuffing it in his coat pocket with a grunt of satisfaction. He moved back to the chest of drawers and took down the photograph of Tatyana Nowak and her husband on Westminster Bridge.

The MI5 man picked up the telephone and pressed the digits with the forefinger of the same, left hand. His right still held the revolver. Blanche wanted to be clever and memorise the way his finger moved across the numbers but she could not maintain the concentration after the first four. Instead, her eyes strayed to his gloved hand. It was neat and elegant, with cool, long fingers. She heard the muffled trill of the ring. A sharp click sounded at the other end of the line and a voice muttered something. Whoever it was must have been waiting by the telephone for the call. 'Yes. It's me,' said Urquhart. His voice was nervous and conspiratorial: he knew the person he was speaking to quite well. 'I found more than we bargained for – including that policewoman Hampton.'

He paused as he listened. 'God knows. I thought she was off the case as well.' Blanche made out the murmur of the other voice. 'No. Don't worry. She won't get in the way. And I've found what we're looking for. I'll bring it round at seven. Is everything fixed?' He glanced up at her.

She thought she detected a grunt of assent from Urquhart's unknown colleague.

'Seven o'clock then.'

The gloved hand – like a fat, black spider – delicately placed

209

the telephone back in its cradle. Urquhart breathed deeply and glanced round the room. He edged backwards to the wall. Her fists gripped the armrests of the chair so tightly she made out the taut ligaments running from her wrists to her knuckles. He bent down and yanked out the flex that connected a standard lamp to the mains. He pushed over the lamp, wound the wire around his left wrist and then, with a foot on the base, tugged aggressively at the flex. It offered no resistance and Urquhart was almost thrown off balance when it slipped free.

He stood silent beside the sofa, the black disc of the revolver trained on her, his face half in shadow from the harsh light shining down from the ceiling. 'Get on the floor, chest down. Hands behind your back.'

She did not respond. 'What's this all about, Robert?'

Urquhart flicked his gun menacingly and stepped forward. 'Get down,' he shouted.

Never one to try and out-stare a person holding a cocked gun, Blanche jumped out of the armchair as if it were spring-loaded. She feared Urquhart was going to kill her. She kept repeating to herself that it was an irrational fear, but logic did nothing to quell the lurking terror. She had no idea what the MI5 man was aiming to do, or to whom he owed his ultimate loyalty – except himself. The only certainty was that she had a few seconds to act. Urquhart had broken off the lamp flex for a purpose – to strangle her or tie her up, or both. He was toting the gun for a purpose – to shoot her through the head or knock her unconscious, or both. After either of them had happened, she was finished.

Urquhart tiptoed forward with a respectful air, as if he were approaching an altar. He was about ten feet away. His eyes clung to her like thirsty leeches, watching for any movement, the revolver trained on her back. He was about four feet away when his foot caught in the electric flex he was dragging and he stumbled forward off balance. Blanche flung herself across the floor and rolled on to his feet, at the same time throwing a punch up into his genitals. Two dull cracks resounded as bullets bored through the ceiling. Urquhart crumpled. Blanche had found her target. The gun lolled in his hand. She jumped up and punched him in the kidneys before landing a fist on the point of his chin. He flopped to the floor. In her panic, and to make sure he stayed unconscious, she hit him twice over the head with the base of the standard lamp. He groaned and lay still.

Blanche rolled her erstwhile lover on to his chest, untangled the flex from his left glove and tied him up with his hands and feet behind him. She pulled the white cord so tight it cut red weals into the white flesh. She hoped they hurt. The chief inspector listened to his breathing and for a moment found it difficult to separate it from her own rasping pant. It was steady and normal. It looked as though she had not fractured his skull. She ripped a cushion cover into strips and used them to make a gag.

As Blanche snatched up the telephone and listened to the reassuring hum of the dialling tone, she caught sight of herself in the mirror on the wall: the shimmer of sweat on her forehead, eyes wild, face haggard and pale, hair stormy and unkempt, knuckles bruised and sore. The phone rang for ten minutes, or so it seemed, before Dexter answered. His voice was distant and fogged with irritation. 'Who's that?'

'Me.'

'Oh, shit,' groaned the detective sergeant without malice, and he coughed three or four times to wake himself up. 'What do you want at this time of night? Psychological counselling?'

'Shut up, Dexter. It's not your mind I'm after. It's your body,' she said, amazed at her good humour. 'I've got a man trussed up here on the floor like a Christmas turkey.'

'I didn't know you were into bondage, Blanche.'

She smiled thinly. 'When he wakes up he could turn nasty. That's when I want you here to keep a watch on him.'

'A friend of yours, is he, by the way?'

'He's not a friend of mine. Especially by the way.' Dexter always irritated Blanche when he tried to be clever when she was tired. 'Just get over here, will you?'

'Where's here?'

'The Nowaks' house.' She gave the address.

'What the hell are you doing there?'

Blanche thought for a moment and assembled a smile. 'I'm not quite sure.'

She hung up. Dexter would appear in about half an hour. She staggered over to Urquhart. A thin trickle of blood was

211

darkening below his mouth where her ring had torn the skin. With difficulty she rolled his dead weight first to one side and then the other to search his pockets. From one she extracted the brown exercise book, more creased and folded than when she had first set eyes on it a quarter of an hour or so before. From the other she took the photograph – now with the glass cracked – of Tatyana and Zbigniew Nowak on Westminster Bridge.

With fatigue hanging in lead weights from her shoulders, she remembered the telephone number Robert Urquhart had dialled. To refresh her memory she picked up the telephone, closed her eyes, and recalled how his gloved finger had moved over the first four raised knobs of plastic. He had dialled 373–7. She could recall nothing more. The number echoed back from the past. It seemed familiar: 373 was an Earls Court exchange. She took out her notebook of numbers and addresses on the Graham Mills murder case and found the number she was looking for – Jozef Taczek's ex-directory one, which began with those four numbers. Dexter and she would deliver Urquhart there for his rendezvous at seven o'clock that morning. She had always been suspicious of Taczek, and here was yet more evidence implicating him with people she no longer trusted.

Urquhart had come to the Nowaks' house, Blanche thought, for the same purpose as her – an illegal search for clues about Marek's past activities. He must have managed to purloin a copy of the house key from somewhere and was obviously astounded to find someone already scouring the house, especially her.

The glass in the photo frame still held together but it was difficult to make out the five faces beneath. Someone wanted that photograph badly.

She unfolded Marek's exercise book and began reading the spidery writing where she had been forced to stop. Her eyelids burnt with tiredness.

'Slowly I found out more and more about my marvellous father and though my mother – or perhaps because my mother – cherished his memory like that of nobody else, I found out she had lied to me about him. For he was not killed in a car accident. My father went back to spy for MI6. But in the

212

British Secret Service was a Judas and that British Judas betrayed my father to the Polish Stalinists.'

Marek went on to tell the same story as Tait had narrated to Blanche the day before in the circling car – of a brave man who was betrayed, tortured, castrated and shot.

'It was an old Pole called Poniatowski, now in exile in Paris, who told me the awful, ghastly, horrifying details. He worked for the KGB at the time and he knew everything because he was involved in the secret inquiry that was set up into the "incident", as he called it. Then he worked for the British.'

Blanche nodded. Poniatowski was how Tait must have known.

'Poniatowski told me the Party decided that silence was best. The interrogators were quietly sacked and sent to work in the coal mines. Poniatowski said both of them were now dead.

'I could not have my revenge on those sub-human creatures who actually killed my father, but I swore to myself that I would find the British Judas who had betrayed him and have revenge.'

The chief inspector shivered with an indefinable dread, the fear she always experienced when faced by a hatred that could only be satiated through violence.

'I narrowed the possibilities down to five with the help of Jozef Taczek. Two had died. That left three. But it wasn't Jozef who finally told me the truth – which of the three suspects had taken the pieces of silver. Jozef put me in contact with an old acquaintance of his, who still works for MI5. He told me to keep my links with him secret, and I have, from everyone else. He's called Hugh Capron.'

Capron was Urquhart's boss, the head of K8, the man who had ordered Urquhart not to see her again. Capron was also the fifth face in the photograph that Urquhart had wanted to take from the Nowaks' house.

'We met near the Albert Memorial one afternoon in July. I had to wheedle the information out of him, but Capron said he was the senior case officer on the investigation into Mills, and could confirm absolutely that it was Mills who was the Soviet agent who had betrayed my father. He told me it was scandalous that Mills had gone unpunished. Many lives had been lost because of Mills' treachery but the government was unwilling to do anything about it. As he walked away into the twilight, I felt fired up. Suddenly he walked back to me and said I ought to avenge my father's death and that he could help me. He could even provide me with a gun if I needed one. He gave me a phone number to ring. I was exhilarated. At last I knew the truth about my father's betrayal and death. I had the conclusive evidence I needed. I was to be an avenging angel: Justice, putting right what could not be done through the courts. Mills had murdered more people than just my father. Capron talked about hundreds of lives having been lost. I was wielding the sword of justice, the son seeking revenge on behalf of the father.

'I knew my mother was fond of Mills. He was a kind of platonic lover, an admirer who'd come round once a month and help her live out her fantasies. Tea at the Ritz. Dinner at the Dorchester. He bought her clothes and jewellery. There was never anything between them. Just an old, sentimental friendship. He tried to be nice to me but something rebelled inside me. He seemed – in a way I can't really explain – to be protective towards me and also ashamed of me, for the sake of my mother perhaps.

'It went so smoothly. It started with the phone call asking to meet him. Capron had lent me the gun, and suggested the ploy of telling Graham that I had found new evidence that would clear his name of the allegations that he was a Soviet agent. Clear him! When the evidence that I had confirmed it all! The suspicion in Graham's voice turned to puzzlement and then to excitement. I was surprised by how quickly he agreed to the meeting, as though he had some sort of obligation towards me. And he ended the conversation mysteriously, saying he had something important to tell me too.

'I waited for Graham to arrive on Hampstead Heath – the hunched figure I knew so well tottering down the tarmac path that clings to the side of the hill in the twilight. There was still a little colour left in the sky. I told him to meet me inside an isolated summer house. The seats inside face away from the path and I thought it would be safer like that. I watched him arrive and disappear into the black shadows. I decided not to say anything to him. He knew he was guilty. I just had to kill him. I crept round the side. His mouth dropped open when he saw me standing in front of him, carrying a gun. I ordered him to turn round. He just had time to say, "Marek, you don't know what you're doing." Then the first bullet went into his head. There was less blood than I thought. He made a strangled groan and swayed. I fired again, calm and yet so full of fear, so full of fear I forget how often I fired. He whimpered no more and lay on the concrete, silent.

'That's all the memory I have of what happened. I can't remember what I did with the body next. I know I took a saw with the idea of cutting his head off so that the body couldn't be identified. The newspapers say Mills was half buried under branches and leaves. That must have been it. I was in some kind of trance. The memory of him lying there doesn't worry me, nor the memory of the blood trickling out of his body. I seemed to be watching myself acting in a film. It was all over so quickly. I must have buried him. I ran off and drove away in the car. I had to get rid of the gun as soon as possible. When I looked I found I had not only a gun but also a kitchen knife and a saw. They were covered in blood. I had no idea why I had brought the knife and what I'd used it for. I think I dumped them somewhere. I threw the head weighted down with stones into a canal. I was in a dream.'

Marek must have castrated the corpse to fulfil his revenge, Blanche thought. His father had suffered the humiliation because of Mills' treachery and so the traitor should suffer in the same way. But the memory of what he had done to the corpse was so painful Marek obliterated it from his mind.

'I had done it,' Marek crowed, 'I had killed the man who had betrayed my father, and I was exhilarated. I rushed back from Hampstead Heath, flush with a kind of triumph. At last I had avenged the ghost of my father. I hoped it would stop haunting me. But as I approached home, I was filled with a sense of shame, of uncertainty about how Mum would react when I told her. I decided, as I arrived, to keep the revenge to myself. Mum noticed I was in a rather strange mood. I walked on air for a couple of days. It was euphoria. She asked me straight out once what it was, but I did not want to tell her yet. The secret should be kept as long as possible but, the longer I waited, the harder it was to tell her. I thought first of all that I'd wait for the newspaper reports of the killing and use those as an excuse. But the body wasn't found for over a week. I thought there might be some kind of cover-up. I feared as well that Mills might not be dead after all, that he'd recovered miraculously and decided for some reason not to go to the police. I didn't know. I didn't dare return to the place where I'd killed him because I could easily arouse suspicion. So I had to wait in suspense.

'The good mood evaporated. I sank into gloom and depression. I knew Mum rarely read a newspaper so she wouldn't hear of the killing that way. I telephoned Jozef to tell him what I had done. But his damned lover answered the telephone. The little, promiscuous slut of a cheap – it's no good going on. The number of sleepless nights I've had over that smooth bastard moving in and Jozef kicking me out of bed.'

The chief inspector paused, squinting with concentration. Marek and Jozef must have had an affair. Unclear mysteries came into focus. The Voice had come between them. Blanche understood at last why Marek, in his frenzy of desperation after the first attempt to kill him, had named Jozef Taczek as the killer of Mills. Revenge. His was the jealousy of the jilted lover as well as the clever move of the cornered murderer.

She heard muffled groans from the corner of the room by the television. Urquhart was coming round.

'I was in such a fury I hung up. I had to ring twice more before Jozef answered the phone. He was furious with me for ringing him. He told me I was turning into a jealous old queen but before he slammed the phone down he agreed not to tell Mother about the death. "It'll hit her worse than you think," was what he said. He told me he wasn't planning to see Mum straightaway but that he'd call round in a couple of days to comfort her. When he said that, I knew the pressure was on. I had not considered the possibility that it might be me who would have to tell her of Graham Mills' death. But I had to. I shied away from the prospect. The longer I waited to tell her the harder it became. But in the end, it was Mum who broke into the circle of silence. I wish she hadn't.

'When I came home that night she was still up. Normally she would have gone to bed. She was beside the gas fire, just staring. She told me a policewoman had been round and announced that Graham Mills had been found murdered. I acted very cool and saw my chance. I had been drinking before. I had been trying to pick up a barman in a pub in Hammersmith. I poured myself a huge whisky. I swallowed it in one gulp and almost died of coughing. Then I launched into the confession I should have told the priest – the one I have written down here. I could not look at her while I spoke. I told her that at last I knew what really had happened to my father, her beloved husband, the man who had laid down his life for his country. That she had lied to me, that my father had been betrayed by Mills and that I had avenged her husband's memory. It flowed out in a torrent. I expected her to interrupt. But she didn't. I looked up. She simply sat there, her head sunk down. I wanted her to praise me. Tell me I had done the right thing. After all, I had taken vengeance on her behalf as well as mine. She was the one who had always gone on about what a paragon my father was. Instead she said nothing. Her head sank on to her chin and a kind of blank look misted over her eyes. She sat like that for what seemed like ages while I tramped round the room, nervous and on edge and blabbering with the excitement. All of a sudden, she whined something about me not knowing what I had done and she broke down into tears. I tried my best to comfort her but she was beyond consolation. She rocked backwards and forwards with my head in her lap – for I was in tears as well by then – and moaning. We sat like that for what seemed like hours until we could not cry any longer. About midnight she suddenly got up and, without saying a word, went into her bedroom and slammed the door. I heard her lock it. I knocked and asked, begged, to be let in. I heard nothing inside. She did not seem to be moving around. I could not hear any sobs. I carried on knocking on the door and begging to be let in. I thought of smashing down the door but the idea seemed ridiculous – knocking down the bedroom door of your own mother. Finally I slumped down outside it for a while and went to bed myself. I could not sleep. I rolled and tossed and kept thinking of Mum, and only fell into a doze at dawn. I woke up a couple of hours later. I went to Mum's room. I called out. There was no reply. I called again and a panic came over me. I had to smash the lock.

'She looked so peaceful. Her eyes, her beautiful eyes, were wide open, staring up at the ceiling. There was no note. She had left me with nothing. Nothing. Not a word of gratefulness and not a word of forgiveness and not a word of love. Nothing. And I had killed her. I only wish I had the courage to do the same as her. Mary, Mother of God, please forgive me. Help me in my hour of need.'

The manuscript finished at that point. Marek must have been interrupted or decided his confession was over. Blanche sat slumped in the armchair, arms, legs and shoulders aching. Marek had confessed to the murder of Mills. He had carried out the killing. There was no doubt of that now. Marek had been led to Graham Mills partly by his former lover, Taczek, but the conclusive evidence was provided only by the shadowy Hugh Capron. Capron had even provided the gun that had been fished from the pond on the heath. People in the secret services wanted Graham Mills dead and Marek was a tool that came conveniently to hand.

If Marek was right, Tatyana had taken her own life less as a result of the news of the murder Blanche had brought, than of her son's dreadful confession. But something still troubled the chief inspector. Mrs Nowak had impressed her as a strong woman, a woman inclined to fantasy perhaps, but resilient and not inclined to despair. Blanche could imagine her weeping with her son over his confession but, like Marek, she was a little puzzled that Tatyana had not shown even a spark of joy at the revenge he had taken. A sense of betrayal was stamped on all her words and gestures when the chief inspector spoke to her, betrayal of herself, her husband and of Poland. Yet when the vengeance was exacted she showed no joy. An element was still missing from the equation of Tatyana's suicide and Blanche was more convinced than ever that Taczek possessed it. He knew Marek – more intimately than she had ever imagined. He knew Tatyana. He knew Mills. He knew Capron. All four were silent. Only he could speak.

Urquhart's muffled groans became more frantic. She translated his grunts to mean he wanted to talk to her. His blue eyes implored her to take off the gag. She enjoyed watching him wriggle. She untied the knots and removed the saliva-sodden strip of cushion covering from his mouth. Urquhart inhaled deeply and flexed his firm jaw. Neither of them said anything. They looked at each other warily, circling for an opening remark.

'So Jozef Taczek will be waiting at seven o'clock for the exercise book and photo, will he?' she asked finally.

Urquhart squirmed on the carpet, stared at her in confusion for a second, and then nodded. She found herself enjoying the sight of his embarrassment and frantic need to buy thinking time. 'Look, Blanche, you've got to let me go. You don't know what you're doing.'

'I'm getting fed up with people telling me that, because I think at last I do know what I'm doing. That's why you're tied up on the floor and I'm aiming a gun at you.'

'Just untie me and let me go. Please.' He tried to look full of rakish charm by pulling on a weak smile.

She snorted with nervous laughter. Urquhart said nothing. It looked as though he was sulking. 'Why don't you tell me who you really work for? Did someone send you to go through Marek's things, or was it you who made the decision?'

His face was pale, his forehead puckered with apprehension. He gripped and released his fists again and again, seething with anger, frustration and despair. It must have been like this watching a man being broken on the rack, Blanche thought. 'I want to tell you,' he gasped. 'I want to tell you the truth. But if I do, it's the end of me. There'll be no escape. I'll be trapped.'

'What do you mean trapped? What the hell *are* you involved in?'

Urquhart turned his head away. She realised she was gripping the gun with two hands and had trained it on his chest, as if she expected him to leap up at any moment and lunge at her. She slipped the safety catch into place and deposited the gun on the coffee table beside her. The back of her throat rasped as if someone had been scraping it with a razor blade: she needed a drink. There was a full drinks cupboard in the corner. As she swilled out a whisky, she caught the burning, envious eyes of her captive.

'Please,' he groaned.

She took the gun and sat down in the armchair at Urquhart's head. 'You can have a swig for every secret you tell me.'

He wetted his lips in a theatrical way and a glimmer of humour flickered in his eyes. Then the earnest, sad look returned. 'What if I tell you the whole truth? What do I get for that?'

She sighed. 'I don't think you know it. MI5 hasn't *let* you know it. Besides, you have problems yourself sorting out lies from the truth.'

Urquhart smiled: a line of white teeth, as classical and regular as the white columns of a Greek temple. The curling mane of blond hair, she noticed, had a wisp of baldness at the front, suggesting experience and gentleness. He really was remarkably handsome, even when he was trussed up like a turkey ready for Christmas. The smile melted into a chuckle.

'Why did you tell me Mills was a KGB agent, when he wasn't?' she asked.

'Who's so sure he was not?'

She took a provocative gulp of scotch, savouring the aroma of burnt peat. The helpless man on the floor looked up greedily. 'A man called Tait,' she said. A crease of apprehension tucked itself in his forehead. 'Is that why your boss, Capron, gave Marek Nowak a gun to murder Mills?'

'Is that what Tait told you?' He tried to hide his surprise by mumbling in a drawl.

'The whole story's in that exercise book I found.'

He thought for a moment. 'Oh God,' Urquhart sighed and he turned his head away from her. 'We're done for.'

'Who?'

He lay in silence for a moment, gazing at the louring prints of eagles on the wall. 'Me at any rate. A traitor. A KGB spy.' He waited to harness his thoughts. He looked up and sought Blanche's reaction to his confession.

She was numb. She had guessed Robert and others were manipulating her as a chess piece in a game whose rules and ultimate aim were a mystery. But only now did she have confirmation of the full extent of her betrayal by Urquhart. The way he had misled her, Blanche thought, was heinous enough if his loyalty had lain with the same country. But if Urquhart were speaking the truth at last – and she wondered whether yet another web of deception was being woven about her – he had forged her into an unwitting tool of the Soviet Union. The numbness was inched away by a mixture of anger and sorrow.

'Do you want that drink now?' she asked, the sorrow predominating.

He was motionless. She poured out a generous measure of malt whisky and positioned the glass in front of his nose. Urquhart's eyes were closed, the lashes like black feathers. The firm lips pouted in a sulk. His nostrils quivered when they caught the perfume of the scotch. One blue eye opened and stared at her without blinking. She rolled him on to his shoulder and two cornflowers stared at her. She flushed. 'Why did you do it?'

He sighed, as if the answer were much too complex for words. 'Thatcher, I suppose. God, how I hate that woman.' She slipped her left arm behind his head to cradle it while her right hand brought the whisky to his mouth. 'I've seen my own country laid waste and no one seeming to care. The rich getting fatter and sleeker. The poor getting thinner and dirtier. No one seemed able to stand up to her, to dent her. So I thought I would. In my own wee way.' He paused to think, staring at her. 'Also, help Gorbachev a bit. I've got more time for him than either our lot or the Americans,' he added bitterly. Blanche listened and said nothing. A crackling silence tiptoed round the room. His lips sucked eagerly at the golden liquid. 'I lost hope, I suppose. Lost hope in my country. Because it's being betrayed by the people who are meant to govern it. I became an exile in my own land.'

Urquhart smiled, his eyes chiselling into hers with hypnotic intensity. 'I'll have a lot of time to go back over the past in the coming years, I suppose, wonder whether I made the right choices at the right time.' He arched his neck upwards and pressed his lips against hers. His earthy sweetness filled her nostrils. 'I love you, Blanche. Let me go, please. Let me go,' he murmured.

The front doorbell rang. Dexter had arrived.

She scrutinised his face, as though he were a stranger. Then Blanche – with a cool and deliberate swing – threw the remnants of the whisky over it.

'The magic's stopped working,' she hissed, as she retied the gag. 'You've told so many lies, the truth isn't enough any more.'

Chapter 22

When they left Blanche's flat at half past six the sky was an intense, brooding blue. The wind had died and the almost bare sycamore trees along the road sighed in expectation of the dawn. The rain had cleared, leaving only a cloud shaped like a mackerel skeleton picked clean by scavengers. The silver arrow of an early morning jet glided westwards to land at Heathrow. The chief inspector shivered as they walked the few yards to the car, because the air was so damp and heavy. It was like swimming through cold treacle. Drops of moisture hung from the tips of the bare branches, swelled until the surface tension could no longer contain them, and fell with a scarcely perceptible pat on to the pavement. A sodden thrush croaked out the first few notes of a premature dawn chorus but lapsed back into silence when no other birds bothered to take up the refrain. Urquhart shuffled along beside Dexter, his right wrist handcuffed to the sergeant's left, the revolver thrust into his rib cage. The sergeant knew he was committing a firearms offence but was too tired to care. Blanche regretted once again that Dexter and she had only one gun between them that morning. She felt in her pocket and fingered for comfort the kitchen knife wrapped in a tea cloth.

Blanche cut through the empty backstreets, bejewelled with puddles, and they were soon on the A4 into central London. Her eyeballs felt as if they were stewing in vinegar, the lids drawn irresistibly to each other. Her bones throbbed with exhaustion and an aeroplane buzzed round inside her skull dropping cluster bombs of pain.

They turned right into the Earls Court Road. Plastic bags and cardboard boxes stood on the kerbs outside the restaurants waiting to be collected, each with a dribble of black liquid flowing to the gutter. An old man with a large red nose shuffled along holding a Marks and Spencer carrier bag.

Blanche drove into the square and parked about fifty yards from Taczek's flat. There was a flush of peach in the east where the sun was waiting to rise. The trees knotted the pale sky into their network of black branches, their tops just brushed by the diffuse, pre-dawn light. The light did nothing to cheer the heart. It etched the attic roofs, the bedraggled roof gardens and balconies, the disused chimney pots with cold clarity. Moss was already growing on the pavement on the side of the square where they were: the sun would not touch it for another five months. Odd branches, snapped off by the strong winds the night before, lay scattered on the wet road, their wounds white against the black tarmac. Urquhart stirred. He reminded Blanche of a deer that has scented the approach of the hunters and must flee or die.

A custard-yellow British Telecom van drew up five doors down from Taczek's flat. Two engineers jumped out and began dismantling a junction box set back from the road with uncharacteristic energy. The chief inspector wished they had not come. She wanted as few people about as possible. The curtains of Taczek's flat were still drawn tight. One telephone engineer glanced at her suspiciously when he saw her looking there, so she gave him a benign nod.

Her plan was risky. It depended on Urquhart's cooperation. He had looked pale and nervous but nodded when she told him what she wanted him to do. He was obviously as keen to talk to Taczek as she was. It was five minutes to seven. She nodded to Dexter.

They walked swiftly down the road, Dexter frogmarching Urquhart, with Blanche in front, the click of their footsteps mingling with the chattering of a few tone-deaf sparrows and the distant rumble of the city. A young man – sporting a grey wool overcoat, briefcase and the worried look of the ambitious – clattered down the steps of one house and pretended to ignore them. He ostentatiously revved up his malachite-green BMW and sped away with a squeal of rubber and puff of exhaust. In a moment they were under the portico of the house and hidden from view. She pressed the buzzer and waited. It was two minutes past seven.

The answerphone exploded into a hum of static. 'Hello?' She looked at Urquhart and nodded. 'Hello?' The voice was not Taczek's.

223

'It's me,' whispered the Scotsman. 'Robert.'

The buzzer sounded. They climbed the steps up to the flat. Blanche pulled out the kitchen knife and a ball of Plasticine. She flattened the sticky globe over the fish-eye lens on the door and then knocked. Someone inside strode up and tried to look out through the lens. Puzzled at seeing only black, he asked through the door sharply, 'Is that you, Robert?'

She held her breath. Dexter ran his tongue over his lips and glared at Urquhart, stabbing him in the ribs with the gun.

'Yes. It's me,' he said finally.

A bolt was laboriously drawn back and the lock turned. As soon as the door moved the chief inspector threw her full weight against it and tumbled inside. The door caught the man by it and sent him reeling back into the room. Jozef Taczek was sitting in an armchair and jerked upright when she rushed in flailing the knife. He stood motionless and open-mouthed. The other man edged back towards the wall, watching her knife with alarm. She thought at first she had never seen him before. He was in his late fifties, quite tall and stocky, with a long, thin face. His nose and eyes were pinched and suspicious. The pair of spectacles he wore was so anti-quated they could have been there from birth: black, plastic uppers with wire curves beneath. Dexter came in behind her and kicked the door shut. Urquhart and the man in the antiquated spectacles exchanged worried glances.

'I'm afraid you m,m,must be making some mistake . . .' he began coolly, despite the stutter.

She advanced a couple of steps and flashed the kitchen knife towards the man's belly. 'What's your name?'

'What's yours?' he replied with a curl of the lip. 'What are you doing here?'

His coolness irritated her. It was the coolness and superiority of all those she had met in the previous few months, people who held secrets and were not willing to share them. She wanted to slap his face and send those stupid spectacles flying on to Taczek's pile carpet. Instead she imagined the face without the spectacles, and remembered a fresh-faced young man lounging on Westminster Bridge with the Nowaks and Taczek.

'You're Capron, aren't you? Hugh Capron?'

He looked hard at her. 'What if I am?'

'I've come to arrest you. First, on a charge of murder. It was you who gave the gun to Marek Nowak that he used to kill Graham Mills.'

His suntanned face wobbled like a jelly. 'Rubbish,' he snorted and stepped towards her. She jerked the knife at him and he stopped.

Hypotheses raced through Blanche's mind. And then, suddenly, she understood. Capron was the missing figure in the equation of deceit. 'It's not rubbish. It's why you sent Urquhart round to Nowak's house last night to check whether there was anything incriminating. First that old photograph you didn't know about until I talked about it to Robert. But also the confession written by Marek. You wanted Mills dead and Marek appeared right on cue to be your assassin.' Near the door against the wall were two suitcases. Capron was dressed as though he was going on a business trip, in a tweed jacket, grey flannels, white shirt and tie. He breathed out deeply and clenched his fists. 'I'm arresting all three of you, Taczek, Capron and Urquhart, on a charge of espionage.'

Silence hovered in the air like a hummingbird. Without pulling his brown beads of eyes from her face, Capron murmured across her, 'What happened, Robert?'

'She knocked me out.' He managed to say no more before Dexter jerked the gun into his ribs and hissed at him to shut up.

Taczek regained his composure and ability to speak. His voice was querulous and confused. 'Is this true, Hugh – what the policewoman says – that you supplied the gun to kill Graham?'

Capron ignored him and continued to stare at the chief inspector.

Taczek prodded at his spectacles and gesticulated wildly with his hands. He began to shout. 'Is it true, Hugh?' He stepped towards Capron to attract attention. 'You were only meant to tell Marek who the traitor was – not organise a murder. Did you give him the gun? Tell me.' He ended a couple of feet from Capron. In his slippered feet and paisley-patterned dressing gown, Blanche found him vaguely ridiculous. His final cry was one of betrayal, whose echoes were smothered in the thick folds of the Liberty curtains. 'Tell me!'

They were all suddenly aware of another presence in the room: the Voice had lolled his way from the bedroom like a drunken kitten. He yawned and ran a hand through his skein of black hair. He was naked. 'I got woken up by all the noise,' the Voice whimpered. 'So I came to see what it was all about.'

'Go back to bed!' snapped the Pole.

The Voice swung his hips provocatively. 'Only when you come with me.'

'Cover yourself up for God's sake, boy. You've no sense of decency.'

The Voice flushed with anger. 'What do you mean – no sense of decency? I've got more decency than you –'

Taczek spun round in a fury. His features were creased like a bundle of intestines. 'Get out! I don't want you here. Get out, you stupid fool! Get out!'

The Voice lost his confidence, pouted and scampered back into the bedroom, slamming the door behind him. A fraction of a second too late, Blanche saw Capron draw a gun from the inside of his jacket. Before Dexter or Blanche had time to react, he fired two shots. Dexter's revolver lolled in his hand. He crumpled to the floor, clawing at his white shirt, blood oozing between his fingers. By the time she realised the danger and was close enough to strike at Capron, it was too late: she was staring at the same sight as a few hours before, the black, round barrel of a gun pointed at her chest. She threw the knife to one corner. While Dexter writhed on the carpet, Urquhart kicked the revolver free from his hand. Above Dexter's hoarse breathing the buzzer on the door sounded.

'That's him now!' said Urquhart.

Capron rifled through the wounded man's pockets for the keys to Urquhart's handcuffs. He could not find them straightaway and started to slap Dexter's face in irritation. 'What have you done with them, you black bastard! Where are the fucking keys?'

'Leave him, for Christ's sake,' Blanche screamed. She lunged at Capron but only looked into the gun barrel, which had already lost its metallic chill through firing two bullets into the sergeant.

Capron found the keys and freed Urquhart. He lumbered menacingly towards the detective. 'Now throw across what you found in the Nowaks' house last night.'

'She's not that stupid,' Urquhart interrupted. 'She hid them in her house somewhere. Let's just get out of here for Chrissake.'

Capron glanced across, donned a weary smile and nodded.

'The least you can do,' Blanche said acidly, 'is call an ambulance.'

Urquhart's colleague was motionless, his voice artificially calm. 'You can do that when we've gone.'

'But he might die.'

Capron shrugged his shoulders.

Taczek stared about him in amazement, like a figure in Second World War archive film emerging from the bombed ruins of his house. He had lost all sense of orientation. The sound of petulant sobbing, amplified for theatrical effect, penetrated the bedroom door. Taczek ignored it: he threw his spectacles on to the sofa and dabbed at the tears that glittered on his cheeks. 'You bastard, Hugh,' he sobbed. 'All these years I've known you, you've worked for *them*.' He spat out the last word as if it were pus. The ring of conspiracy binding Capron and Urquhart was clear and there was no room in the circle for Jozef Taczek.

The buzzer on the door rang again in two brief bursts, demanding attention. Capron ordered Taczek and Blanche to carry Dexter into the bedroom. The door was locked behind them. The policewoman heard movement in the reception room, footsteps, rustling, and the flat door slamming with a sullen finality.

The Voice redoubled his whimpering when he realised Jozef was in the room, and the Pole started to comfort his lover with soft words of affection. As Blanche covered Dexter with a luxurious silk eiderdown pulled from the bed, guilt seeped through her. He had been hit twice – once in the arm and once in the stomach. Dexter's face shimmered with sweat and twitched with the occasional spasm of pain. His eyelids were glued down tight against the pain. She had led him into this trap and now both of them stood to be sacked, even prosecuted. She hurled herself against the door in anger and frustration, but it only gave way when she dragged Taczek away from his lover and·they smashed down the frame together. Jozef returned to give solace to his brat.

Blanche heard sirens wailing in the streets but had no time to investigate why. She tried to call for an ambulance but the telephone had been ripped from its socket. An explosion flashed and smoke swirled into the room from the flat door. Blanche dropped, choking, to the carpet and the fog solidified into the two telephone engineers she had seen outside and two policemen dressed in flak jackets. They stood in the identical pose taught by the police firearms training course, feet apart for greater stability with both hands supporting the gun. Following up behind was a sprightly and cocky figure: Inspector Dickinson of Special Branch.

'I was told you were here,' he said with a swaggering sneer.

She started to raise herself from the carpet, smearing Dexter's blood on the pile.

'Stay down there,' he shouted. 'Don't move 'til I tell you.'

She hesitated and then hauled herself up.

'Don't move!' he ordered again.

She slumped in an armchair, too tired to care, mumbling something about an ambulance. Two more uniformed policemen arrived and carried her down the stairs. She was too exhausted to resist. All she wanted to do was sleep. Outside the flat a line of police cars was drawn up, the occupants scurrying about to stop the curious coming out of their houses. At the far end of the square she glimpsed the lurid, revolving light of an ambulance among a chaotic knot of cars. She was handed over to two burly men in plain clothes, who looked as though they were waiting for her. They said nothing and she was too tired to speak.

She dozed off on the back seat, lifting an eyelid to register their progress northwards through the imposing mansions of Holland Park, past the black-tiled bleakness of Kensal Rise, and on to the crowded tarmac of the North Circular. With each successive vignette the flush of peach in the east grew stronger until it bleached the sky with wintry sunlight. Blanche remembered one ray catching the grey bristles on the driver's neck before the slush of the tyres, the hum of the engine and the stifling air from the car heater sent her back to sleep.

She was shaken awake. They had parked outside a house in a street of detached thirties villas with wide bay windows. Most were pebbledashed and oozed an air of prosperity. A young mother in scarlet wellington boots walked by, pushing her son in a tripper. The house was partially hidden behind an ill-kempt privet hedge and two overgrown japonicas. The curtains upstairs were drawn completely, those downstairs had been opened a few feet to allow in shafts of the morning light. The house looked deserted and in dire need of a coat of paint, but when one of the minders knocked on the front door with a gloved fist it was opened almost immediately by a middle-aged woman in twinset and pearls. She showed Blanche into the front room and asked if she wanted a cup of tea. She said no, and promptly fell asleep on the sofa.

Chapter 23

'Thank you,' he said, as the grey-haired woman in twinset and pearls left the room and closed the door behind her as if it were made of thin ice. Blanche shut her eyes again. The grumble of the central heating was counterpointed by an irregular tapping as the water gurgled through the pipes. A train rattled across an embankment somewhere in the distance. She half opened one eye. Tait, who had just spoken, was the only other person in the room.

'Good evening, Chief Inspector. I'm sorry I wasn't able to see you earlier but it has been a busy day, what with one thing and another . . .'

His thick lips chuckled over the non-existent joke he had just made, revealing a regular set of yellowish teeth. She was still lying on the sofa facing the bay window. Someone had thrown a blanket over Blanche and placed a cup of tea before her. The curtains – cream nylon with a sprinkling of corn-flowers that reminded her with a sad start of Urquhart's eyes – had been drawn against the chill night. The carpet was a symphony of lilac whorls and umber curlicues with strategically placed trills of lemon yellow. Two standard lamps played their gentle light on the room. Around the pipes of the radiators, where they emerged from the walls, were circles of pink plaster: they had been recently installed and there had been no time, or money, to redecorate. Tait sensed her reaction. 'It's hardly Chatsworth or Castle Howard. The Prime Minister likes us – but not to the extent of giving us a blank cheque. We have to take our safe houses as we find them.'

He suddenly whipped a silk handkerchief out of his breast pocket and snorted. 'Haven't had a cold for years,' he mumbled. 'When we were married twenty-two years ago, my wife told me to take a vitamin pill and cod liver oil every day, and I did. During that time I never had a cold. Then I forgot two mornings on the trot last week and suddenly I'm struck down.'

He blew his nose again with a flourish. 'It's all a stinking mess really,' Tait added abruptly, as if he were referring to the cold. 'There's been a string of betrayals, one feeding on another.' A podgy hand, like a kipper, flapped at his bow tie with irritation. The armchair, as solid and well fleshed as the person it held, creaked as the MI5 man leant towards her. His tone became cold and formal. 'I've come to ask you some questions.'

Blanche was so disoriented she had forgotten Dexter. She had left him fifteen hours ago lying in a pool of his own blood and vomit. Tait told her, with the glazed look of boredom in his eyes, that Dexter was recovering in hospital after an operation. She asked about Urquhart and Capron.

Tait shuffled his weight in his armchair and stroked his beard. Blanche found she was tense and watchful with Tait: his rotundity and tweediness were a source of uncertainty rather than comfort. She respected him but did not trust him. She trusted no one any more.

His colourless eyes appraised her. 'The most satisfactory solution would have been to catch them both. But we were unlucky.'

'You mean one of them got away,' she flared, angry at the incompetence of Special Branch.

'I didn't mean that,' replied the MI5 man. 'I should have said catch them both *alive*. You see, their driver swerved to avoid a road block and smashed into a couple of parked cars at the end of the square. The driver was knocked unconscious. Capron and Urquhart scrambled out. Capron understood what was happening straightaway and gave himself up. Urquhart, on the other hand, took out a gun and made a run for it along the pavement. He managed to wound a Special Branch chap before he was brought down by a bullet in the leg. He fell between two cars and we couldn't see him any more.'

Tait's voice quavered with irritation: he was still angry, very angry because things had not worked out as he planned, but determined not to show it. 'A couple of seconds later we heard a shot from where he was lying. The stupid man had killed himself.' He flapped his hand at his bow tie to ensure it was square. It was askew and kept returning to that habitual angle. 'I hate loose ends. I wanted Urquhart badly. I needed to debrief him. Your . . . intervention certainly messed things up. What on earth were you doing there anyway? Come to arrest Capron yourself, had you?' he added with the trace of a sneer.

She smiled to defuse the tension and sat upright on the sofa. 'As a matter of fact, I did arrest him. For espionage, along with Urquhart and Taczek. But having slept on it, I realise I made a mistake with Taczek. He's never spied for the KGB.'

Tait sniffed and dabbed at his blocked nose with his handkerchief. He wanted to change the subject and regain the initiative. 'Anyway, that's why I came to see you: to find out why you were there.'

It was time for Blanche to change the subject. She knew she was in a feeble position, possibly facing dismissal or worse, and needed to discover whether she had any weapons to fight back. 'Did you find the brown exercise book and the photo, by the way?'

A quiver of interest passed across the MI5 man's placid face. 'The brown exercise book and photo?'

Blanche paused. Marek's brown exercise book and the photograph, hidden in her wardrobe at home, were her best protection. 'Hasn't Capron mentioned them in interrogation?' she asked with false innocence.

Tait paused. For a second too long. Blanche knew she was not completely defenceless. 'Oh, of course he has. But we need your account too.'

'What *has* Capron said so far, by the way?'

Tait folded his fleshy hands together again over his bulging stomach like a closing flower. The detective waited for another question about the exercise book and photo. But Tait did not ask it. 'Please don't forget your tea, Chief Inspector. It's getting cold.'

To ask immediately would have exposed his vulnerability, Blanche knew, and Tait understood how dangerous it was to expose a weakness at the beginning of an interrogation. She sipped from the edge of the cup. The tea *was* cold. It had a cracked, oily skin: a sure sign that the beverage had been brewed with a tea bag.

'I am as much interested,' Tait went on, 'in what you have to say about young Robert Urquhart as about Capron. Did he confess to you – explain his motives for spying for the Russians, for example?'

She took another sip of tea. It was so awful she abandoned it. 'Why should I tell you?'

He lifted his head back so that a double chin came into view, and narrowed his eyes. 'It's a matter of national security. Besides, you face a number of disciplinary and criminal charges.' He counted off the charges on the fingers of his left hand. 'You arrested Jozef Taczek without proper evidence. You were told by your senior officer to stop work on the Mills case and you deliberately flouted his orders. You ruined a carefully planned Special Branch operation.' He did not mention the illegal search of the Nowaks' house, Blanche reflected, because he had no means of knowing about it – except Capron, who probably had not talked. Tait unsheathed his yellow teeth. Blanche wondered whether their perfection was because they were false. 'You really ought to tell me everything you know.'

'I will.'

The MI5 officer smiled with surprise at her pliability. His mouth began to phrase a question.

'On three conditions.' His lips froze. 'First, that I'm given immunity from any criminal or disciplinary charges. Second, that in exchange for me answering your questions, you answer mine.' A flurry of rain whisked against the window. Away in the distance another train rattled through the night. 'And thirdly, you switch off and wipe all the tape that's been recording this conversation.' Blanche had no choice but to strike boldly. Having uncovered areas that Tait was ignorant about, she had to exploit them mercilessly. She had to bargain her route out of trouble.

The chief inspector had only guessed at the tape recording, but when she mentioned it, the spycatcher compressed his lips into a prim line. Blanche had been right. 'I don't think you quite understand your position.'

'Oh, I understand it only too well. You see I was called in to investigate a murder, the murder of a former MI6 agent called Graham Mills. It seems a long time ago now. That long,

233

hot summer. It was my duty as a police officer to find the killer. And, in the end, I have.' The discs of Tait's pale grey eyes did not blink. He sat motionless, as though meditating, pretending nothing of this was new. 'Obstructions were put in my way. I'm due an explanation as much as you think you are.'

Capron must have undergone interrogations all day but, Blanche guessed, decided not to talk. He was probably hoping for an offer of immunity from prosecution in exchange for a confession. Although he had tried not to show it, Tait needed the chief inspector to talk, to provide him with evidence to trap Capron.

Tait thrummed his fingers on the arms of his chair. The fingers were surprisingly thin and delicate to protrude from such a well-fleshed body.

She leant back in the sofa. She was not going to be recorded on tape as saying that she possessed invaluable written evidence against Capron or would leak the whole story to the newspapers if Tait refused her terms. Whatever else he was, the policewoman knew Tait was clever, very clever. She trusted he would weigh this possibility in the balance. She shrugged her shoulders and tried to guess where the microphone had been hidden. In the light fitting? In the coffee table? Behind the Gauguin print on the wall? She had no idea. The bugs used by the Force's Criminal Intelligence Branch were sophisticated enough yet MI5 were sure to have even more sensitive technology. Blanche spoke out for the benefit of her concealed listeners. 'Whatever happens, I will of course offer my full cooperation to the Security Service and wouldn't dream of breaching the Official Secrets Act.'

Tait flashed his yellow teeth again. By now, she was convinced they were false. The MI5 man blew his nose again before he heaved himself up with a puff and ambled over on his stubby legs to the bay window. The spy pulled the curtains apart and glanced outside as if he wanted to consult the stars before deciding. Whatever he saw there gave Tait inspiration, for he waddled over to the door and picked up his coat from a chair. He had received and understood the message. 'I think we could do with a breath of fresh air, Chief Inspector. It's stopped raining.'

Chapter 24

Tait had lied. It *was* still raining. Pellets of water bit into their skin like deep-frozen mosquitoes. The MI5 case officer tugged his trilby down against the wind and adjusted his scarf as they wandered along the pavement. 'Zbigniew Nowak was betrayed first,' he began wearily. 'Not by Mills, mind, as you found out. Nowak was betrayed by a young man called Hugh Capron.'

The road was deserted, the street lamps reflected in the globules of water on the roofs of the cars. In their sulphurous light the lines of suburban houses with their sodden, trimmed gardens looked menacing and alien. In the lulls between the gusts of wind, the steady dribble of water tinkled from the gutter into the drains.

'Capron was recruited in the late forties,' the MI5 man continued. 'It was the start of the Cold War. Liberals were disgusted with the way the West suddenly stopped cooperation with Stalin. Capron was then Mills' number five in the Soviet-bloc department of MI6 and one of the department's jobs was to run covert operations against the new communist regimes. Estonia. Lithuania. Hungary. Albania. Poland.' The spy spoke like a lecturer, repeating a talk he had given too many times before. He ambled along, ponderously transferring his weight from one leg to the other, as if each movement required careful calculation. Blanche was reminded of a brontosaurus lumbering through a primeval swamp. 'Capron leaked details of some operations to the KGB, and he saw a chance in Mills to cover his tracks. One of the operations that he betrayed was Zbigniew Nowak's return to Poland. You know all about the false suspicions that fell on Mills as a result.'

Tait wanted to tell someone the secrets he held, flaunt his knowledge of the dark side of the state. All he had lacked until that night was a listener. Now he had one, and an excuse – satisfactory at least to his own mind – to reveal what he had learnt. His face maintained an expression of detached contentment. The MI5 man stopped suddenly and pursed his lips, as though he had divined Blanche's thoughts. He studied his shoes but needed to crane forward to do it because of his paunch. 'I don't know why I'm telling you all this. It's most unorthodox, this exchange of information.' He looked at her, as though seeking commiseration.

'What's more orthodox than the laws of the market?' She shrugged her shoulders. She wished Tait would walk faster. Chill water was seeping through the soles of her shoes and her feet were cold. 'I have information to sell and you want to buy it.'

'That's what we're always being told, I suppose,' murmured the spy with a sly smile. 'Obey the laws of the market and all will be well.' He began walking again, cursing that he had not bothered to put his wellington boots on before coming out. He said he always carried them in the boot of the car in case it turned wet. 'To discredit Mills, Capron used information partly furnished by the KGB. They hoped – rightly as it turned out – that Capron would eventually take over from Mills at the top of the Soviet-bloc department.'

They reached the curve at the bottom of the road and she spotted a wintry profile on the corner by a post box: a Special Branch man. She twisted round and saw another one thirty yards behind. Their footsteps had been muffled by the wind and rain. Tait glanced behind after her and shrugged apologetically. 'The laws of the market, I'm afraid, Chief Inspector. Information is valuable, so protect anyone who's got some that you want.'

They walked on a little, past the beckoning lights of a pub whose hubbub spilt on to the road when a young couple emerged. Further on was a novelty shop and a newsagent's, which were both closed. They finally paused outside 'The Continental Supermarket'. It was empty except for a beautiful Asian girl in a saree who sat by the till, eyes unfocused, lost in her daydreams.

'Mills finally resigned in 1962, didn't he?' Blanche asked.

'Yes. He harboured a grudge against Capron that rankled for the rest of his life.'

'Why didn't he try and fight back against all these allegations?'

'He did. Sour grapes, they said, tossed at Capron, who was a tried and tested officer, by an unreliable one. Everyone – except Mills – liked Capron and thought he had a safe pair of hands. So Mills resigned and Capron stayed. He drifted up the hierarchy and then in the seventies Capron transferred across from MI6 to MI5. There he stagnated, doing immense damage to us of course, but stagnating.'

'Perhaps he was burnt out,' the chief inspector commented.

'Perhaps,' Tait sniffed with irritation. He did not like being interrupted. 'Anyway, the KGB knew Capron's retirement was coming closer all the time. They told him to keep his eyes peeled for a replacement. Some time in 1980 Capron spotted a possible new recruit who'd just joined his department.'

'Urquhart?' she said.

He nodded. 'It was a clever move. Capron wanted to ensure his succession. Pass the torch from the generation of Philby and Maclean to the young men of the eighties and nineties. It almost worked. Urquhart was well regarded.' Tait stopped and fussed with his gloves. It was a typical gesture: a perfectionist's prissiness. 'Did Urquhart ever say anything to you in detail, by the way, give any . . . hint?'

She did not want to answer the question straightaway. She was not going to be smothered in the patronising embrace of Tait's words and unload any of her cargo of information yet. 'You sound almost as if you admire Capron.'

They had stopped again outside a shop selling bric-à-brac. The MI5 man leant forward so that his nose was almost against the glass and raised a gloved hand above his eyes to kill the reflection. 'I *do* admire him. As one professional looking at another. Makes Philby look like an amateur. A superb dissembler.' Tait hissed out the sibilants, luxuriating in the word. He stared intently through the glass for a moment and then walked on, clasping his hands behind his back. 'As only, I suppose, we English can be. We hide our real feelings in ordinary life, so it becomes second nature to show false ones when we're spies.'

Tait sniffed good-humouredly at his own cleverness. 'By the way, you didn't answer my question. Did Urquhart ever give any hint . . . about why he went over?'

They turned back into the road where the safe house was.

237

The two Special Branch men still provided a shadowy escort. 'He was angry and disillusioned,' was all she could murmur, aware of the inadequacy of the reply.

'Angry and disillusioned about what?' said Tait, spreading his pianist's fingers in a gesture of incomprehension. 'Sex? Money?'

She spoke to herself more than to Tait, trying to explain for her own benefit why he had betrayed his country. 'Inequality. Poverty. Thatcher. Elected dictatorship.' She looked up and found Tait scrutinising her. 'He came from Scotland, remember. He saw his own country and the north laid waste. And no one seemed able to fight back. So he did.'

The MI5 man stroked his goatee beard. 'So he was a Scots commie?' said Tait dismissively, nodding at his own perspicacity. 'There's a long tradition of it up there. Working-class bolshevism. Clydesiders.' Tait plucked a stray hair from the arm of his jacket. He wanted to tidy Urquhart up, package and despatch him in his report for the MI5 Registry.

'But none of those Scottish communists became KGB spies –'

Tait's eyes sparkled querulously. He had assembled his explanation and brooked no challenges to it. '– you never know with the Scots.'

'In England we seem to have recruited them specifically.'

'Water under the bridge, Chief Inspector. Things are different now,' countered her companion jovially. 'New recruitment procedures. Different atmosphere. No one could have told that Urquhart was unreliable when he was recruited.'

She could not be bothered to prick the balloon of Tait's self-satisfaction. Urquhart, she knew, was a novel sort of British spy, a spy of her generation. Not a son of the rolling downs of the south, the public schools and Oxbridge, who betrayed the ruling class from which he had sprung out of a sense of mischief and idealism. Urquhart was a son of the consensus that ruled for almost forty years after the war – the consensus of sympathy for the poor, of the National Health Service, of state schools, of giving the working class what they should have rather than what they want, of profit not being the ultimate arbiter, of conciliatory government. He joined MI5 to support that consensus and then saw it levered to one

238

side. He had wormed his way up through one of those midden heaps of the Old World that had been left to rot by governments who were powerless to stop the decay. When he had emerged at the top and sniffed clean air, he had found himself charged in MI5 with sustaining a government he despised. There were other Urquharts, she was sure, burrowing away as she talked to Tait in the featureless London suburbs that October night. They were frustrated fools, Blanche believed, but there was some holiness in their foolishness.

Capron was a different sort of spy from a different generation. Tait's generation. 'If Capron was such a professional how come you caught him?' she asked.

Tait started, as if shaken out of a dream. 'It goes back to that KGB man I mentioned to you in the car. "Nikolai". Do you recall? The one who met Mills a few times in Moscow?' He glanced at her with his pale grey eyes to confirm she had remembered. There was a velvety note in his voice that suggested he did not necessarily expect her to, and that he was used to dealing with fools. She nodded.

'"Nikolai", it seems, was charmed by Mills. Trusted him implicitly, even after just a couple of evenings together. Anyway, "Nikolai" became increasingly fed up with the Soviet Union. He had a couple of foreign postings and acquired a taste for the good life. He decided to defect. So in the early seventies he approached the British. And because personal contacts matter in this business as in no other, he asked for Graham Mills by name.'

Tait paused to pull out his handkerchief. 'No one else would do, he said. Only Mills. MI6 was very alarmed. Here was a potential defector of the very highest level, a colonel in the KGB, and he wanted to speak to a man who'd been forced to resign from the Service, under suspicion of having been a Soviet agent. I ask you?' Tait snorted into the handkerchief and then carefully folded it up, before replacing it in his pocket. 'So Taczek was called in to make an approach to Mills and sound him out. Mills refused.'

Blanche recalled to Tait a fat second-hand-car salesman smelling of whisky, slumped in his office and telling her a story. Years and years ago a man with a foreign name, he said, had come to Mills' caravan office and provoked a quarrel.

239

That man must have been Taczek. Only then did the chief inspector know why voices had been raised. Taczek was trying to persuade Mills to come and help out people in the Secret Intelligence Service who Mills believed had betrayed him.

Tait's wrinkleless head nodded back and forth, appreciating her understanding like a fine wine. 'My, you are sharp, Chief Inspector. Anyway, Mills said no and just at the same time, "Nikolai" got a KGB promotion. So he decided to remain contented with his lot for the time being and stay in Russia.'

'Mills was an old hand,' Tait went on. 'He sniffed around, put two and two together and guessed who the potential defector might be. So, he decided to go on holiday to Russia. He knew his visa application would be processed by the KGB and he knew there was a faint chance, and no more, that "Nikolai" might try and get in touch. Mills was lucky. "Nikolai" did get to hear of the visit and his superiors approved of a meeting. Who knows, "Nikolai" argued, perhaps Mills is still so angry with his old service he might tell a few tales.'

'Did he?'

'Who can tell? What we do know is that "Nikolai" told some tales to Mills – above all that Capron was working for the KGB. Mills didn't tell us, the old fool. He was probably too resentful. He wanted to go for Capron in his own way.' Tait tugged down his trilby against the freezing rain. 'Finally his chance came. He almost went bankrupt when companies he'd invested in in the Far East went bust. So, desperate for money, Mills started to blackmail Capron nine months ago. We were watching Capron's bank accounts by then. The KGB paid up for a time. They didn't want to get involved in any messy assassination business and also wished Capron to stay where he was as long as possible. But Capron became increasingly edgy when he smelt suspicion on the air – people, he felt, didn't trust him any more. He assumed Mills had talked to somebody. The KGB was behind with its laundered payments to cover the blackmail. Capron had had enough. He wanted a safe passage out of England straightaway.'

'And did Mills talk to you?' she prodded. 'Was that how you found out about Capron working for the Russians?'

The old spycatcher smiled and ambled on a few steps before answering. 'The real reason we were investigating Capron was information from another source. "Nikolai". Life was increasingly unbearable under Gorbachev. A crackdown on corruption and vodka. New boys were moved in over him. "Nikolai" put out feelers to MI6 again, after telling them of a KGB mole in London in Capron's department of MI5.'

They stood in front of the safe house again. When they stopped the two Special Branch men halted too. The rain had halted and a quiet murmur had settled over the invisible city that was all about them, beyond the roofs and chimney pots. Tait clasped his gloved hands in front of him with an air of menace. His voice was harsh and clipped. 'That's my side of the bargain. Now what about yours? Who killed Mills, and why?'

Chapter 25

She suggested they went for another turn around the block.
Tait nodded. She wanted time to think through what he had
said before she spoke, add it to the knowledge she already had.

'The trouble was,' Blanche sighed at last, after they had
walked fifty yards or so, 'Capron was not given his safe passage
out of England. The KGB must have wanted him to stay in
MI5 as long as possible, feeding back secrets. Capron lost
patience. He wanted Mills dead. He could, I suppose, have
hired a contract hitman but instead a stroke of luck came his
way. Marek Nowak appeared.'

Tait's face seemed to throw off its flabbiness and become
taut with concentration, his colourless eyes riveted to hers. His
gaze was so unwavering she found it disturbing. 'The son of
Mrs Nowak? The one researching Zbigniew Nowak's death?'

Blanche told him about the events of the night before and
summarised Marek's confession. She told the MI5 man that
she possessed the exercise book that contained it. The spycatcher regarded her with a mixture of annoyance and admiration. 'Tell me, by the way,' Blanche hurried on to change the
subject, 'who was watching Mills in the weeks leading up to
his murder?'

Tait narrowed his eyes. 'Well, it wasn't us.'

'Urquhart said it was.'

'Well he would, wouldn't he? It must have been the KGB
or some freelancers employed by Capron to keep an eye on
Mills.'

'And who was keeping an eye on us?'

Tait looked even more puzzled. 'On you?'

'Yes. On Urquhart and me.'

'No one. Special Branch and MI5 only had instructions to
tail Urquhart from very late yesterday. It was only then we
got the final evidence that he was working for the KGB. And

then they couldn't trace him. Luckily he turned up at the flat. He and Capron were run by different KGB controllers, apparently. They were friendly at the office but Urquhart was ... well, so young. He didn't automatically come under suspicion when Capron did.' Blanche realised the sole purpose of Urquhart being put on to the Mills case by Capron was to make sure she came nowhere near the truth about the murder of Graham Mills. Urquhart relayed all her moves, as she made them, back to Capron. What a shit, she thought, kicking an empty drink can off the pavement.

They stood in front of 'The Continental Supermarket' again. The beautiful Indian girl had been forced to stop dreaming and start counting the money in the till. She had turned out some of the lights and was no more than a black profile against the back of the shop as she stood the coins in piles. She arranged the piles elegantly, as though they were a work of art. Blanche lined up the new facts in her mind like the piles of coins. The pattern they formed made sense.

'You haven't finished the story of this man "Nikolai", have you? He's defected, hasn't he? He finally came across.'

Tait displayed a flicker of concern. 'What makes you think that?'

'My guess is that "Nikolai's" defection sounded the alarm bells in Moscow. The Russians told Capron and Urquhart to get out. You knew Capron would make a run for it and you trapped him, except that when you looked in the net you found there were two fish rather than one.'

'For an amateur you're rather good.'

'I may be an amateur spy but – unlike most of you lot – I'm not a professional shit.' The words spurted out with all the accumulated antipathy for the way she had been manipulated and misled over the previous months.

Tait winced like a diner in a superior restaurant who sees someone eating their sauce with a knife. 'We have a very difficult job to do. We can't defend ourselves in public.'

'Just tell me if I'm right or not.'

'Substantially yes.'

'Why "substantially"?'

'I never like to be over-committed,' he said with his Buddhist smile.

Blanche tried to feel some sympathy for Urquhart but found none. He had forfeited any right. Instead she found her thoughts drifting towards another victim. 'I assume it was the KGB who tried to murder Marek?'

'Of course. Who else? Despite all the rubbish in the papers, we're not allowed to. Capron must have seen that Marek was getting more and more unpredictable. Take for example your arrest of Taczek. Taczek had left various messages with different people about how to contact his friend, Capron, should he ever have a problem. That was what happened. Capron pulled some strings at the Cabinet Office and Taczek was released straightaway. I approved it.'

'You approved it!' Blanche was outraged.

'That's right. It made you look stupid but by then Capron was under surveillance and we had to show that his authority was undiminished, otherwise he might have become suspicious.'

Blanche thought it through. If Marek could accuse Taczek like he did, Capron thought Marek might turn on him at any moment with the same apparent irrationality. But with Marek and Mills dead, Capron and the KGB believed he would be safe again. Capron would be able to spy as before. No more blackmail. No evidence from Mills to any enquiry into him. The KGB sent in one of its assassination agents to complete the botched job outside the school.

They stood once again in front of the safe house. The curtains were twitched apart and the lady Blanche had seen earlier glanced out through a mellow rectangle of light. She remembered her cold and soaked feet. Another train – perhaps the last one of the evening – clattered by, away in the cutting behind the lines and lines of houses. The clanking rattle was surprisingly loud outside, carried in gusts by the chill wind. When the spycatcher spoke next, the chief inspector wondered at first whether she had heard him right.

He repeated it: 'With luck, Marek Nowak will never recover.'

'That's cruel.'

Tait looked up. 'How do you know?'

'Only a spy could wish a human being to stay a cabbage.'

'I'd rather be, if I had to face what he'll have to if he comes out of the coma. The fact that he murdered Mills is bad enough but . . .'

Blanche knew Tait was keeping something back, corralling a secret that was perhaps darker than the rest. The MI5 man moved purposefully towards the door. There was a tacit understanding between them that once over the threshold they would say no more to each other. The whispering of secrets, the mutual confession, would be over. Their meeting might never have happened. The words they had exchanged would have been heard only by the wind, the street lights and the parked cars. She touched Tait's arm and noted the flash of white in his eye as he turned – whether of irritation or embarrassment she could not tell. 'Why don't you stop being so bloody coy?' she said.

'Haven't you guessed?' he murmured with a patronising flash of his teeth. 'You seem to have worked out everything else.'

The chief inspector stood in her damp overcoat, hands in pockets, eyes rimmed scarlet with fatigue. 'Just tell me.'

'Tatyana Nowak's marriage was unsteady. Her husband was apparently as much of a ladies' man as Mills. Just before Zbigniew Nowak went back to Poland, Mrs Nowak and Mills had an affair.' Tait shuffled on his feet with the suppressed excitement of a housewife about to relay a choice morsel of gossip. 'Marek was the result. If you were born out of wedlock then, of course, you were a bastard, and Tatyana didn't want that for her son. So she and Graham Mills pretended the affair had never happened.' The MI5 man stroked the raindrops from his goatee beard with a gloved hand. 'Marek ended up murdering his own father.'

Tait's mood changed abruptly. Once told, he realised his story was not to be chuckled over, a piece of bar-room hilarity. The spycatcher was still a schoolboy at heart, Blanche reflected, who sometimes spoke without thinking. He took his trilby off and turned the brim round and round in his hands as a form of apology.

Blanche knew at last why Mills, although suspicious, could hardly refuse the rendezvous on Hampstead Heath: he was going to meet his natural son. And she knew why, exactly, Tatyana Nowak had committed suicide. When Marek blurted out the details of what he had done – full of passionate self-justification and panting for her approval – a frost settled on her heart. A sense of hopelessness, of the vanity of fighting fate, made her stare in disbelief at the imploring eyes of her beloved son, eyes which reminded her of the innocent man he had murdered, and the eyes of her lover, of long, long ago. Tatyana passed from disbelief, to anger, acceptance and finally despair, foundering in guilt. Her son murdering his own father. If only she had told him the truth. She realised the ghost of the past would never sleep. It would haunt her for ever. She saw no alternative to self-destruction.

The scudding clouds had been blown away to the east, and the same moon Blanche remembered from the night before shone cold and clear. She wanted to say something profound but could not. She looked up at the moon. A waxy halo softened its hard outline.

'It makes me wonder sometimes, about whether there's any justice in the world,' Tait said.

'Really? I thought that word didn't mean much to spies.'

'Oh, it means a lot,' grunted Tait, his breath hanging on the night air, peeling off his gloves and placing them in his hat like chicks in a nest. 'Rarely comes about of course. But the *idea* means a lot.'

The Special Branch car did not wait at the hospital where Dexter was. 'Sorry,' said the driver, 'but we're not a taxi service.'

Blanche arrived too late for evening visiting but after she explained to a sister who she was, the nurse allowed her into the ward. Dexter had been operated on that afternoon and was due to wake about then from general anaesthetic. A bullet had been removed from his stomach and, although very weak, Dexter would make a good recovery. Their whispering voices made his big mahogany eyes flicker open. They blinked into the half light of the ceiling, probing and empty, until the black pupils focused on the chief inspector's face.

She sat down beside him.

Dexter's voice was no more than a croak. 'I feel like shit.' He gulped and the effort caused the veins on his temples to swell with pain. 'Did they get the bastards?'

'One. Urquhart shot himself.'

The detective sergeant closed his eyes.

'I'm sorry, Dexter. It's all my fault.'

'Lot of good that'll do.'

A furrow of bitterness she had never seen before had dug itself across Dexter's forehead. The stubble had grown round his chin during the day and now stood out thick and bristly. She leant forward, kissed him on the cheek and walked straight out. She did not want to cry in front of him.

Early the next morning, Blanche phoned her brother. They had an unwritten agreement not to talk much about their jobs, so she only hinted at what had happened and they agreed she should stay the coming weekend with the family in the country.

Spittals rang a little later and told her to take a few days' leave. 'I don't know how you've pulled it off, Blanche, but you're in the clear. The commander's been squared by somebody or other and we've all been told to forget about it.'

The chief inspector sighed. 'Thank you, sir.'

'See you in the office Monday.'

Blanche made herself another cup of coffee and nursed it in her hands. She made her mind up. She had nothing to lose. She was her own woman and there was no obligation.

'Is that you, Roger?' She realised how unfamiliar her husband's voice had become.

'Blanche. What a surprise! Hope you haven't got a problem about next week?'

'Well, I have actually. I wondered whether you could make it tonight instead. I need someone to talk to.'

Her husband paused. 'Yeah. OK.' Then more confidently: 'Sure.'

She had one other visit to make that day. Marek Nowak lay unchanged, his face sad and wizened. His eyes were closed, his lips slightly apart. The only sign of life besides the gentle rise and fall of his chest beneath the sheets was a twitch which flickered on his right temple. Marek's face was noble and distant, beyond the concerns that agitated the nurses and doctors who occasionally scuttled by. His face gave no clue to what he was thinking, indeed whether he was thinking at all, but he gave the impression of being sad. Perhaps it was just an effect created by the drooping moustache which had encroached over his lips. Blanche wondered whether Tait was right: that it was better for him never to wake. He was impervious now to the concerns of the world, undisturbed by the hushed hum and clatter of the hospital, as timeless as a marble statue on a tomb. A doctor and nurse approached with the respectful tread of tourists who tiptoe up to such a monument in a church, whispering to one another.

The doctor was the one who was treating Marek. He said the poison used by the assassin had been an extract of shellfish toxin. Marek's life had been saved for the moment only to shelve him in a state of animated death, alive yet not living. Marek murmured the odd phrase in Polish but nothing that made sense. The doctor saw little hope of recovery. He coughed with embarrassment and asked who Marek's next of kin were. Blanche said she thought they were all dead.